BEYOND BARLOW

JASON R. KOIVU

ISBN: 978-1-61296-942-8
PUBLISHED BY BLACK ROSE WRITING
www.blackrosewriting.com

Printed in the United States of America
Suggested Retail Price (SRP) $19.95

Beyond Barlow is printed in Adobe Caslon

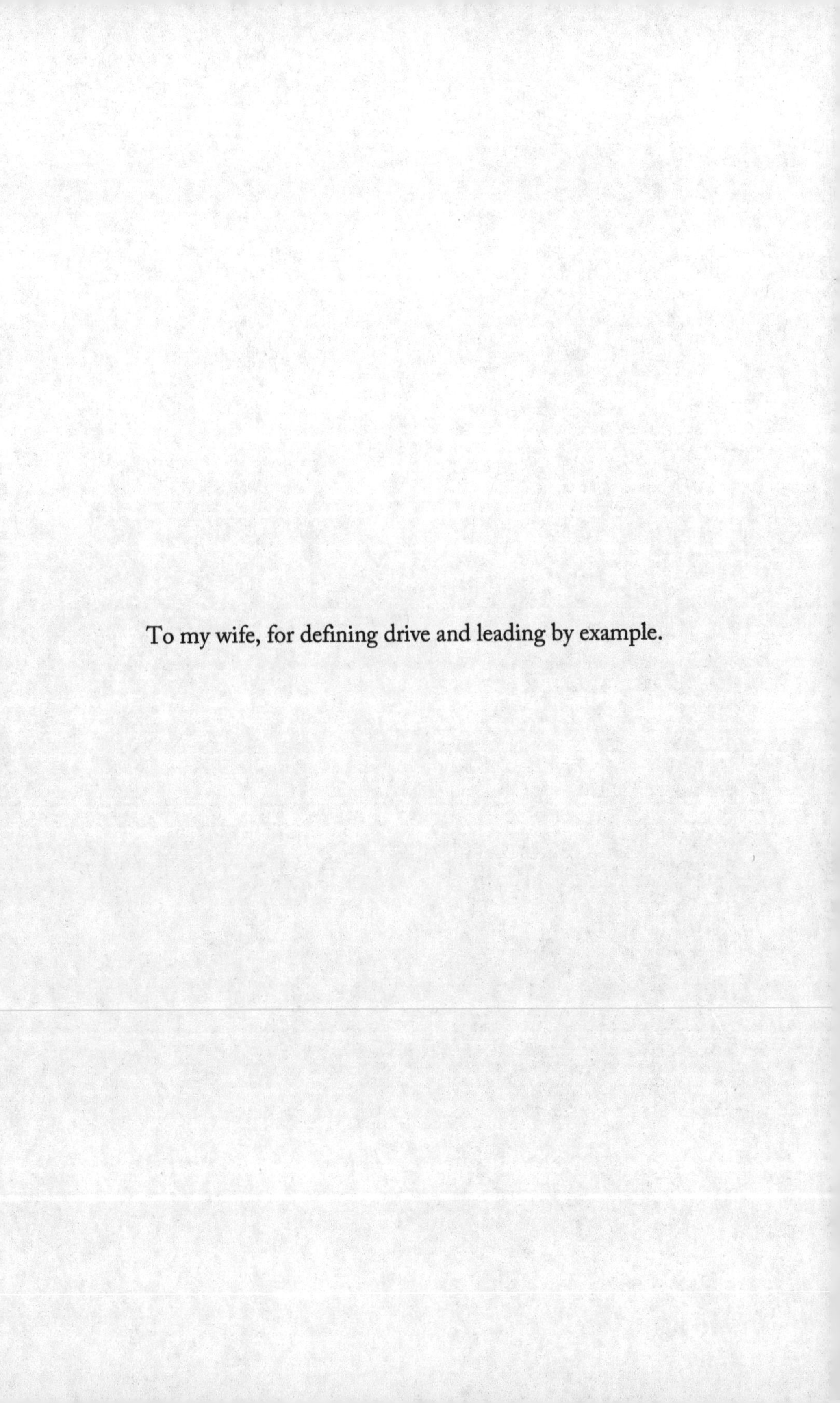

To my wife, for defining drive and leading by example.

BEYOND BARLOW

Contents

Chapter 1
The Battle by the Llyn

This might be the end, the end of them all. A prospect daunting and exhilarating to Ford Barlow, a woodcutter's giant of a boy running wild alongside friends and family over a lumpy field and wondering all the while if this thrill within him were born from eagerness for victory or fear of death. His untutored mind, all but untethered by a spirit finally set free, could hardly cope with such weighty ponderings, least of all at a time like this. Thoughts of valiant victory torn from eviscerating defeat dizzied his senses. Vague notions of what it was like to stab and be stabbed by spear or sword flooded his vision blind. Then he tripped over a jutting rock and fell on his face.

"Get up." His father's level, but insistent command propelled him to his feet as much as the man's calloused hand hoisting the boy by the arm.

"Hurry!" his nerve-rattled brother Leoffred cried, while pulling at Ford's other arm.

"Get down, get down!" Ford begged of the dog sniffing, licking and jumping on him. His enormous wolfhound Stinky would not be put off until he knew his master was unhurt.

"Make haste or get left behind!" bellowed a marchog, an armored warrior on horseback corralling the nearly two hundred other men, women and children bounding through high, bearded grass. All of the people, including a half dozen trained marchogs, belonged to the fork-bearded, red-faced Barwnig Blackoak, a sturdy and tenacious clan chief. Their fire-breathing barwnig rode at the fore, whipping his ax over his head, rallying them with whoops and cheers so robust he went hoarse. There wasn't a boy among them who didn't want to be him.

All of his people were happy to fight, but this chasing about the countryside after the Staneards, an unwilling and elusive rival clan, had gone on much longer than usual for a simple dispute between two local chiefs. Disregarding a border they claimed to be erroneous, the Staneards had made a quiet grab for a parcel of arable Blackoak land to add to their rocky territory. When roaming Staneard sheep were found repeatedly grazing on the wrong side of the border, Barwnig Blackoak mustered a force upon the disputed spot. The Staneards met them, but outnumbered they turned and fled. Demanding reparation, the Blackoaks gave chase. Normally with these feuds a bargain was struck, otherwise a brief battle ensued with the side taking it hardest on the chin relenting. But the Staneards were playing a new game and the chase had carried on for nearly a week now. With each passing day the people grew more restless, anxious to end this dispute and go home where work and families awaited.

Back and forth they tread over the fields of friend and foe with nights spent sleeping in forest and orchard. The footpaths traversed between villages could be counted in miles, but now it looked like the chase might finally end. A scout, Gil of Iselbryn on his cranky pony, reported the Staneards hiding in a village over the next rise. Forgotten were the aches and pains from days of trekking all over the land, the monotonous waiting for a scout to return, the boring afternoons foraging from hastily deserted villages. All around Ford people of the earth like himself, enthusiastic as hungry dogs after a wounded deer and armed with axes, knives, spears, and even farming tools, sprinted through a sunken field, a shallow bowl of a valley rimmed by squat, tree-lined hills. Silvery-skinned birches stood in a row along the western ridge, dicing the horizontal afternoon sun and causing it to flicker between the trees and partially blind them as they ran for the north rim directly ahead, a steadily rising knoll fronted by a head-high wall of bushes.

"Halt!" shouted Barwnig Blackoak. "Halt!"

"Fucking halt, damn you!" hollered the marchog Cenric, the impoverished master of Oren Hall near to Ford's home in Barlow. The people stumbled to a stop, grasped their knees and caught their breath while the marchogs conferred with the barwnig.

"Why we stopping?" Ford wasn't the only one asking, but no one was answering. His father scanned ahead. His exceptional height meant he barely had to crane his neck even when crowded by clansmen standing on their toes or jumping to see. However, he he could see nothing out of the ordinary.

"Maybe it's the Staneards," said Leoffred, who they called Leo for short. Leo leapt to see and failing that, looked to his brother and father. Ford shrugged and their father shook his head. "If we don't hurry and find them, it'll be dark soon."

"Sure will," said Ford, "and we'll miss our chance, again."

Weapons and packs dropped to the ground and then the Blackoaks themselves when it became apparent they wouldn't be moving anytime soon. Ford thumped down on his backside in the grass and laid his hand upon his chest, feeling his heartbeat return to something like normal. His dog plopped his head on to Ford's stomach.

"Maybe we'll make camp here tonight," said Leo.

"Maybe," said his father sitting with his sons.

Rumors swept through them like wind over grass: the Staneards were not in the village ahead.

"Gone. Gone again," said Winhild, a longtime family friend sitting close by with his graying father and relishing the old, familiar routine of passing on information to the Barlow family. He came from Oren, a small village attached to Cenric's meager hall. Diminutive as the village was, it acted as the hub of news and trade for even smaller settlements like the hamlet of Barlow. Accustomed to relaying gossip and realizing he had nothing else to say, Winhild gave a discontented sigh and his attention roamed to Ford's fidgeting fingers.

"What's that you got, Ford?"

Ford held up his hand and upon his open palm sat a half dozen colorful pebbles and stones, mostly marble chunks and pieces of quartz.

"For your girl?" asked Winhild. Ford flushed pinker about the cheeks and up into his ears. He grinned for an answer, mistrusting his lately creaky voice. "You still have an eye for that girl? That…who's it now?"

"Gwen," said Leo with a smirk.

The men goaded Ford to tell them all about Gwen and when he hung his scarlet face, they laughed and blessed "the beautiful Gwen!" Those at hand slapped him on the back.

"Tuck them away good and safe," said Winhild, "so as you don't lose them in the fight." Lost in imaging his stones knocked free and flung irretrievably away, Ford stared horrified and unblinking at Winhild for so long the disconcerted older man broke the awkward silence with a rush of words, "They'll be fine, I'm sure. You boys never been in a battle before? Scared? Scared, are you?"

"Yeah," admitted Ford and immediately regretted it. Making others laugh was a joy, but not in this way.

"You'll be fine. Stick by your pa and you'll be fine."

Ford appreciated the sentiment, but not even Winhild knew what kind of relationship he had with his father. Up until these last few days, he wouldn't have been able to say whether he'd feel safer at his father's side than on his own. For all of their time together, nearly ten years, their bond had been tenuous and restricted, but this week Myer Barlow had shown his son more warmth than usual, more than Ford could remember.

"There's worse ways to die than getting killed in battle," said Winhild's father, slipping this insight into the pause like a frayed leather belt drawn soft and dry over cloth, in the end cinched tight and true.

"True, quite true. But," said Winhild waving as if to disperse the gloom, "you boys wouldn't mind dying in battle, would you?" Leo shook his head, but Ford mistook the question and answered with a nod that started the men laughing again.

"Smart lad," said Roddick the smith of Oren, leaning back from his own circle of friends into theirs. The few occasions he sharpened a sword or shoed a horse for the local marchog had somehow transformed him into a battle-hardened warrior, though he'd seen little of war himself. "The best way to go is to die fighting, but if you can, fight dying." Most didn't get the joke, which he'd stolen from the marchog, so he tried it in summary, "Die fighting or fight dying!" repeating it louder and louder until the people around him were hooting. Only then did he sit back content.

Horns rattled the ears of the Blackoaks and flushed flocks of squawking birds from the trees. Thunderous drums rolled over the valley. Shadow fell upon them as bodies blotted out the solar radiance from the west. With weapons drawn, horns blaring and drums beating, the Staneards stalked through the trees and down the slope, coming on like a wave gathering force enough to wash all away before it. The Blackoaks scrambled to their feet and gawped at the unexpected host before them.

"There's twice as many of them as before," cried one of the marchogs.

"Where'd they come from?" demanded the barwnig riding out in front of his people.

"It's devilry," someone declared and it was plain by the people's shrinking posture and involuntary steps backward that many believed some dark magic must have brought the mysteriously swelled enemy so swiftly upon them.

"Very well," started Barwnig Blackoak in a casual tone that rose to a growling bark, "we'll fight them right here!" He wheeled his horse around the open valley and rode into the middle of the Blackoaks. "This is what we've been waiting for! The worms have finally stopped wiggling!" The people raised fists and weapons and let forth a howling cheer. Ford thumped his spear repeatedly into the ground with the others and added a cracking wail to the clank and clash of metal blades crashing together. The marchogs prodded the people into a line, disorderly but determined to stand firm. The Staneards neared the valley floor and broke into two ranks, a second line slipping discretely behind the first. The barwnig and his marchogs sat high in their saddles trying to see what they were about.

"Where'd they all come from," asked Winhild, giving voice to what all wondered. The number of enemy had indeed doubled since the last time they had been seen scurrying away. Sharper eyes picked out gray rings around the upper arms of half of them.

"Bledwins," muttered a Blackoak from a village Ford had never seen nor heard of until a few days prior, and yet he had an instinctive liking for the stranger and an instant hatred for these Bledwins; this was a clan name new to his ears, but uttered with a strain of disgust that made it clear nothing good could come from any of them. For the Blackoaks, nothing good would come of the Bledwins, not for the foreseeable future. They'd been bought by the Staneards and together numbered well more than two hundred.

As the enemy mass pressed on, the Blackoaks gripped their weapons tighter, took up a wider stance, rocked back and forth to their own clash-stamp beat, and laughed loudly when the Staneards and Bledwins pulled up short.

"What are they doing," asked Leo.

"They turned coward again! Give it to them good, boys!" shouted Roddick the smith before drawing in a deep breath and resuming his mocking laughter with a sharper edge at the Staneard force gathering at a distance beyond the range of a hurled spear. Taunts from both sides couldn't be made out over the hundreds shouting simultaneously, but the enemy was close enough that there was no mistaking their bared teeth and sly grins a moment before death fell upon the heads of the Blackoaks. They looked up in confusion at the swarm arching high above with a whooshing buzz like gnats in flight. A sharp screech spun Ford around and there was Glenys, the marchog of Wygrand's stout and indomitable daughter, with an arrow shaft pinning her hand to her thigh. A man in the front swore and fell to his knees. Someone down the line yelped and hopped about on one foot.

"The scum are using bows," said the barwnig in disbelief. As if providing confirmation, an arrow thudded into the head of a man before him. The man dropped back against his horse and the horse reared and sidestepped, letting the man fall lifeless to the ground. Without bows of their own, some Blackoaks threw stones and even sticks at the enemy. When there was nothing more at hand, they shook their fists and hurled insults.

"Dung-eating bootlicks!"

"Milk-livered maggots!"

"Mule suckers" was Ford's favorite. Some simply stuck with "Cowards!" for this most cowardly of all acts perpetrated against clan tradition. Ancient inter-clan code demanded hand-to-hand combat, so that a warrior might look into a foe's eye and seek the righteousness of the deed within one's own heart. If a life were to be taken, it should be justifiable and done so in earnest. It was true, the old ways were fading, but more to the point, the Staneards were in decline, their numbers fewer now than of old and their territory shrinking. In desperation they'd sunk to using the bow and arrow in battle, tools for hunting beasts. Their use on another human being, rival clan member or no, was tantamount to calling that person an animal.

The second volley of arrows shot into the air. Barwnig Blackoak tugged at his horse's reins and pointed his ax northwards. "To the higher ground!" he commanded. "Never show your back!" He summoned his mounted warriors and together they charged the enemy, galloping against the tide of their own streaming people, whose packs, blankets and cloaks were forgotten or cast aside and trampled upon. The barwnig and his marchogs scattered the archers and drove back the Staneard force a pace, giving the Blackoaks time enough to fall back beyond the range of the arrows. They made for the higher ground of the north rim, veering away from the encroaching, broken eastern rim and the sodden ground of a swamp beyond. The people feared a swamp at night and the horizon was devouring the sun.

Almost immediately the enemy barwnigs and their marchogs countered with support from their rallying troops, forcing the Blackoaks' mounted warriors to break off the attack or risk becoming engulfed.

The Blackoaks retreated at angles, always keeping one eye on the enemy as they first ranged this way and that, seeking safety without seeming to flee. Lacking the graceful singularity of a flock of birds or school of fish, many bumped into one another. Ford stepped on the heels of the man in front of him and stumbled to his knees with an inward curse for his newly lanky and untrustworthy legs. Eventually they all arrived at the line of bushes fronting the valley's north rim rise, only to discover it proved too thorny to push through, effectively barring their way and forcing them either west into a barrage of enemy arrows or east into the dreaded swamp. There was no advantage in being pinned against thorns, but having followed orders as far as possible, they wavered in indecision and awaited their barwnig's return, watching as the marchog of Wygrand, trailing his comrades, fell from his horse in a hail of arrows.

"Go back!" cried Barwnig Blackoak and the remaining marchogs to Wygrand's daughter as she passed between them, heading straight into the heart of the enemy. Hobbled and one-handed though she was, Glenys staggered like a three-legged bull to her father lying face down in the field. As the enemy surrounded her, she ran her spear through the first man to oppose her, lodged her broad-bladed short sword in the neck of another and fell over her father's body like a shield, where she died, pierced through and through.

When Barwnig Blackoak reunited with his people, he commanded them into the swamp, but it was the arrows falling all around them that hastened the more hesitant among them into the forbidding marshlands. They would have stayed for a fair fight, but this was slaughter. Some did balk. The stone-fisted smith of Oren flatly refused to enter the swamp, swinging his hammer at the thorny bushes in an attempt to escape through the thick growth, only to be swallowed by the rush of the enemy's mounted warriors.

The Blackoaks splashed through a stream dotted with heaping tufts and were funneled into a deepening gully that grew thick with immature trees, the full-bodied balsam firs of the valley meadows giving way to thin red maples with a strong attachment to the waterway. Hundreds weaved through the laurels, no one speaking above the swish of pant legs, the scrape of limbs on cloth, the crunch of leaves and twigs, and the enemy's drums and horns pressing from behind. They spread out, each picking the path he or she thought best, passing wooly-mammoth-like willows that cast them in an ever-increasing darkness and stifling silence under the fortuitous canopy that kept the lobbed arrows at bay. The evening descended like a lid upon the pot of a sulfurous, sour brew of dead leaves and mud in long-standing water.

Ford followed his brother, Leo followed their father, and their father raced ahead with long-legged strides. Neither boy could remember ever seeing their father run before. His speed surprised them and they feared being left behind; not only by him, but the whole clan. Blackoak folklore brimmed with legends of wanderers becoming disoriented by the enchantments of spirits and hopelessly lost in forsaken places such as this. Swamps especially were notorious haunts for the dangerously entrancing will o' the wisp and any secluded water might hold an alluring nymph. Although, attractive women tempting their victims into the depths didn't seem an entirely bad thing to Ford. The Barlow brothers could be dismissive of certain tall tales and imaginings, like the story concocted by a frightened friend about a ghostly white demon with a long spiked tail he'd seen flying backwards over marshlands, which Leo assured him was nothing more than a normal crane flying forwards. However, both of the boys heartily believed the legends handed down through the generations as well as the horror stories of their own making. How could anyone deny the existence of "that damn leshy" who misplaced their father's ax so often? But shapeshifting pixies playing tricks were nothing compared to the fear evoked by the knucker waterwyrm, an enormous aquatic lizard inhabiting deep pools in wetlands. The beast was fresh in Ford's thoughts since hearing someone ahead hiss, "Look out, a knucker hole."

"They driven us here on purpose," fretted another.

Ford and Leo skidded to a stop in front of an oval pool, their feet up to the ankles in mud and sinking deeper. Ford wiped sweat-matted hair from his eyes and both boys stared mesmerized at the coppery water. A violent ripple tore across the surface. Stinky circled the water's edge, occasionally lowering his head for a tentative sniff.

"That's a knucker's hole if ever there was one," said Leo.

"Surely is," said Ford urging his brother on with a hand to the back and then passing him with soupy, slurping high steps.

"I'm stuck." Mud seeped over both of Leo's knees and up his thighs. He jerked about and flailed his arms for a nearby sapling. Ford stopped and darted a wary eye at the pool. The ripples over its surface were dissipating when the enemy's horns blared through the trees ever sharper.

"Come on," said Ford, rushing back and reaching out for his brother. "Give me your hand."

"I'm trying!"

"Be quiet."

"You be quiet."

Ford caught Leo's fingertips, gripped his hand, then the other and leaned back. Leo fell forward. Ford's legs plunged back into the mud. Leo's fingers gripped his pants and dug into his legs. Neither of them were getting anywhere but more stuck. Ford reached over his shoulder and caught the nub of a root. Stretched to his fullest with the weight of his brother on his legs, he could do nothing more than hold on. Stinky darted continually from the pool to the boys, barking at them, at the water and at the nearing horns and drums.

"Can you climb up?" he asked, but Leo was already scaling his prone brother, hand over laborious hand until his legs finally slid free and he found solid footing. He planted his heels on the root and helped Ford struggle to firmer ground. Both lost their shoes and neither knew it; their tough-soled feet so caked in mud as to be indistinguishable from leather.

"Come on, boy, come on," Ford called in a soft and tender voice to soothe his dog, who was soon panting away, happily loping alongside and ahead, guessing which way they might turn next. But they hadn't padded far over a carpet of moss when Leo stopped.

"Where is everyone?" he whispered. Stinky came back and nuzzled his palm. No one but themselves could be seen or heard in an ever-thickening fog resting upon water which stretched out randomly before them to the left and right. Hollow stumps and rotten logs surrounded the vast, choked pond, while in its midst white-gray spindly trees like skeletal arms with gnarled hands and uplifted fleshless fingers clawed at the sky for salvation from the inky depths beneath. In the old dead trees Ford saw faces with mouths gaping in silent lamentations and black eyes piercing his soul. Seeing phantom faces in the dark corners of his world was nothing new, and after an initial shudder, he ignored them. "Do you see anyone?" asked Leo peering all around them. Ford shook his head, but he leaned forward on a stump for a better look in the diminishing light, straining to see across the water and into the shadows beneath the distant trees.

"Listen!" Ford said, holding up his hand for silence. They heard nothing but the cheep-cheep of countless frogs, the dissonant trill of red-winged blackbirds and a rumbling that made Ford clutch his stomach the same instant the stump crumbled beneath him, a solid chunk thudding to the ground and rolling into the water with a peace-shattering splash. The boys tore off into the woods and flew nearly blind into a veritable blockade of briars.

"Back! Back!" they both warned one another.

"This way," Leo suggested, though he could not say why, other than a natural path seemed to open before them and lead around the swamp. But soon they were stumbling into water, wading through lily pads, and grasping at cattails to pull themselves on to a mushy mound. Ford turned to see his dog stopped in the middle of the water. Almost at its side, the pond erupted with a loud smack upon its surface like a boat oar brought down with a mighty slap. The dog leapt straight up, bounded away with the water frothing around his legs, and jumped into Ford's comforting arms. They gritted their teeth and clenched their fists. Leo closed his eyes and Ford hugged his dog tight. Certainly some grotesque monster would emerge and devour them.

"Dam," murmured Leo when a length of time elapsed and nothing had come along to make a meal of them.

"What?"

"It must've been a beaver. There's a dam back here."

The very mound they'd mounted was an integral part of a dam, but what worked for the beaver would not help the boys. The spot left them exposed, so they moved on, climbing carefully over thin limbs woven together with their jagged ends pointing out here and there. Ford slipped and caught his ankle in a hole. He yanked it out and ripped his pants, painfully scraping the inside of his calf, but the injury was nothing compared to their real problem. The beaver pond was on one side of the dam, while the other side spread out into a vast body of water, impassable unless they wanted to swim through it at night. They did not.

Leo pulled at Ford's sleeve and led him tiptoeing off the dam on to thin a sandspit. At the end of the soggy strip, a tree recently fallen on to some bushes created a heap of leaves that might provide a place to hide if only they could crawl in between the jagged limbs. Comfort would be hard to come by, but by pushing aside branches and twisting about, they were able to insert themselves into the somewhat crushed bushes deeply enough to be mostly hidden. There was no need to lure the dog in as Ford feared. Once he sat, Stinky dove in and curled up on his lap - or at least his rump fit upon his master's lap.

No sooner had they settled themselves when their blood froze at the sight of someone or something darting through the woods, splashing around the beaver pond and over the spit. Stinky's roaring bark shocked whatever it was into the water for a few steps before it carried on out of sight. Whether the stringy-limbed, heavy-breathing creature was naked and naturally black and slick-skinned or whether that was but an illusion of the night, neither boy could tell. It had long gone when they finally relaxed enough to realize that defending themselves from whatever it might have been would have been difficult.

"Your spear?"

Ford threw up his hands. "Where's yours?"

Leo squirmed while Ford stroked his dog's back in hopes of calming him. Another outburst like that while the Staneards were at hand might be fatal to them all. Leo bobbed his head about looking through the branches and leaves back in the direction they'd come from. Ford had a mind and eye for the stringy-limbed creature and kept a watch-out in the direction it had gone, hoping it wouldn't come back. Both pricked their ears, expecting voices, footsteps, horns and drums. In a far corner of the pond a throaty bullfrog ripped into a rhythmic croaking. A fish jumped somewhere off in the distant water. Little else stirred and after seemingly unending hours, boredom overtook Ford. He laid his head on Stinky's rump and couldn't tell whether his eyes were open or closed.

Though it seemed strange, what he could see clearly was the knucker hole they'd passed earlier. No, it was the beaver pond. Or was it? He couldn't be sure. Funny, he thought, the fog seemed to hang in the air like a bloated cloud blotting out everything and yet he clearly saw a scaly claw creeping out of the water and two diamond eyes glowing red. Another claw broke the surface and an enormous wyrm crawled out of the water, its glistening green body uncoiling to the length of three men. Rippling gills along its sinewy neck snorted in and out a putrid and pungent air. Spiked ridges like ax heads ran along its muscular back and its chest expanded to the width of an ancient oak in one mighty heave before it shot hot, black slime from its nostrils. Locking eyes with Ford, it launched itself out of the water and slithered toward him. Ford tried to back away, but his feet slipped in the mud and his fingers clawed futilely for something to grip. The creature caught Ford's foot and its long gray tongue flickered ever closer while it hissed in his face. The tongue withdrew, the hissing stopped, the wyrm cocked its head and with a look of annoyance, began poking him in the ribs.

"What's—" Ford began, but there was Leo pressing a hand over his mouth. Beyond his brother lights dangled in the periphery, swaying and dancing in the blackness all around them. They streaked between the trees like magnificent shooting stars or hovered as flaming golden suns might were they to shine in the evening, all of these wonders reflected off the water in a dazzling display of celestial brilliance. One of the fiery lights snapped him out of his reverie with a crack and a spark that sizzled in the water. Only then, when Leo was sure his brother would remain silent, did he release his hand and ease back.

"Watch it. Don't fall in," came a voice from a spot by the beaver pond. Footsteps squished in the damp leaves. Ford realized why he could make out Leo's face so clearly: they were surrounded by torches, dozens and dozens of them. His breathing seized up, his nervous gaze dropped to his dog, thankfully asleep, and then passed on to Leo. Creases marked his face and underscored the pervading fear his brother fought to suppress, a fear that might unbalance him at any moment with disastrous consequences. Ford leaned his weight back, felt a stick bending behind him and stopped. It was enough to slide his hand out from under his leg for the pins and needles of returning circulation to spread through it. He clenched and released a fist, then slowly reached out and laid his hand upon his brother's arm and held it there, steady and unmoving. The tension slowly eased out of Leo. A torchbearer drifted toward them, orange-lit and half hidden by shadow with one arm ending in flame. Feeling exposed, Leo turned away from the light and Ford buried his face in his dog's fur. Twigs around their bush snapped underfoot and the footsteps passed on. By the time Ford found the courage to lift his head, the last of the torches were bobbing off into the forest.

"It will be dawn soon," Leo whispered when they were alone again. It was wishful thinking and they both knew it. Dawn didn't come for hours and neither boy slept the entire time. Even after the sun rose gray behind the trees, they weren't drawn out of hiding until they began to hear occasional and distant shouts. Stinky was already up and about investigating the new smells around pond, but the boys crept reluctantly on to the sandspit, expecting to be taken up by an enemy lurking in the forest nearby. In the dim morning light the boys could make out a village scattered far off beyond a long stretch of water. A crowd massed upon a field rising behind the few tiny huts.

Eager though they were to rejoin their people, fear of the Staneards kept them from rushing through the woods and out into the open. Instead, they picked a careful, quiet path around the lengthy stretches of water and skulked behind the last of the trees, huddling together in search of friendly faces amongst the crowd sitting about fires sharpening weapons or finishing off morsels of meat that made Ford's mouth water. Bushes rustled behind them and Leo cried out, "Father!"

"There you are! They're here!" Myer called over his shoulder as he strode up to the boys. Leo flew into his arms, Stinky jumped around them and Ford stood by smiling, watching his father squeeze his brother in a warm embrace, both parting with glassy eyes.

"Well, well, look who's joined us," said Winhild coming up alongside Ford and patting him on the shoulder. "It's a blessed day indeed! You had us fretting something awful, but you made it all right and that's the important thing. Now hurry on, hurry!" he said guiding them out of the woods and over the fields. Ford didn't understand why he was being pushed ahead until he turned to see, beyond a line of rushes and much closer to them than the Blackoaks, the Staneards encamped in a field left fallow this season. "You good as walked right into them!" Their jolly neighbor laughed as if that would have been a hilarious sight to see.

"Eat! Eat!" urged a few concerned Blackoaks when the boys arrived among them and Winhild's father offered the remains of their meal that morning, which they devoured long before their appetites diminished.

"You were right behind me, why didn't you follow me out of the swamp?" their father demanded of them both. Leo launched into a floundering explanation with scant help from Ford.

"What about that knucker hole, eh? You run into that, did you," asked Winhild and with that prompting the boys suddenly found they were able to turn their experience of the night before into somewhat of a fireside story, a traditional pastime beloved by all the clans of the region. Their ambiguous description of the torchbearers' led Aran, a goat herder from the rocky hillside village of Celyn, to nod knowingly and utter, "Will o' the wisps," from out of the middle of a growing audience of Blackoaks. While they listened, the last drop of the ale discovered in the nearby village was drained, and a warm glow spread within each man, woman and child.

The boys plied the others with questions of their own and learned that the Blackoaks had gathered in the field above the village the night before. They thought the place might be Llyn o' Doreithiog. The inhabitants fled fast and were guessed to be up on the hill still watching them from the trees.

"Them Stained Ears and Bleeding Whinies been right there just about half the night," answered Winhild. "Whoop there, look out! Stinky's off to visit the neighbors!" When Ford called him back, the dog was already halfway to the enemy, negotiating a leap over a pebble-strewn stream washing down from the forested hill above and through the village.

"Better do something with him," said his father when Ford finally led the dog back. "See if you can't find a rope and tie him up down in the village."

Ford and his dog walked among the ramshackle huts, each with its own traps, nets and lines hanging from posts or lying wrapped in coils in small boats pulled ashore and tied to a rotting dock. By the largest hut, a fortified hall in comparison, a group of boys no older than Ford tended the horses of the marchogs from both sides, who sat or stood quite close to one another right outside the closed door. A somewhat strained, but surprisingly companionable exchange between them died away at the sight of Ford.

"What are you doing here? Go on!" commanded a Staneard marchog laying a hand on the hilt of his sword. Ford shoved his dog ahead and hurried off along the shore to the far end of the village.

"Hello!" he called into one of the last huts. Everything within was in turmoil: wooden spoons and bowls upside down upon the ground; a child's shoe and a cloth doll left behind; a light table knocked over in the inhabitants' haste to escape. The family's god had not been forsaken. A tiny shelf over a cutting block, a common place of honor for an idol, was now bare but for dust around a clean spot where the base had rested no doubt for years without being disturbed. Stinky pushed by, stuck his snout into a bowl and licked at a kind of porridge caked to the inside. Ford noticed a battered threshing flail left behind, leaning against the wall by the door. He grabbed it, and with a heavy heart, slipped outside and jammed the door closed with the flail. A quick search of the village and he was soon back with a fisherman's makeshift anchor, a rock the size of a human head wrapped in old netting. He dropped it with a thud and propped it against the bottom of the door. Shutting Stinky up felt wrong, but he wouldn't chance his dog being caught or killed by the enemy. Taking the flail and a dulled-pronged pitchfork he found leaning behind another hut, he walked back to the camp to the sound of his dog's howls and worried what would become of him should they all die in battle. The homeowners would come back and then Stinky would be theirs.

"They'll be good to you," he said, clamping his eyes shut and shouting the words as loud as he could within his own mind in hopes his dog would hear and understand. Such a good dog. It would be terrible to die and never see him again.

The barwnigs and marchogs rode out of the village, veering away from one another and returning to their camps. From this vantage point, Ford could see both sides almost equally well, and although he struggled to count above ten, he could tell they were of roughly a similar size. Hundreds crowded in fields cultivated to provide for dozens. Here were more people gathered in one spot than he'd ever seen in his life.

Looking as pleased as if he'd already won the battle single-handed, Barwnig Blackoak called his people to him and said in a resounding boom, "They're giving up their damn bows and filthy arrows!" He waved down a spite-tinged yet grateful cheer, and continued. "But we have to give up the hill." The cheer dissolved into a discontented grumble. They would lose a great advantage in giving up the high ground. "No hill means no arrows and we finally get our fight!" And just like that, he had them in hand once more and led them stomping down the slope, their anger reignited by the indignation of the past week's chase after an insolent quarry that dared steal the land out from under them. Their simple battle cry turned bloodthirsty and pitched into a maniacal, murderous fury in which they hurled insults at the enemy, goading them until the Staneard and Bledwin archers finally discarded their bows, drew out their long knives and cudgels, the two sides flung themselves at one another with a wild and savage frenzy.

"Stick by me!" shouted Myer. Ford would rather have stuck by the barwnig, leading the charge so he imagined, though he could see nothing for the ranks closing fast around him. In between the sharpened points of gleaming metal, the enemy - sun-beaten, bearded, matted hair falling to their shoulders, their faces contorted in hideous hatred, sneering and gnashing their teeth, spitting and shouting curses - all mirrored the Blackoaks. As the two sides came together, Ford's ears screamed with howls and shrieks, horns and drums, the thunder of feet over the field and splashing through the stream. At the resounding crash of the clash, he broke into a deep, fear-driven sweat. And then came the blood. Gushing, spraying, draining out of jerking and writhing men and women bitten by steel. The horrid scene shook him and he stood motionless, plagued by a piercing ringing in his head that blocked out all other sound. He clamped a hand over one ear. No sound but the mad ringing as bewildering sights moved about him. Horses leapt by. Blades flashed, glanced off bodies or vanished into them. A Staneard on the ground with a gash in his belly and the skin of his thigh stripped to the knee opened his quivering mouth wide. It worked in sorrow and suddenly Ford heard his pleading for mercy, and a mother like the one the man begged for, stepped over him with her baby strapped to her back, whipping her ax back and forth in wide arcs until it connected with another Staneard. Knocking her foe over backwards, the Blackoak woman took a slash to the ribs as she brought her heavy weapon down upon the enemy's skull, swung it around and buried the ax head up to the handle in the red trunk of the corpse.

A yank on the arm revived Ford and pulled him close to his father's distorted face. Leo, whiter than he'd seen him before, huddled against his father's side without the pitchfork Ford had given him. The flail drooping in his own hands was lifted and shaken.

"Swing it!" Myer shouted, the words seeming to come from deep within some thick forest. "Swing it!" He was thrust into a veritable wall of elbows, boots, backs and the hilts of swords and the butts of spears jutting back at him. Seeing nothing of the enemy he turned back, but his father and brother were gone. He took a few tottering steps forward and still could not see them. An urge to rush after them, to flee the field altogether, rose dangerously high with him. Dangerous, he knew, for the shame it would bring. He turned back towards the throng and saw large pockets of space open upon the field before him in which axes swung free. With the flail held aloft, he willed one foot forward and then the other. Staring rigidly ahead, ready for whatever came straight at him, he missed the Blackoak in a locked grip with a Bledwin mercenary spiraling towards him. The two windmilled by. He sidestepped, twisted and brought the flail down like a club, coming up short and hitting his own clansman in the shoulder. Ford cringed and stepped back, like a child expecting punishment. Like so many ineffectual blows before it that day, it went unnoticed. Again he tried, the flail hovering over his head, awaiting another opening. The Bledwin spun around toward him and stepping forward, Ford slipped on the slickening grass, crashed into both of them and fell. He knelt to stand, but someone from behind bumped him, tumbling him back to the ground and into the stream. Two thrashing marchog steeds pranced by his head, kicking up water while the warriors upon them slashed recklessly at one another. The Staneard warrior's horse faltered and the only Blackoak marchog Ford didn't know by name struck a hard blow that overshot his moving target, throwing him from his horse. He sprang to his feet with surprising speed, wheeled about and took a jab to the shoulder that dropped him to his knees. The Staneard rode over him and a Bledwin pinned him to the ground with a spear. Blackoaks from his village panicked, fell back, and exposed the flanks of others to attack. An arrow shot under Ford's chin as he got up. Another flew overhead into the Blackoaks as they were giving ground step by step across the once fertile-green field, now churned mud of brown and red.

"Brother!" Ford cried from his hands and knees into the mass of his retreating clansmen and his hands dug convulsively into the mud seeking something firm, seeking some kind of support at the sight of his people's waning strength. His fingers wrapped around what he thought were the two pieces of the flail.

"Blackoaks to me!" his barwnig commanded as Ford held up one half of the flail and an ax. The handle was straight and thin, the head small, but it was an ax. He threw down the broken flail and shoved and shouldered his way into a gap where he could swing the tool-turned-weapon he knew so well from working with his father.

The massive horse of Barwnig Blackoak galloped through the crowd. Ford lunged out of the way and turned in time to see a man dashed to the ground and kicked in the head by a hoof. The horse might have been riderless, he couldn't tell. A blindside jarring thump to the shoulder made him jerk his arm up in a defensive reflex in time to absorb another bone-rattling blow, this time upon his elbow. His arm went numb. With his good hand, he swung the ax blindly around and it thudded into something. When he whirled about there was no one there, nothing but a flurry of weapons, fists, kicks and ramming shoulders. The mass of bodies crowded around him, everyone fighting and dying. A tingling brought life back to his arm. He shook it out, flexed his hand and found himself bent double, fighting for air that would not come.

"Can't breathe," he wheezed. Blood ran from under the hand he pressed to his convulsing stomach. Above him a Staneard with a hungry sneer and the warped joy of a kill in his eyes, yanked back a wide, sharp-bladed hoe, lifting it above Ford's head. A blur of fur bolted by and bashed into the enemy's chest bowling him over. Ford's wolfhound growled and thrashed, tearing the man's tunic open. The Staneard scrambled backwards like a crab, screaming and kicking at the jaws snapping at his groin and belly until he and the dog were swallowed by the sea of legs.

Still kneeling, Ford pulled at his tunic and the cloth, now dyed red, around a hole three inches long over his stomach. A young Blackoak tripped on a drum and fell over him, knocking Ford on his side, from where he watched a long-armed Bledwin whipping a scythe back and forth, widening the space around him. His crazed eyes, white-wide and rolling side to side expecting attack from any direction, landed upon Ford. Ford scrabbled for the ax, the Bledwin rushed him and the young Blackoak going for his drum stepped on Ford's hand. The boy ran off, Ford's fingers clutched at the handle and he felt the air sliced a hair's breadth above him. A shadow overhead cloaked him. He took the ax in both hands and drove it skyward right under the Bledwin's chin. The scythe flipped away and the man collapsed with the ax still lodged in his jaw.

Ford crouched with fists balled, but when the Bledwin didn't move, when the ax handle remained stock-still and pointing straight up to the heavens, he realized he'd killed a man and his legs folded under him. He sat in a stupor staring at the body next to him, feeling sick and sad, like the first time he'd been made to strangle the life out of a chicken. Of all the horror and death he'd witnessed that day, this was by far the worst.

The battle encircling him subsided and he knew not why. Like a wave receding, the enemy gave way, turned and ran, and the Blackoaks roared. The retreat, the chase, the celebration, Ford noticed none of it. His stomach threatened to turn, but then he felt himself lifted to his feet and gradually became aware of his father.

"Good!" said Myer with an arm around him. Ford blinked and looked up at him. "You did good, son!" he said beaming the most wonderful smile his son had ever received from him. Son, thought Ford, something he was seldom called and never with such pride, never such affection. Hearing it felt better than anything he could imagine. If this was what it took to gain his father's respect and love, Ford would kill again, gladly.

Chapter 2
Scream It to the Nothingness

The Blackoaks tore into and devoured greedy mouthfuls of flesh. Beards ran red with the blood of a bull bought by the barwnig from the local villagers. They all drank far too much: pilfered wineskins from the decimated Staneard camp, a barrel of ale exchanged by surviving Bledwins for their lives. Whatever they could get their hands on, the Blackoaks ate and drank. Some stretched out under the sun and slept the afternoon away. Others told and retold their battle stories in the high tones of elation.

When the battle was over, Ford and Leo sat in the circle around a cooking fire and made the mistake of facing out over the battlefield all covered in blood-flecked grass, broken blades and cracked wooden shafts sticking up at odd angles between naked corpses. Ford tried to keep his eyes locked on the fire, but caught himself staring out on to the field, unable to blink away memories of a young man clutching his baby while he slumped over, resting forehead to forehead with his gutted wife, the woman Ford had seen fighting with the baby strapped to her back. He wouldn't soon forget the sight of Winhild cradling his father, blood running from the old man's head, the skin torn back and the skull caved in.

During the fighting Ford had been fine, but after it was over he vomited and remained a few yards away leaning over with hands on shaking knees, feeling better but too embarrassed to return to the others, who seemed so at ease, lighthearted even.

"Came for me he did," said Aelgar Tanner of Iselbryn continuing on with his story, "and well you can believe I swung hard." Here he hung and shook his head. "Clear missed. Missed everything, went head over teats flat on my back." Some around him commiserated and a few chuckled. "I'm laying there and this ass-ugly Staneard, he's right over me, got this huge ax" —he held his hands apart to show an impossibly wide blade— "right up over me and I says to myself, there goes my head, and what happens but he swings down on me and clear misses everything! Same as I!" Astonishment swept through the listeners. "It's true. On my honor. Missed my nose by inches. So, that old boy fell flat on his back, same as I!" A burst of laughter had them slapping their heads and holding in their stomachs. "Then, I don't know how it was, but some fool came along, tripped over us both and we all three were laid there like we was taking a nap together!" Someone spit up his ale, a few were left gasping for breath, and tears flowed.

Ford couldn't understand how they could be so jolly after what they'd all just been through. He needed to get away from them and wandered off, turning into the dazed faces of those tending to the field of the dead. His eyes fell upon the young man mourning over his slain wife. He still shook uncontrollably and now the baby cried, too.

"What's his name?" asked Winhild, stoically recovered from his own loss and kneeling gently beside them.

"Elyan," said the young man, allowing the child to be coaxed from his arms.

"Well, Elyan," said Winhild smiling down at the baby, "you and me we'll go play so your pa can do what needs doing." His voice dropped to a murmur and the baby calmed somewhat as he rocked the bundle in his arms and walked about in slow, easy circles while the young man attended to his wife's body.

Ford stood transfixed by the remaining carnage upon the field and recalled what he'd seen and done after the battle: Blackoaks crawling over the bodies, finishing off the wounded with a precisely placed knife thrust, then pawing over the corpse in search of loot. Myer had pressed his boys to do the same. Ford found very little, only a ring, but the recollection of wrenching it from a cold finger, something he'd not soon forget, was nearly blotted from memory by Barwnig Blackoak beheading Barwnig Staneard. The act was an ancient rite, a victor's privilege and an all-but-forgotten tradition, now reserved for a particularly hated foe with hopes that by removing the head from the body it would keep their souls from cluttering the warriors' heavenly paradise.

"One less to worry about," the Blackoaks' loquacious bone mender had said when he grabbed Ford to help with a patient who had an open arm wound. Some menders were divinely imbued with the power to heal, but like so many, this one was no holy man, rather a butcher with some knowledge of how the body worked. "If a cut's not too deep this way," the mender later explained with a gesture down the length of the forearm, "chances of surviving are good. But if it goes crosswise the blood will usually drain right quick." Ford followed along all too closely and felt his own blood draining as he knelt beside the wounded man with his big hands wrapped around the other's arm. "Cleaning a wound is just as important, if you survive, that is. A dirty wound will as like kill a man as the wound itself. Just takes longer is all." While the mender strung a needle, the gash pooled with blood that ran between Ford's fingers and loosened his grip on the lips of flesh. "Hold it still, nice and close." With methodical care, the mender pushed the dull needle through the skin. His writhing patient screamed and Ford passed out on top of him.

"That's it, hold him down. Good!" the mender exclaimed, pinching the skin and pulling his needle back through. A wild spasm of pain shook Ford awake and he found the twitching, wounded man biting down on upon his forearm. "There we go," said the mender tying off the stitches. "Well done, son."

The next thing he knew, someone was leading him away, pressing a flagon of ale into his hands and helping him back to the others. He sat alongside Leo, who had dried vomit down the front of him, and picked at the ground. A nugget of quartz gave way under his bloodstained fingernail and though it wasn't worth much, he added it to the pouch of rocks and trinkets he was collecting to give to his girlfriend. Thought of her was enough to bring back her sweet breath blown into his face after chewing wintergreen berries, as well as times spent laughing together or hooting like owls across a valley during one of their slow walks over the bush-covered hill between their villages, or lying nose to nose hidden in tall grass when she would run her hand up and down between his legs. He couldn't wait to touch her again, to fondle her breasts and for her to touch him. His hand rubbed over his crotch briefly before he pulled it away, looking around to see if anyone had caught him. But no one was paying any attention. He laid back and stretched out. Stinky rested his head upon his chest and the two soon fell asleep.

That night those Blackoaks who'd not yet left for home celebrated with a modest feast at marchog Bachbel's hall, the nearest at hand. Every inch of the low-ceilinged dwelling was packed with those who'd fought and the families of those from the village, so that even the marchog's prized sow was penned outside to make room for the night. Toddlers crawled over young girls and boys listening with envy about the battle. The old and infirm wished they could have been there and praised those who had. Diminutive wives clung to their husbands and showed pleasure at their return with kisses and hidden caresses. Infused with the joy of being alive and of going home, the Blackoaks ripped into juicy haunches of meat around a blazing fire and congratulated one another, then drank to the health of all, especially those who would never make it back. They threw their arms around one another's shoulders and sang beautiful songs terribly. Then they would laugh, drink more and sing louder.

Ford sang the songs he knew and mouthed along to those he didn't. After a while the songs sounded disjointed and his mug seemed to fill and empty of its own accord. Each sip of the strong, flavorful brew begged for another. Before he knew it, he'd finished his third ale, was well into his fourth and was feeling fine, aside from his uncooperative eyes, which tended to unfocus themselves.

Having exhausted talk of the battle and grown tired of singing, the people returned to the old tales to while away the remainder of the evening. A lull between stories left the group smiling and nodding off, except for Ford. Infused with good cheer and a love for this newfound camaraderie, he leaned over his brother and pulled on his father's arm.

"Pa. Pa, tell the one," —a belch slipped out— "tell that story, the one you telled, told to me." Myer ignored him, but Ford persisted, yanking on his sleeve. "You remember, you know the one, that one about the weird lady." With his heavy-lidded eyes half closed, Ford missed the irritation looking down upon him along the length of his father's long nose, made crooked from the time his wife caught him across the face with a pan.

"Stop it, Ford." Myer jerked away his arm and Ford flopped into his brother's lap, confused as to how he had ended up there. Leo helped set him upright again. Most pretended not to notice or feigned sleep. Myer got up, muttered something about relieving himself and walked outside.

Ford cringed at the return of the old, familiar knot in his stomach, a constant complaint for the boy with a father practiced at shooting him down, sometimes unexpectedly like this and at other times quite subtly. Myer spoke to him so infrequently and never at length about what was right and wrong, so Ford wondered how he was to know, particularly when the wrong was a story Myer told him so many years ago on a rare occasion when it was just the two of them. Ford only wanted to hear again about the enchantress who had ensnared a man's heart, a heart belonging to another, so that the woman and the baby born of this unlawful union were driven away. And how the woman had returned one day and left the child for the man to care for, then mysteriously disappeared, Myer believed, to the western city of Mortre Porth, where she no doubt lived to this day. Ford couldn't imagine what was wrong with the tale, partly because he didn't even understand its meaning. All he knew was how much it reminded him of how his own mother had once left him to be cared for by his father. Some soured souls insisted she must be dead. Myer gave him no answers. As he had done a hundred and more times before, Ford tried to put it all out of his mind.

That night in the crowded hall, lying wedged between his dog and the marchog's lively young niece who was gradually pushing her backside into him, he dreamt of becoming a warrior who went off to new lands to fight battle after battle with never an end to the thrill and companionship, and that feeling of making his father proud. He could get nothing like it at his unhappy home, but he hoped life might change. After all, he felt a change within him and perhaps others would take notice and treat him differently from now on.

The following day Ford and Leo took their turns at the litter carrying Winhild's father home with the marchog of Oren leading the dwindling party. Over a stone bridge, they followed along a chatty, rocky stream for a while before climbing out of a valley and over a windswept hill. On the other side, their footpath joined with a cartroad lined with pines. Ford recognized this land.

"Oren?" asked Leo. Myer nodded. The trees along the road ahead parted for the fields and houses of the village the Barlows knew second only to their own. They emerged from the forest road and shouts rang out from the old and young coming from the fields to greet them. Doors flew open with cries of joy and they were surrounded by all of the remaining two dozen or so villagers. The hugs, well-wishing and eagerness for news soon subsided at sight of the dead. Winhild's aging mother squinted about the crowd and spotted the graying head of her husband laid out upon a litter.

"Rhys," she cried out, falling to one knee and into the arms of her daughter-in-law. She pushed free and crawled on hands and knees to her husband. When she reached out and touched his cold skin she gasped for air in vain and thought she might never breathe again. Nor did she want to. Her son and his wife fell in beside her imploring, "Mother…mother." With the children crying and the villagers hanging their heads, Myer and his sons said a prayer and left them to their grief.

Passing from Oren to the top of the hill where the cartroad met a low stone wall and turned south, to the east a cluster of homes forgotten by the outside world could be made out between the trees on the other side of a stream below. Another hill beyond crowded the whole of the settlement into a small, uneven patch of cleared land. Normally after such a long time away from home, Leo would have jumped and shouted for joy at the sight. Happy but weary, now all three of them raised little more than a grin at seeing Barlow.

A squeal shot up the hill. Their little sister Nia with her beaming eyes and face-stretching smile, leapt about, yanking the cloth tie from her hair to wave it back and forth over her head. On the last leap, she spun around with a cry of joy, plopped down into some thick grass, then jumped to her feet and ran for them with her dress whipping about her legs. Stinky galloped down the hill and the two crashed together into a blueberry bush. He came bounding up with his tongue lolling out. She stayed down and a gradual sob rose from the bush.

"Oh no," sighed Leo and Myer shook his head, but Ford ran for his sister.

"You're all right. Don't cry. Please don't." Ford cared deeply for his sister, but the dog was his responsibility. He lifted her out of the bush and found her smock blotched by mushed berries on the back with two dirty paw prints and a tear down the front. The dog lapped at the girl's face so much she could scarcely breathe and could only flail about trying to elude his affection. Ford pushed the heavy beast away and after a deep breath, his sister let loose a pitiful sob.

"What's wrong?" Little else could stamp joy out of Ford and seize up his heart quite like that voice. Without having to see, those simple words etched the scowl of Milda Barlow's disapproving face in his mind. The stabbing condemnation embodied her quick temper and the speed with which she rushed to judgment with the sympathy of an executioner. Ford had never heard her laugh. Witless prattle she called it. If she had possessed a sense of humor at one time, a once-faithless love had driven it from her.

However, it couldn't be denied that she was a hard worker and staunch defender of her children. That made matters worse for Ford. He looked down at Nia and wished the tears she fought back wouldn't come, but she was only four and he couldn't blame her when the tiniest droplets rolled from the corners of her eyes.

"What happened? What did you do?" With her sharp nose pointing the way, Milda stalked toward them, her spotless smock rustling as her legs churned and her elbows thrust side to side. Not long before, Ford had noticed that the woman was all points. Her knees, chin, shoulders, even her knuckles had an edge to them. He was not fond of bones and she had a bucketful.

"Nothing," Ford replied, but he'd long since stopped looking her in the eye when speaking to her and she mistrusted him for it.

"Nothing?" She gripped the fabric around the tear in Nia's smock. "Then what's this?" Ford began a fumbling explanation, but she turned away to Nia. "How did this happen?" The little girl couldn't gather breath enough to answer and her angry mother's frantic behavior only increased her sobbing. "You should be ashamed," she said to Ford, taking her youngest into her arms.

"It wasn't Ford," said Leo, as he and his father approached with caution. "Stinky knocked her down. He didn't mean to."

"That dog is nothing but trouble." Milda gave Leo and her husband each a kiss on the cheek before going on about Ford's dog, while she herded her sniffling daughter back over the stream and along the path to their house. "Well, I'm glad you're home safe. Tilly's been ill and in bed since yesterday. I'm worried it's the - scrape the filth off those feet before you even think of coming in! Where are your shoes? Lost them, I suppose. Well, you'll have to wait until I can sew up some new ones. It won't be soon. I've a heaping hill's worth of work ahead of me." She flicked a finger at Ford. "You, put your clutter away neat, then tie up that dog of yours!"

Ford grumbled, swore after the last of his family passed into the house, and dropped everything he was carrying on the ground except for the pouch tucked into his belt and made for Gwen's village. He didn't give a second thought to his sore feet or tired legs on the way over the hill east of Barlow, even though mounting the granite ridge felt more like climbing a mountain.

The lazy watchman in the shaky, wooden tower on the hilltop snored away behind the shuttered windows, instead of leaving his comforts and scouting the wilderness as he was paid to do. It was a regular and sweet sound to Ford, a herald mere moments before Mewn Gulch came into view.

Though the people there were not of Ford's clan, they were on good terms with the Blackoaks and treated him well. Ford wished he were on good terms with Gwen's family the Maips, but the only one he liked was her mother, a kind if somewhat loony woman. On the occasion when her mind came fleetingly back to the present, she went out of her way to make him feel welcome, a stark contrast to the treatment he received from her husband and son. Whenever Ford could, he avoided Gwen's father and brother. They laid hands on her, hit her for the slightest thing. "It's nothing," she would say. She could take it, she'd insist. Ford didn't doubt it. She was solidly built, but so were her father and brother.

"Shouldn't lay hands on no one who can't defend themselves," Ford's father had said about two years back when his eldest daughter Tilda brought up Gwen's recurring bruises after a day of swimming. The words stuck with Ford. He pondered and repeated them until they were so ingrained that one day when he actually saw Gwen's brother slap her, Ford tore into the much older boy before he realized what he was doing. The fight dragged on until both boys looked like they'd lost. On that day Ford made not only an enemy, but a lifelong friend, both of whom lived under the same roof.

Anticipation can make one miss important details, just as Ford missed the large bowl of fruit and bread by the door, as well as the maple leaves hanging over it upon ducking into the Maips' home and finding the family quite subdued. Gwen's mother burst into tears at the sight of him and placed an elm tree sprig in his hair. When he left the house and really looked about, he saw that the whole village was in a somber mood, having taken part in Gwen's interment only the day before.

Ford couldn't remember walking home. When he arrived he went straight to the barn and crawled into the narrow loft where he slept above the animals. He propped a foot against one of the rafters and lay silent for a while, then kicked the beam. He kicked it harder, then again, harder and faster each time until he wore himself out. The sucking of feet in the muck by the doorway had him hurriedly rubbing his eyes dry on each shoulder.

"No Stinky, not for you. No. Down," came Leo's voice from below. Ford dug a piece of mica from his pouch and starting picking flakes from it just before his brother's head appeared in the loft.

"Hungry?" Leo asked holding out a chicken leg. Stinky whined at the base of the ladder.

"No," said Ford.

"You sure?" Leo's hand stretched closer. Ford shoved it back.

"I said no!"

"All right, all right."

"Just leave me alone." Ford rolled on to his side facing the wall. Leo said nothing, sighed ever so slightly and eventually left.

The following morning a powerful hunger, stronger than his misery, compelled Ford up and out of the barn. His father and brother sat on a bench by the house carving a small wooden totem. Ford guessed it was for the Maips. It would be in the likeness of Gwen and they would float it down the river on the far side of Mewn Gulch with their blessing for her in the afterlife. Leo's face melted into pity for him. His father kept his head down. Ford walked by them into the house where he found Milda cleaning out a pot at the family's largest basin, a vaguely pale Tilda lying by a weak fire and Nia on her hands and knees pretending to be a deer.

"Now he's hungry," Milda said without looking up. "I told you he'd come around soon enough. That boy is ruled by his belly."

"Am not," said Ford.

"Don't you talk back."

It never did to answer Milda and Ford wasn't sure why he'd bothered. He tightened his lips, looked away and Milda was satisfied. "Well, you're too late anyways. There's none left, so you'll just have to go hungry." She moved her clean crockery back to the table and continued on with plenty to say about being late for a meal, the rudeness of talking back, and more, but Ford stopped listening.

"Don't," Tilda said to Nia, who was threatening to leap over her – or at least attempt to. Nia hopped away, directly into Milda's path, nearly tripping her. She hopped around the table, jostling one leg and rattling the crockery.

"Go outside, child!" Looking around the room to find a chore, Milda sputtered out, "Go and get me some watercress." She turned back to Ford. "And another thing! I haven't heard an apology out of you. Leo was only trying to do you a kindness. I said, don't bother, he won't appreciate it. He'll be in there carrying on and he won't thank you for it!"

"What's watercrush?"

"Watercress!" hollered Tilda across the room in a full, hardy voice. Her mother shot her a calculating eye and the girl forced out a dry cough.

"The round, green leaves. By the stream," said Milda, taking Nia by the hand and leading her to the door. While repeating her instructions and pointing downstream, Ford sneaked a handful of strawberries from a hanging sack.

"Mam!" shouted Tilda from within the blanket wrapped tight around her head and shoulders. "Ford's taking strawberries."

"Get your dirty hands out of there. Oh, that reminds me." Milda took down the sack and handed it to Nia. "Fill that up while you're out there. Try along the hill."

"I don't know which—" started the girl.

"Oh for the love…" muttered Milda, dragging Nia by the arm out the door.

Ford stomped across to his sister by the fire and hovered over her. Tilda cowered deeper within the blanket. Checking that no one was looking, Ford pulled back his fist and swung at Tilda's face, stopping an inch away and grinning with satisfaction when she flinched.

"Pa!" she cried.

"Come outside," called Myer.

Ford slumped down beside Leo and they watched their father digging at the arm's length of wood in his large, rough hands. Normally all three would have been out in the forest working, but it was decided a day of rest was in order after what they'd recently endured. Besides, with carving work to do, it was a good opportunity for his sons to learn the skill that benefited the family in a little extra coin and trade. The boys weren't as attentive as they normally would have been, especially when it wasn't their turn with the knife. Leo watched Ford from the corner of this eye.

"I'm sorry," he eventually said. Ford shrugged it off. He didn't like pity, especially coming from someone to whom he owed an apology. "I mean about Gwen."

"I know." He could still feel Leo's eyes upon him and perhaps Myer could, too.

"Pay attention," he told his boys, but what he was doing was nothing they hadn't seen countless times before: shallow scalloping gouges, this time to indicate long wavy hair. It didn't exactly match the thick mass that once flowed over Gwen's shoulders, but the reminder was bitter enough. Ford couldn't bear to watch any longer.

"I got to go," he told them and ducked behind the barn where he normally relieved himself. From there he drifted off towards the stream and around the edge of the forest, lost in his own thoughts and walking slower with each step. Still looking to avoid his family, he passed behind the cottage of the Woodmans, an old couple and the only others living in Barlow. The Woodmans had no surviving offspring, only a widowed and reclusive daughter-in-law still living with them, so Myer had had the fortune to take over as woodcutter when the old man's enlarged joints became too painful for him to swing an ax. The door creaked open and a voice crackled out to Ford.

"Come. Come," he heard the old woodcutter's wife say from within the darkened interior of the old house. "Bless you now and take this." She handed him a small sack when he came to the door. "Take it. Spread it 'round the…'round the trees there." She waved her white, spotted hand vaguely towards the forest. Ford knew what she wanted done, so he took the sack, remembered to smile and began spreading horse hair clippings at the forest's edge. The old woman and many others did this to ward off or appease spirits or fairies, Ford couldn't remember the exact purpose. Years now he'd been doing this for the old woman without question. Someone had to do it. She didn't get around much and neither did her husband. Their pale-skinned daughter-in-law managed their animals and made their meals, and she was only seen coming and going as needs must due to her diminished health after a long, torturous grieving of her lost husband and three children. The Barlows were often helping out what was left of the Woodman family.

The horse hairs sprinkled from his fingers landed on tree stumps and their off-shoots or dispersed into the wild grass. He took his time. Leo's pity, his apologies and debts owed, and thoughts of Gwen slowed Ford almost to a standstill. When one lazy toss rubbed his wrist against the pouch filled with rocks at his waist, he realized he could fix at least one of his troubles. He had planned to give the ring to Gwen as a gift and perhaps even ask her to marry him, but this new idea would serve another purpose just as well.

"I'm sorry what happened before, what Stinky done…did," he said back at the house in a quiet earnestness with a slight twitch of annoyance at the error in words, a mildly punishable crime under Milda's roof. He had knelt beside Nia where she played on the floor with a wooden doll her father had carved for her. "Here, this is for you." He put the pouch in her hand.

"Now Ford's telling secrets to Nia," said Tilda just as she hid her face from Ford behind a blanket. Focused on the apology, Ford had forgotten about his other sister buried in the bundle by the fire.

"I can't wait until you're all out of this house again," said Milda wiping her hands dry on a cloth and coming to investigate. "We have no secrets in this family. What is that?"

"He gave her something," came Tilda's muffled voice.

"I can see that. What is it?"

Nia dumped the contents of the pouch on the floor. Her delighted eyes spotted the ring amongst the pebbles and held it up to admire it in the fire light, a loving smile spreading across her face. Milda snatched away the ring, stalked to the window and turned it around in the light.

"What is it," asked Tilda, rising up in her bed.

"It's for Nia. I gave it to her," said Ford.

"This is the family's," Milda said hurrying from the house with Nia on her heels. "Shut that door. Do you want Tilly to get worse and die like that Gulch girl?" It was a warm evening, but Ford slammed the door after them and swung around to face Tilda, who turned paler than she had been since the start of her illness.

"Mam," she shouted when Ford grabbed a knife from the table and stalked towards her.

"Go back inside," Milda ordered Nia. She had to pry the reluctant girl from her skirt and push her at the door. "Go!" Nia scurried in. "And you, go check on the chickens." Leo jumped up, called for the suddenly excited dog to come along with him and disappeared into the barn. Milda rounded on her husband. "Did you know that son of yours was hiding this?" She held the ring before his eyes. "He was going to give it to Nia. Just give it to her! What's a girl her age to do with something as valuable as this?"

"He meant it for the Maips' girl," said Myer. "I suppose, because of what happened—"

"You were going to let that idiot boy just give this away? It's silver!"

"He won it in battle."

"What does that matter?"

"It's tradition."

"Tradition? Nonsense!"

"It's his to do what he will."

"It most certainly is not! I'm struggling just to feed this family and this—" A terrified scream, more piercing than Tilda's usual shrieks, cut Milda short. They rushed in and found Ford sitting by the fire with Nia's fretful eyes upon him as he calmly scraped the knife along the length of a piece of wood while Tilda wailed away, making wild claims that he'd threatened her.

He denied it and since apparently nothing of great import had happened, the matter was dropped.

"Don't," said Milda taking away the knife, "use my good knife on wood. I told you, you'll dull the edge."

"It's nothing," said Myer from the corner of his mouth on his way back out the door to Leo, who was just rushing in.

"We're not done," said Milda following her husband outside.

Ford smiled to himself, pleased to have gotten away with frightening his sister in retribution, until he noticed Nia wrapped around one of the legs under the table staring at him and nearly in tears. His brother and his youngest sister were the only people left in the world that he loved and seeing one of them look at him like he was the stuff of nightmares made his heart sink. He slunk out of the house and heard Milda say to his father, "You're going to take this to your brother when next you're in Lewiston and have him tell you how much it's worth."

Even inside the barn he could hear her clearly. He did his best to block her out, but when she began talking about Gwen, he couldn't help but listen.

"It really was the most pathetic thing you ever saw. That poor girl just faded away. And so fast. She was always a sturdy girl, but Tilly, she paid a visit and she said the girl just laid there all skin and bones. Don't know what could've been the matter with her."

"You afraid Tilly's caught it?"

"No, I don't think so. More than like, the way she's been carrying on, it's just a cold. I've taken precautions though." She listed all the herbal remedies she'd administered over the past few days and Ford was thankful she'd moved on from talking about Gwen. He didn't want to think about her. The pain was too great, and yet, a moment later he found himself vowing never to forget her. Prayers for the dead stuttered from his lips, followed by demands for the gods to treat her well in the afterlife.

"Please," he begged when he'd been finally worn down to tears, "please just let me see her one more time."

In the days and weeks ahead, his love, loss and anger would find triggers in nearly everything: whiffs of the lilac or lavender Gwen had once used to scent her skin; a sip of soup sounded like kisses stolen with her in the tall grass at the back of fields or at the edge of the forest pressed against a tree. Memories sent him spiraling into depression. Over time he bounced back quicker, but he would never completely forget her.

That night he was quick to abandon sleep and lay out under the stars with his dog.

"Nothing's changed," he said so softly that Stinky didn't raise so much as his eyes to him. "It's worse really. The bad's gotten worse and the good things are gone."

· · · · · ·

One of the last unbearably hot days of the year fell on a holiday and after prayers, the children of the surrounding villages spent as much of it as they were allowed swimming in what they called The Pond, a relatively deep pool of water in the shallow stream that ran past Barlow into the lower fields below Oren. Wearing nearly nothing or, in the case of a boy they called Brown Bum, absolutely nothing, children screeched and laughed as they splashed and dove and chased one another around the water almost endlessly.

Those who knew how to swim or at least hold their breath underwater were in a contest to see who could stay down the longest. On the count of three, they all took the plunge, Ford among them. When he opened his eyes, the water was so stirred up he couldn't see much beyond his own nose, but he could hear the muffled splashing of children giving up and surfacing or fighting to stay under. A hand or foot struck him in the mouth and bubbles burst from his lips, but he held on, clamping his eyes shut and enduring the burning in his lungs and mad desire to breathe. Then he relaxed, let his body float backside up so that his face remained submerged, and began thinking of anything else that would come to mind. The initial panic died away and in its place arose a self-assurance that he could go on doing this forever. So sure and confident of his own abilities was he that he sank down into the water and opened his eyes again, hoping to spy who was left in the game. A ghostly face, like that of death itself, nearly touched him nose to nose. He screamed and bubbles roiled the water before him. His flailing limbs kicked up more mud. Then he stopped. The face he'd seen belonged to Col, the boy always first to quit the game and rise for air. Ford broke the surface gasping and wiping his eyes to the cheering of the children around the edge of the pool. Col, still submerged, had outlasted everyone. When he remained underwater longer than natural, the cheering died away.

"Help him," screamed Col's horrorstricken sister pointing at her brother's body. In the confusion, Leo dove in, grabbed the boy by the hair and dragged him to the edge, where he struggled to lift him out of the water. Ford splashed through the pool, hefted the boy in his arms and threw him on to the bank. The boy landed hard on his back, choked up a mouthful of water, coughed and sputtered out some more. He rolled on his side and breathed deep, desperate breaths.

"I'm all right," he said, his eyes fluttering and his voice still hoarse. Seeing he wasn't going to die, the others lost interest and went back to swimming. Ford and Leo collapsed on their backs in patches of sunlight to catch their breath. Stinky came loping up to check on them with a rider, little Cy of Oren, clinging to his back. Before long the boy lost his grip and slid off. The dog bounded away with Cy chasing after him.

A few of the cold and tired among them joined Ford and Leo in the sun creating a lull in the excitement that the ever-energetic Brown Bum would have none of. With his arms and legs spread wide, he repeatedly thrust his hips out so that his peanut-sized penis bounced about. In this manner he hobbled after screaming children. Hiding from him behind some bushes with her face a mask of confusion, Nia circled back to her brothers and slumped down with her head on Ford's leg, grabbing his hand and dropping it over her eyes. She smiled up at him through his fingers, closed her eyes and soon fell asleep.

Ford thought about his little sister more these days than ever before. He no longer took her affection for granted, but it was more than just fondness that made him ponder Nia just then. She'd turned five the day before, the approximate age he'd been when his mother walked unheard of miles and left him to be raised by his father. Later that day so many years past, Milda's studying glare took in the boy and the man. If the unusually tall child standing next to her long-legged husband didn't erase all doubt, few could deny their strikingly similar dipping and rising eyebrows and how they gave both boy and man a leaden gaze that fell hazily somewhere between vacant and that of the thinker; a look that made others wonder if they were all-knowing or if they knew anything at all. Myer remained mum on the subject of the boy, neither admitting nor denying he was the father, merely accepting Ford like an expected burden and paying for his transgression every day since.

Though she seldom let him forget what he'd done, to her credit, Milda stuck with him. Some rumored she had her eye on his family's lucrative trade. Certainly ambition flowed through her, but it was nothing to her stubborn pride and fear of aging without the family she envisioned around her. The vision skewed by another woman's child was still the vision, warts and all. In the meanwhile she held out hope that Myer's well-to-do family might welcome him back. After all, she'd seen him carve and assumed he was just as skilled in the crafting of precious metals, so perhaps one day she might change her name from Barlow to Goldsmith.

If the Goldsmiths had been farmers in a remote village all might have blown over and been little more than an embarrassment, but as respected craftsmen in town their name was as valuable as the metal they worked. Myer's father had cut him out entirely, halting his apprenticeship and forbidding any potential partnership Myer and his elder brother might have had in the future. Myer's mother was more forgiving, helping him buy a country farmstead. Misfortune and his ineptitude as a farmer ran it into the ground a few years later, so that they had to sell it for a pittance and use the remainder to move to the even more remote Barlow.

At first, getting away from the scorn and shame was a relief, but Milda chafed at the instability and the distance from her kinsmen. Faced with a wife whose anger often boiled over, the naturally reserved Myer turned almost mute and went about quietly doing her will as a means of placating her. Since she was not unreasonable for the most part, they learned to live with one another. Eventually, the years-long chill between them melted significantly enough to bring about the birth of Nia.

Ford beamed down upon his sister. An ant sped across her arm in a zigzag course and he flicked it off. He plucked a long blade of grass within arms reach and tickled her ears and nose with it. Every now and then she waved a languid hand at the imaginary fly, then rolled on her side. Ford shifted with her and jerked involuntarily from a sharp pain shooting through his leg. Nia's head bounced and she sat up straight and defensive, but saw Ford grabbing his leg and grimacing.

"What's the matter?" The anxious question didn't come from Nia, but rather Leofy Bawgwaith hovering off to one side with clasped hands. Leofy could have been Tilda's twin, at least in age and frailness. She came from a village almost a mile away, but the Barlows had seen a lot more of her since the passing of Gwen: a visit to wish them joy after their return from battle; the delivery of a gift of lamb sweetbreads from her family and to give her condolences. "That's nice, but why us?" Milda had asked, voicing what all but Tilda failed to understand.

"It's nothing," said Ford to Leofy, rubbing his legs, "they just hurt sometimes."

"Oh," swooned the girl moving in close and laying her hand on his leg, "it happens often?"

"Kind of."

"Oh, that's horrible!"

Ford stopped rubbing his calf muscle and stared at her hand upon his leg. She froze, caught his eye and ran off into the bushes.

"That was weird," said Ford.

"Yeah," agreed Leo, distracted by a boy with a frog. "Hey Morris, bring that over here." The redheaded, hollow-chested Morris stood ankle-deep in the water amid the limbs of a branch accidentally ripped down by someone trying to swing from it into the water. Dirt still clung to Morris, who had spent most of his day out of the water scouring the weeds for his prey. He held his cupped hands tight to his chest. "Come on, I just want to have a look. I won't steal it." His main worry abated, the boy came to them and held out a thick-legged bullfrog looking quite bloated due to the tight grip about its waist.

"I've caught bigger," said Morris running a critical eye over the frog.

"I know. I've seen. But still, it's pretty good," said Leo leaning in for a closer look. "Can I hold it?"

"I don't know."

"Just for a little bit?"

"Well, only you, for a short while."

"Did you know frogs have two sets of eyes?" Leo asked Ford, taking the frog in his hands and holding it for his brother to see.

"I do. One, two," said Ford pointing in the direction of both sides of its head.

"No, I mean it's got four eyes."

"Sure he does. So where's he hiding the other two?"

"On top of these two," said Leo pointing and inadvertently poking one of the frog's eyes. Ford winced with the frog. "One set for above water and one for below, for swimming. Haven't you noticed when they go underwater?" Ford didn't know much about frogs, but he knew they'd dry out in the sun and eventually burn to an emaciated crisp without water.

"Put him back in the pond and show me." They crawled to the edge of the water and Leo dunked the frog.

"Um," said a worried Morris hovering at their side.

"Did you see?" Leo pulled the frog out and dunked it again.

"Oh, yeah."

"Wow," said Nia hanging from their necks and leaning between them over the water to see.

"Oh, I knew that already," said Morris. "Give me my frog back now, would you?"

"Let me see." Ford took the frog from Leo, held it under the water and loosened his grip imperceptibly. The frog slipped free and swam away.

"Aw, nuts! Now I have to catch him all over again," said Morris splashing back into the weeds.

"Poor frog," said Leo. He and Ford sat for a while dangling their feet in the water.

"Maybe this will make you feel better," said Leofy appearing as if from nowhere behind Ford and dropping an apple in his lap.

"An apple?" Ford left the apple where it landed.

"The least you could say is thank you," said Tilda on her way over from her usual spot under a tree to stand over her brothers with her hands propped on her hips. "You're so impolite. He really isn't worth your attentions, Leofy." Leofy turned a shade pinker. "Well?"

"Well what," asked Ford. "Leave me alone."

"There she goes again," said Leo at the sight of Leofy dashing off through the trees.

"You are plain rude. And dumb," said Tilda leaning in close to point in Ford's face. "So, so dumb." Ford made a grab for her finger and Tilda fell back, stuck out her tongue and ran after Leofy.

"You know that girl likes you," said Leo.

"I know and I don't care."

"Why not?"

"She's weird. And all bones. And she's Tilly's friend and I don't like any of those things."

A splash drew their attention to Morris leaping in the shallows.

"Nuts!"

"What did the frog do to the paper?" asked Leo.

Ford floated away into deeply aimless thought before answering, "What paper?"

"No, there's no paper. It's just a joke."

"The paper's a joke?"

"There's no paper, just the joke."

"Then why didn't you ask me what the frog did with the joke?"

"Because that's not the joke."

"You mean the paper?"

"What about the paper?"

"The paper's not the joke."

Leo's eyes narrowed in his attempt to follow Ford's thinking and his already long face, resembling his father's now that he'd shed the rounded cheeks and chin, lengthened further in a scowl from patience wore thin. "Listen, forget all that. Just, when I ask the question, say what. What did the frog do to the paper?"

"What?"

"Rip it!" A smile lit up Leo's face as he waited for a reaction, but he got nothing. "Rip it! You see? Rip it?"

"Why do you keep saying ribbit?"

"No, rip it! The frog rips the paper. Rips it, ribbit, rips it? Get it?"

Ford's belly jumped and a muffled chortle buried deep within him rumbled out like a wagon rolling over bumpy ground; the start of a stampede of laughter.

"I know one. Why did the frog jump over the stream?" asked Nia, but as always, before anyone had a chance to answer she shouted, "Get it?" and laughed herself silly along with Ford roaring out of a love for jokes, poorly told or not. They went back and forth telling more or posing riddles to one another. Ford floundered terribly, unable to keep them straight and usually premature in giving away the punchline, which made everyone laugh as well as himself.

On the frog-catching side of the pond, Cy made a leap for Stinky's back, the dog dipped his hip and dumped the boy face first in mud and weeds. Seeing the other children laughing and pointing at him, the open-mouthed boy started to cry. His brother led him into the water to wash up until he looked human again. Tilda returned and sat with her brothers.

"Well, she's gone," she said in grand declaration, throwing the weight of blame their way.

"Give up?" Leo asked Ford.

"Hold on."

"What is it? Let me guess," said Tilda, a clever one for riddles.

"Hold on!" Ford didn't like to give in that easily, at least not without giving it his best shot. He always felt that if he just closed his eyes and thought long enough, the answer would eventually come to him. It worked on occasion, so he dropped his head and shut his eyes tight.

"Tell it to me, I bet I can get it," said Tilda.

"Don't tell her," said Ford.

"Come on, I won't guess."

"All right," said Leo. "Name a thing that you can catch, but you can't throw."

"Oh that's easy!"

"Don't say it," said Ford.

"A cold," said Tilda, punctuating the answer with a crunch of Ford's apple.

"I told you not to!" Ford opened his eyes and they fell upon the apple. "Hey!" He scrambled to his feet and would have dove at her, but Tilda threw the apple over his head. It bounced twice and rolled down the bank. Ford chased it into the water.

"You've still got some on your face," said a girl with a scrunched up nose to Cy, who went on furiously wiping his cheeks. One particularly slimy brown glob wouldn't come off. "It's a leech," screamed the girl, setting off the kind of panic and chaos normally caused by invading hordes charging over the hills. The children closest to Cy stumbled backwards and started a general flight from the boy, whose crying increased when he pulled at the elastic creature fastened to his face.

"It won't come off! It won't come off!" he screeched.

"Come here," said Ford, washing off his apple and holding it in his mouth, so he could work at the leech.

"Look at him, he looks like a pig. Oink! Oink!" said Tilda laughing loud. Ford tried to ignore her and focus on carrying out the difficult operation on a particularly squirmy leech and boy. The children gathered around, not repulsed enough to overcome their curiosity. Ford pinched his fingers where leech met skin, pulled with a sharp jerk and the leech finally came off. Blood gushed down the boy's cheek and started another riot. Boys and girls ran away, some bent double pretending to retch; one particularly squeamish child ran home. Ford held up the leech in triumph and catching a glimpse of Tilda, his lips lifted around the apple in a wicked grin.

"No!" she yelled, backing away and waving her hands to ward off his sudden and determined approach. Through the stream and around the pond they went, she ducking the apple hurled, he wiggling the leech in the air and cackling at her screams. This was good fun for the others, some getting so absorbed within the game that they chased the pair around the pond. "Get away!" Tilda demanded. The next time they came around to where the stream fed the pond, Brown Bum bumped against her. She missed her jump and fell in the water. Ford caught up, but Tilda rolled on her back on the bank and kicked at him, keeping him at bay for a moment before he fell on top of her. Sitting on her stomach dangling the leech over her face, he pinned her arms under his knees with his free hand. The children chose sides, goading Ford on or calling him a brute amid Tilda's screams. Ford heard none of it, not even his brother telling him to stop. There was nothing else in his world then but the vile pleasure of giving her the kind of retribution he'd been meaning to for a long time. He lowered his hand slowly and choked out horrid laughter as the leech's wet tail licked against her nose, making her thrash about from side to side. He reached down and tickled her ribs. "Stop it!" she cried. His hand darted up and he shoved in the leech, clamping her mouth shut with the other hand. She stared unbelieving up at him for an instant before screaming into his muffling hand and digging at the earth. She kicked and bucked and Ford nearly fell off, but he was too strong and far too heavy for her. Even after fighting one arm free, she couldn't even pull off his hand clamped over her mouth. He laughed into her face a horrible laugh that frightened some of the younger children. She went limp and began to sob just as Leo crashed into Ford, knocking him off Tilda.

That afternoon and evening at home Ford caught an earful; all the while Nia drizzled water over dirty potatoes that Tilda cut for a pie Milda was making with the dough she kneaded on the table. No one would listen to his side of the argument, he complained, while trying to explain how Tilda had started what led to the trouble with the leech. Little could be heard above Milda's shouting. She yelled at him from across the room, yelled at his face and kept on yelling with her back turned to him as she stood at the washbasin cleaning the potatoes abandoned by Nia. Leeches disgusted her and the whole scene, described in detail by Tilda, sent her into a fit on her daughter's behalf. Ford was sent hungry to the barn for the night. Pray as he might, Leo never showed up with anything to eat and Ford eventually fell asleep with nothing but a bellyful of resentment.

The next morning, Myer led his boys into the forest and none of them had much to say. A few hours into their work, the boys were left piling wood on to their sled while their father searched for suitable trees to cut down at a later date. Ford turned on Leo and let his annoyance come out, "Why didn't you say anything last night?"

"What do you mean?"

"You could've stuck up for me." When Leo avoided eye contact as he did now, Ford knew they had a problem.

"You went too far," said Leo, frowning and shaking his head. "Mam says you could've killed her."

"Killed her? That's ridiculous. With a leech? How?"

"I don't know," said Leo kicking at a rotting stick. "Maybe if she'd swallowed it it could've gone down and sucked all the blood out of her and she'd have died." Aside from the little he learned from the mender, Ford understood how the body worked even less than Leo did, so the theory sounded fairly plausible to him.

"Bah," was his only defense.

Leo seldom took sides against Ford, and never so adamantly. It drove an odd, unfamiliar wedge between them. Neither spoke to the other for the remainder of the day.

Milda came down hard on Ford after the leech incident, heaping on extra work around the house when he wasn't helping with the woodcutting. Consequently, Tilda found herself with free time, time she used to keep an eye on Ford and criticize his every misstep: he didn't clean the breeches fully; there was food still stuck to a spoon; often the fire was too low or too hot.

After a couple days of this, Ford's obstinate side made him drag his feet while doing chores. When there was suddenly never enough water for the washbasin or for boiling, Milda banished him from the house. However, the past few days made Tilda realize the power she wielded within the family and her relationship with her brother worsened because of it.

On the other hand, by the end of his household servitude, the rift between him and Leo was mended, even though Ford did go back to his old ways, without remorse and without having learned much from his punishment. He didn't think he was to blame, couldn't see his own faults: the curt answers, mood swings and taunting. All he could see were two tyrants jerking the reins of his life. One was untouchable, but the other one he could deal with. He envisioned ways to go about it that night over a bowl of fish soup, while staring across the table at Tilda.

"Stop it!" she demanded.

"Leave her alone," said Milda.

"He's still staring."

"Stop it." Milda faced Ford and held up her spoon in warning. He rolled his eyes and Milda's flashed a barely contained fury. Knowing punishment was coming, having seen it all before and being thoroughly tired of it, he sighed. "Out! Get out now!" she shouted with a vehemence that rocked everyone back from the table. "I won't have this in my house!" Ford got up and strolled out to the barn, a little surprised at how angry she was over nothing more than a stare across a table.

"You'd think I'd killed somebody," he said while patting Stinky, his preferred companion these days. He was just as happy to be alone where he could drift off into fantasies of far-off places or daydreams of winning glory in battle, even enjoying a recurring nightmare that began with him slaughtering a swarm of bloody-minded Staneards. Lately the dream would find him pitted against a faceless foe that wouldn't die no matter how many times he thrust a spear into him. One night recently, this anonymous warrior had morphed into Tilda and he'd found himself on top of her, pressing her down with his weight, she sneering back at him in recrimination for each of his repeated spear thrusts into her. Jolted awake, he spent hazy moments in ambivalent confusion questioning the mix of loathing and joy he derived from the dream.

Wandering back home the following day on an errand for his father, he stopped to admire a favorite tree with a peculiar bend. In another moment's dallying by the stream to watch the water flow, the scent of Milda's chicken broth drew him home and was full in his nostrils by the time he stepped from the edge of the woods. He had to admit that she knew how to cook and could do a lot with very little.

Their house had few windows, but the shutters of the nearest were thrown open and Stinky shot ahead for a closer smell, dancing at the window on his hind legs and tramping the patch of herbs beneath it. Ford cupped a hand around his mouth, thought better of shouting and ran to his drooling dog and pulled him down. Milda's disapproving face appeared in the window.

"Get out of my garden! What are you doing here?"

"Smells good," Ford blurted out.

"Go on! Get," she said waving them away and turning vexed at seeing Ford coming into the house. She moved to block the doorway. "Why aren't you out working?" Ford brushed by her with his head down. "Well?"

"The ax broke," he said grabbing the hammer, the hatchet they used for kindling and a spare ax handle. "I was told to say we won't be home 'til late."

"Then you'd better bring something or they'll faint away." She quickly diced a few skinny, pale carrots and threw them into the broth, considered handing him the pot and reconsidered. His hands were full and she didn't trust him with it anyhow, sure he'd drop it or stop halfway and drain the pot. "The boy eats like a horse and a pack of wolves put together," she had often complained.

"I'll take it," offered Nia skipping up to her mother.

"It's too heavy. You'll only drop my good pot," said Milda. "Tilly, you take it out to them."

"Go on now," said Tilda to Stinky sniffing at her side and occasionally jumping to get closer to the pot as the three of them passed into the woods. "It feels good to be outside in the fresh air. It's so stuffy inside. It's like a holiday," she said with a cheery ring in her voice. She took in a deep breath and let out a long sigh. Ford couldn't relate to her enthusiasm, having spent nearly every day working outside in almost all weather. He considered saying something nasty, but he couldn't precisely express his annoyance, so instead he mocked her by skipping ahead, twirling around, throwing his head back and smiling like an idiot.

"I'm so happy I could die," he sang out gaily before stopping to lift his leg and pass gas that ended with a prolonged ripple.

"Ew!" Tilda stopped to let him go on, but Ford backed up towards her. "Stop it! You're sick!" Though hampered by the sloshing broth, she still managed to push by and get ahead of him. He tried to pass her, but dropped further behind when the ax handle slipped out of his hands and disappeared into the fallen leaves. "Ha, ha!" From then on she stayed in the lead, regularly shouting insults back at him. "You're disgusting!" she'd say and then moments later ask, "Am I going the right way, piggy?"

"Shut up," he finally shouted and smashed the dead stem of a pine tree branch with the ax handle. Stinky ran back to him, barking.

"Oh, you're so strong!" she said over her shoulder. "You can break old branches. How strong you must be!" The ax handle whirled over her head.

She spun around shouting, "I'll tell Father!"

He drew back to throw the hatchet and growled low, "I'll do it."

"You'd better not," she said. The cold anger in his eyes made her turn and run. Seeing her flee was like the signal to the start of a game in his knee-jerk mind. He let loose the hatchet and watched it fly towards the back of her head.

CHAPTER 3
AMBUSHED

The hatchet somersaulted through the air and regret flashed through Ford, who wished it back in his hand the instant it knocked against the back of Tilda's head and bounced away. She crumpled to the ground as if all the bones of her body had been shattered. The pot broke at the base of a tree and Stinky dove upon the remains. For untold time, Ford couldn't move and when he finally did, he could only will himself to lean forward, to stretch his neck for a look at her to see if she was dead.

"Tilda," he said quite softly. Nothing. He took a step closer. She wasn't moving. He couldn't even tell if she was breathing, but there was blood trickling between the hairs down the back of her head. He stepped closer, stood over her and whispered, "Tilly? Tilda?"

"They're over here," he heard Leo call through the trees. Ford bent to snatch up the hatchet, but hesitated when he saw long strands of his sister's hair buried in the handle. The crunch of Leo's footsteps grew louder. Ford wiped at the handle and tucked the hatchet into his belt.

"Good gods, is she all right?"

"I don't know," said Ford taking a step back and throwing up his hands, "I don't know." Myer crashed through the bushes, pushed the wolfhound aside and knelt beside Tilda.

"What happened?" he said to no one in particular. The splayed fingers of his hands hovered over Tilda's sprawled body for an instant of indecision before he gently rolled her onto her back. Stinky nuzzled into the shards of pottery and yelped when Myer elbowed him away again. "Get off! Take your mutt away." Leo and Ford pushed and pulled the dog out of the way. Myer put his ear to Tilda's nose.

"Is she breathing?" asked Leo, his voice taking on a slight tremble.

"I think so," said Myer and immediately Tilda started slurring incomprehensibly and kicking her legs as if trying to run. Myer held her down. She convulsed and heaved gasping breaths violently in and out, her eyes flickering, darting. Eventually her frantic thrashing slowed, her eyes focused and she began crying.

"It's all right, it's all right," Myer told her in a stiff, yet gentle tone as he took her into his arms and examined the back of her head. Over her shoulder he turned to Ford and asked with a penetrating eye, "How did this happen?" Ford fumbled for words and bought time when the dog pulled away and went back to the pot shards. Myer became impatient. "How did it happen?"

"It was, well, Stinky was jumping up," he stopped and tried again, "she sort of bumped her head," but he could see by the look of malice his father shot towards the dog that it was too late. The damage had been done and his dog would take the brunt of the blame. An awful, sick feeling flowed over him along with a nascent urge to tell the unadulterated truth, but before it could fully form in his mouth, Tilda calmed enough to be pressed with questions. She couldn't remember what happened, didn't even know how she'd gotten out into the middle of the woods. However, when she saw Stinky greedily lapping away at the pieces of Milda's broken pottery, she started to cry again.

"Mother will kill me."

The wound turned out to be no worse than a mean scratch and a sizeable bump, however, once she was on her feet, dizziness overcame her and she had to be carried.

"Ford," said Myer staggering to his feet with Tilda in his arms, "you go finish the hatchet work, fill the sled and bring it back." He nodded at the largest piece of broken pottery, the base of which still held a good amount of the broth, "Leo, grab that. It might be saved." He stalked off, carrying Tilda home, with Leo trailing behind.

Ford was often tasked with the heavy labor like pulling the laden sled back home, and although he wasn't fond of being alone in the woods, on this day he didn't mind. Better that than catching the brunt of Milda's anger when she saw the state of Tilda and found out what had become of her prized pot. Ford stripped logs of branches, piled up their sled and hauled it by a strap over his shoulder most of the way home so quickly that he decided it would be best to sit for a while patting his dog with Barlow just in sight through the trees. "We'll wait this one out." Stinky looked up at him and let out a small, impatient whine. "Trust me."

While the clouds darkened on an already overcast day, Ford spent the time racking his brain for some way to make right the wrong he'd done. All the while a shrill word or two from Milda could be heard coming from within the house. Apologizing outright would be tantamount to an admission of guilt, he'd learned that the hard way some years ago, but he wanted to set things straight for his own peace of mind. There was the ax that still needed fixing. He could do that much and make his father happy. It was a start. As for Tilda, he could think of nothing. The problem was that although he hadn't really wanted to hurt her, not seriously at any rate, he also disliked her so much it prevented him from thinking kindly towards her.

When the ruckus died down, he pulled the sled into the clearing and brought the ax head, the new handle and the other tools over to the house. Myer met him at the door.

"I'll do it," he said taking the tools. "Head over to the quarry. There's still time enough to put in a half day."

"What about the rest of the wood?" Ford asked, watching his father drop the tools and seize Stinky by the scruff.

"Leo and I'll take care of it." Myer dragged the dog into the barn and shut him in. Seeing Ford's questioning face he said, "He stays in there for now. Don't let him out, no matter how much noise he makes."

All of the marchogs who had participated in the battle earlier that year were receiving rewards from Barwnig Blackoak for their service. Over in Oren, the barwnig was having the old wooden palisade around the marchog's hall repaired and expanded to take in some of the village. Stone needed for some of the construction was obtained from a quarry to the west and families under the marchog's protection were required to provide a day's labor there per week. Within the Barlow family, Ford was always chosen for this duty, because "Leo's time," said Milda, "is better spent in study or with his father learning the trade that will support the family." She had a point. If Myer ever took over the legal rights to the old woodcutter's trade, he would pass it down to Leo, not Ford. Tilda and Nia stood a better chance than Ford.

The quarry site looked rough and the landscape foreign to anything Ford had ever known. It was as if a rampaging giant had ripped up the earth, tearing away the lush green ground and exposing the dirt and rocks beneath, leaving behind what looked to Ford like a disgusting mess. He hated working the quarry, but that afternoon he welcomed the chance to get away from home. Halfway there, he met with Winhild and others from Oren. Their clothes were soaked through.

"Rain's been coming down hard all day," said Winhild. Not so much as a greeting, noted Ford, who missed the jovial, welcoming Winhild of the days before the battle, before the loss of his father. "Can't move the carts for the mud. Work's been called off."

"How can it be raining there and not at all here?" Ford might as well have wondered the words to the wind for all the answer he was likely to get from the exhausted workers coming from the quarry. Even Winhild ignored him.

"Go and tell your pa to work on timbers. The barwnig's man'll be over soon enough asking for more."

A strange thing happened when Ford crossed the stream back into Barlow. Myer emerged from the woods with a spade, his ax and a short length of rope, which Ford thought unusual. Myer looked surprised and displeased to see him.

"What are you doing here? I told you to go work the quarry."

"They called it a day," said Ford as his path converged with his father's. He repeated what Winhild had told him, all the while taking particular notice of Myer's paling complexion.

In the background, the old woodcutter swayed in his doorway complaining, "Something got at the chickens last night," and Myer seemed pleased for once to go speak with him. The old man often had extra work for Myer and his boys. The week prior they had been tasked with finding and mating a billy to his nanny. There was nothing for it; they were beholden to the man.

Hunger and a desire to face the inevitable and be done with it compelled Ford inside, where he found the rest of the family quietly about their work.

"What's that old thorn want now?" Milda speculated from the tips of her toes while leaning over the brook trout she was gutting to squint out the window.

"Something got at his chickens," said Ford.

An abnormally white-faced Leo dropped the kindling he was chopping and said, "I'm going to go help him," as he rushed outside. Sniffles came from under a bundle of blankets upon the bed. When Nia peeked out, tears slid down her cheeks and she started bawling.

"What's wrong?" Ford asked and Nia blubbered out something incomprehensible. "What?"

"Stinky's dead!"

"Shush," hissed Tilda.

"What?" Ford was sure he hadn't heard right or that Nia had things confused. She so often muddled her words and ideas. Tilda groaned.

"That stupid dog nearly killed me." It was a simple statement lacking venom, an explanation edged by sadness. Ford rounded on her and his mouth fell open, but Milda stepped in front of him, her voice low and controlled at first, but rising in malevolence.

"Your damn dog broke my perfectly good pot. It ruined another meal. It hurt Tilly bad and one day…who knows!" She stopped, regained her composure, let out the sigh of someone finished with a tiresome, unsatisfactory chore and went back to her work. "If you'd trained that cur better or kept an eye on it, but no. It's your own fault. That was the last straw. I had your father put it down."

The house was small and the distance between them short, so that when Ford charged at Milda, she only had time to raise the knife and strike down at him. The blade caught the tip of his chin and disappeared between them when their bodies collided. His hands clamped around her throat and choked off her cry of surprise. One of the girls screamed. Ford's bulk held Milda down, her back pressed firmly upon the table that creaked under their weight. His fingers dug into her neck. The jarring clangor of the room rang in his throbbing ears. Milda's frantic eyes reflected terror, sought escape. Her legs thrashed the air. She pulled his head back by the hair and scratched at his face. Something jabbed persistently into his stomach. He pushed back to see what it was, but her fingernails bit into too much of his cheek for him to disengage. When he reached up to pull her hand away, a pounding jolt like an ox ramming into his ribs sent him vaulting off Milda and crashing through the house wall. A plethora of dried, hanging herbs showered down, jars toppled from a shelf and shattered on the ground. All the air in him grunted out from the pressure of Myer falling hard and fully upon him. Ford rolled and squirmed to get loose, but after a quick scuffle, his father pinned him down, gripping whole clumps of Ford's clothes and skin at the chest. He'd never seen his father's eyes so full of pure animal ferocity.

"Let go!" Ford shouted over and over as he thrashed back and forth. Myer lifted Ford's body and slammed him back down, knocking his head into the ground. Whenever Ford struggled, Myer slammed him down again. "You're hurting me!"

"Get out!" growled Myer into his son's face. "Get out!"

A shuddering gasp from inside the house stopped them both. Looking up, they saw the rest of the children gathered around Milda leaning on the edge of the table with the knife handle protruding from her stomach. She gurgled and choked up blood that ran down her chin and neck. Both girls screamed. Myer left Ford on the ground and ran inside, standing before his wife not sure what to do. Still sprawled upon the ground, Ford watched the scene unfold through the hole in the wall where weather-worn and poorly-made wattle and daub had given way. Hunched over and hesitant to touch his wife, all of Myer's body heaved with unbridled strength, anger and confusion. He looked from the hated knife to Milda's agonized face and back to the knife, and with one swift and violent jerk, he wrenched it out and a fountain of blood gushed on to him. Milda's grasping fingers reached out as if to catch it before she tottered, swayed and collapsed.

Ford was up and running before she hit the ground. He made for the barn on unsteady legs and leaned on the door for support. Tilda's hysterical screams and Nia's wailing shot a gut-clenching flood of panic, guilt and regret through him so powerful that his knees buckled. A howl of such anguish as he'd never heard his father utter drove Ford into the woods, dodging between the trees, scraping his shoulders, stumbling and falling in a flailing sprint.

The stream appeared sooner than he expected. Without thinking, he went directly to the pond, dropping beside the warped tree with the trunk bent into a perfect child-sized seat. This was where Leo had found him years ago after one of the many incidents that had labeled Ford a trouble-child. He had been hiding there for hours after a violent spat with his sister, an eruption brought on by his mother's abandonment of him just months prior, as well as his inability to integrate into his new family. On that day, Leo appeared, laid a hand on his shoulder and said, "It's okay, it's okay," in that simple way one child shows another compassion. It was enough to defuse Ford's anger and allowed him to grieve.

Tears brimmed in his eyes from the memory and from his current misery. Rage over the loss of his dog mingled with guilt for the part he had played, along with images of Milda, her twisted face pressed so close to his. He was sorry and then in the next moment remorseless. It was an accident he wished had never happened, yet part of him wished her dead. It had all happened so quickly that he didn't know what to think and needed time to sort it out, some place where he'd be undisturbed. From here he could still hear cries coming from the house. This would not do. They would find him here, he realized, so he ran deeper into the woods along the stream where thorny brambles didn't crowd the open areas along the banks, following trails the children and animals had made over the years, and when those died away he tore through tangles that ripped new holes in his old clothes. Bushes and low hanging limbs clustered together to block his way, but he pushed on, twisting and thrusting his shoulder through them until he burst into the clearing where a path from Oren met the stream. Leaning over the water with a stone in one hand and a soaked shirt in the other, Winhild's wife's mouth hung open.

"Ford," she finally managed, "you scared the life from me!" The kindly, middle-aged woman relaxed. "What are you about, eh?" Crouched as if to pounce, scratched all over, sweating and panting, he was a strange, unsettling sight and the woman's drooping face showed it. She placed the stone and shirt aside and took a measured step toward him. "Your chin bleeds. Come, let me have a look." He reached up and dabbed where Milda had cut him.

"Ford," came his father's mountain lion roar like a damnation. Ford rushed by the astonished woman. As he vaulted into the woods, she called after him and it mingled with the frightening "Ford!" of his father. Again and again the tormenting call through the trees pushed him faster and farther until finally, falling down beside the stream with his lungs afire and legs wobbling, he gulped water until his stomach hurt. Water washed away the blood and stung the cut on his chin. It ran down his chest and red bled into the brown and gray cloth. Propping himself on one elbow, he strained to listen and heard nothing over the noisy, bubbling stream.

Up again, he plodded along so slowly he might as well have been walking. The gray, threatening sky threw all into dim shade that only grew dimmer as Barlow receded. People seldom ventured this far in, not even woodcutters, which allowed an abundance of maple, ash and oak to mature and cast a wide, overlapping canopy. The solitude was perfect for one needing a place to hide. But what, Ford asked himself, would he do out here after dark, all alone and with nothing to defend himself?

Sand and smooth yellow-white pebbles against the greens and browns of the forest signaled the farthest point he'd ever been in these woods. Twice before he'd come to this tiny peninsula created by an extreme bend in the water's course, once with Leo and later alone. The most fantastic feature of the spot, one which still impressed him, was the outside curve in the stream and how it rose sharply into a ridge twenty feet high and more, hugging the water like an embracing mother. The peninsula left the stream and began to rise in an easy slope, the way eventually walled off by a lengthy thicket of brambles. In the clearing by the bend stood a rotund fir tree like a stout and gloomy sentry and on the ground beside it sat a battered tin pot with a broken handle.

"Someone's been here since," Ford muttered after a scan of the landscape around him. His attention was arrested by a certain tree up the slope beyond the fir where the forest growth took hold once more, a beech that held out its sprawling branches most invitingly. It was one of the best climbing trees he'd ever found. From its top branches a person might command a relatively wide, panoramic view of the area, even over the top of the curving ridge. Ford got hold of the lower branches, much more easily now than in years past, but they seemed altogether less substantial and he climbed only halfway before deciding they wouldn't hold his weight. Besides, the waning light provided a poor view from any vantage point.

Spread out under the beech, bluebead lilies with a few overripe berries still holding on posed a temptation that brought on a piercing hunger. Being almost certain they weren't good to eat, he checked the brambles instead and found the berries there ripe but picked almost clean. Only by reaching high and deep into the thorny bushes was he able to gather a mouthful, which he ate back at the strip of sand while sitting on the remains of a rotted tree stump he'd kicked over two summers ago. He flicked pebbles about with his toe so that they clicked and clacked against one another or plopped into the water.

There was no wind and yet the branches of the fir rustled. Ford sat bolt upright, moving only his eyes around to peer at the tree. Some of its lower branches swayed and stilled. He squinted into its dense, pitch-black body. Nothing dangerous could be in there, he decided, as the branches were too thick and the needles too prickly for anything larger than a bird or squirrel. For a measure of reassurance, he tossed a stone tossed directly into the middle of the tree. Nothing came of it. All the same, the branches had definitely moved and so he kept watch upon the fir.

His thoughts wandered back to his present troubles and the horrible scene back at the house. Over and over again the vivid images flashed before his eyes, the tortured screams rang in his ears, his guilt mounting into a desire to turn back time and undo the fact that he'd killed Leo's mother, Nia's mother. He drove his foot into the ground, kicking up a spray of clattering stones. A twig snapped. Maybe she wasn't dead, he hoped. "Probably," he muttered and chucked a rounded stone into the water, then grabbing another at random and tossing it over the stream into the high rising bank. It stuck soundlessly into the leaf-strewn ground, still moist from rain. Another he hurled over the ridge into the bushes atop it and they burst to life as if he'd flushed a whole warren of rabbits. Seeing nothing, he tilted his head to one side, straining to hear. Again, nothing.

The sun went down, the forest descended into shadow, and trees, boulders and bushes morphed into strange beasts and malformed bodies in his lively imagination. Leaves crunched, but from where he couldn't tell. A shiver ran through him and he crossed his arms, holding them tight to his body, while willing his eyes to pierce the dark. He truly doubted he had it in him to spend so much as a single night out here alone.

"It's only natural and nothing that'll pester you. It's only natural and…" he repeated in hopes of believing that it was nothing more than his senses playing tricks, like the faint glimmer atop the ridge presaging the coming of dawn. "Dawn don't come at dusk, nor move all around." The light shifted and waved over the branches, acting more like the haunting will o' the wisp than anything he'd ever seen. He watched the light play upon the leaves and realized shapes like bodies were forming upon the ridge before his eyes. He gripped the log under him and demanded, "Who's there?" The idea occurred to him that it might be his father with an angry mob hunting him down for murder and that was almost a relief. One of them leapt from the ridge and plummeted down the bank, plowing through leaves and plunging into the water. With his attention diverted, he didn't notice crouching figures shambling towards him from upstream and down until they were close enough to touch. He jumped back into the arms of one, pushed away, spun around and could just make out in the dark that he was trapped between ragged creatures entirely covered in long, matted hair, their faces drooping with a leathery, decayed skin. One had horns atop a head too long to be human. A full, bright flame jumped and flickered upon the ridge and Ford turned to see a tall being holding the fire aloft before sliding down to the stream and nimbly leaping over the water. Mesmerized and panicking, Ford had no notion of the shadow creeping out from behind the fir tree until something stung him in the back of the neck.

Chapter 4
Life and Liberty

A hastily built fire crackled and spit an erratic, wavering flame that lit the sandy bend, caught the steal of knives and illuminated the strange creatures peering at Ford from sunken eyes. How many surrounded him he couldn't tell with them wheeling around him and skulking in the dark, but he guessed between six and ten. When one of them laid the point of its knife to the back of Ford's neck, he gave up the idea of fighting back. They could have killed him, but they hadn't yet, so he stood still as they crept about him. His eyes adjusted to the light and he could see that they weren't covered in matted hair, but shredded clothes. The leathery skin upon their faces was indeed pieces of leather they'd cut into masks. The tall one, who had seemed to hold fire in his hand, actually carried a torch. A grunt slipped out of Ford as they grabbed him, forced him to his knees and bound his hands to his ankles behind his back.

"We should cover his eyes, so he can't see us," came a reedy voice from one of the scrawnier of the band, his whispered suggestions slithering into the ear of the tall one.

"Don't tell me what to do," said the tall one. By their voices, Ford assumed they were human, quite desperate and starved humans in filthy, motley rags, but at least human. Immediately he second-guessed himself at the sight of one of them waddling from the stream without a mask on, revealing in the light of the fire a rough face below a sickly pink, scarred forehead without eyebrows and only a thin patch of short stubbly hair atop its head.

"What're you looking at?" it snarled at him, placing a pot it carried on the ground, careful not to spill the water within. Ford recognized the kettle-like pot with the broken handle he'd spotted earlier.

"Cook, where's your mask? Put it on," chided the tall one.

"I ain't wearing no mask," said Cook, pulling out a sharp knife and going to work on a plucked chicken that had been left on the log after the noisiest of the band had hooted and danced in front of Ford shaking the dead bird in his face while others tied him up. "You want we eat this bird some time tonight? Then fuck the mask. Can't see a damn thing with that nonsense over my eyes."

"He's seen your face now," said the reedy voice.

"Yeah, now we gotta kill him!" said the noisy one, whose horned head in the light proved to be deer antlers, slender horns still attached to the skullcap that had been sewn into his hooded mantle. Underneath the mantle he wore a patchwork tunic of many colors. Skipping circles around Ford, he sang in a high-pitched giddy child's voice, "Cut off his fingers, snip off his toes! Pluck out his eyes, slice off his nose!"

"Shut your hole!" ordered the tall one. "You'll be the one sliced up, starting with your tongue, if ya don't hold it." The noisy, colorful one stopped singing, slumped down in front of Ford, threw off his mask and crossed his arms. Though the fire was not bright, it was plain to see that he was nothing more than a pouting boy and it puzzled Ford as to what he was doing in company such as this.

"Why'd you take yours off too?" asked the tall one. "Oh forget it!" He ripped off his own mask and threw it on the ground. As if released from bondage, the rest removed theirs as well. All were boys. One or two might have been older than Ford, but most were his own age or younger. His taut muscles relaxed somewhat and he eased back into a more comfortable position. The tall one saw this and leaned his gaunt, severe face closer. "You've seen us and that's no good for you." He knelt, drew out a long knife and aimed for Ford's heart.

Ford had little love for a world that showed him little love. With no home or family to go back to, no one left who he cared about or cared for him, ending it all might have seemed like a tidy solution to his problems, but some remnant of hope remained, if only in instinct, and he recoiled from the blade as much as his bonds would allow.

"No, I'm not going to kill you," announced the tall one, pulling the knife away to an expectant titter of malignant pranksters' mirth from those surrounding them, but he jerked a thumb at the largest of them all, a smirking barrel-shaped ghoul of a boy, and said, "he will."

"Duff! Duff! Duff!" they all chanted. The thuggish Duff pulled his thumb out of his pug nose and mucus ran into drool and dropped in a big gob from his chin. He lurched forward like a ravenous bear, but was restrained from beating their bound prisoner lifeless. His eyes narrowed to slits and the fuzz growing in the unusually long, smooth space between his nose and thin lips spread in a grin that bared broken incisors and sharp canines. Again Duff lurched for Ford, pounding his fists against his own head in excitement and frustration. Ford wasn't very smart, but smart enough to know that this snorting and slobbering fellow was too stupid to know he was stupid.

Behind him, while the tall one worked at the knot at his wrists, Ford heard the reedy-voiced boy say, "If you let him loose now he might slip free in the dark." The tall one considered this and was on the verge of agreeing when the noisy, colorful one slid in between them.

"We could wait 'til morning," he said, mocking the reedy-voiced boy's sly manner.

"Don't be a idiot," said the tall one yanking the rope from Ford's hands. "Gather sticks, bunches." They bundled sticks, lit them in the fire for makeshift torches and made a circle on the sandy ground around Ford and Duff, who stamped his feet in the pebbly sand, dropped down to pound the ground a dozen times and clumsily hopped up holding his nicked fists under his chin as he came at Ford again, the tears in the skin upon his knuckles tinting red. Though standing a full head shorter than Ford, it was as if Duff's missing height had been compressed into girth and meaty arms.

Ford's shoulders down to the tips of his fingers were stiff from stifled circulation and he lifted his arms wide to stretch just when they let Duff go. Only a reflexive dodge saved Ford from being bowled over. Duff flew by him, ripping at his clothes and falling into the fir tree's branches. Cursing and thrashing out of the tree with a club-like branch, he hunkered down at the shoulders and stalked after Ford, who bent his arms and beat them on his sides to work the blood back in, all while retreating backwards around the fir tree to buy more time. The others laughed at him and Duff snorted, hurling the branch at Ford's head and charging. As the two collided, Duff's powerful arcing punches caught Ford's tucked elbows and ribs. Ford stumbled back, launching a single, desperate punch. Duff's head flew back, his jagged teeth cracked together from the shot to his jaw, his eyes rolled back. Bending to seek a stick or rock, Ford saw and felt the soaked front of his shirt and realized it was his own blood from his wounded chin. He tottered forward and his vision doubled, only briefly, but enough to cast a haze before him. Sound deadened. Overcome by a need to sit, he grabbed his knees to hold himself up. The excited boys, eager for more, whirled in a circle around the bewildered fighters, urging them on. In some far off corner of his distorted hearing, Ford made out a muffled growl and footsteps galloping closer just before Duff plowed into him.

"Watch it!" hollered Cook, grabbing his pot and ducking out of the way when Duff drove Ford back toward the bend, lifting him in a bear hug to throw him down on to the stones. Ford clung so tight that Duff could not let go of him and his momentum sent them both splashing into the water. The other boys ran to the edge of the stream, falling over themselves in laughter. More than one was pulled in as Ford and Duff tried to scramble back out. Many of the torches were doused so that only the campfire they trampled precariously about gave off any useful light. Out of the narrow bend crowded with bodies came Duff, slamming head first into Ford, throwing the wide punches that worked so well for him. Amid a hail of fists, Ford grabbed a clump of the coarse, knife-cropped hair ramming into him, twisted and fell to his knees, rolling the heavy boy over his back. Duff flipped over and landed chest-first on the log. A sharp, desperate braying like a panicked donkey bleated out of him and silenced the cheering boys.

"Can't breathe…can't breathe," he finally gasped as Ford climbed on top of him and rained down unrelenting blows until he was pulled off by the other boys.

The raucous echoes in the stream bend died away, leaving only Duff's labored breathing and Cook's grumbling. None of the boys rushed to Duff's side, but rather dispersed, wandering aimlessly, quiet and confused. They turned away as if too ashamed to even look at Ford, leaving him to guess what would happen next, what would become of him and how they would punish him for beating their champion. Not all losers lose well. Some demand revenge. Ford eventually realized everyone was ignoring him, so he backed away from the circle of light as slowly and quietly as possible, not turning away or making any sudden moves.

"Get back here!" the tall one called to him. When they caught him after a slow, clumsy chase, Ford dropped to the ground before their fire, a spent deadweight unable to fight off even the frailer of the boys, who tied him up with ease. Bound by the hands with a line to the beech and another from his feet to the fir, he lay listening to their mutterings for half the night and learning quickly not to speak after being silenced by shouts and kicks. Nothing but the occasional word could he make out, but he guessed they spoke of him and what to do with him. They ate, offered him nothing and bedded down in the driest leaves and softest patches of sand. Some draped cloaks over low-hanging limbs to provide a cover overhead or just bundled up as best they could. At the first sign of rhythmic breathing and wheezing snores, Ford worked at the rope about his wrists. He pulled at a loose end, which only tightened it. Twisting his hands almost to their limit, he still couldn't reach his fingers around the knot with enough force to free it. Time and again he tried until he finally resigned himself to failure and his whole body slumped. Though exhausted, he couldn't stop the steady flow of worry and useless thought. Once he realized he wasn't thinking straight, he gave up trying. Almost instantly the idea of sleep hit him and, after writhing about until he'd worked a pebble out from under his back and doubting the entire time that he'd catch so much as a wink of sleep, his head bobbed.

When his eyes popped open the camp was quiet, save for some light snoring. Only orange coals remained from the fire. A shadow passed in front of its weak glow and the outline of a wide body moved closer. A void of blacker night and heavy, open-mouthed breathing hovered over him. One of the other boys stirred and sat up.

"Shut your mouth," Duff growled through his teeth quite close to Ford. Others stirred now.

"Kellyn, Duff's messing with our prisoner," called out one of the youngest boys.

"What's going on?" said the tall one so named Kellyn, sitting upright and speaking with barely a trace of sleep in his voice. "Go to bed!" Duff tossed a thick branch into the coals, ripped off the tattler's cloak and rolled up in it on the ground.

Ford breathed again, kept his eyes on the spot where Duff had bedded down and was still awake at first light when one of the older of them, a lanky youth, got up and strolled quietly out of camp. For what reason, Ford hadn't the foggiest of notions.

Eventually the rest of the boys roused themselves, each at his own desire. The lumpy form of Duff rose and fell to a rhythmic snoring. Cook stirred the coals and put on a pot of boiled oats with butter and milk. Lack of sleep, hunger and a nagging thirst drained Ford, so that he felt more tired than he did at the end of a long, hard day of work. While the boys ate and drank directly from the stream, they watched Ford, unsure what to make of him.

"Here," mumbled one of the younger ones edging closer and holding out his waterskin. Desire flared in Ford's eyes, but he gestured that his hands were tied. After slight hesitation, the boy put the waterskin to Ford's lips and carefully tilted it back. Ford swallowed every drop and asked for more. More was brought to him. "My name is Ham," said the boy in halting but eager speech while tilting the skin back with care. "I was the one who stopped Duff." Ford showed no recognition. "Last night. When he was going to hit you with the stick. That was me."

"Oh. Guess I owe you…twice now," said Ford nodding at the water. Ham lowered his head to hide his pleasure. "You think maybe I could get some of that?" Ford was eyeing the pot. "My stomach's just about eating itself." The boy nodded and ran off.

"You want seconds?" Ford heard Cook holler at Ham, "Jakes ain't even had his firsts!"

"But it'll go cold and hard before Jakes ever gets back," Ham reasoned.

"Forget Jakes," said Kellyn across the camp to them, "He's probably off somewhere, you know…" He held his fist by his crotch and jerked it about until everyone had had a good laugh.

"Yeah! He's probably doing this," said the noisy one, pinching his cheek and pulling on it vigorously so that it made juicy slapping noises.

"Gross!" cried the smallest of them.

"Cut it out," said Kellyn.

"Why's it that every—?" started the noisy one.

"Why's it you're still talking?" said Kellyn. His command was absolute. Ford noticed that all the boys went quiet whenever his harsh tone cut one of them short. "Give him seconds," he told them and watched Ham take the oatmeal-filled mug over to Ford and offer it to him. "What's he supposed to do with that?" Ham shrugged and to the surprise of everyone, Kellyn went to Ford and untied his hands. He took the mug from the boy, waited while Ford flexed his fingers and then handed it to him. "No spoon? Where's the spoon? What's he supposed to eat this mush with, his fingers?" Cook grunted, turned his back and let out a long stretch of oaths under his breath. Ham jumped to it, searching the camp for something for Ford to use, but Ford was licking the last of the oatmeal off his fingers when he returned. "Little hungry, eh?" he said and Ford nodded. "I'll see if we can't spare some more." Cook whipped his disbelieving face around and his cock-eyed glare killed the question at the source. "Looks like that's all we got."

Ford grimaced from more than just hunger. Pain from last night's bruises throbbed throughout his body. Not even during the battle with the Staneards had he been so knocked about.

"What's your name? Where you from?" Kellyn asked him.

"Ford. Barlow."

"Ford? What, were you born in a river?" The air filled with the cruel laughter of children glad to direct scorn at anyone other than themselves.

"Barlow, eh?" crowed the noisy one with a knowing leer at Ford. "You know what comes from Barlow?" Ford guessed the fool had never heard of the place before, but it didn't matter. It wasn't a real question, just a setup for some slur against his hometown. He prodded Ford with a finger. "Do you know, huh? What comes from Barlow?"

"Better pieces of shit than you," said Kellyn.

"Better pieces of shit," laughed the noisy one with the daydreaming air of one storing a delicious morsel in safekeeping for later. Kellyn pushed the boy away.

"Don't mind him. He's half a idiot. We ain't figured out what the other half is yet. So, Ford of Barlow, why you out here in the middle of nowhere in the middle of the night? You a spy from the towns out here after the Wayward Boys?"

"Who's the Wayward Boys?"

"Us. That's what we call ourselves. Stop asking questions." He threw up his hands to stop Ford before Ford had even thought of another question. "You ever heard of the Second Sons?"

Everyone across the land knew of the infamous Second Sons, those loose bands of thieves, roaming vagabonds who burglarized homes, pilfered purses in the towns and preyed upon merchants and tradesmen traveling remote roads. By law, the firstborn inherited everything. Most siblings shared out the wealth to a degree, but in some cases greed or sheer poverty meant no one but the firstborn and his or her future family benefited from what little their parents had built after years of hard work. So it came to be that most bandits were the younger sons, and sometimes the unfortunate daughters of poor families. The Second Sons may have been comprised mostly of the disinherited, but they'd also become a sort of moving midden for any societal outcast, be they thieves, rapists or murderers. Ford was well aware of their reputation, and knowing he was a captive of such bandits made him rightfully nervous.

"Wayward Boys is just a name we use to," Kellyn turned to the reedy-voiced boy, who Ford could now see was cleaner and better dressed than the rest. "Chandler, what's that word?"

"Distinguish." Without looking up from cleaning his shoes, the rather delicate and handsome one they called Chandler rattled off the word like he had another dozen just as impressive to whip out if anyone wanted.

"Right. To dis-*tin*-guish," - Kellyn drew the word out mockingly - "ourselves from the other, um, fellows."

"What's that?" murmured the smallest boy.

"I don't hear nothing," said Kellyn. In the distance leaves rustled and trotting footsteps grew louder. Everyone reached for weapons or dove for cover. A head popped out of the bushes upon the ridge above them and the boys relaxed.

"It's only Jakes. Who's on watch?" asked Kellyn counting heads and mouthing names.

"No one," said Chandler, his disgust undisguised. Kellyn wheeled about and was ready to lay into him when the lanky boy took a step off the ridge and slid down amid a mini avalanche of rocks, earth and leaves that crashed into the water. The way he pulled up short and leapt over the stream impressed Ford as something more akin to a deer than a human.

"Did I miss anything?" asked Jakes, an airy and guileless young man whose bright eyes saw the world through a dreamy prism.

"Your breakfast," Cook said as if pronouncing the guilty verdict to a crime only outdone in magnitude by Ford's, who he stabbed a finger at, "which *he* ate."

"Well, least someone enjoyed it." Jakes sat down beside Ford and smiled at him. "It's always good and delicious, no matter what Cook makes, right Ham?" Ham was lost in staring at Ford and jumped at the sound of his name. "Well so and you won last night. Beat our Duff, that tough old dog. Good for you! I'm Jakes, by the way."

"Ford."

"Ford. Good name. You look hungry. Have some," said Jakes handing Ford a handful of berries from his pocket. Seeing Ford's hesitation he said, "Go on, they're all right," and threw a few into his mouth.

"Ham," Kellyn shouted to get everyone's attention, "get up that hill and keep an eye out!" Reluctant to leave when something interesting was afoot,

Ham dallied a moment too long. Kellyn stamped his foot and feinted towards him. It was enough to make Ham hop and scurry away over the stream and up the ridge.

"Chandler." Kellyn jerked his thumb over his shoulder in an upstream direction. "And Smith," he said turning towards the noisy boy. "No, not you, *you*." His pointing finger fell upon Duff, who was just waking up. "You get extra duty. Head downstream and make sure nobody sneaks up that way." Duff hung his head, and when Smith made a small mocking sound as he passed, Duff cuffed him.

"You never answered me. You a spy?" asked Kellyn. He and the remaining boys gathered closer to their prisoner, some of them picking their teeth with their knives.

"No," said Ford, his concentration immediately taken up by thoughts of escape. With so many of the boys gone, he might fight off the rest and get away. However, he wasn't going to be able to untie the rope from his ankles with all these eyes on him.

"Why you out here then? Thought you'd have a holiday by yourself in the woods?"

"I left home." Ford almost came clean with him, but thought better of it. Regardless of the Second Sons known reputation for harboring murderers, Ford wasn't ready to admit to anyone what had happened the day before, accident or no.

"You left home," said Kellyn as if he expected it, expected it and yet wanted to think about it. He got up to pace along the stream. An expectant hush fell upon the remaining boys and their eyes followed their leader. Ford placed his hands over his ankles quite naturally, as if he were resting them there for no reason aside from comfort. No one took any notice, so he went to work on the knot. "You left home," repeated Kellyn, pausing over each word with a sort of slow contemplation. "So what's the matter, grow tired of home or home grow tired of you?"

"No…I…" Ford stopped and started a few times before giving himself a moment and going on in a low, almost inaudible voice, "I don't have a home no more. I got no place."

"Why can't he just join?" The half-hearted mumble came from the smallest, most meager member of the group. When he was done talking, the little boy plugged his thumb back in his mouth. It may not have been a promising recommendation, but it was in his favor and it was enough to rouse Ford. He turned from the boy to Kellyn.

"So, you want to join the Wayward Boys," said Kellyn. Whether it was a statement or a question Ford had no idea, and didn't know what to say. His hands pulled back from the knot, but otherwise he was too stunned to react. "Fact is, we could use you, we can always use muscle, and you need us."

"I do," asked Ford, but in his confused state it came out flat and Kellyn mistook it as confirmation.

"I told you," Kellyn said in triumph. Looking around for Chandler and remembering he was on lookout, he turned back to Ford, "I told him. It's the old story. See, it stands to reason, nobody goes out into the woods alone for no reason, so you tracked us down. There's always a reason and reason is you need a place and you came looking for us." Still trying to absorb this strange turn of events while Kellyn meandered on, Ford considered his position. Without a home, occupation or so much as a single coin to his name, his options were limited. "Am I right or what?"

Having missed some of what Kellyn said, Ford nodded as the safest bet and went right back to wondering what he was going to do now and where he was going to go. But it wasn't long before he became aware of the quiet all around him. Assuming he'd missed another question, he looked up to find Kellyn pacing by the stream again, avoiding the spot where Cook worked at cleaning his pot. After lolling aimlessly waiting for the conversation to continue, the patience of the other boys wore out and they began throwing stones or splashing one another. One by one, the lookouts wandered back into camp and blended into the pack without a replacement being sent back out. Instead of anger at Chandler for leaving his post, Kellyn appeared almost happy to see him and they spoke alone together out of hearing. The rest played games with wooden dice, told jokes or spent their boundless energy throwing each other to the ground time and again in wrestling matches. It seemed to Ford a grand way to spend the day. Seeing them for who they were and getting to know each individual a little, these boys didn't seem so bad to him. Perhaps they pilfered now and then, a hard charge to deny when there was an open sack with dead chickens that looked like the old woodcutter's and Chandler had been admiring a lady's hairbrush before combing out his hair with it, but aside from this kind of lax morals, Ford could see himself enjoying the freedom of this life. Joining the Wayward Boys would be just like starting over.

"What do you say, Cook?" said Kellyn upon his return to the bend.

"Think you can keep a big boy like that fed?"

Cook's features curdled worse than ever in his brief study of Ford before passing judgment. "He'll eat us clean bare."

"I don't doubt that." Ford didn't catch it, but to the other boys this must have sounded like acceptance coming from their leader, because they gathered around Ford welcoming him or congratulating him and introducing themselves.

Runt, he learned was the youngest and smallest of them, so named only because he'd forgotten his own name at the time he'd attached himself to the group.

The noisy boy jumped forward and blurted out, "They call me Joker."

"We ain't called you that since you stopped being funny," said Kellyn.

"All right then, Goldy." The boy untied the horns and pulled off his hood to reveal a wavy, blond mass matted to his head.

"Not that neither. It's just Smith. Or you can call him Shithead," said Kellyn.

"Just call me Smith."

"On account of he's from a smithy family," said Runt, obviously proud of his knowledge, but only managing to sputter out half of what he wanted to say before Kellyn talked over him.

"Hold up, hold up. Before the big welcome, before we throw open our arms to the new man, he's got to show us what he can do. If you want to join us," said Kellyn coming up square in front of Ford, "you'll have to prove your loyalty."

"How?"

"We're hitting a place tonight and you're in on it."

"Where we doing tonight?" asked an eager Smith.

Kellyn's eyes locked on Ford and twinkled with mischief as he said, "Barlow."

CHAPTER 5
HITTING HOME

"Barlow? Why," asked Ford, frantically searching for good reasons not to go to Barlow.

"Why not," said Kellyn. "You know your way around, know where everything is and all. It'll be easy. And what better way for you to show your loyalty?" There was no hiding his prideful smirk at having thought of something so clever.

"But they'll be looking for me."

"Good, then nobody'll be home." As Kellyn moved through the band of boys playing their games or lying by the water, Ford marveled at how he seemed to have an answer for everything.

The day dragged on and in between quick drops into necessary sleep, Ford began to doubt if they were ever going to go. Not until sundown did the boys stop messing about and begin preparing. Most everything was set aside, but for weapons, masks and sacks.

"I can't go back there," Ford finally told Kellyn.

"Thing is, you are."

"Bring me back something I can use this time," said Cook from over by his pot, dumping in beans to soak. "No more of them scrawny hens!"

"And no more of them fucking beans," said Smith under his breath in his best impression of Cook.

Kellyn led them south out of the wilderness. Every few hundred feet of creeping along the stream was punctuated with a smack to the back of the head, for the younger boys would not stop talking until Kellyn, or Duff at his boss's command, did something about it. Smith seemed incapable of keeping quiet regardless of the punishment he endured. Ford was never touched. He wasn't the talkative type, but even so, he was far too nervous to speak. His nerves doubled when they came to the clearing where the people of Oren bathed, washed clothes and gathered water if their well was dry.

"Which way?" Kellyn asked Ford, who pointed the direction with his chin. He wished he could have come up with a way to throw them off, change their minds and make them think it was better to go after some other prize, but he already knew he couldn't compete with the clever Kellyn.

Forced to the front, Ford led the boys around the edge of the woods, keeping just out of sight on the backside of Barlow.

"Here. This is it," he whispered when he stopped them and they all crouched behind trees and bushes.

"What, this is Barlow?" Kellyn asked with a disgusted look at the scant few houses and the two meager barns that comprised one of the most pathetic hamlets he'd ever seen. "We was just here," he said massaging his forehead.

"Aw shit, yeah, we just hit this place," said Smith. "There weren't nothing here then."

"There will be even less now," put in Chandler.

"They've a big dog," whispered Runt searching for it with eyes of worry and hope. He loved a big, shaggy dog, at least the good ones.

"Maybe try some place else, Kell," suggested Jakes.

"No," said Kellyn without hesitation. "Our new friend here's got a job to do and this is where he's going do it. Right here. Yeah, we been here and there ain't much, but I'm sure Ford knows something we overlooked?"

To an outsider, the darkened windows and lack of life made the place appear deserted, but Ford knew better. The old woodcutter's family turned in early and his family would be inside mourning or out after him with a search party. If Milda was dead, they might be at her burial on the far side of Oren. Ford pondered the chance that she might not be dead right up until Kellyn's elbow jabbed him in his bruised ribs.

"I said, you're gonna get in there and grab us something good, right?" Ford nodded. "Which one's yours?" Ford pointed at his house. "Take something from there." A mask was thrust at him and he was given a shove towards the village, but Kellyn pulled him back for a final warning. "Remember, you call out, raise any alarm or such bullshit and we'll come back for you and your family. Count on it." Kellyn knew he was taking a risk, but he also knew his boys could easily melt back into the forest if something went wrong.

With the exception of Duff, Ford should have been the last of them sneaking around. To be fair, he didn't have the full cover of night, but still, stealth was not his strong suit. He ducked and dashed from tree to tree like a woolly mammoth playing hide and seek amongst sunflowers.

"If he don't get caught it'll be dumb luck," said Kellyn to the other boys watching Ford flounder in a bush.

For a tense moment or two longer it would remain darker inside than out and anyone watching from a window would be more likely to see Ford than he them. He ran to the back of the old woodcutter's house and ducked under the single shuttered window. From here he could stop unseen to listen, calm his heart and quell the pounding in his ears.

"What do I take? What do I take?" he kept asking himself, hoping to think of something to appease the boys. Their expectant, smiling and he thought perhaps laughing faces were just visible peeking at him over bushes and from behind trees. The ring came to mind and with it the awful feeling of stealing from Nia. Milda's jar of coins and trinkets on the other hand was the sort of thing the boys would appreciate and Ford had no scruples about taking. Thinking of nothing more valuable, he set his sights on the jar.

In two long strides Ford spanned the short gap separating the old woodcutter's house and the abandoned one he'd built years ago for his son that now housed their chickens. Peering around the corner he could see his family's house and barn. A breeze tossed dry leaves into summersaults across the intervening ground, the only disturbance in an otherwise oddly quiet evening. Getting this far had been easy, too easy he thought. What was going on? Was the place truly deserted? The eerie feeling that perhaps he was walking into a trap was just forming in his mind when, from his family's house some dozen yards away, a mournful wailing drifted light upon the breeze. Note after high, sailing note aimlessly rode the air like waves.

"Nia," he muttered and stepped out into the open, closer and another step closer. His feet stuck in the earth at the sight of someone or something moving about at the side of the house, an elusive form, a tall, shadowed figure in a billowing cloak. If there was a face, it was hidden or he couldn't see it in the low light, and Ford's tiny-holed mask wasn't helping. He threw it to the ground just in time to see the figure flip and wave like the fins of a giant ray. Possibilities flooded his imagination. Another gust whipped the cloak about and the light slap of cloth against the house deflated the whole imaginary mass into an ordinary sheet hanging over the hole he'd made in the wall when his father crashed into him. Ford stumbled forward and fell against the house. The wailing stopped.

"What was that?" asked Nia from within. Ford hoped hard that his inquisitive little sister wouldn't investigate. He held his breath and waited, pressed against the house beside the cloth cover. No movement stirred within. Then Nia started singing and Ford exhaled. It was possible that the girl was alone, and if so he could go in, take the jar and she might not say a word. His excitement didn't gain much of a footing. More than likely, he reasoned, she would scream if the man who had stabbed her mother walked into the house. For a brief phrase or two, the girl's rambling song coalesced into something recognizable: a lament, heartfelt, if off-tune and missing the occasional word. Listening to even that erratic melody lulled him into a drowsy lethargy. Exhaustion fomented a mild queasiness in his gut. The song stopped and then picked up again, this time with a coherence that was almost enchanting.

Curiosity took him. Ford clipped the cloth between his fingers and lifted it enough to see a sliver of the dimly lit interior. He made out nothing and inched closer, then pulled the cloth back further. Lying half-covered upon the table was Milda's waxen corpse. The cloth slipped out of Ford's hand as he recoiled, but it was too late, the image was imbedded. He could even see in his mind the vast bloodstain on the floor beneath her.

Deep breaths, gritting his teeth and telling himself the battlefield had been far worse steeled his courage enough so that when the breeze died away and the cloth over the door stilled, he peeked through the hole and made out Tilda's bristle brush sitting on a stool, the sorghum-made broom, and his bedding rolled up against the far wall.

"Shush now, honey," murmured Tilda, so close she could have been whispering in his ear. Ford fell back a step, shuffled away from the opening and would have bolted at the very next sound if it hadn't been a sniffle from Nia. "Oh, don't cry. Don't." Ford had never in his life heard Tilda speak so tenderly, with such compassion and the kind of lilting sadness that could only come from one filled with her own grief. Nia's sniffles continued. "Don't waste tears, not on him."

A weak shout came from the other side of the house. Ford's head swiveled about, but there was no one in sight.

"Who is it?" Nia pleaded to know. "Are they back?" Her scampering feet crossed the floor and the door opened with a creak coinciding with the old woodcutter's cackling call.

"Probably nothing," said Tilda. "Just the goat getting loose again." The woodcutter's wife's shriek cleft the air. "Oh my, something must be wrong!" Ford knew that if the girls were looking out the door, then they were facing away from him, so he lifted the edge of the cloth again. A hand grasped him around the arm and he nearly jerked down the covering from the hole, but it was only Chandler who'd sneaked up behind him. Chandler lifted his open hands palm up and raised a questioning eyebrow. Ford shook his head and Chandler had a peek inside for himself. Astonished by the brazen way in which the boy stuck his face into clear sight, Ford pressed his back against the wall and from this sharp angle saw the shelf upon which sat Milda's jars. The one containing her collected valuables was missing. It must have broken in the fight, he figured, since its coins and various baubles were left piled behind larger jars of salt and what little spice she had possessed. The shelf was high and Chandler short, and so when he pointed something out to Ford, it was at a sack of cornmeal hanging below the shelf. Below the sack was Myer's ax propped against the wall. Chandler nudged Ford, who edged forward, wincing at the sight of his sisters' backs by the door, but he slipped the sack off its peg and drew it painstakingly slow from the house. Chandler snatched it before it was halfway out and nudged Ford again, a clear command for him to grab something. He looked to Milda's scattered pile of valuables and saw the ring amongst them. He looked to the ax, that vital tool of his father's. He hesitated. Chandler prodded him again. Ford lifted the ax out with a thump against the wall.

"Hey there! You! Stop, thief!" Ford froze at the sound of the old woodcutter's shouts. When he looked around the corner, there were the Wayward Boys running hither and thither about Barlow. Jakes was leading away the old woodcutter's goat with Smith gleefully smacking its rump. Feathers filled the air around spooked chickens wildly beating their wings and running from Duff and the smaller boys who were futilely chasing them around the yard. The girls were screaming. Chandler was already gone. Though it was quite dark now, Ford shielded his face from sight with one arm and sneaked around the back of the houses. The boys fled into the woods, their hooting laughter fading away from Barlow, leaving behind the hobbled old woodcutter bent and cursing by his doorway.

Carried by wind and echo, a few feet into the forest Ford heard Nia say, "Where are they taking Nanny?" and it ran on in his mind over and over as they passed along the stream fast as they dared in the dark, tripping over every root and rock, branches thrashing their faces, the goat slowing them down, and Smith falling against trees, laughing so hard Kellyn had to slap him about and threaten to do worse if he didn't keep quiet.

Not much farther on, Kellyn held up a hand and they came to a halt. The crunch and crash of stomping footsteps came fast through the forest behind them. Whatever it was would overtake them. The boys instinctively ducked behind trees or hid in bushes. A man, tall and determined, went careening through the trees right by Ford and stopped. Ford crouched low and crept behind a tree. The man looked about him, listened and started off again, making for Oren.

When his footsteps faded away, the scattered boys began again, each heading on his own to meet up and continue on along the stream. Ford sat tight and watched them go, feeling the handle of the ax beneath his fingers, rocking back and forth on his heels to the tug of war within him. Standing and turning towards Barlow, he found little Runt crouched behind him. The boy stood and looked up at him, waiting for Ford to lead the way.

"Go. You can still catch them," said Ford, but no sign of the others could be seen or heard. "Just follow the water." He realized the stream couldn't be seen or heard either. "It's just there. Somewhere over there." Runt slipped his thumb into his mouth. "I'm going now." When Ford took a step towards Barlow, Runt followed. "You can't come back with me." He stepped again and again the boy came with him. "Ah damn it, come on." The two of them picked their way down to the stream where they found some of the boys waiting for them.

"We got to get out of here," said Kellyn when they found the campsite and fell in breathless heaps upon the bend in the stream. "If they find us, they'll hang us for sure." Squatting by a full pot of beans boiling over a white-hot glowing fire, Cook looked them over and went back to stirring his pot. "We got to go, Cook. Pack up."

"Bah." Cook flipped a hand in his direction. "They won't come after us in the dark. You're getting all excited for nothing." No matter Kellyn's insistence, Cook proved immovable. "You want me waste these good beans? Besides, pot's too hot to move and I'm not leaving another good pot behind. If any you fools got a good way to move a pot without no good handle and what's heavy and hot as that, I'm happy to hear it."

"Dump the damn beans!" shouted Kellyn.

"I'm not dumping no fucking beans!" Spittle flew off Cook's lips into

Kellyn's face. They both knew it was an accident, but it killed Cook's venom. Finally settling on a compromise, they prepared everything they could for a quick departure at the first sign of danger. The beans would be eaten the moment they were in the least bit edible, but if Cook had to leave his pot behind, then so be it.

In the meanwhile, Kellyn suggested they get some sleep while Cook stood watch over them and his beans. With his hands shaking and his thoughts racing, Ford very much doubted he'd sleep, but he did. Soon enough they were all settled and wrapped in dry, warm bedding by the fire only to be startled awake soon after by Cook banging the side of his pot with a spoon.

"Listen!" he hissed and in the distance they heard a rapid clanging bell.

"Is that from Barlow?" asked Ham. "I wished we hadn't of gone there."

"That's Oren's bell," said Ford. The more substantial settlements, those with a temple and even smaller villages like Oren that played the significant role of meeting place often had a bell. Oren's small iron bell hung outside the marchog's hall and was tolled in different ways for various reasons: fast for emergencies like fire; slow and deliberate as a call to prayer and afterwards lessons for the likes of children such as Leo, Tilda and even Nia.

"I hate them damn bells," said Kellyn. "Let's go." His command was obeyed, but the boys moved without hurry. They knew that the tolling bell was an alert to the surrounding villages, that the people would migrate to Oren, and the news of bandits would be spread, but it wouldn't be until morning that a search would be made. By the time dawn arrived the boys would be long gone.

"Center's still hard as stone," said Cook spitting out a bean and throwing his spoon back into the pot with disgust. "Water weren't hot enough."

"We'll find you another pot," Kellyn told him while lighting torches, "one with a good handle."

Though there was no great rush, some of the younger boys were nervous and left behind their masks or mugs. Runt would have forgotten his blanket if Jakes hadn't picked it up for him.

"Damn shame," moaned Cook casting a last glance over his shoulder at his beloved pot sitting over the embers that lit the bend in the stream in a warm glow that faded from view as they made off into the woods.

They kept to the stream much of the time, but impassable thickets or a lazy desire to take the easiest way set them upon a winding and, it seemed to Ford, a haphazard path. The land rose and fell, but that was all he could make of it, other than the poking and scraping branches upon his face. He'd never been this far into the forest and that made him stick close to the torchbearers. When the distant ringing at Oren was nothing but a memory, he asked of anyone willing to answer, "Where are we going?"

"To the Kingdom of the Valley," Smith sang out right beside him, throwing the words with all the pompous majesty his wavering boy's voice could muster.

"The Kingdom of the Valley," some of the others uttered reflexively. Ford had never heard of it, but he didn't want to say so and insult his new friends as he had done with the name of their band, but when the boys broke out in a loud chant of "All hail the King of the Valley," he could contain his curiosity no longer.

"Who's this King of the Valley?"

"I am," said Kellyn.

CHAPTER 6
HUNTING THE HERDER

All this time he'd been talking to a king and he didn't even know it, Ford marveled while twice bumping into the confused goat, running into a tree, tearing his pants on thorns and knocking the top of his head on a low limb. Eventually, the absurdity of Kellyn being an actual king dawned on him and he stopped tripping in the dark.

"I'm Runt," whispered the tiny boy at Ford's elbow. Enough of the glow from the dying ember at the end of his torch caught his upturned, smiling face.

"Yeah, I know," said Ford smiling back.

"My stick went out."

"I see."

"What should I do with it?"

"Why don't you stick it in your pocket and save it for later?" suggested Smith. Runt looked at the pocket sewn into his pants, looked at the stick and shoved the glowing end into his pocket. Ford whipped the stick out and Smith burst out laughing.

In the darkness ahead, leaves kicked up, and branches clattered. They all stopped and yet footsteps everywhere thumped furiously upon the ground. Runt and Ham yelped involuntarily. Ford braced himself for a stampede of night demons. The boys clung to one another. The unseen flurry and thunderous rumble faded and flew away, as if sucked into the void ahead.

"What was that?" Smith stuttered out and fought to pull his knife from his belt.

"Deer. Just a bunch of deer," said Kellyn striding forward. "Look, here." He held his dying torch close to the grassy ground. "Beds." Nearly a dozen depressions the size and shape of a curled up deer's body clustered together in a small clearing of overgrown grass.

"It's still warm," said Jakes with his hand in the grass at the moment Kellyn's torch snuffed itself out. Kellyn blew on the end without result.

"I guess we gone far enough this night," he said and the boys immediately began unburdening themselves. After Jakes finished tending to the goat, getting her water and the bit of feed he could scrounge, he tied her up with the rope they'd bound Ford with and was the last to curl up in the grass and go to sleep.

The next morning Ford awoke from a dream and the dream marched straight into his consciousness, refusing to dissolve away as most others did. Without getting up he turned towards Kellyn and scratched his backside.

"You been to Barlow before."

"Yeah."

"Did you steal some chickens?"

"A couple."

"No one caught you?"

"No one even saw us. It was just me and Chandler. No fuss, no noise. Got in, got out."

"Is that all you took?"

"I think so. It was a shit night."

"We meant to see about the next place over," said Chandler smoothing down his hair and itching behind his ear, "I believe you called it Oren, but seeing the marchog hall, we decided against it."

"You don't want to fuck with those guys," said Kellyn, "They'll hunt you down and string you up without so much as asking your name."

"Something's eating me alive," said Smith digging into his armpit. Immediately, Ford reached down the back of his own pants. Something didn't feel right down there. A lump appeared where he'd never found one before, a small and slippery dome, not very skin-like at all. He plucked at it, pulled it, pulled it hard and off it came, the plump body and writhing legs of a tick.

"Ticks! Ford's got ticks in his ass!" Smith announced.

"I've got one too," said Jakes holding up his find. "It happens."

"I'm going to throw up," said Smith, crawling out of his grassy deer nest.

"Quit playing the damn fool!" said Cook swatting at Smith even as he twisted round and round trying to scratch his own back.

"We got bigger problems than bugs. We got to get moving before that marchog or Rover or whatever he was catches us up again," said Kellyn. By

Rover, he was speaking of the Wilderness Rovers, that brand of brave, some said foolhardy, adventurer paid to scout the wild borderlands for trouble.

"I think it was my father," said Ford. Kellyn doubted it, but Ford knew what he'd seen and continued to ponder the previous evening while the band of boys wound through the forest that morning. Over the course of a half mile, Ham worked at falling in beside Ford as nonchalantly as he could. Once there, however, he remained mum in a way that disconcerted Ford, who wished to be left alone to think. Ham ached to say something, but "hi" was all he eventually managed.

"Hi," Ford replied and that was that. They walked along a shelf of granite jutting from the side of a hill, not a word passing between them. Still somewhat tired, few in the group made a sound above the shuffling of their feet. Not even Nanny, a chronic bellyacher in Ford's opinion, complained as she trotted placidly by Jakes' side ahead of everyone else. But Ham looked livelier than the rest, making his silence perplexing. "So," began Ford when he grew weary of the quiet boy beside him, "they call the small one Runt and they call the one that cooks Cook, so why they call you Ham?"

"Because that's my name," Ham said and went on staring silently at him.

"Are we almost there?" Ford shouted ahead to Kellyn and picked up his pace to join those at the front. Not much farther on, at the peak of a broad-shouldered hill, Runt ran before them all and was the first to the head of a descending, zigzagging path.

"Welcome to the Kingdom of the Valley," said Kellyn waving at all before him when he reached the peak. Most of the trees had already lost their brown and yellow leaves, aside from the evergreens, so that much could be seen of their Valley from this vantage point, and yet Ford saw no sign of any kingdom below. He wasn't expecting any grand city or castle ruled by a jewel-bedecked, crown-wearing king, the sort told of in tales of foreign lands, so when they at last reached the valley floor he wasn't disappointed by finding little more than the knobby, uneven ground of climbable trees, groves in a clumpy sea of dried grasses, rounded boulders like giant bald heads sticking out of the ground, and a sodden log bridge laid over a stream that wound crazily around it all.

"That's something," he said to Kellyn's satisfaction as they stepped gingerly over the bridge and came upon their "watchtower," a platform made of interwoven branches like a flattened bird's nest in an oak. Runt scrambled up the side of the tree with the help of a knotted rope.

"That's his favorite place," said Ham, indicating the high platform with a slight grimace that said it wasn't a favorite place of his own.

"Only a couple people fit up there, but it's a good place to keep an eye out," said Kellyn, his chest thrust out from leaning back to look up, a stance that made him appear strong and proud. He was proud of having built the lopsided and dangerously leaning platform, just as he was proud of all of his Valley. "Come on, there's more."

A few yards on they passed between two mature apple trees.

"These still give off good fruit," Cook said, giving one of the trunks a pat on the way by. "A little mealy, but good enough."

"And this is the stockyard," said Kellyn laying a hand on a ramshackle fenced-in mess of logs, branches and the odd plank tied together with bits of rope and vines. It was an area just wide enough for the goat to turn in agitated circles after Duff lifted the rickety gate and Jakes led her in.

"She won't like this, I tell you," Jakes said to their backs when the rest of them walked on to a palisade of thin logs and thick branches sharpened to a point at the top and bound together with all manner of rope, bark and even strips of cloth. The wall's height varied, but went no higher than the top of Ford's head. Its smooth-planed wooden gate, formerly a door to someone's house, sat loosely hinged with twine in a heavy log frame that leaned outwards against a boulder poking up from the ground like an overgrown tooth. Duff dutifully dragged the gate back over a well-worn arc of bare dirt.

"Good sir, welcome to the Great Hall," said Chandler who, standing by the gate, made a low sweeping bow with upraised palms. Kellyn pushed him aside and everyone filed in. Cook set to work at a fire pit. Duff yanked the gate back into place and enclosed them within the palisade's narrow confines. Hands grappled Ford about the neck and someone jumped on his back. He wheezed for breath and clawed at the arms around his throat. Bending deep at the waist with a quick jerk forward, he flipped his attacker off his back and it was Smith who landed in heap at his feet. Ford leapt away from them all with the ax at the ready and his back against the wall, but none of the others came at him. Smith laughed and groaned while rubbing where his shoulder had hit the ground.

"Cut it out! I'm trying to show him the place," said Kellyn, drawing Ford's attention to the palisade. "See now how when the door's closed we can defend from anything that wants to have a go at us?" Here and there gaps large enough for a man to poke his arm through were quite visible. "And this is where we sleep at night," he said, pointing to a shambles of a house to which the palisade was joined, completing the enclosure. Well-hewn, mortared stone of a ruin formed the house's solid foundation for the first few feet, but the remainder was a congealed stew of rough rocks, shards of slate, hand-sized stones and mud haphazardly packed right up to the roof, which looked like a dumping ground of forest debris. "Nothing can get at us in here." He held aside the patchwork cloth and leather flap doorway. Ford hunched over and passed through. Inside, Runt sat on the floor amid a pile of blankets and sacks. "Where'd you come from?" Runt pointed up at a gap in the roof. Kellyn jumped on to a box, stuck his head through the gap and called to Ford with a lighthearted voice, "Here, check this out. It's a secret trap door." Ford popped his head above the roof a moment, then helped replace the planks that covered the gap. "Anyways, you can see how the place is big enough to fit everyone, even you, too, if we all squeeze in. Might be a little tight." It was getting more than a little tight with most of the boys pushing into the dank, one-room house.

"This is about as crowded as it gets," put in Chandler. "At least one of us is usually up the tree keeping lookout at night and of course someone else keeps watch on the fire," said Chandler.

"Cook is almost always by the fire," said Ham from behind everyone else.

"Anyways, plenty of room in here," said Kellyn.

"There's never enough firewood," they heard Cook complain outside. "How am I supposed to keep up the heat without wood?"

"Whose job was it to bring in firewood last?" asked Kellyn, herding them out of the house. "Come on, who's not doing their job?" Some of the boys went shame-faced and others threw blame about until a brawl nearly broke out.

"Don't worry about firewood," said Ford holding up the ax. A wood-gathering party with Ford at the lead soon stockpiled enough to satisfy Cook and Kellyn, and everyone's ill temper blew away.

Enthusiastic, good moods abounded in those who wished to show Ford their favorite Valley features. Ham wanted to draw him away from the others to the stream, which they called "the river," with its short but edible brook trout. Ham lingered longer than necessary in showing off their fishing gear. Runt dragged him around the Valley to point out the rest of the ruins remaining from a long-abandoned settlement.

"That's an old well," said the boy, skirting a stone well covered over with sticks held down with rocks.

"Why's it blocked up?" asked Ford.

"So no one falls in," said Chandler slipping in beside them. "The water's all mud now."

"And so the monster doesn't get out," said Runt. Ford looked from Runt to Chandler and Chandler shook his head.

Out of all the ruins, the place they called the Face was the most complete and impressive. Carved with a blunt nose and sunken eyes, the huge rock sprung from the side of a hill facing in towards the Valley, seeming to glower down upon all before it. Age wore smooth its finer features and whether it was male or female was anyone's guess. The stream slipped under its chin and wrapped around it, so to get to it from the Valley without soaking themselves to the knees, the boys made a rope swing. Smith demonstrated it twice before Duff knocked him off and took a turn. After that, Ford felt sure it would hold him and followed the others over with a running start that swung him with a body-jarring thud into the steep ground beside the Face. Kellyn and Jakes caught him from sliding back down into the water and helped him up to "the ear," as they called the entrance. Following Kellyn, Ford slid in between the cold rock walls to reach a cramped chamber dimly lit from the entrance and a small hole chiseled through the rock to where the mouth was on the outside. They sat shoulder to shoulder on a shallow ledge and Ford looked out through the hole at a narrow view of the Valley. In his direct line of sight was "the table," a nearly six foot slate slab not far from their Great Hall, set horizontally upon rocks about waist high.

"It's cold in here," said Ford wrapping his hands around his shoulders on his way out of the Face.

"Makes a good storehouse in the hot months for cheese or butter when we can get any," said Kellyn. Duff replaced the crudely fashioned wood grate they laid over the opening. "Keeps animals out."

Ford surveyed the Valley from beside the Face. He'd never seen ruins quite so intact before. His look of awe made the boys happy. All the same, the entire time he was being shown about, there was but one thing on his mind, "When do we eat?"

"Hey, we got a goat now," mumbled Smith a while later through a mouthful of Cook's bland-but-filling cornbread.

"You just figure that out?" asked Kellyn.

"You can get cheese out of goats," said Smith. "I love cheese."

"My god, you're almost as smart as Chandler."

Undaunted, Smith jumped to his feet and looked with eager yearning towards the stockyard. Ford's mouth watered immediately, and he wasn't the only one with an excited gleam in his eye.

"You know how to make cheese?" asked Cook. Smith and all the boys who'd hopped onboard the idea had to admit they did not. "No, you don't and neither do I. No, what we got here is a walking bag of milk and that ain't bad."

"That ain't bad," muttered Runt, a touch of hope plucking up each word. As if her ears were burning and she wanted to know why, Nanny leapt out of the pen, knocking down some rails as she did so, and trotted over to them looking proud and happy.

"Told you she wouldn't like it," said Jakes through his laughter. After sniffing over Ford, the goat turned to Jakes and bleated, then started in on the clover patches about the valley floor.

In the late afternoon, each boy curled up in a patch of sun warming his body through. Most dropped off to sleep. Before his eyes closed completely, Ford peered about him at the Kingdom of the Valley and thought it would make a fine new home.

. . . . .

The diminishing sun glistened within clinging ice along the edges of the stream. The onset of frigid mornings and nights calmed and quieted the Wayward Boys, and made it almost impossible to budge them from their wraps beside the fire. If not for Kellyn, nothing would have gotten done, but at his insistence, they slipped into villages, lurked about towns and stole into barns in the night, carrying off valuables whenever and wherever they presented themselves. Fresh meat was highly prized, but they also made runs to stashes of grain sacks hidden away in rock nooks when past hauls were too heavy to transport all the way back home.

During the midday of these dreary autumn weeks, the Valley came briefly back to life with laughter. Now and then, Smith came out with a genuinely funny joke, and when Ford laughed harder than he could ever remember laughing before, Smith couldn't help but love him for it. Everyone but Kellyn and Cook played practical jokes that often proved bitter as the day was cold. Ford didn't mind joining in and even learned a few new ones, like the time Smith sneaked up behind him, sat on his head and broke wind. Ford chased him in circles around the Great Hall, then up and down the Valley. A lot of fighting resulted from these pranks and most of it was good-natured, though bruises were commonplace. Having always fared well against Leo, Ford thought highly of his own ability until he learned from Kellyn and Jakes the value of quickness in a fight.

The songs they sang and the stories they told around the fire at night, these were what Ford held most dear. While shepherding before joining the Wayward Boys, Jakes developed a smooth, carrying voice over years of singing to his flock and he knew some particularly beautiful songs. Though Ford couldn't sing and could only recite a few stories, hearing the others was an absolute joy to him.

Early on, Ford's worth rose steadily among the boys. All the work he saved them with his ax and the strength with which he wielded it set him on a kind of hero's pedestal in their eyes. He chopped down trees, hewed limbs and roughly fashioned pieces of wood that went into the repair and improvement of the Great Hall's roof and palisade. To show their appreciation, the boys outfitted him with everything he needed: a lengthy fur to wrap up in at night; a nice though tight jerkin; deerskin leggings; a leather belt; his own knife. The boys took him in like a brother. He was fitting in so well and quickly, in fact, that after only his second day in the Valley, he woke to find Runt nestled against his ribs, blissfully sound asleep. Even Cook complained a little less about how much he ate. Only Duff remained distant, still chafing at no longer being clearly the strongest in the band of boys.

"Still no milk?" Ford asked Jakes through chattering teeth. They stood in a few inches of new snow expanding and strengthening the rails around the stockyard. Jakes shook his head.

"Not a drop." The usual smile on Jakes' face dropped into a pensive frown. "I told Kellyn, she won't milk until she has a kid."

Ford had heard Jakes argue this before, but his family being such poor farmers, he knew little of animal husbandry. He liked animals well enough, he just didn't understand them. But Jakes did, and in the middle of winter, when food was running low, he found himself pitted against just about all the other boys, who called for goat meat.

"She's fattening herself up good," said Smith earlier that day, while licking his blue-tinted lips and gesturing to the goat's hanging belly.

At first, Ford sided with Jakes, if only because he liked Nanny and didn't want to see one of the few reminders of the home he had left slaughtered. But lately his hunger was overruling his fondness for the animal, and it was hard to deny that Nanny refused to yield a drop of anything drinkable. She stood outside of the stockyard, nipping at the shorn grass, then holding her head up high and keeping an eye on them.

Days passed and neither threat nor kindness could coax forth milk. Jakes never gave up on her. He would run his hand along her back in long, soothing strokes, massage her udder and whisper close by her ear. She would lick the side of his face and go back to scraping at the snow in search of roots or twigs she'd missed. As long as there was still bread, no one raised a complaint any louder than Ford's own stomach.

"That's the last of it," said Cook upending and shaking a sack of rye not a week later.

"It feels warm almost. Maybe winter's over," said Ford, tilting his head back, tossing hazelnut crumbles into his mouth and having a look at the noon sky through the bare trees.

"We're right in the middle of winter with months to go," Chandler said, soured at seeing the last of the nuts vanish. On the following day, when the snow fell hard and a driving wind pierced their Great Hall, the boys' superstition kicked in and they cursed Ford for tempting the wrath of the gods by putting voice to his desire for an early spring.

"Too much damn snow this year," said Kellyn pitching in with the small group clearing off the frozen stream and breaking through the ice to scoop out water.

"There won't be any fish, not for a long time now," said Ham to Ford, dipping the bucket in the hole and handing it to him. "Kellyn tells me I have to do the fishing, but I don't mind at all," he admitted in a quiet aside. "I like sitting by the river, thinking."

"Me too," said Ford and that pleased Ham, who would have liked nothing more than to have a friend to sit with silently by the river while he fished and thought. Nanny stuck her nose in the hole and sniffed. "Get!" She sniffed once more and, uninterested, pranced over the stream and found a snow-covered area to scrape at in search of the elusive grass, having stripped the twigs and bark to the limit of her reach all around the Valley.

"The trees look naked," giggled Runt in the midst of a discussion on that very problem when they were all within the palisade huddled around the fire ruminating on their hunger. The scrawny little boy in particular looked more gaunt than usual.

"That damn goat's eaten everything," said Cook.

"There's just about nothing left for her," said Ford and a quiet moment lapsed before he realized what he'd said. He couldn't think fast enough to change the subject and make the others forget about Nanny.

"He's right," said Chandler, sliding closer to Kellyn to whisper to him in a voice gone hoarse from illness. "Come on, let's butcher the thing before she starves to death." He turned and coughed, and pulled a matted pelt tighter around his head.

"She still got meat on her," added Cook, and everyone's eyes fell on Kellyn to see what he would say.

"You don't kill the does," burst out Jakes from across the circle, looking angrier than ever they'd seen him. Those flanking Jakes scooted away.

"Watch yourself," warned Kellyn, his steady eyes locked on Jakes. Chandler waited for the tension to pass, and then leaned towards Kellyn again.

"We could split up and some of us try our luck in the towns." It was a reference to the practice bandits had of breaking camp for the winter and scrounging on their own as beggars or lone-wolf thieves within the larger towns where they might survive more easily alone.

"No one leaves." Kellyn's words marched out with the stamp of finality, like a declaration of law. The miserably cold boys went quiet, each lost in his own thoughts of despairing hunger, resigning himself to his fate or plotting an alternative. Kellyn too sat in heavy thought, eventually stirring to say, "I don't see no choice but the goat. We got no food and we can't get none with this snow."

"Why not?" asked Ford.

"What you mean, why not?" he said rounding on Ford, but seeing his simple ignorance he explained, "Cause you walk into a place in snow, they see your tracks walking back out. That's why not."

The wind picked up, moaned through the trees and blew the snow off branches on to the roof.

"It's snowing, it's snowing," sang Smith over and over until Duff slapped the back of his head.

"It is snowing," said Ford.

"No, it ain't," said Kellyn, then he leaned out the door. "Shit. It is. Again." Chunky flakes plummeted to the ground all that afternoon, and by the time it was dark they abandoned the idea of slaughtering the goat until the next day.

When they woke to an icicle-strewn valley of twinkling crystals, the goat was gone. Nanny's tracks led away from the stockyard and eastward, down along the stream. Beside the hoof marks were a set of human-made prints.

"Where's Jakes?" hollered Kellyn looking around at all the drowsy faces that peered half-aware back at him. "Damn him, that son of a bitch!" He stomped in and out of the palisade gate, glaring at and then kicking at the footprints in the snow. "Someone's got to go after him and bring that goat back." The boys ducked inside or curled up on the ground and stared blankly at the fire. Smith pretended to have fallen immediately back to sleep. Kellyn prodded them each in turn, shouted commands and threatened banishment, but no inducement would move them. The bitter cold and lack of food brought on a lethargy that had been dogging them for a few hard days. This new setback sank their spirits even lower.

"I'm not chasing after our meals and cooking them too," stated Cook before turning away to dig for wood within their buried pile.

"You're the one," said Kellyn turning his attention on Ford. "You and that sheepherder didn't want to lose your precious pet. We could be filling our bellies right now if not for you." Ford stayed tightly wrapped in a warm bundle, averting his eyes from Kellyn's. "All right, fine. Duff'll go." Duff would go, knew Ford, and he would also likely beat Jakes into a bloody mess if he caught him. Ford wrapped the fur tighter around his shoulders and stood.

"I'll go."

As he trudged through the thick drifts that caked about his ankles, Ford considered leaving the Valley forever. He liked being a member of the Wayward Boys, but he didn't like the idea of starving or freezing to death. His only other option, as far as he could see, was to crawl back to Barlow, beg forgiveness and endure whatever punishment the family piled on him. Warmth, comfort and a full belly were strong temptations, but he knew it would be more than punishment from the family. Accident or not, he'd killed someone and his fate would be in the hands of the law.

The snow carpeting the ground and clinging to everything created a claustrophobic barrier to sight and an almost enveloping void of sound. All he could hear was the soft crush of snow under his feet and his own labored breathing as he exhaled white puffs into the still air. Out here where his imagination allowed anything to linger in the shadows under the evergreens, he felt alone, like the loneliness he had endured as a child sleeping by himself in the barn back in Barlow. The ghostly remnants of old nightmares of some approaching unknown terror flooded back to him. A chill penetrated his clothes and prickled his skin. Just a few short months with the boys at the Valley had removed his dread of the unknown wilderness. However, on his own once again, the old familiar feelings returned and his steps began to drag through the snow as he lurched forward into that eerie silence.

"Ford!" It came faint, and so deep and distant as to have been a mere deception of the wind now sailing through a shallow ravine where he fell against the nearest tree and wrapped an arm around it for support against his buckling knees. He listened. When he thought it might be one of the boys, he hoped for a repetition. When his mind wandered and he thought it might be his father, he despaired the repetition. None came, but the words "Turn back, turn back!" repeated in his head so loud he was sure they'd been spoken. His hands itched for the ax. Before leaving, Kellyn had pushed it into his hands and told him to use it if he had to, but Ford had left it, saying he'd do the job without it. Now he wished he'd at least thought to bring his knife. He was cold, he felt vulnerable and he wanted nothing more than to go back to the boys in the Valley. His inner voice even devised promising schemes. *You could tell them the tracks disappeared.* It was almost true. Jakes had made some attempt at covering his trail by walking over any available patch of exposed ice along the stream or using the branch off an evergreen to sweep behind him, but after a while he'd given up and the tracks were plain to see. Going back now would only anger Kellyn, he would undoubtedly be thrown out of the gang, and Duff would be sent after Jakes. Besides, he'd said he'd do it and so he would.

Loping with abandon through the drifts as a way to defy cowardice and make up for lost time, Ford followed Jakes' trail across undulating land, over and around boulders capped with snow, and returned to a parallel course near to the stream. Now and then, where a branch hung low and bare, Nanny's tracks stopped and then there would be long streaks in the snow as if she'd been dragged. Ford held up his ear, listening only briefly before moving on, for again the encompassing nothingness infested his waning courage.

"What in the name?" he muttered while staring down perplexed at four sets of tracks in the snow by a rotted, overturned stump. It appeared another person and another goat had joined Jakes and Nanny and then carried on. He followed slowly and with keen glances about him, scanning between the trees for signs of the four. Perhaps stranger still was when the tracks broke off, one set continuing on in the direction Jakes had been traveling all along and the other veering away down to where the stream had eroded the bank into a steep gully, too wide to leap over and too deep to crawl into and out of without help. These tracks went along the gully before turning away from it and eventually circling back around to join with Jakes' original tracks, back where Ford had found the four prints coming together for the first time. Eventually it dawned on him that the extra prints were duplicates of Jakes' and the goat's. He'd been tricked and was on his guard when later he came upon tracks that seemed to break off into three different directions. This was just the sort of thing his brother used to do for fun. After fooling him when they were children, Leo had shown Ford how this particular trick was done. Lots of careful backtracking into one's own footsteps was needed. It was clever, but time-consuming.

A companion or two at this moment would have been handy, he reflected while running along the first trail, which led down a hill and stopped abruptly at the stream. The next one shot ahead with long strides, but then ended soon by wrapping itself around and around a tree. Ford ran up the hill after the last trail, only then realizing that he should have paid attention to the goat's tracks. Nanny couldn't be expected to backtrack her own prints. There was only one set of her and Jakes' prints going forward on this trail. Ford clenched his fist and knocked the side of his head.

Over the hill the trail led deeper into the still, dim world under the snow-laden evergreens. Branches broken by the weight stuck out at odd angles like the arms of shadowy figures. The blanketed limbs, massing impenetrably thick overhead, thinned the snow underfoot to a dusting. In some places the ground was bare of snow and tracks altogether. Running this way and that with his head down searching for any sign, worry haunted him that he might have lost the trail. Losing the goat would be bad, but he also hoped to bring Jakes back. He liked the jovial, hard-working and kindly sheepherder. He'd never met anyone so consistently cheerful and friendly, and he liked having that in his life.

Kneeling down for a closer look in the poor light at a bare patch of earth, he figured it for nothing and was about to sit down to rest and think, when he noticed the pine needles pushed aside. Unable to see, he felt within the fresh scrape with his fingers and realized it was an imprint in the shape and size of a goat's hoof. That one print led to others, which took him right up to a towering, lopsided boulder looming over him like a frozen mammoth, and here the trail ended. Circling the boulder three times with his eyes desperately searching the ground and finding no prints, he stopped and let out a somewhat caustic laugh of relief. Now he could return to the Valley and tell the boys that the tracks had simply vanished, because they truthfully had. What Kellyn might do or say and what they would all do now to keep from starving, left Ford wondering right when a jolting weight landed fully upon his back and bent him over. Arms wrapped around his neck, the weight shifted, he spun around and there was Nanny. The goat hopped off the boulder and away.

"Stop!" he gasped, but the arms held tight. His vision went blue, white blotches swam across his eyes and he whirled around, nearly floundering under the extra weight before slamming Jakes against the boulder. The two of them fell to the ground. Ford got up and rested with his hands on his knees to regain his senses, while Jakes scrambled to his feet and faced off with him, poised to spring again.

"Don't do this," Ford pleaded, but Jakes' determined scowl and stance held firm. They circled one another, neither attacking. Nanny trotted back to watch their curious dance. "I'm not fighting you." Ford straightened up and shivered from the chilled sweat running down his back. "It's cold, Jakes. Let's go home." Ford lunged for the goat, but Nanny scampered off and led him and Jakes on a chase out of the dim evergreen grove to the relatively light and airy world of the taller trees and snow-covered ground. Just as Ford reached Nanny's rope, Jakes caught him from behind and they wheeled about together, tripping over each other's feet and going down in the snow. For the moment, Ford had the advantage and pressed his weight down on Jakes, grabbing his arms and pinning his legs, but Jakes was quick and slippery as an eel. With a few rapid jerks he broke free and wriggled away.

The struggle for the goat went on for some time with neither getting the upper hand. They didn't really want to fight each other, but they wouldn't give in either. Every time Ford went for the goat, Jakes came at him.

"Give up the goat!" shouted Ford.

"You're not getting her!"

"Give her up!"

"No!"

Eventually the fighting devolved into pushing and shoving until both were so tired that they dropped to their knees and resorted to throwing snowballs at one another.

"Look," said Ford after a while, holding up his hands to stop Jakes' next throw, "I don't want this and you don't neither, but it's happening one way or other."

"Maybe not." A glob of snow and pine needles flew by Ford's head and plopped down a few feet behind him.

"If you don't come with me, Kellyn and Duff will come after you. They're probably coming now. You can't get away."

"I might," said Jakes appearing to weigh more than just the snowball in his hand.

"Maybe," Ford seemed to agree before slipping into a near trance while puzzling how to win the argument. A snowball smashing into his chest brought him back. "Not in this snow, you won't. They'll track you down." Triumph rose within when he saw Jakes seriously ponder this. "They're starving back there, Jakes. Runt and them, they look like skeletons. You're walking away with the last of what we got left. Do you want everyone to starve? 'Cause they will."

Snowflakes floated to the ground, each taking its own lazy path, in no particular hurry to land. For a time, the sun shone bright behind the cover of clouds, casting a dazzling glow and a modicum of warmth. In all ways Ford walked with a lighter heart back to the Kingdom of the Valley. Not only did he have the goat, but Jakes as well. Both hiked beside him willingly, though Jakes remained sullen.

"What'd you do before, when they killed your sheep you herded?" asked Ford after a long stretch of silence.

Jakes shrugged, "I was a herder, not a butcher. The only slaughtering I've seen's been chickens. And I hate chickens." They stopped to let Nanny rip at a branch. "That's not true. I just don't like them much, is all."

As predicted, Kellyn and Duff were on their way, following the tracks at a trot when they all finally met not far from the camp. At first Jakes caught an earful of abuse and threats for what he'd done, but they were all so hungry it was soon forgotten. What was not forgotten were the sacred rites due a beast of such importance to them. Within the enclosed palisade, the boys knelt in front of the goat and lifted their forearms. Each made a fist and held it to their hearts.

Kellyn muttered, "Mother, Father, Great Provider, bless us and protect us. Nourisher of earth, Sustainer of life, we thank you for this bounty." Some of the words were wrong or missing, but Ford hardly noticed. He had other things on his mind: the goat; the ax in his hands; a stomach once rumbling, now tightening. As Kellyn finished, they lifted their arms high and each of their fists burst open with fingers spread wide. They stood and gathered about Nanny in curiosity. At Kellyn's command, Duff grabbed hold of the goat's rope. Jakes laid a hand on her back and Ford positioned himself at her side.

"Right there," said Cook pointing at the middle of her neck, "good and hard."

Ford raised the ax in his two unsteady hands.

"Do it quick!" cried Jakes, hanging his head and holding his hand firmly upon her back. Ford jerked the ax down fast and with as much muscle as he could muster in what he hoped was a single and merciful stroke, but the ax head flew wide and the handle thumped down on Nanny's neck. A hideous, uncontrollable grunt sputtered out of her as her eyes rolled back and she staggered drunkenly to and fro. Some boys screamed, others yelled at Ford, and Duff laughed.

"Hold her still! Hold her still!" shouted Ford diving after her, swinging at her swaying neck. The blood splattered upon the snow and squirted onto the boys. A last, crunching blow upon her neck dropped her. Runt started to cry.

Cook dug his knife into her belly. Out rose steam and stench as the intestines sloshed over the ground and sank through the snow. The boys covered their wrinkled noses and edged away. Jakes couldn't look up.

"Are those worms?" whimpered Runt, wiping his runny nose and creeping closer behind Ford, who stood rigidly holding the bloody ax and watching without seeing anything.

"Them's the guts," replied Cook sinking his arm up to the elbow and feeling inside the chest cavity for the heart.

"Looks like worms."

"Nah, they's guts. And that right there's the liver or kidneys and that's the stomach," said Cook leaning back and pointing with his knife at a bulbous gray sac, "or no, that's it, I think." His knife moved towards another, larger sac, somewhat deflated and lumpy. "You can learn a lot about an animal by their stomach."

"How?"

"You cut it open and see what they ate." Cook stabbed in his knife and tore the sac open. Two uniformly flesh-colored, partially formed kids, smooth, hairless and coated in clear amniotic fluid flopped against his knees. He howled and fell over backwards. The boys dove into the house or fled the palisade.

"I told you," Jakes cried after them, "I told you! You don't kill the does!"

Ford dropped to his knees and the ax fell out of his hands.

CHAPTER 7
AN ILL-TIMED JEST

The Wayward Boys including Jakes put the trials of winter behind them by releasing pent up energy in warming chases and races run half-naked over the spongy ground and among its sprouting weeds and the exploding puffs of white and pink blossoms of a swiftly greening Valley. Two nights prior, a successful raid on some sleepy villages secured enough barley flour, cured meat and maple syrup to last for weeks. They even managed to bring back live chickens for a new coop built with a few tools recently seized.

As if this wasn't enough for a pack of half-starved boys accustomed to a winter's deprivation, the earth too brought forth its own bounty. With Cook's instructions ringing in their ears, the younger, more shiftless among them were compelled to gather dandelions and other edible greens, as well as to pluck up the right roots and mushrooms.

Smith did his best to disrupt work and cause mayhem at every opportunity, leading whoever would follow in various idle escapades: contests to see who could hang from a branch the longest; dangling Runt upside down over the water; hiding beetles in bowls of beans; and dropping worms into unfortunate sleepers' ears. The pranks and teasing seldom ceased. Playful wrestling returned and quarrelsome fights declined. With heavy bellies and light hearts they ran about the forest like wild animals, kings of their own secret world among the trees.

The joy of spring was enhanced by a great event that season, the carving of their very own totem. The boys had always wanted one, but none of them had the will or skill for such an undertaking. Now they had a carver amongst them. Ford doubted his own ability, pointed out that he didn't have the right tools for the job, and really wished he hadn't been the one to point out their lack of a totem.

"It won't look good," he warned.

"Something's better than nothing," Kellyn kept telling him until the project was underway. Starting with heads full of enthusiasm late one afternoon when there was barely enough light left to see by, they hewed the largest log they could handle and stuck it in the ground by the rock outside the gateway to the palisade. Without Duff's help, lifting and holding the massive log in place would not have been possible. Ford still didn't like him, but had to admit that they worked well together at times. Yes, the two of them had set the totem a little lopsided, but the important point was that it did stand and stood taller than the tallest of them to boot.

Once he started carving a generic tree image on the log, Ford regretted all the trouble they'd gone through in securing it upright in the ground. If he screwed up now, they'd have done all that work for nothing. Ignoring the others who grumbled about him dragging his feet just to get out of doing hard work for a while, he took his time, planning ahead just like he'd seen his father teach Leo to do by first sketching out an outline before committing to a gouge or scrape. In the end he had the most crooked tree he'd ever seen, adorned with only a half dozen animals and flat human faces etched into oversized leaves and acorns before he ran out of room and patience. It didn't matter, the boys were impressed. For the first week they all saluted the totem whenever they passed by and from then on that was the spot upon which they said their prayers, prayers that soared with uplifted spirits and pride at owning their own totem.

On a muggy full-moon night, after having slipped in and out of a poorly guarded tithe barn and returning heavily-laden with a jingling, coin-filled coffer, a small party of the boys walked back to the Valley through a forest illuminated as if by the sun. Exhausted from doing most of the carrying, Ford dropped right off to sleep and fell deeply into the hands of his father. At least, he was fairly certain that's who was manhandling him in his dreams. He always kept his eyes averted from the man gripping him about the chest, pushing, shoving and pressing down so hard that Ford often woke gasping with a scream caught in his throat on the many nights he succumbed to the dream. On the most recent night it happened, he'd fought the arms holding him down, thrashing with his whole body.

"Wake up! Wake up!" Cook's scarred face hovered inches above his own and Ford slid back with a frightened yelp.

After the mud-churned waters of spring cleared, Ham took up fishing again and would talk Ford into coming along whenever he could. Having hiked upstream to a place they simply called the Swamp, the two were attempting to retrieve Ford's line for the third time that day.

"I don't know why you whip it around over your head like that," said Ham, while keeping an intent eye on the cluster of leaves where the fishing hook had snagged a branch as he was lifted by Ford into the tree. He dearly hoped to free it and untangle the precious tackle without snapping the line. "You can just drop it in the water. It works just as well."

"I think my father is after me." Ford's blunt statement came so far out of nowhere it caught Ham quite by surprise.

"What?" he repeated two, then three times before Ford's far-off gaze focused on his face.

"I think my father's after me."

"What makes you think that? Higher. I almost got it."

"Can't say. Just a feeling."

"Well, there's got to be a reason." Ham glanced down in time to catch Ford's shrug. "There's always a reason. Little higher. I need to stand on your shoulders. There."

"For revenge, I guess."

"Revenge? For what?"

"I killed his wife." Ham's knees buckled and he almost fell. Sensing his terror, Ford quickly added, "It was an accident. It wasn't my fault."

"I got it. Let me down," said Ham after an interval of quiet, and Ford lowered him to the ground.

"Partly it was my fault, but I didn't mean to do it. Anyways, I been having these dreams, nightmares really, all to do with all that and I think they're trying to tell me something." Ford explained it all and in more than enough detail to satisfy Ham's curiosity. It was a lot of information for the boy to take in all at once and although he believed in Ford's innocence wholeheartedly, he had little to say at the moment. "Don't say anything to anyone."

"I won't."

The unseen far end of the swamp erupted in an unnervingly loud splash. Ham was already gone by the time Ford had all the tackle and fish they'd caught in hand. Just before he was about to bolt, Ford stood on his toes and craned his neck to see what he might over the rushes. Ripples from the splash reached the shore at his feet. A deep, throaty "gah-lump" groaned across the water and Ford no longer cared what it was.

"Hurry," called Ham from behind a tree and the two ran home together.

Strange noises were not unheard of in the forest, especially around the Swamp, and both boys forgot about it soon after they got back. For his part, Ford was more intent on catching Smith, who would not stop calling him "sucker," for that was what they called the kind of suction-mouthed, bottom-feeder fish he'd caught. Smith latched on to the word and wouldn't let it go, calling him a "sucker lover" and making obscene gestures. Eventually Ford had had enough, and chased him to the ends of their Valley and back, their legs swishing through ferns, their feet splashing in the swollen stream. When Ford's heavy step sucked in and out of mud, it vaulted Smith into a whole new barrage of name-calling. Unable to catch him, Ford went back and sat by Cook, who was looking over his fish.

"They ain't best for eating. They got bones, little bones."

"We can't eat them?"

"Sure you can, all's you do is slice them up," he explained as he made incisions in the fish, "then cook them good and hot and they's fine."

By the time the fish was on the fire, Smith's boredom got the best of him and he came back, leaning in and sneering over the fish. Ford collared him, dragged him through the palisade gate and down to the stream, where he lifted Smith bodily over his head, shook him while howling like a wolf in triumph, then threw him into the water. Cook shook his head when Ford walked back in and sat by the fire.

"Thanks for showing me that," said Ford, "I learn more good stuff from you than anybody ever taught me." Cook waved off the compliment and turned away, pretending to look for his knife in order to hide the merest of smiles. Leo had always taken the time to teach Ford lessons, and although Ford was a poor student, he did love to learn. When Kellyn needed help with his traps, Ford naturally leapt at the chance.

"This string attached to this stick here," explained Kellyn when he and Ford were out in the woods kneeling in front of a heavy box, one end of which was propped up precariously with a stick, "this goes inside the box there and over that nail. See it? The other end is wrapped around that chunk of meat. The meat hangs there like that or sometimes I use an apple and anyhow, if I'm lucky some dumb animal will grab it and yank on it and that'll pull down the stick and then *whomp!* Down goes the box and the stupid thing's trapped."

"Does it really work?" Ford asked crouching down and twisting around to see underneath the box.

"Does it work? Yeah it works," said Kellyn frowning. "All my traps work. Where you think all the rabbit and coon come from? I only wish we had more of them."

"That's pretty smart. How'd you learn to do this stuff?"

"My ma was a trapper," said Kellyn jumping up and striding away, leaving Ford to follow with the new trap they'd finished making the day before slung over his back.

"More like she was a poacher, if I'm speaking true," Kellyn admitted when Ford caught up. "Guess it was just easier to take what was already trapped, but she knew a thing or two." Animosity brewed within, and his next words spilled out like a challenge, "She knew how to make traps good as anybody."

"I bet. I mean, I'm sure. What your pa do?"

"Don't know. Never met him. It was just me and ma. Then she died."

"Oh. Sorry," said Ford, scratching the side of his face and looking around while he thought of something to say. "You didn't have no brothers or sisters?"

"No. None what lived long enough to grow up."

"So it was just you by yourself?"

"Yep."

"What'd you do?"

"Huh?"

"How you get on?"

"I did just what I'd been doing, trapping and thieving."

"You never got caught?"

"I got caught. Got caught lots."

"What happened?"

"Got the shit kicked out of me, that's what happened." Kellyn glanced around him and changed direction slightly. "After a while I guess they had enough of me and it was either run or…" Here he mimed the chopping off of one of his hands. "So I ran."

"Where'd you go?"

"Went out and joined the Boys, only they was called the Bag Jackers then. An old man and his lady, a couple others. It was nice. Anyways, I knew where they camped sometimes, so I went out there and just waited 'til they came. Like what you done. Watch it!" Kellyn slapped a hand against Ford's chest and prodded the ground ahead. It gave way with a springy bounce under his toe. "Pit trap. We only got one of them. No one wants to dig holes." While Kellyn threw half of a pungent squirrel into the bottom of the pit, where it landed amongst a few wooden spikes sticking up from the ground, Ford thought about trying again to convince him that he hadn't intentionally tried to find the Wayward Boys, but decided there was no point.

Kellyn smoothed over the covering of the pit and headed off. They hiked the rim above the Valley, staying upwind of the camp. Though no great height, one could see between the tree trunks a long ways down the slope from which they came. Ford loved views like this and would often stop and gaze off into the distance, taking it all in with nothing in particular on his mind. He'd been called back from such deep reveries countless times before by his father.

"Let's go!" shouted Kellyn from far ahead before disappearing out of sight.

"Wait up," called out Ford, the thatched conical trap bouncing off his back in time to his hastened, stomping gait. Reaching the spot where he had last seen Kellyn, he found no trace of him. "Hello?" A beastly snarl and a startled cry froze him with his hands cupped about his mouth for another call. "Kellyn!" he shouted and edged forward through the trees on half-willing, stilted legs. Not far ahead he found Kellyn sprawled out on his back with another conical trap rolling around on the ground in front of him. From within the trap a hairless creature with leathery, wrinkled red-brown skin emitted a low, dry growl broken by the occasional yap and a strange nasal whinnying. Without a second's thought, Ford whipped the trap off his back and brought it crashing down on the other, scattering splinters everywhere.

"What is that," shouted Ford over the creature's incessant growling.

"No fucking idea! It sounds like a coon, but that ain't no coon I ever seen!"

Ford helped Kellyn to his feet and the two boys huddled side by side leaning on one another, falling back in step when the creature lashed at the sides of the weakened trap. With each jerk and thrust, the bones of a carcass rattled around its brittle cross-hatched sticks.

"Coyote, maybe," said Ford.

"You ever see a coyote that look like that?"

Though a naked dog in appearance, its hind legs were stronger and its shorter, thinner forearms ended in nimble, clawed fingers. It glared at the boys down a long snout with dark, beady eyes. Scratches and crusty scabs oozed blood about its nose, head and upper body where it had tried crawling back out of the trap and got cut up on the spikes pointing in around the opening through which it had first easily squeezed in.

"Look at it shake," said Ford. Whether it shook out of fright or ferocity, neither could tell.

"I ain't losing that trap." Kellyn took out his knife, even took a step forward, but stopped. "I was just thinking, what if it's got disease or something."

"Surely it could, just look at it."

Kellyn found a long sturdy stick and sharpened one end to a fine point, then stepped forward and jabbed at the trap. The shaft slid through a gap, narrowly missing the creature, which whirled about and snapped off the end with its sharp fangs. The boys retreated a few yards. Out of sheer frustration, Kellyn found a few stones and threw them. They missed or bounced harmlessly away, each throw angering him more until he swore and threw a heavier rock that smashed in one side of the trap. The creature went wild, circling round and round, crashing against the sides until it broke free.

"Look out!" cried Ford and they both dove behind a tree, crouching and listening to a mad scramble in the leaves. A black flash in Ford's periphery fled into the undergrowth and all was still, but for one of the traps rolling down the hill. When it finally stopped, they kept listening, but could hear nothing more of the creature.

"Is it gone?" asked Ford. Kellyn held a finger to his lips.

"I don't know," he whispered after a while. "Why don't you have a look?" Ford poked his head out and Kellyn yanked him back. "I was kidding, you idiot." More anxious than annoyed, Ford kept looking.

"Anyhow, I don't see it." It took some time before they both relaxed enough to creep out and return to their trap setting.

"Don't tell any of them others about this," said Kellyn while examining the old, destroyed trap. It wasn't a command, so much as a request. "I seen shit like this thing out here. Not the same, but like. I tell you, I seen…weird things."

"Yeah?" asked Ford, wanting and not wanting to hear what he'd seen.

"Yeah, and them others back at camp, they don't need to know about this or any of it. Got that?" Ford gaped as he took it all in. "You got that?"

"I got it."

"There's weird things out here, sure, but ain't nobody got hurt, so ain't nobody need know about it. Them fools'd only get spooked."

Ford nodded. Kellyn may have been disagreeable at times, but he was beginning to see the burden of responsibility he took on for the good of the boys. His respect increased as well as his understanding of the faith the others placed in Kellyn's leadership.

"Fun's over!" Kellyn bellowed to the few boys sitting around playing a game with rocks when he and Ford walked in through the palisade gate. "Pack up your stuff. We're heading out." Ford looked at him, surprised. Kellyn hadn't mentioned anything about this during the hours they'd been setting traps together. "We're going out again, before we run out of stuff."

"Sounds good. Anything to get away from these flies," said Jakes swatting at the black cloud of insects that appeared to swarm up out of nowhere just a few days before. They hovered about the heads of all the boys and drove them mad.

While Jakes might have been making the best of it, some of the younger boys were never happy about leaving the Valley. So long as they weren't starving, they were content and Kellyn's concern seemed unfounded to them. They were as well stocked with provisions as they'd ever been, so Ford guessed that Kellyn just needed a break from the forest after what had happened earlier.

"He always makes us do raids when we don't even need to 'cause we got plenty a food," complained Ham, dawdling along behind Ford on a deer path leaving the stream up and out of the Valley the following morning.

"He does that," explained Chandler walking behind them, "because it makes sense to, before we run out of things."

"I do my part," said Runt dragging his feet on the path ahead, slowing down those behind him.

"Sure you do," said Chandler.

"I do!" said Runt, twirling about to stick out his tongue in Chandler's face.

"Whatever you say, little man." Chandler yanked Runt's mask down over his head.

"Stop it!" Runt swung a tiny fist at Chandler and then fell back in step with Ford. "I don't like Chandler," he said confidentially. Ford smiled and caught a bending branch about to slap across Runt's face and probably bring the little boy to tears. Later when Runt was walking alone, Smith slipped in beside him to whisper something in his ear. They both giggled and nodded, and soon Runt was skipping along merrily.

The proud village of Farnod, tight-packed within its high wooden wall, pressed against a new-growth forest of spindly trees and thick bushes in a remote valley glen. Most bandits would have passed Farnod by at the first sight of its wall. However, its distance from neighbors enticed Kellyn, who saw it as a "rich nut to crack" and gathered his boys in the thick bushes on the outskirts at nightfall.

"It's too high to climb, but its posts are tied by old rope and leather strapping. Should be easily to cut," explained Chandler in a discreet hush after infiltrating the village earlier in the guise of a messenger in search of a recipient, a traveling merchant whom, it just so happened, he'd only barely missed according to the villagers.

Truth be told, the boys hadn't missed the merchant. They'd waylaid him on the way to the market town two miles up the road. The bigger boys had held the guards at bay while the smaller boys had stood back from the road among the trees holding sticks that made convincing bows to one being robbed by bandits. The two men guarding the wagon would not surrender their weapons, but that wasn't necessary, as the merchant was quite willing to hand over his small purse of copper coins. Kellyn considered trying to take the wagon and its entire load, guessing there were more valuables secreted within, but he knew the limits of his band and settled for what they could get.

"Some of the new posts they replaced the old ones with aren't even dug into the ground." Chandler paused here to raise a highly arched brow and give a big nod.

"So, they just got lazy and tied them in with the rest," said Kellyn.

"Precisely. Should be easy to move them out of the way."

Many of the new, loose posts were made from the spindly trees near at hand. The people had indeed neglected their wall, preferring instead to spend their time tending their fields which stretched out beyond a brook, across impressively extensive cleared land that Ford found somewhat familiar, at least from what he could see while peering from behind a tree many yards deeper in the woods than Chandler and Kellyn. However, the sun was going down and soon all that could be seen were points of lights from candles and fires shining through windows and peeking through gaps in the wall. Ford focused his flagging attention back on Kellyn, who was giving the last of his instructions.

"Got it? Good. Go."

Ford followed Duff, sneaking up to the wall where a house butted against the posts. When Duff bent at the waist and interlocked his fingers, Ford nudged him down lower against the wall. Chandler ran up, stepped into Duff's hand cradle and before Ford could get a helping hand on him, he was hurled completely over the fence, landing with a muddy splat beside the house. His moaning started a dog barking. Jakes, arriving just behind them, had a piece of raw meat ready to fling over the wall. Another piece held through the posts had the animal literally eating out of his hand.

"That dumb lump," growled Kellyn jumping up and running down to where Duff was staring blank-faced through the wall at Chandler lying on the ground. Kellyn silently berated Duff, snarled instructions in his ear and soon was standing on his shoulders, as Chandler was meant to be, cutting away at the straps binding the loose posts at the top. Ford sawed away at the bottom straps.

Within the village, a light passed from house to house. It was a small oil lamp in the hand of the village joiner, an irritable man who worked wood into tables, benches and chests during the day, and who took his turn as watchman one half night a week. His business suffered from his impatience, impatience that forced his strong hands into making frustrating mistakes that set off frequent bouts of anger, which he took out on his wife and children. That night he was armed with a knobbed cudgel and a long knife, both of which he'd used before on man and beast.

When the oil lamp flickered through the gaps in the wall, Ford stuck his fingers in his mouth to whistle the agreed upon alarm. The problem was, he couldn't whistle, not in that manner, nor very well in any other when it came down to it. Nothing but air blew between his fingers. Back in the trees, Cook also saw the roving light, but no one could hear his distant signal. The others, who heard Ford trying to whistle, spotted the trouble and sounded various alarms. Smith hooted, Runt crowed and Jakes whistled like a hawk. The tiny lamplight hovered in mid air, changed course and came closer towards the wall. The boys dropped flat against the ground.

"Who's there?" called the joiner, creeping alongside the house nearest to the wall with his lamp held aloft. Chandler crawled back and shoved himself between house and posts in a fit so tight he had to exhale to squeeze in. The oil lamp illuminated but a small sphere about the man. He lifted it higher to cast light upon the corner where the house and wall met. "Who's there?" he demanded in a louder voice.

"No one's there, Mervyn," said a man from within the house, "so shut your fool mouth and let us sleep!"

The joiner grumbled and walked away. Light from the oil lamp remained in the far end of the village from then on. Still, half the night seemed to pass and Ford began fighting off yawns before Kellyn allowed the boys to start working on the wall once more. Eventually one post lay in the long grass and Duff held another aside, creating a gap wide enough for any of them to shimmy through.

Chandler stood within the walls waving them in like a welcoming host. As planned, Kellyn took Ham with him towards what they thought might be a grain barn and Chandler limped off the other way to fill a sack in the dovecote. Smith grabbed Runt around the neck and dragged him along after Chandler. Ford and Duff kept a lookout from a spot near the opening in the wall. Kellyn didn't trust them lumbering about in the dark. Jakes stayed with his arms wrapped around the relaxed dog. When the boys passed by into the village, it gave a concerned whine, but Jakes ran massaging strokes down its side and spoke to it softly. Cook remained hidden in the woods, waiting for their return with a hooded lantern he would unveil to show them the way back.

A darting shadow now and then was all those nervously waiting on the outside ever saw, and all they could hear were the snores of the villagers, until the bear growled. At least that's what Ford thought it was, perhaps a small one. The tiny roar set off an eruption of noise and confusion. The dog began barking uncontrollably and others joined it from within houses throughout Farnod. The anxious coos and beating wings of dozens of doves flew overhead. A chicken coop exploded in squawking. The galloping of whinnying horses thundered somewhere out of sight. Toppled crockery crashed in one of the houses. Doors and windows slammed open, while others closed. Shouts rang out from all corners.

"What's going on?"

"Who's there?"

The whole village lit up with the light of lamps, lanterns and torches. The boys ran at random between the houses. Ford saw a small figure he was sure was Ham darting into view, ducking under the railing of an animal pen,

105

knocking his head against the bottom rung and dropping flat upon the ground. Ford forced himself through the posts and bolted across the yard, bending low to make himself smaller thinking he might not be seen rushing straight through the middle of a village filling with light and curious onlookers.

"A bear!" a villager shouted from the crack of her barely open doorway. Ford found Ham lying face down in muck. He plucked him up, threw the boy's limp body over his shoulder and ran back. "It's grabbed a piglet!" cried the woman with a quiver of hysteria. Ford dashed for the wall and collided with Duff between two houses.

"Two bears!" hollered a terror-stricken man from across the village.

"Grab his legs," Ford ordered Duff as they got to their feet. With Ford going one way and Duff the other, they stretched Ham out to his full length.

"They're ripping that pig apart!" wailed the woman, flinging a kitchen knife out the door at them. Ford and Duff grunted angrily at one another and settled on the same direction. Catching sight of Chandler stuck midway through the gap in the wall, Duff dropped Ham and at a full charge, rammed into Chandler and sent him with a rip and a scream through the wall. Ford shoved Ham through the gap and was halfway through himself when the dog got hold of him by the ankle and yanked him back. The loose post clamped down on his chest and held him from going forward or being drawn back. Jakes jumped in beside him and dragged the post away enough to set him free, but as Ford lunged forward the dog fought back and his pants slipped from his waist.

"Go on, dog!" pleaded Jakes. Too busy trying to kick his leg free, Ford never saw the joiner sprinting towards him with his knife drawn, his cudgel brandished over his head and a concentrated grimace.

"Help!" yelled Ford at Duff lumbering off up the hill. A few feet away, Ham fell about on all fours, trying and failing to put one foot steadily under him. The joiner bore down on Ford, his eyes gleaming with such malicious intent that he was blind to Kellyn diving for his legs. The joiner went down hard. Kellyn leapt up and drove his foot into his ribs and brought a tin pot down with a clang on his head. After a yelp from the dog, Ford felt his foot finally stop thrashing back and forth. With a shove and a pull, he tumbled through the gap with Kellyn following fast after. Another clang behind him spun Ford around in time to see Kellyn fighting to pull the wide pot through the wall. He gave up, leaned back in and hurled it over.

Firelight grew and clustered within the village.

"Thieves! It was thieves!" some were beginning to shout.

"They killed Mervyn!" cried the joiner's wife.

Fear abated and anger rose until a ball of fire and fury moved as one toward the wall.

"Ready the horses! Arm yourselves! We'll have them and hang them by morning! No one thieves from Farnod!"

The boys ran for the forest, scattering every which way until Cook's lantern gradually drew them all together and they slunk off as one, passing through the trees like a half-blinded, beaten and exhausted snake recoiling to the safety of its den.

CHAPTER 8
IN BLOOD AND BONES

The sun rose all too soon that morning for a pack of hunted bandits. The Wayward Boys marched deeper into the woods, feeding their hunger on dried meat and freezing their bellies with hurried gulps of cold stream water. They stopped for a brief rest, sitting with their backs against the edge of a bare slate shelf that crowned a knoll. Kellyn stood atop the rock with a hand cupped to one ear.

"They got dogs on us," he reported without breaking his concentration on what could be heard between the distant blasts of horns calling to one another. A flurry of baying from an excited pack of hounds found its way between the trees to send chills through the boys.

"I hear them. I hear the dogs," whimpered Runt.

"Be quiet," demanded Kellyn. Back and forth, the horns and the hounds called to one another until it was obvious there were at least two parties in search of them. The hunt sounded as far away as the village itself. Kellyn jumped down from the rock and stood before the boys with his hands on his hips, shaking his head at them. "Look at you!" he said and spat from the pent up disgust he felt for the still somewhat dazed Ham with a bump on his forehead, for Chandler dabbing at his scraped chest and fiddling with his ripped and bloodied shirt, and for all the others, many of whom had lost pieces of their gear. "Where's your mask?" he demanded of Duff. "Where is it?" Duff searched himself in disbelief, but by then Kellyn had already moved on. "And yours?" he asked Smith, who patted himself down with a rising mix of confusion and suspicion playing about his face. "Cut the act." Kellyn stalked amongst them, his features souring. "Damn you all!" He tripped over Ford's long, outstretched legs and kicked them until Ford tucked them in close. "Fool! You're all fools, you know that? If they catch one of you and they finger your face from last night, then what?" Smith dropped his open hand down upon his other wrist and then mimicked the motion of being hung and pretended to choke to death. "Right. It's your hand if you're lucky and your neck if you're not." Kellyn threw himself down on the ground next to Cook. "You all wear me out." He pulled his knees up and laid his head on them, glaring sideways at the boys. "Gods on earth, you wear me out." He sighed and closed his eyes. "We went through all that, and what we got to show for it?"

Rhetorical question or not, Smith answered by lifting up Chandler's loot bag. "Chandler got something." The bag was handed over and Kellyn dumped out its contents. Two broad, white pieces of cloth dropped on the ground.

"Great," he said grabbing one and standing with it held out, "you can sew me up some new underwear. Pathetic." He threw the cloth in Smith's face.

"We could make masks out of it," Smith ventured.

"White masks? We might as well try sneaking into town with torches blazing! Suppose it wouldn't be much different from what happened last night. What did happen last night? Did I hear someone roar like an animal?"

"He did," said Chandler with a scowl and a finger pointing at Runt. "He snuck up behind me and growled like a bear!"

"I scared you good," gloated Runt with a happy smile lightening his tired face.

Smith was about to say something when Kellyn charged over to Runt, lifted him by his shirt and slapped him. "What's wrong with you?" he asked in a shout so loud it echoed off the rock. He slapped the boy again and shook him. Tears filled Runt's eyes. Ford, Jakes and Cook converged on Kellyn, prying him from Runt, holding him back and imploring him to keep his voice down. Kellyn struggled free. The boys stood between him and Runt.

"Don't lose your head," said Cook.

"You," said Kellyn pointing a finger at Runt, "you're banished! Get out! Get out of here!"

"No, you don't mean that," said Jakes.

"You better believe I do," Kellyn said, driving the words home with cold sincerity. Try as they might, there was no calming Kellyn, no changing his mind. The group went quiet, except for Runt, who stood in place with his hands dangling limp at his side, raising them only to wipe away tears and watch Kellyn with a mix of despair, hatred and hope, a hope soon dissolved into uncontrollable sobs. Ford stood behind him and held him by the shoulders. Smith slipped away behind a tree, pretending to urinate. The sound of horns and hounds bounced from their left and right.

"I smell smoke," said Ham standing on top of the rock sniffing the air.

"They're carrying torches," wondered Ford, "in the morning? What, are they gonna burn us?"

A horse whinnied, followed immediately by others. The boys ran on to the rock to listen and look.

"They're on horses," said Jakes.

"On either side of us, too," said Kellyn. "All right, we move. Now!"

They gathered their belongings, some with sweaty, shaking hands. At Kellyn's command to head deeper into the woods, they filed down the knoll with Runt following in the rear.

"Not you," said Kellyn barring him, "you go the other way."

"Kellyn," said Ford coming back and laying a hand on Kellyn's shoulder, "don't…"

"Go," said Kellyn, brushing away Ford's hand and dismissing him with a wave. When Runt tried to dodge around him, Kellyn grabbed his arm and threw him back. Runt tried again. Kellyn drew his knife and pressed it against Runt's chest. "You're not one of us no more."

No knife could sting Runt quite like those words. He collapsed to the ground and curled up in a ball with his head buried in his arms while the band withdrew from him. They could hear his heaving gasps long after they left his tiny crumpled form behind.

The dogs' relentless barking grew louder, sharper. The horns blasted through the forest in a crisp call and response. Kellyn pushed the boys on harder and had Duff beat the laggards. Ford took a jolt to the back for constantly looking over his shoulder and slowing down. Ham was kicked for having to go back for his dropped knife. Cook caught an earful through Kellyn's grinding teeth when his wooden spoons and his new tin pot clanged together as he ran.

The shorter-legged among them, like Cook, were not made for this kind of travel. His overstuffed pack didn't help matters, regardless of adjustments made on the fly. The beatings at the rear stopped only when Duff – sweat-soaked, heaving and wheezing – fell behind despite his running in spurts to keep up. The lighter and quicker Smith and Chandler pulled ahead. Jakes outstripped them all and soon their line stretched out of sight from one end to the other.

Kellyn knew the villagers would be on them soon and could see it was hopeless to run. As things stood, some of them might escape, but others would definitely be caught. They needed a place to hide out, yet the farther they pressed on, the thinner forest cover became, with its tall, straight-trunked trees like masts rising high above the undulating land flowing before them as smooth as waves on a calm sea. The high vaulted canopy blocked the sun quite thoroughly, so that only the occasional solitary bush persisted upon an otherwise barren ground. A shrieking whinny closer than anything they'd heard that morning stopped them dead, leaving them gawking about them and looking to Kellyn with questioning, even pleading eyes.

"What do we do now?" asked Smith.

Kellyn held up a hand and they held their breath. The thumps and thuds of galloping hoofs beating the ground sent them flying for cover. Some ducked behind trees. Chandler and Smith shared a bush. All melted as best they could into the landscape, all but Ham, who ran to a tree and was pushed away by Duff. He spun around in a circle seeking another spot, but the galloping grew so loud that when a dark form dashed into view from behind a tree, Ham let out a yip and fell to the ground in a ball with his hands over his head. The four-legged shadow darted between the trees ever closer, leaping high with a twitching, white tail raised like a flag. Ham peered through his fingers and saw a deer skipping towards him with its head held high and its vigilant, dark eyes opened wide in search of a trailing foe. Just feet away, it spotted the boy on the ground and sprang to one side, bounding around him and out of sight. The boys left their cover and gathered together ashamed, but relieved.

"I thought we were done for," said Ford.

"A deer running mad like that usually means something's coming right behind it," whispered Jakes. Kellyn waved them on, twirling his arms like a watermill in spring to get them to follow fast after Jakes, who led them on a perpendicular course away from the path of the deer. They hurried on, pushing their tired legs and soon running out of breath.

"I feel naked out here," Ham gasped when the land flattened out and the boys could see for long distances all around without so much as a single bush to block their view.

"But listen," said Smith slowing his pace, "we're putting distance between us and them dogs." A horn sounded three quick blasts somewhere close behind them. Smith's shoulders jumped and most of the others stopped. The signal repeated a moment later.

"I think they found our trail," said Chandler fingering the handle of his knife as he scanned the trees they'd just passed through.

"Or caught Runt," said Ford. Some of the boys looked shamefaced, but Kellyn held his chin up.

"Here! Look!" called Jakes from well ahead. He was pointing at weather-beaten stones that dotted the ground. Further on, the stones grew in number and formed the remainder of a crop field boundary wall from some former civilization.

"Come on! The stones'll cover our tracks," said Kellyn stepping on top of the wall and hurrying along it as quickly as the uneven, sometimes loose stones allowed. "Pick up the pace! Let's go!"

The wall went on for a hundred yards before it was crossed by another wall. A stone framework built into one corner of the cross was all that remained of a house. The blocks stood knee high, providing no shelter or concealment, and so the boys passed it by without so much as slowing.

"Straight on!" said Kellyn. The wall continued another hundred yards before being crossed again and ending abruptly.

"Which way now?" asked Smith.

"Have a look at this!" said Jakes pointing beyond the stone wall through the trees to a hill too perfectly round to be natural. They stepped down from the wall, crossed a wide but long-dry riverbed at the foot of the hill and ascended to the top, a plateau fifty feet across.

"There's nothing up here," said Ham.

"There was something," said Chandler from the center of the plateau, his toe tracing a few feet of a large square outline, an indent where heavy stone blocks had once sat.

"Can't see nothing!" spat out Cook standing on one side of the hill and wrinkling his face into a displeased squint. The view from the top was blocked by the full, leafy boughs of the trees surrounding the hill.

"This ain't no good," said Kellyn. "Let's get off this thing." He sprinted from one side of the hill to the other, looked around and in the end, led them away in the same direction they had been heading.

"Another one up here," said Jakes when the flat-topped hill was barely out of sight. They hurried ahead to a second earthen mound, this one domed without a plateau and only half the size of the first.

"Is that what I think it is?" Smith asked Jakes in a worried voice while they ran around it.

"Fraid so."

The heap of piled earth was a crypt in the old style, nothing more grand than a mound of rock and earth with a single, stone-framed entryway. A layer of dead leaves covered it and a solitary tree grew out of one side, its roots creeping over the mound like fingers clutching a skull. The thin stone slab that had once served as the door was gone, leaving open a gaping black hole like a toothless mouth in mid-howl.

"Looks like we found ourselves a hole to hide in," said Kellyn with a glimmer of hope.

"I ain't going in there," said Smith taking a step back.

"No one asked you to." Kellyn slowly approached the mouth and peered in. A stack of bones could be seen close to the entryway.

"Strike up a light," said Chandler.

"No time for that. Get in there, you shivering lambs," Kellyn commanded, but not a single one of them moved closer. "Cowards." He laid a hand on the stone framework of the opening, took a long but cautious step over the threshold and, seeing that he hadn't been struck dead, walked in. When he crossed into the darkness, the others followed, their eyes eventually adjusting enough to make out more piles of bones. Ford brushed against a stack of femurs and recoiled.

"It's cold in here," whispered Ham from the opening where most of the boys still clustered together.

"What's that?" shouted Smith gripping Duff's shoulder from behind and pointing over him at the back wall, where a human skeleton stood facing them with its arms raised wide. The crypt rang with an ear-piercing screech. Bones rattled in the dark. Something shot out of the shadows beside Ford and he jumped back, knocking Jakes over into a pyramid of skulls that crashed across the floor. The boys in the entryway pushed each other in a desperate scramble to escape. A squat quadruped, its thick body covered in gray hair, scuttled through the skulls emitting an inhuman squeal much deeper than all the others. It made for Jakes. Ford lunged at it, but too late. Jakes screamed as a broad-shouldered wild pig bit into him. The boys leapt aside when five brown, furry piglets the size of rabbits skidded over the bones, skirted the human intruders and slipped through the entryway and out of the crypt. Duff, who had his hands over his ears and was gritting his teeth, pulled out his knife and drove it hard into the back of the big sow's neck when it tried to escape with its young. Jakes rolled around below the skeleton hanging from the wall. Blood poured over the crypt floor between the scattered bones. The boys who had run away ran back into the crypt.

"Horses! Horses coming!" cautioned Smith high-stepping over the bones towards the back.

"Hide," said Kellyn, but he needn't have. Every one of them, even Jakes crawling over the floor, found some place to conceal himself. The smaller boys ducked behind the stacks of bones still standing. Kellyn leapt into a box with a skeleton. Duff crouched with Cook in the deepest, darkest corner they could find. Ford jumped into a hole half filled with bones and Jakes rolled in after him. They remained still, but their rapid breathing echoed so loud it sounded like the crypt itself was panting. Ford muffled his mouth, as did others, not only to keep down the noise, but to keep from inhaling the musty, swirling dust.

Outside, a man and a woman carrying pitchforks rode up to the burial mound on swayback workhorses. The dirt under their fingernails and in the wrinkles of their skin hung as naturally upon them as their coarse, patched clothes. A horn swung at the woman's belt.

"Marks. All around here. Should we blow the horn?" asked the man.

"Maybe," replied the woman, but she continued to ride around the mound examining the kicked up leaves and pausing over the feet and hoof prints with a look of grim determination. When they stopped at the entrance, she jumped off her horse.

"I'm not going in there," said the man pulling back on his reigns.

"You're worse than an old lady," said the woman, refusing to look at him. She loosened a knife at her belt, gripped the pitchfork in both hands and held it out before her. Heel to toe she stepped up to the mouth of the crypt. At the entrance, she caught sight of the blood spread out over the ground around the numerous bones and skulls strewn about. Her ruddy complexion went white and she fell on one knee to steady herself. Trembling prayers tumbled out of her.

"What?" cried the man, jerking the reigns and worrying both horses. "What is it?"

The woman held a fist to her chest, brought it to her lips to kiss it in blessing and backed away, never blinking or taking her eyes from the entryway until she reached her horse. The two galloped off, throwing nervous glances over their shoulders.

The boys lay rigid amongst the bones of the dead well into the afternoon when the horns finally ceased. Squirming and shuddering, Smith jumped to his feet and ran out of the crypt at Kellyn's word. The others pushed aside the bones they'd piled upon themselves and emerged from the shadows. Kellyn brushed off small cloth fragments stuck to him from the disintegrating robe worn by the skeleton with which he'd shared the lavishly lined box. Ford helped Jakes out of the pit and pulled off his shoe for him. All gathered around to examine the bite on his foot.

"I was on my back and I guess my feet was in the air when it got me. It hurt like nothing I've ever felt."

"How's it feel now?" asked Ford gently turning the red and swelling foot into the light.

"Throbs something fierce, but it's all right."

A scurrying in the leaves outside had them all standing at attention.

"Sounds too small to be horses," said Kellyn. "Probably Runt come to weasel his way back in."

Five small-eyed, snouted faces poked around the entryway. Their oinks turned to squeals when Duff stamped after them and drove them away.

"What happened back there with Runt?" asked Ford, failing to hide the anger he still felt for the boy.

"What you getting at?" Kellyn caught Ford's eye, whether in warning or a dare, Ford did not know, but he stared back and pressed on.

"Why'd you kick him out? That wasn't right."

"Wasn't right? Wasn't right? Listen to this guy! I'll tell you what wasn't right." Kellyn strode up to Ford, stood chest to chest with him and punctuated each sentence by jabbing a finger into his chest or thrusting his head as if he might head-butt Ford on the nose. "He almost got us all killed, that's what! I did what was best for all of us! Or did you want to die back there? Huh? Huh?" When Ford refused to respond, Kellyn turned his back on him and stalked about the crypt, kicking bones aside and creating an enormous clattering racket.

"Calm down! They'll hear," said Ford. Kellyn jumped at him. Ford pushed him back. Murder flared in Kellyn's eyes and he sprang at Ford again, but Cook and Chandler wrapped him up. Duff stood by with clenched fists ready for anything, his leader had but to command.

"You're out, too!" Kellyn spat at Ford and pushed Cook and Chandler away. "Anyone else?" No one spoke, and most turned away or pretended to stand as lookouts outside.

"Me too then," said Jakes struggling to his feet. "It's not right, throwing a child out on his own."

"Great! You're out, too. Anyone else?"

"You can't go throwing everyone out," said Cook. "There won't be nobody left."

For a disquieting moment, Kellyn studied Cook with an intensity few of the others could have endured, and then he broke into unhinged and spiteful laughter.

"This is a joke! I can't do this, I can't do that?" He kicked at a skull rolling about his feet and sent it cracking against a wall. "I do this shit for you ungrateful bastards and this is what I get in return?"

The crypt grew quiet within and without, but for the boys' shuffling feet and an angry huff from Kellyn now and then. The piglets returned and Duff once again chased them away. Cook got Ham and Smith to gather wood for a fire, while he cut pieces off the boar. Life went on without a word spoken, all of them silently stewing in their own fear or anger, even a touch of embarrassment.

"Leaving Runt behind might've been the only thing that saved us," Chandler eventually said and hurried on when he saw Ford tense up and raise a finger at him, "I mean, Runt might've saved us. While they were stopped to grab him, maybe it gave us extra time to get away."

"Whatever happened, happened," said a calmer Kellyn. "What's done is done and now we got to just keep moving on. I think we're safe here tonight, but this ain't no place for us."

When night fell they ate and tried to sleep, but the piglets came back and their whining squeals could not be ignored.

"Put the sow out there," said Jakes. Ford and Duff dragged the pig's carcass out of the crypt and left it for the piglets, which dove at it, pulling at the teats relentlessly. In the relative peace, the boys fell asleep.

"I never want to do that again," Smith said upon waking up inside the crypt the next morning. When he stepped outside into the light and breathed deeply, it was clear in his drawn face how all the blood and mirth had drained out of him overnight. The piglets were gone and only a smear of blood and gore remained where the carcass had been.

"Where'd it go?" asked Ham from the middle of the group gathered at the entrance.

"Look here," said Chandler, pointing at a wide scrape marking the ground where it had been dragged off into the woods.

"Something as fat as that ain't carried away easy-like," Smith said with panic enough to infect them all.

"Probably just a wolf or two and nothing more," said Kellyn, grabbing Smith tight by the arm and giving him a short, sharp shake. "It's nothing to worry about. Got it?"

He surprised the boys by letting them eat at their ease. As the morning light gradually revealed the gruesome interior of the crypt, Ford followed the decorative pattern of the bones stacked against the walls, organized layers of femurs and skulls, and couldn't guess why Kellyn didn't have them on the move.

Kellyn too spent time within the crypt that morning, musing over the skeletons laid out in decayed robes like the one he'd climbed in next to. Hours he'd already spent thinking over their situation, his fingers running back and forth over a thick coin he'd found hidden in the folds of fabric lining the coffin-like, lidless box he'd hunkered down in. With the dust rubbed off, he could feel its intricate design on both sides. Holding it in the light showed it to glint gold. The stroke of fortune bucked his spirits, but his thoughts this whole time ranged well beyond a single coin.

"Give me that," he said emerging from the crypt and pointing to Chandler's bag stuffed with the nice, white bolts of cloth. "I got an idea."

CHAPTER 9
THE BROTHERHOOD OF THE VALLEY

Along the road to Port Morton, that unfathomably vast and distant city in the west, the forest gave way to a wide clearing of cultivated fields and millponds. On a rise in the middle stood Melynbren, a modest but prosperous market town filled with content inhabitants. Comfort and good fortune were the byproducts of the safety afforded them by their vigilant barwnig and the town itself, half of which was surrounded on one side by a river snaking around it and on the other by a ditch with an earthen mound topped by a sturdy palisade. Small but strong gatehouses controlled the road running right through Melynbren. At the town's center, two-story houses and tradesmen's shops surrounded a lively square, where the people transacted most of the important trade for miles around.

Walking upon the road, two priests in white robes with young acolytes following close behind, passed by cottages bunched around a mill. Their somber procession joined the steady stream of water boys and washerwomen walking to and from the river to the town center. They entered Melynbren under an open gate where the guards were hanging garlands from the eastern gatehouse.

It was plain to them, as it would be to any stranger, that this was not a normal day for the town. Flowers filled pots in windows everywhere. Early daffodils adorned hair and smartened up buttonholes. Even a truculent old mare's halter and a tired ox team's yoke were beautified by daisies. Oak leaf and twig wreaths with acorn clusters hung over doors. Ribbons drooped from signs and were wrapped around the pillars lifting the dome atop a partially open-air temple that rose high above them all at one end of the square. Fresh paint coated the facades of the houses and shops. Opposite the temple, the barwnig's hall gleamed a most bright yellow from the ground up to the eaves. Even its guardhouse out front enjoyed a new coat of lime white.

Townspeople passed the procession of holy men with a mere cursory glance if any. Street sweepers barely halted their vigorous attack upon the clean cobblestones to allow them to pass by. Vendors from a double row of fruit and vegetable carts held up orange and green tomatoes or yellowish cucumbers while calling out their "good, fair prices!" A cattle auction was finishing at an animal pen erected on one side of the square. The proud son of a farmer led away his family's new bull. The bewildered farmer himself appeared relieved to be walking away from the intense bidding war. A line of people with buckets and basins chatted together while waiting their turn at a well. Above the continuous rumble of it all could be heard the steady *ping! ping!* rhythm of hammer upon metal from a blacksmith shop off the square.

"Who are you?" The question came from a frowning, cross-browed boy at the head of a pack of idle and inquisitive children, who passed for urchins in this close-knit town. The boy stood directly in front of them and when the priests ignored him and walked on, he kept pace backwards.

"What are you supposed to be, priests? I never seen any priests' robes like that afore." The other children giggled and skipped around the procession. The priests pushed past the boy and left them behind. The boy hurled a rock at their backs and then ran off with the children in tow.

A brown-skinned and bent old woman with a basket of herbs held a sprig of rosemary under their noses as they passed. A spotty-scalped cordwainer stepped forward, bowed and presented a pair of soft leather shoes for one of the priests to inspect, but he slid back and everyone made way for a team of drovers guiding a flock of sheep into the square. Farmers gravitated towards the nervous animals, scrutinizing them, while they were steered and prodded into the pen.

As if led by their noses, the priests stopped by the town's bakers, all three of whom shared a building next to the barwnig's hall. An exceedingly long house had been built and quartered for each baker's family, with the brewer of Melynbren working out of the basement of the fourth lodging.

"Welcome!" hollered one of the bakers to the priests, waving them closer with a chubby hand. The procession closed ranks and reluctantly, but irresistibly moved as one up to his counter. "That's it, under the awning. Looks like we have a storm rolling in." He took stock of each with a friendly regard. "I don't think I've seen you here afore. You're not with the Order, now are you?" When he received no reply, his welcoming demeanor deflated somewhat. The priests willfully refused to answer. His saddening gaze passed from them to the young man coming out from behind them.

"We're from the Brotherhood of the Valley," said Kellyn stepping up to the counter.

"Honored, I'm sure," said the baker, who wasn't honored at all, but still delighted by the prospect of a sale. "I'm sure you brothers are good and blessed holy men." Here again he tried to speak directly to the more noble-looking Ford and Duff in their long white robes, little more than cloth cinched with rope, "but I confess I never heard of...what was it now? The Brothers whom?"

"Brothers Ford and ah...they, ah...they don't speak."

"Taken a vow of silence," Chandler whispered to Kellyn. "Taken a vow of silence, both these two," said Kellyn indicating Ford and Duff with a jerk of his thumb. "I speak for them. We are their, what you call, servants." His thumb jabbed at Chandler, Smith and Ham, who leaned out from behind the wide, billowing robes to smile and wave.

"That's peculiar," the baker said to Kellyn in an undertone with a hand shielding his mouth from Ford and Duff, "Silence? What'd they do that for?" Kellyn looked to Chandler for an answer, but only received a shrug.

"Search me," he finally said to the baker.

"Any road," said the baker with a returning smile as he stood tall, "what can I do for you?" Kellyn bought a few two-copper loaves just out of the oven. While they waited for them to cool, the baker couldn't keep from asking, "What heathen's hole in this awful world do they make you poor lads keep your traps shut? What I mean to say is, where'd you say you boys hail from?"

"We come from," Kellyn struggled to think of anything better and blurted out, "Kell...town."

"Never heard of it, but never mind. To what do we owe the pleasure of your visit?"

"Eh?"

"Why you here? Did you come for the wedding?"

Half of "What wedding?" came out before Kellyn caught himself and nodded.

The boys' expedition, verging on failure every step deeper into town, would never have happened if Ford had had any say. Though it had been years since his last visit, at the first sight of Melynbren he recognized it as the seat of his clan's power, where Barwnig Blackoak had his great hall built. He begged Kellyn to turn back for fear the people there would know him. Desperate for a proper score and sure of his plans, Kellyn refused. Ford asked to be excused and in reply, Kellyn stung him with shame.

"Turned coward?"

"No."

And that was that. All he could do was hope to go unnoticed. He pulled the cloth over his head like a hood to feel less conspicuous, but as it looked nothing like a hood, it had the opposite effect.

Waddling to the front, the baker's brother absentmindedly handed over the fresh loaves and leaned out the window to look around the corner at his son with a cumbersome sack of flour hoisted upon his shoulder shuffling unsteadily out the door.

"He's fine, he's fine," said the baker watching the boy from over his brother's head. The beaming guard sitting on a stool next to the open guardhouse door with a mug in one hand and a girl in the other, nodded the boy down the lane beside the great hall. The barwnig's porter pulled open a side door and guided the baker's boy into the kitchen. Out poured the sweetest scent any of the boys had smelled in some time. When the two bakers turned back, their customers were gone.

"Remember, don't say nothing," said Kellyn with an annoyed look around the square as the boys cut through the crowd to the other side. "These people with their damn questions."

They passed along the Green Hart down a deserted lane to the inn's back door, where they gathered in a circle devouring the bread.

"I'm thirsty," said Smith with a full mouth.

"Finish what's left," said Kellyn handing over his nearly empty waterskin, "and we'll get a drink later"— a nod indicated the inn— "if you do your jobs. If." He stared down the three boys acting as priests' acolytes, rather grubby and ill-dressed acolytes, then turned his attention to Ford and Duff. "And you two stay away from that temple. If a real priest starts asking questions, we're sunk."

Chandler, Smith and Ham stole back to the square and dispersed into the crowd. Kellyn sent his two priests to the pen to silently watch the sheep auction and then wandered alone along the shop fronts and under a hanging sign with a pair of rusty shears tacked to it, pretending to casually look over clothing and cloth. One glance at his filthy appearance and the owners of the shops, a tailor and weaver, both cast their icy glares back to the elated traveling clothier with his handcart on the corner surrounded by giddy young women in smart pelices and thick-soled shoes pawing over his unusually bright multicolored garments.

"It's bluer than the bluest sky!" said an amazed girl wearing deep greens and immaculate whites holding up a kirtle. A young woman with a plunging neckline snickered with another at a pair of pink stockings. On the other side of the circle, two of them grabbed hold of the same crimson skirt at the same time and a squabble might have broken out, but for one immediately yielding to the other.

The winner of the skirt, a plain girl of fourteen with long, fleshy cheeks and bushy eyebrows was shown deference by all the young women for the simple fact that she was the barwnig's daughter and it was she who was soon to be married. When she held the skirt up for the others to admire, the girl with the plunging neckline slipped the clothier some coins, turned away and shoved the pink stockings deep down her bosom.

"Don't know who he thinks he is," said the weaver's wife leaning out her wide window for a confidential word about the traveling clothier with the oldest daughter of the tailor next door. "Coming here from where, only the gods know, with his fancy this and thats. Oh, that's rain." Sticking her hand out beyond her uplifted window shutter, she caught a few drops to confirm it.

The clothier's smile faded. The rain would ruin his business and although the young women had already made a purchase or two, they were far from decided on the items that would truly fill his purse. The barwnig's daughter held the skirt in one arm and a gown in the other, asking the others to choose and then questioning their choices. Her own opinion waffled and nothing was settled.

"Ladies, the rain. I must pack up. Have we arrived at any decisions?"

"It's more, but I think the gown," said the barwnig's daughter for the third time.

"Nice dress," said Kellyn pushing into the crowd and pressing up against one of the girls, who took one look at him and recoiled.

"Get off, you!"

"All right, no need to shout," he said backing off.

"Now just look at these!" exclaimed Chandler, his eyes twinkling in the newly washed face he thrust into the crowd. He ran his clean fingers over the material. "Oh my, but that is lovely."

Kellyn longed to know how Chandler had gotten hold of the new, unsoiled jerkin so quickly, but while his accomplice in this scheme whipped and twirled about a piece of silk to the delight of the young women and the consternation of the clothier, he had work to do. His hands dove and his fingers plucked. Then he slid alongside the clothier and put an arm around him in a friendly embrace.

"Finest wares this side of the Valley, my friend," he announced, jostling the clothier a little too hard and nudging him into the young woman at Chandler's side.

"Thank you," said the clothier with his eyes still distracted by the silk in Chandler's hand. "What valley?"

"What's going on here? Is everything all right, ma'am?" The guard from the hall stood behind Kellyn scowling over his shoulder as he surveyed the scene, his wide fists gaining a better grip on the studded truncheon at his waist.

"No, Wyot," said the barwnig's daughter. "I can't decide between these two. What do you think?" She held the two garments before him.

"Oh, you know I have no idea of such things, young ma'am," he said slipping into an embarrassed smile, the likes of which few in the world but this girl ever saw.

As the girls dove back into the dilemma of the purchase, the guard laid a vice-like grip upon Kellyn's arm and another upon his neck, holding him tight while he spoke into his ear. "I don't know what you're up to, but be off!"

"I'm not up to nothing," said Kellyn, wrenching free and walking away. When the guard turned to confront Chandler, he found only the young women still tormenting the clothier with their indecision.

Kellyn and Chandler blended back into the crowd, each their own way and each with new, but discreet bulges lightly jingling about their person. Above the business dealings and idle gossip, Kellyn easily picked out Smith's laugh and spotted him running circles around the well with the Melynbren urchins. Without acknowledgement, he passed by Ham patiently listening to two old women who had him cornered and were chastising him for his filthiness. The increasing rain did nothing to dampen the vigor of their reprimands. Over at the auction, Ford and Duff leaned against the top rail of the pen with a foot each upon the bottom railing, shoulder to shoulder with the farmers appraising the remaining scrawny and dejected sheep. They went mostly unheeded and only drew a few peculiar looks whenever they spat or grunted along with the rest of them while listening to offers and counter-offers.

"Who'll take these last beggars off this poor woman's hands?" asked the auction master.

"Worthless!" said an angular man in a loose smock tied tight above his bony hips. He'd been insulting the quality of the sheep since the moment they were penned, punctuating his remarks with dismissive waves at the startled animals. The owner of the sheep, a stooped woman with rounded shoulders clung fast to the last of her patience against the heckler's draining onslaught, ignoring him and concentrating on the interested customers.

"Coat's not pretty, but they's good breeding stock, gentlemen. You've my word on that." With unwavering eye-contact and a forthright manner, she spoke directly to the last two competitors, a couple of tight-fisted provincial farmers.

As their incremental offers rose, so rose the volume of their shouted bids, and the sheep couldn't stand still. When the price hit its peak, both farmers turned shy as lambs. In his excitement, one of the two had inadvertently bid beyond his means. It was no great fortune, but neither was a rich man. The auction master asked for more bids once, twice, and then the angular man shocked everyone by putting in his first ever bid and taking the last of the sheep. He led away his small flock with a puffed-out chest and a high step.

The stir he'd caused eventually calmed down and the farmers headed home or to the inn venting a few final gripes to their friends. This left Ford and Duff almost completely alone and, with no auction to watch, they felt lost for what to do next. Ford scanned the square, hoping to spot Kellyn. Duff's breathing took a husky, rapid turn and he started smacking one of his thighs.

"Cut that out," whispered Ford.

"I'm sweating like a pig," complained Duff.

Lacking a better plan, the two play-acting priests stayed anchored to the pen and waited for Kellyn.

"He can't bring four stinking cows in on time," mumbled the auction master by the pen gate with his hands on his hips. Forgetting the rain clouds, he sought the sun to see where it sat, but finding only overcast skies, he climbed the railing for a better view of the town gate. "Bah!" He jumped back down and stomped off, cursing as he passed a young father and child.

"Fuck!" repeated the boy of less than two years.

"Don't say that," said his father without much conviction. He lifted the child off the top rail and cast a wistful glance at the empty pen sighing, "Better luck next time, eh Elyan?"

"Ness tine," said Elyan, more intent on plucking at a thread in a loosening seam upon his father's frayed shirt.

The man hoisted his son into his arms, but when he turned to go he stopped and faced Ford. "I know you." Ford straightened up, but kept his vacant gaze straight ahead. "We fought at the Battle by the Llyn, you and me. You were with your father. Don't you remember me?" He stepped up to Ford and held out one arm in Ford's line of sight, so that it became impossible to ignore him. "I'm Dafyd."

Ford inclined his head in the smallest of nods and tried to smile, but it looked more like someone was yanking a thorn out of him rather than greeting him.

"Hello," he finally said, grasping the arm and shaking it.

"This is my boy. You remember him? He was just a little squawker then, but he's grown, ain't he?" The boy stared long and hard at Ford and Duff. Sweat beaded up on Duff's fuzzy upper lip and he took a couple steps away, turning his back on them and pretending to seem interested in something across the square.

"Tough fight that was, eh?" said Dafyd.

"Yeah."

"Not a good day."

"No," said Ford, now recalling how this man had knelt over his slain wife in the midst of a field of bodies.

"Move on, that's all you can do, right Elyan?" The boy snapped out of his daze, twisting away from the two oddly clothed people in front of him and clinging tighter to his father. "We came over today hoping to grab us a sheep or two. Looking for a deal, but" —here he shrugged— "there's no deals in this town. No sir, too rich for my blood." Dafyd looked Ford and Duff over and asked the question he'd be meaning to all along. "Looks like you moved on all right. You're a holy man now?"

As if summoned by the very question, the priest from the Order of the Word of Alis stepped out on to the temple's stoop. Feeling the rain, he drew his cowl over his head and then folded his arms to bury his hands in the sleeves of his elaborate robe, all while contemplating the false priests. The contrast in quality between his robe and the crude ones worn by Ford and Duff was glaringly apparent. Ford was sure the game was up. He hung his head and tried to concentrate on how to get out of this situation. Dafyd was still talking, asking more questions. The priest stepped off the stoop towards them, one hand held aloft in greeting. Ford watched him come and held his breath. Duff turned his back on the priest and huffed louder. A hand clasped about Ford's arm.

"Come brothers," spoke Kellyn loud and clear, "let's get you out of the rain." Ushering his priests through the square, he whistled for Ham and Chandler. One appeared from around the corner of a shop and the other popped out from behind a beekeeper's stall. "Where's that fool?" asked Kellyn, but no one knew where Smith was.

The rain emptied out the square. Shopkeepers shuttered their windows. The produce vendors abandoned their carts, keeping an eye on them through the inn windows.

"Hello there!" called the priest "Hello there! Hello?"

"Ignore him," said Kellyn through his teeth.

Sharp, shouted accusations from over by the garment sellers stopped everyone in their tracks. The traveling clothier, all packed and ready to bolt, was being held up by an irate customer, a tall woman who had him by the collar with one hand while shoving a fading red skirt in his face with the other. Red dye stained the front of her smock pink and ran from the skirt ran down her sinewy forearm.

"I've done nothing!" cried the clothier, jerking away from her iron grip.

"You won't be doing nothing when I'm done with you!" shouted the woman.

Kellyn steered the boys toward the fray. They passed the squabble right when the woman was hitting the clothier about the head and swearing because the balled-up skirt in her fist softened the blows, leaving only dyed red marks on his face instead of the bloody ones she'd intended. The weaver's wife and the tailor's oldest daughter joined in and shouted down the clothier, occasionally delivering a kick or slap.

"Stop that there!" pleaded the priest, hastening to them. "That's enough of that now!" When the irate customer relented slightly and the others held back at seeing the priest, the clothier broke free and dove down a street leading away from the square. The small mob chased after him with the priest following behind begging, "Order, please! Restrain yourselves!" Kellyn squeezed through the laughing crowd by the inn door and led his boys inside.

The entertainment over, the Green Hart's delighted patrons continued their fun back at their tables, each recounting what they'd seen or heard, guessing what it was all about, and cursing the clothier for a thief. A popular place for such gossip, the only inn in town had gotten its start when a tavern owner had bought the building next door upon the failure of a glazier. The tavern had soon expanded into an inn, the owner letting out the upstairs rooms to travelers and creating a large, L-shaped common room on the ground floor to better serve the growing population and tradesmen passing through. While not a miser through and through, the landlord did stow away income whenever possible, so during a day like today when he declared it "warm enough," the fires were not lit and the only light came in from the windows. Black coals with a hint of orange, last used at breakfast, remained. Still, out of habit, the tables closest to the two fireplaces were already taken. A few idle cattle drivers and some of the town's shop owners waiting out the rain took up the bench seats at the long tables against the walls. A small group of men and women from town sat at a round table playing a card game. Farmers from outlying villages watched over their shoulder. At their feet, a cat lay in a shallow bowl set by one of the fireplaces. A dog curled up around the bowl. The boys negotiated the crowded room, where even the antlers at eye-level were tacked to a post, and found a lopsided table in a corner by the back door.

"Keep an eye out," Kellyn said to Ford, and sat against the wall with him next to a window, "and holler if you see that damn priest coming." Ford leaned back. He could see down the lane to one corner of the animal pen out in the empty square.

After seeing to everyone else first, the Green Hart's landlord finally made his way over and stood in front of them, passing a critical eye over each boy while still making up his mind whether or not he wanted them in his establishment. When Kellyn pulled the copper coins out of the purse lifted off the merchant days prior and pushed them across the table, the landlord eyed them with momentary suspicion. *Never refuse a paying customer* being his motto, he swiped the coins off the table into his apron and soon his snaggletoothed wife in a worn-thin, low-cut blouse returned to pour a strong amber ale into mugs all around the table, partially revealing her wizened breasts when she leaned forward and ducked to keep her frizzy hair out of a fly-caked rag soaked in maple sap hanging from the ceiling.

"Did you see that?" asked an excited Smith when she had gone. He leaned forward and juggled invisible balls at his chest. Because it got Ham giggling and a snort out of Ford, Smith kept juggling, even after Kellyn moved on to more important business.

"What you all get?"

Nothing was expected from Ford and Duff and they had nothing, however, Kellyn gritted his teeth when Ham showed his empty palms and Chandler handed over a nearly empty purse of copper coins.

"I got these too from the tallow man," he said when laughter erupted from the gaming table at the culmination of a particularly bad run of luck. Shielding them from the rest of the room, he revealed two slender candles and a small pot of honey.

"Two candles," said Smith, "Ha!"

"Oh yeah, and what'd you get?" asked Kellyn. Smith gave a meandering excuse for having nothing to show for his efforts until he was cut off. "That's what I figured. Nothing, because you were too busy fooling around like always." Smith reddened and mumbled a gripe so low as not to be heard. "What?"

"Nothing."

"That's right. You got nothing." Kellyn might have been sucking on a lemon the way he looked. "You people are lucky to have me." He dropped a pouch on the table with an enticing jingle of coin. The landlord's wife, whose hearing was keenly attuned to that very sound, came right back to the table and Kellyn ordered plenty of food for his boys, including something to bring back for Jakes and Cook.

Ford checked the window and thought of Jakes and Cook waiting for them out in the woods, and naturally his mind passed on to Runt. Between his own worries, he often spared a thought or two for the forlorn boy since they'd left him behind. Where was he now? What were the chances he was still alive, and how might he be found again? Ford considered these things and came to no satisfying conclusions. His stomach gave a great groan at the sight of their dinner arriving.

"Eat up, eat up! There's plenty more," said the landlord, helping his wife deliver lamb chops, greasy pieces of duck and a tureen of mutton broth. If the shabby clothing or odd robes the boys wore didn't grab attention, the way they ripped and gorged, gulped and guzzled definitely did.

"It's like they never eaten afore in they lives," said one of a half dozen local field laborers hanging around a tapped barrel. They were a hearty crew of hired hands in thick with the landlord. Eventually they resumed their ruminations regarding the coming wedding, which would strengthen the ties of loyalty and service between the barwnig and the marchog Bachbel, but more importantly, what it might mean for them in the way of more work. Those speculations had been exhausted days ago, so that even these simple fellows were soon bored with it and moved on to another topic.

"You heard of the ol' goat herder bringing in what's left of his herd? Osgar tells me they been ravaged something fierce."

"By what?"

"No idea."

"Wolves?"

"Could be, but whatever it were, something got into them up in them hills, that's for sure. Poor fella. Says he's given up herding. Says he's selling off his entire stock. Giving it up for good, he says."

"What'll he do now?"

"Anyone's guess."

"You hear that?" Chandler asked the other boys, who'd slowed their eating to listen in. "Sounds like the same thing that dragged off that sow."

"Yeah," Ham agreed, fidgety with worry, "and it might get Jakes and Cook." Ford's thoughts returned to Runt.

"Nah, that was nothing but a bear," said Kellyn calm as he could, "one of them little black ones."

"Maybe it's a man-eating bear," said Ham, and Ford wished the boy would shut up. His nervousness was contagious.

"He might be right," said Chandler.

"He's not right," Kellyn insisted, "but either which way, we ought to go back. We pressed our luck here, for all the good it's done. Besides, them two'll be worrying where we are."

Ford leaned back and looked out the window. The rain appeared to be easing and there were signs of life outside again.

"It's letting up," he said, but then something caught his eye and he sat upright. Of the few people milling about the square, one woman looked vaguely familiar. Ford squinted and then squinted all the harder, because he could have sworn he was looking at Aedalin, the old woodcutter's daughter-in-law. The idea was absurd, he told himself. The woman barely left the house, never mind Barlow. Nothing more than a figment of his imagination, of that he was certain, almost. He had another look. Ham's heel pressed down on his foot and Ford elbowed him in the shoulder.

"Sorry, but look." Ham pointed across the room where Smith was sitting amongst the cattle drivers, laughing loudly.

"I tell you, I could beat any one of you," said Smith - and it occurred to Ford that it was the third or fourth time he'd overheard this boast. "No! Two at a time!" Smith drank deep from his mug, slammed it down and when some ale splashed out, he laughed all the harder. "Bring on your best!"

"What," said Kellyn banging the tabletop, "is that dolt doing over there?" He leapt to his feet.

"Wait!" said Chandler grabbing his wrist.

All the cattle drivers were massing about Smith, grinning and smacking their palms together.

"We'll show you!" said one and "Shut his trap for good!" shouted another as they settled in to watch Smith thumb-wrestle two of their mates at the same time. They hooted and whistled, becoming more boisterous the longer Smith lasted. Putting up a credible but doomed fight, he congratulated both men. They slapped him on the shoulders and he sat back as if exhausted. The two victors leaned across Smith and commenced the champion's match.

"What's he think he's doing?" snarled Kellyn, who was ready to jump out of his seat again when he saw Smith's hand slide down the back of the man sitting next to him towards a small bag tucked into the man's belt. They weren't the only ones with a view. The landlord's wife, bringing a fresh pitcher to the cattle driver's, walked up to the table on the side where Smith's hand had wandered where it shouldn't. The darkened room might have cloaked his deed, but the rain clouds above had passed on and the windows glowed, lighting the whole room more brightly than if both fires and all the lanterns were lit. Everything stood still at the boys' table. The landlord's wife put the pitcher down and returned to the washing tub behind the sturdy plank they used as a bar.

The arrival of the sun sent the shopkeepers out to reopen their stalls. Even with the farmers in town for the auctions staying put, the room was anything but crowded now.

"He'll get caught and get us all killed," hissed Chandler into Kellyn's ear.

"Get off!" said Kellyn shouldering Chandler away. "I know that! Don't you think I don't know that? I'll straighten him out." But once again, he got up and sat back down. The landlord and his wife were looking right at them and whispering together.

"That's not a good thing," said Chandler sliding lower under the table.

"Get ready, boys," said Kellyn out of the corner of his mouth. The landlord, his wife and the half-dozen field-hands were headed right for them. They gathered around the table, blocking any of the boys from leaving.

"What did you boys say your business was?" asked the landlord, his tone stern, his frown damning.

"We're holy men," replied Kellyn, voice steady and chin up.

"So that's your game then?"

"We're on a pererindod," put in Chandler, referring to a kind of pilgrimage common to the area.

"Yeah, we're heading to a holy place," said Kellyn, punching his words with more confidence.

"Oh yeah? To where?"

They didn't have a ready answer for that and floundered to come up with one.

"Port Morton," said Ford, and the others sighed in relief.

"Right," said Kellyn, "that's it."

"Sounds like a cartload of bullshit," said one of the field hands.

"That's what I thought," said the landlord reaching for something at his waist. Kellyn tried to rise, but one of the landlord's men pushed him back into his seat. The landlord produced the copper coins Kellyn had given him earlier.

"Couple days ago a traveling fella came in, said he'd been robbed. Said they didn't get much, just a light purse he keeps ready for just such problems. He hands it over and they let him go. Says it works most of the time. Pretty smart, eh?"

"Wouldn't know," said a sour and sullen Kellyn. "We don't know nothing about all that."

"You don't know nothing about these?" The landlord held a coin out so its sailing ship design caught the light. "It's a rare coin in these parts, it is. You don't see many around here. Strange they'd crop up twice in so many days, first him and then in the hands of you boys."

"Boys with sticky fingers," said his wife through her sneer.

"Boys with sticky fingers indeed," said the landlord. Those at the gaming table stopped playing and started eavesdropping.

"I said, we don't know nothing about that," said Kellyn.

"So you did," said the landlord, losing patience, "and I don't suppose you don't know nothing about the robberies of late neither, do you? Out there in them villages?"

"No."

"You see them over there, the big lads your friend was laughing it up with? Them's Farnod folk—" The landlord paused and smiled when the boys' table shook from the jolt of jumping knees under it. "Yeah, Farnod from down the road. I thought you might've heard of it. I bet you ain't surprised to hear they got robbed not two nights ago." Ham went pale, Ford's mouth fell open and Duff began to sweat. "Funny how it happened right around the time that traveling fella came in and said he's been robbed on the road near there. Not robbed very well," he laughed, "but robbed all the same. But you boys don't know nothing about that now, do you?"

The men standing around the table turned quite grim and shuffled closer, pressing in on the boys like top-heavy walls that could come crashing down on them in an instant. Kellyn's hands slid off the table to where he hid his money-pouch and knife. One of the landlord's men, a farmhand who worked and ate with the same voracious appetite, stood closest to Kellyn, his shirt loose about his thick neck where a straining vein throbbed ever quicker.

"I bet you never seen nothing like this," said Kellyn drawing out the intricately designed gold coin he'd found in the crypt and holding it up to the landlord's face. "How much can this buy us?"

The boys around the table were just as stunned as all the patrons.

"Where'd you get that?" asked Smith, wedging himself in between the landlord and his wife.

"Well?" asked Kellyn.

"That could buy plenty," said the landlord mastering his amazement, "if it were real."

"It's real," said Kellyn handing the coin over as if it meant nothing to him. The landlord held it in the light, examined it front and back and then slammed it down on the table. The coin bounced, flipped about and landed with a slap in his hand.

"That'll buy you plenty, my friends, plenty and more." His lips rolled back over his brown teeth.

"As much drink as each man can hold and then some! For everyone,"

Kellyn shouted. Everyone heard and shouted back their pleasure. Drink flowed. Laughs followed. Blessings were asked of Ford and Duff. Smith downed one too many and danced up and down the length of a bench with his arms and legs flailing like a madman's, while the locals clapped and cheered him on. Kellyn's benevolence made the Wayward Boys heroes of the Green Hart.

All were happy, but for one haggard and fretful farmer from Farnod. Sad when drunk and speaking at random, he complained with a sodden tongue, "They killed one of our men."

"They did, did they?" inquired his new friend, a townsman leaning upon his shoulder and looking down at him with sorrowful, bleary eyes.

"No, but they beat him pretty bad."

"That's awful!" At the townsmen's prompting, they drank to the beaten man's health. "Sure it was them boys?"

"No."

They drank again.

"Is the poor fella here at all?" asked the townsman with a keen look about the room.

"No."

"Well then, another drink in his honor!"

While the other boys caroused with the locals, Ford stayed put at the table. The priest was long forgotten and the apparition of the woodcutter's daughter-in-law was gone from his narrow window. Nonetheless, the latter wrapped up his thoughts until he was doing little more than staring into space in a feeble attempt at making sense of it all.

"What are you thinking about?" asked Ham beside him.

"Nothing," said Ford, trying and failing to recall if the boy had always been there.

"That's what you always look like when you're thinking."

Ford smiled at that. Ham was now the youngest of the gang, yet for his age he had a mature sort of intuitiveness when it came to people, which Ford admired in a way. He admitted he was thinking and related what he'd seen.

"Least that's what I thought I seen. Sounds mad, don't it?"

Ham offered nothing more than a shrug. Empathy was his strong suit; worldly experience was not. The boy could form no opinion on such matters and Ford was left feeling foolish, like a paranoid worrier spooked after the scare at the animal pen with the man and his child.

"Probably just looked like her, is all. Nothing but one of them things."

"Could be a doppelganger," the boy offered.

Poking his head in the door, a much jollier auction-master hollered, "Them goats has finally come in!"

The cattle drivers, field hands and farmers dragged themselves and each other out the door, leaving behind empty mugs, overturned benches, a two-legged stool that had once had three legs, one agitated cat and one over-stimulated dog.

"What you two gabbing about by yourselves like a couple lovers?" asked a slightly tipsy Kellyn. The click-clack of hooves shot by Ford's window, followed closely by delighted screams of children and an exhausted herder.

"I thought I saw Barlow folk out there in the square," said Ford. Kellyn let out a long sigh of beery fumes.

"I think you're nuts, but hey, if it makes you feel better, leave out the back door and meet"—here he belched— "meet us up on the road outta town."

Ford did just that. No sooner was the door shut behind him than he stripped off the robe and discarded it in the alley behind the inn. Rounding a butcher's shop on the far corner, he could see straight down the lane to the pen in the busy square. In his distraction he had to dodge a cart with a pig carcass in it and ducked between a post and a pig hanging upside down from iron hooks in the rafters.

"Step off," cried a girl kneeling on the ground with a bowl carefully catching the blood dripping from the neck of a newly slaughtered lamb.

"Sorry," said Ford, dancing aside amid the bits of gore. His toe caught the lip of a pot, flipping it over and dousing the girl. As he fled, he shouted apologies to the stunned girl with the blood dripping from her face.

The vile stench of burning flesh met his nose and turned his stomach when he passed the town tanner working on a hide. Hurrying away, he came to the end of the lane where a stone embankment provided defense and held back the river from flooding the town. Atop the embankment was a quiet, narrow way wide enough for only two people to walk abreast. It passed all along the curving river with dilapidated housing on one side and a ten-foot drop-off to the water below on the other side. He crept forward until one end of the bridge into town came into view. No sign of his friends, though. Kellyn probably had them trying their luck again in the square, he guessed. If that were the case, they wouldn't be along any time soon. No one was about, so he dallied, waiting and hoping to see a familiar face.

"Ford!"

A chill enveloped him. Many months had passed since Ford last heard his name spoken like that, so harsh and unyielding, perfectly tyrannical. He turned and there was his father standing at the corner of a building. At the far corner of the same building, Ford took an involuntary step back and fought the urge to run, while the vivid recollection of his father trying to strangle him flooded back. If Myer took so much as a single step towards him, Ford was ready to bolt. Whether sensing this or not, his father remained where he was.

"Someone said you were here. I didn't believe him." Myer kept a steady eye on Ford, who couldn't find his tongue for his reeling mind. All of a sudden, the sun seemed intrusively, painfully bright and he feared his tearing eyes might run. His father spoke again, something mundane that Ford couldn't follow in his mind's tumult and desire to explain what happened, to clear his name.

"I didn't—" fumbled off his flustered tongue and he stopped, his mouth twisting in frustration, his head drooping. Finally it came to him, "It was an accident."

A woman in a window on the second floor above them leaned out with a bucket of dirty water poised for tossing and held back from jettisoning it into the river for fear she'd spoil the scene just when it was getting interesting.

"That's what your sister said." He knew then, thought Ford. Immediately his imagination leapt to hopes of forgiveness, of being invited home, and seeing Leo and Nia again. "What's done is done," said Myer turning up his palms at his sides. A glassy sheen masked Ford's eyes and he swallowed hard, wiping a sleeve over his face and blinking to see clearly. A bucket's worth of dirty water from overhead splashed into the river below. Myer cleared his throat. "I don't know what you're up to, don't much care, but you got debts to pay." All of Ford's blissful expectation building within deflated. "I know it was you that stole from us. Aedalin saw you running away."

Ford stepped back, but the way his father spat out "running away" grabbed hold of something inside him. The sting of being called a thief and a coward instantly sowed such a firm resolve within him that he planted his feet upon the ground and would stand there before his father no matter what debt he meant to claim from him.

"I want my ax back," said Myer, seeming to swell in size before Ford's eyes.

"I don't have it," said Ford holding out his arms. It was true; the ax remained with Jakes and Cook back at the crypt. The boys had carried only concealable weapons into town.

"Where is it?" asked Myer, his voice loud and demanding. "What've you done with it?"

Before Ford could answer, a whimper drew Myer's attention down the lane beside him in the direction of the tanner and butcher shops and the square beyond them. Ford watched as his father was struck bemused by whatever it was he saw. Ford's natural curiosity of the unknown gnawed at him, but he stayed put and did not see that around the corner and up the lane, Ham wavered from foot to foot before Myer, holding out his puny knife in a limp hand.

"Put that away and go on, you," said Myer. Aside from shaking, Ham didn't move.

"Daddy?" It didn't matter that he couldn't see her, Ford knew his little sister's voice and could make out Nia's questioning face by her quizzical tone. More than anything he wanted to rush around the corner and embrace her, or even just to see her.

"No, go back!" Myer shouted.

Nia ran down the lane from the pen towards her father with her dirty, worn smock whipping about her legs and a scrawny, confused goat on a lead trotting half-willingly after her. The old woodcutter's daughter-in-law chased behind, wheezing and clutching her chest.

"Go back!" Myer insisted.

Nia caught sight of Ham with the upraised knife between her and her father. She skidded to a stop just behind him, dropping the goat's lead and latching on to Aedalin as she had once done with her mother. Ham turned the knife on them. Myer roared and flew at him. Ham whirled on him and flinched, throwing his hands over his face. Myer snatched away the knife and flung it aside. Ham wilted under his shadow and fled back up the lane, vanishing into the crowded square.

"You all right?" Myer asked Nia and Aedalin, gathering them in his arms. They both nodded. Myer scanned the lane up and down, ushered them almost up to the embankment, and stopped them by the corner of the building. "Stay right here. Don't go nowhere." Without letting his hand slip from Aedalin's shoulder, he stretched to see around the corner and down along the embankment. No one was there.

CHAPTER 10
MANY RETURNS

On the edge of the woods surrounding the fields of Melynbren a widow sat stooped in the doorway of her cluttered yet clean cottage plucking a chicken for her elderly parents, one half blind, the other half deaf, but alive and content to live out their remaining days just over the road from their daughter. On a log fashioned for long, comfortable naps, each rested in the sun leaning back against the simple hovel they had built together when they were young and full of vigor. Only when the squawking of the chickens about the yard and in the road became particularly shrill would the old couple wake. Whenever it happened the daughter would turn a warm smile at them until their eyes closed again, then go back to the task at hand.

The woman hummed to herself, dropping handfuls of feathers into a sack while the chickens pecked at the damp ground and clucked amiably amongst themselves now that there were enough bugs near the surface to please all. Her only living child, a daughter quick with figures and a skilled bargainer, would be coming home soon along with the grandchildren, and the woman's hums flooded with confident gratification that a shrewdly-purchased goat would be added to their small stake in this world. A shuffling of feet upon the dirt road broke in on her reverie.

"Addy, is that you?" she asked, returning her concentration to the bird. More often than not she could correctly predict who was coming from the town, even if she could not see them. A death-rattle from the unseen travelers made her fingers seize upon the bird. When she looked up, her hands flew to catch a gasp and feathers burst into the air. A half-dozen creatures staggered along the road towards her house, towards her sleeping parents. Like actors from a nightmarish play telling of the primeval swamps from which were born rumor and horror, some of the creatures were mud-covered, others walked on the brink of death, hardly conscious, leaning against a stout and occasionally belching comrade in a once white robe. These were the boy priests she'd seen earlier that day, the woman realized, and went back to plucking at the chicken, but with jittery fingers and an unease she couldn't entirely quell, such was their disconcerting appearance and manner. One of the half-dead boys jerked alive and darted behind the old couples' hovel. The woman was about to call for help, but checked herself at the sound of the boy being sick. He reemerged wiping his mouth and hurried to catch up with his companions' solemn procession, as sorry a band of travelers as had ever passed by the widow, a shambles of humanity fading along with the road into the woods.

Out of sight of both town and village, Kellyn sat on a stone marker and started brushing the drying debris from his sodden clothes, which had been sadly soiled when he'd grabbed Ford and dove off the Melynbren embankment with him into the river. The two of them had hidden under the bridge until a guard forced them out. Pristinely dressed in garb he intended to wear at the wedding on the morrow, the guard wanted nothing to do with the muck-covered, stinking strangers and gladly let them escape down the road leaving town where they rejoined their waiting friends.

After an hour's long ramble through the forest during which he'd refused to admit he'd gotten them lost, Kellyn brought the boys to a halt once more, looked about him and said once again, "It's this way."

"How do you know?" Chandler ventured to ask. He was slow to sober and easily annoyed, especially after twice suggesting what he thought was the likely way back to Jakes and Cook and being rebuked for his efforts. Everyone tilted an ear to the air when angry shouts, ever so distant, reached them from deep within the woods.

"Because listen," Kellyn replied with the brash cockiness they'd become accustomed to from him. Not long after, they found Cook hurling insults from one side of the mounded crypt at Jakes, who was sitting with his arms folded on the other side, both oblivious to the boys' arrival. Cook's scarred face yellowed at the sight of them.

"You hear me? I said you're being a horse's ass!" hollered Jakes, limping to his feet and poking his head around to see why Cook wasn't responding. "Oh, hey, fellas."

"You're both a couple of asses!" Kellyn shouted louder than either of them. "We could hear you all the way back in the town!" He went on and on berating them until his throat was sore, then he stomped up the mound and sat alone at the top.

Ford sat by himself, too, though only because everyone else moved away from him. Even after scrubbing up in a stream, he and Kellyn still held an aroma akin to bilge water and no one wanted to be near either of them. He used the time to think over what had happened back in Melynbren, where he'd been made to feel a coward by his father and Kellyn dragging him away surely confirmed it. Ford wished Kellyn had never come along and longed for a chance to do it all over again, to do everything all over again. It had all been a big mistake. Nothing good ever came from dwelling upon regrets over an unchangeable past, but he'd not learned the wisdom of forgetting, and so he fumed and grew irritable when something poked into his back. Shifting and twisting as he might, he sought comfort in vain until, overcome and reduced to growling, he flipped over on to all fours and punched the knobby root sticking out of the ground.

"What you do that for?" asked Ham, and Ford flinched to find the boy standing over him having a look at his bloodied knuckles.

"Damn it, Ham," he shouted and slapped the ground, "don't sneak up on me like that!" Ford ignored the boy for a time, pulling off his shoes to let them dry and air out his feet, then went on searching for a good spot to lie back upon. A few deep breaths later he asked, "How long you been there?"

"I don't know," Ham said biting his lip and scuffing at the earth with his heel.

"Ah, don't be like that. I ain't mad." Finally he decided upon a tree and leaned back against it stretching out his legs and wriggling his white, wrinkled toes. Ham made a lengthy study of the treetops, letting out the occasional soft, insignificant sigh. "Why don't you go back with the others?"

"It's boring. Everyone's sleeping."

But everyone was not sleeping. Smith had passed out, but the others who'd had a little too much to drink at the Green Hart were lying around rather listlessly. With their backs turned to one another, Jakes and Cook gnawed away on bones and licked their fingers. Duff rolled on to his side and passed a steady stream of wind in both directions. As if a fire had been lit under him, Smith sprang to his feet and lurched a few paces away from the others to throw up the little left in his stomach.

"Much better," he said, upbeat and cheerful upon returning, but dismay overcame him at the sight of the others slumped over with half-lidded eyes. "Come on, you dull slugs, wake up! How about a joke? Who's got a good joke?" No one had anything to say. Chandler roused from his stupor, but only to drink some water. "How about a story then? Tell us a story, Chandler."

Chandler recoiled as if repulsed by the sound of his own name and the volume with which it was spoken at him. Smith continued to prod him until he was fully awake and then pointed out how bored everyone was, how depressed Ford looked, and how Kellyn would be in such a better mood if only he had a good story. For the longest time, Chandler's only response was an impenetrably entrenched frown. Then, once Smith had pushed him just far enough, his façade cracked and a malignant gleam entered his eyes.

"All right, you want a story? I'll give you one you won't forget."

Ford heaved himself up, plodded over and plopped down closer to Chandler, who began telling a story about the Sever Man, one of the monstrous people from over the seas named the Severn, known for their broad mouths filled with massive, steely teeth and a voracious appetite for little boys and girls. It was said that the Sever Man would come raiding the land at night, finding the noisiest children in the dark because they wouldn't quiet down. The oft-heard story was told at bedtime by parents to stop their younger children from fooling around, so everyone could get some sleep.

"That one," said Smith with a dismissive wave, "everyone's heard that one. Don't you know nothing but fairytales?"

Chandler's eyes narrowed, his grin widened and he went on, narrating what the Sever Man did to the children, going into much more detail than mothers and fathers ever did.

"Once they returned to their frosty lands in the north, they froze the children in barrels of ice."

"What? What for?" asked an astonished Smith, but Chandler ignored him.

"And when they got hungry they'd break the barrels apart, chip away the ice and snap off the boys' and girls' fingers and toes like icicles. Tasty, blood-filled icicles." Chandler wiggled a finger by way of illustration. Smith's mouth fell open. "Then their cooks would strip off the children's skin—"

"Gross!" cried a horrified Smith.

"No cook's never did nothing of the sort," grumbled Cook, cross and disturbed. Most of the others turned away disgusted, and only Duff wanted to hear more. He got his wish. On and on went the story, and although it was not a cold night, some of the boys shivered. Chandler finally stopped when only one of them was left listening and he doubted Duff could even hear over his own grunting giggles. Soon after he finished Kellyn descended the mound.

"We're staying here tonight," he declared.

"I am not sleeping in there," said Smith gesturing towards the crypt as he and some of the others came back to sit around in a circle together once more, "not tonight, nor ever again."

"Me neither," said Ham so tremulous his voice cracked.

"Little too late for that," said Kellyn walking through the circle and bumping Chandler's head with the heel of his palm. "Good job, smarty. You got them shitting their pants."

"We probably shouldn't stay," said Chandler patting his hair back into place. "It's not safe." Ham nodded without breaking his constant vigil upon the crypt's mouth.

"He's right," said Smith. "That demon that stole our pig could come for us next."

"No demon's coming for us," said Kellyn.

"People from that village might," said Chandler. "We're liable to get caught sooner or later."

"Now you're on to something," Kellyn said considering their situation. "But no one's going nowhere tonight. First thing tomorrow we hoof it out of here. First thing, I mean it, so be ready."

"Where we going," asked Ham.

"Worry about one thing at a time."

The night closed in completely and they bedded down, some sleeping outside of the crypt, some within. Ford tossed and turned, beating at the lumpy ground and figuring sleep for a lost cause just before his snores rippled through the camp.

"My back! I been stabbed!" Smith's screams broke the morning peace.

Kellyn shot up and squinted through the predawn gray at a blanket morphing in agonized thrashings upon the ground. Smith writhed about, his hand clutching his lower back. Kellyn was at his side in a flash.

"Am I bleeding to death? Am I dead?"

"Stop moving! Hold still!"

The camp burst alive. Cook came running around from the backside of the crypt carrying his pot and wiping grease from the Green Hart duck from his hands. Everyone surrounded Kellyn to watch him search Smith in the difficult light for blood. "I don't see nothing. Wait, what's this?" He held up a leather pouch tied off with a string.

"Oh yeah," said a much calmer Smith, "I forgot about those." The string was released, the pouch upended and small pieces dropped to the ground with wooden clicks, pieces to an old game called Strategaeth. "I must've slept on it."

"You're a god-damned fool!" hollered Kellyn, throwing the pouch in his face and calling him a few other names before calming down and gathering his gear. "Get your fool self ready. All of you."

None were truly ready for the day. Smith struggled to roll up in this blanket and took a kick to the backside. Cook fumbled with his cookware and Kellyn turned on him.

"And where was you?"

"Huh? What you on about?" said Cook, refusing to make eye contact.

"I saw you. What was you doing out there alone so early?"

"Nothing."

"Nothing?"

"I needed a shit."

"A shit? With your pot? You ain't shitting in the cook pot, are you?"

While they went back and forth, Smith showed off his game pieces to the others.

"I grabbed them from the inn when they weren't looking." He passed the pieces around.

"Some are missing," said Chandler, counting them and handing them back. "Yes, some pieces aren't here."

"Ford maybe could carve them," suggested Jakes.

"Doubt it," Ford said grabbing one of the simply carved pieces. "Looks too fancy for me."

"Yeah," said Smith thrusting the pouch into his hands, "I'll bet you could carve up the missing pieces just fine."

"A game with missing pieces," said Kellyn elbowing into the crowd, grabbing the pouch from Ford and sticking it under Smith's nose. "This is all you got? All them fat purses walking around and you grab a stupid game and it don't even have all the pieces. Gods be damned, I think we tossed the wrong idiot out of the gang." He threw down the pouch and walked away grumbling. "Get ready. We're leaving. Now!"

"Here," said Smith picking up the pouch and putting it in Ford's hand after the others cleared off, "you have them."

"Nah, they're yours."

"And I'm giving them to you."

"Thanks."

"That's all right. I seen you was down, so, I don't know. You do what you can with them and we'll play sometime."

"Deal."

They rolled bedding, hoisted packs and sacks, and kept mum until they fell in with Kellyn's step. That's when Jakes shattered the tranquility after tripping and falling for the second time in little more than twenty yards.

"We're moving out!" he bellowed to the air while Ford helped him to his feet.

"Gods of the deep," cried Kellyn back at him, "everyone can see that! What are you shouting for?"

"That pig bite's turned him mad in the head," said Smith.

"Or," began Ham, nudging Smith and nodding back at the crypt, "he's been haunted, I'll bet." The boy tapped the side of his head and Smith nodded.

"Sure as shit." Neither had slept in the crypt the previous night and both took long strides ahead to distance themselves from the hobbled former herder, preferring to join Kellyn at the front rather than tempt the gods by associating with Jakes.

A slippery fog wove like ribbon through the trees, slithering toward them and swallowing them wholly as if they were serpent's prey. The unadulterated, singularly straight trees turned to limitless pillars in the white canopy. What direction the boys traveled, if towards the sun or away from it, none could say for certain. The ground dipped and they padded silently into a valley of copses, hidden but for those that emerged from the colorless limbo before them, leafy mastodons in mist.

"See there," said Chandler coming up to Kellyn's side atop a rocky cap upon a sudden rise and pointing ahead to peaked islands in a lake of fog.

"What are they?"

"Houses, I think." Chandler guessed correct. They were the rooftops of houses bunched together and sunken deep in a dell. The boys withdrew, circled the settlement and carried on, crossing a greenway unnoticed into a country of rolling knolls and ancient burial mounds, indistinguishable one from the other.

All the morning Ford trailed behind in support of Jakes, watching his feet kick ahead and fall away, seeing nothing and running into whoever was next ahead when they all stopped.

"Watch it!" said Cook. Ford apologized and, lifting his head, saw that they were at the edge of a clearing. A skull lay half buried in weed and overgrown grass at the feet of some of the other boys. Duff flicked at it with his toe.

"We can't get away from the damn things," said Smith and Ham blew out a fretful sigh.

"Don't worry none about that. Worry about that," said Kellyn pointing ahead to a gap in the trees through which could be seen a tower. How tall it was or how far could not be determined through the haze. "Let's go." And with that he turned and headed away from the tower. Duff pulled back, gave the skull a bone-crushing kick and followed after the rest.

What direction they faced and where they were off to, no one knew. They hadn't seen the sun all morning and this land was new to them, or so they all thought until Ford sensed a vague familiarity about the place brought on by the tower. He caught up with Kellyn and told him so.

"Really?" Kellyn could not disguise his relief from Ford, but spoke in a voice so low and guarded that none overheard. "Stay up with me. " He looked around to check the others and saw they were tired and only concerned for their aching feet to care much what he and Ford were being so secretive about. "If you see anything you're sure of, don't say nothing, just do this so I can see." He scratched his head at the temple. Kellyn was full of silent signals like that, having learned them from his previous band, but he could never get the boys to use them, not as much as he'd have liked. "Got it?"

"Got it."

"Duff, give Ford here a break and help Jakes."

They assumed Ford had begged off work in his whispered conversation with Kellyn and they resented it. No one liked when another of the band got out of a disagreeable chore, even if he'd already done his fair share, so the other boys turned somewhat sour on Ford when they trooped off again.

Around and around the mounds they wound, pushed left then right, trying and failing to keep a straight course, and retracing their own steps more than once. The youngest, smallest and most scared huddled around the tallest or strongest. Jakes with his arm over Duff's shoulder soon lagged well behind again.

Too busy with trying to place where he'd seen that tower or if he'd actually seen it, Ford didn't notice Kellyn fall back a few steps behind him. Their roaming about was conducive to a drifting mind, and so his thoughts wandered back to Melynbren. What brought his father and sister there, he wondered. And why was the old woodcutter's daughter-in-law with them?

"What you thinking?" asked Kellyn.

"I'm thinking my father might've got married again."

"What?" Kellyn looked Ford over quite confused. "I meant, what do you think about where we are? Does any of this look familiar?"

"Um," Ford said, twisting this way and that, "I can't see anything."

"You said you knew where you were going. You're supposed to be getting us back to some place we know. What's wrong with you?" As he spoke, an imperceptible wind lifted the murky veil before them, revealing a dozen yards ahead something man-sized and tubular with an enormous, spherical head. The fog masked details beyond the merest of outlines, but they could make out its thick upraised arms. It stood in a meadow of bracken, like a stalwart herald or some divine messenger waiting and watching or warning, almost entirely surrounded by a smothering circlet of mounds.

"What's that?" asked Ham. "What is it?" he cried and his echo through the fog came back muffled like a child suffocating in a shallow grave.

Kellyn drew his knife, braced himself and demanded, "Who are you? What do you want?"

"Leave us alone!" Smith shouted.

"What do you want?" It didn't move, didn't answer. "Speak or I'll gut you!"

A blanket of fog slipped once more between them and cloaked the stubborn specter. Kellyn silently gave an order for the others to move about into a flanking position, then advanced at a creeping pace with Ford at his side. None of the others had the courage to leave the main group. Without a word, they all followed right behind Kellyn and Ford. The specter emerged once again, first its massive, faceless head, then its arms still aloft, its rod-straight body, legless and naked. Kellyn relaxed.

"It's just a totem," he said and forced out a rather stiff laugh.

The six-foot-tall stone pillar with the gargantuan granite sphere perched on its top was a relic from older days and rites of worship. No longer satisfied with simple images, those seeking self-aggrandizing monuments hewed into solid rock their war-like prowess, holy benevolence, and acts of bravery in the face of impossible odds. No space was left undecorated; there were intricate designs, seals and sigils, fabled beasts, giants defeated and devils cast into darkness.

"How do you suppose they did that?" Chandler asked in admiration of the solid stone sphere, three feet in diameter, resting upon the pillar. The boys walked around the totem and touched the engraved images. Duff ran his fingers along a monstrous cat with a serpent's tail, feeling what was left of its barbs and fangs after the pummeling of wind and weather for untold centuries. He placed both hands upon it, measuring its girth and tried to push the sphere off its pedestal.

"That ain't going nowhere," said Cook.

"Damn stuff won't let up. It ain't natural," said Kellyn, more interested in the fog. "Useless," he said at seeing Jakes waving a hand high in the thick air. A weak, but persistent tug at Ford's sleeve drew him into Ham's spooked gaze.

"Something's following us," said the boy, pointing back to an ill-defined, motionless figure in the hazy distance.

"Nothing but another totem," said Ford.

"But that's where we just came from," said Ham. No sooner were the words out of his mouth than the figure took a few steps back and vanished into the fog. A queer squeal crawled up the back of Ham's throat and both boys stumbled backwards into the others, knocking people down and causing a panic.

"A dead soul's followed us from the crypt!" cried Smith from his knees.

"It probably weren't nothing and it definitely weren't some spirit," said Kellyn.

"I know what I saw," said Ford, "and I saw something."

"Right then. What was it?" Kellyn's words drew out in languorous sarcasm. "Ghost or ghoul? Or nothing but a shadow? Is a shadow coming to get you, Ford?"

"Come on, let's just go," said Ford turning his back on him.

"Where?" asked Chandler. "Where are we going?"

"How do I know? Ask him!" said an exasperated Kellyn driving a finger into Ford's back. "He's the one that's supposed to know. It's his fault we're lost."

"What are you talking about?" shouted Ford, whirling about and knocking away Kellyn's hand as he stepped up to him. Duff drove his wide body between them and butted Ford away with his chest. Everyone gasped to see Duff's head snap back. Ford shook off the pain in his fist from the jolting punch and then they were rolling over the damp grass, grunting and groaning, arms and legs flailing, no one getting the upper hand. Kellyn stepped back with his arms folded and an amused smile playing over his face, letting them go at it for a time before telling the others to dive in and break it up.

"Stop! The ghouls will hear!" said Smith while riding Ford's shoulders around in a circle.

"There's no damn ghouls!" said Kellyn punctuating each word with a pound of his fist into an open palm. The fighters were pulled apart and aside from a reddening bruise on Duff's cheekbone and a dirty scrape across Ford's green-smeared forehead, both suffered from nothing more than wounded pride inflicted by a feeling they'd come up short in the fight.

"We should go. We don't know who lives around here or who might have heard us," said Chandler, dusting himself off rather needlessly since he'd done little to help. The others agreed. Everyone was sick and tired of this place and any reason to leave would do. Kellyn climbed atop one of the mounds to scout around for a way out of the hilly labyrinth. Eventually he guided them through the mounds, down steps overgrown by long grass, out of the fog and into a lightly wooded basin of soft ground and lush greenery, where they found a low, oblong foundation of steady rock to curl up in for the night.

In the morning they traveled into a damper, darker forest thick with mushrooms and fallen, rotted wood. Glad to put a good deal of distance between them and Melynbren and Farnod, they now found themselves in the midst of an endless land of soggy ground. They pushed on and it led them deeper into a swamp. By the afternoon their tone had changed so much they were actually fretting at not having seen so much as a single settlement all day.

"I'm getting tired of wandering around out here forever," Smith grumbled to Ford.

"Seems like a waste of time," he murmured back with a nod. Chandler and even Ham voiced similar displeasure soon after and a revolt appeared inevitable, but for the timely discovery of a lake.

"Finally! I need a drink of something besides muddy water," said Smith.

"Hold your horses!" said Kellyn grabbing the boy's arm before he took off. "We don't know what's what around here. So go slow."

They hid in the trees and bushes by the waterside and stretched their necks to see down the length of the lakeshore. A village clustered along the far edge. Fields cut from the forest rose up a slope behind the houses out toward the trees. A stream split the middle of the cultivated land, and on the side farthest from the village, the slope dipped into flatter lowlands that the boys could barely make out from this distance.

"I know this place," said Ford, and Kellyn let out a snort.

"Heard that one before."

Too excited to be goaded into another fight, Ford studied the village alongside Kellyn as if nothing had been said between them.

"That was where my brother and I came up." He pointed to the swampy end of the lake, then swung his finger the other way to the village and fields. "And right over there was where we fought the Staneards."

None of the other boys had ever been in a battle and had plenty of questions for him. Ford answered their ravenous curiosity with long patience and a swelling pride that gave him a sense that he'd once done something truly great. They wanted to hear about the weapons, armor and bloodshed, and when he told all he could of those things, their interest wore off and they left him frustrated by his inability to explain the feelings welling up from deep inside him. He couldn't describe what it was like to fight for righteous causes like honor and family, and even if he could have, he doubted any of them could appreciate what he'd seen and done. When he really thought about it, by comparison, these boys were thieves without honor, and here he was now, one of them. Not only a common thief, but he'd stolen from his own family. His hands tightened around the ax handle. He wrenched it, twisting and twisting until his skin burned. It looked to the others as if he might snap it.

"It's like he's sleeping with his damn eyes open," Ford heard Kellyn say and realized a conversation about him had been ongoing for some time. "There he is. Awake, are we?"

"I was only just thinking."

"Quit that nonsense and tell me this. Can you get us home from here?"

"I don't know. Maybe."

"We're going home?" asked Smith with a sprightly leap.

"We ain't going nowhere until we get something worth going home with," said Kellyn.

"I'm hungry and I want to go home," said Smith rubbing his belly and letting out a long sigh.

"So? You think the rest of us is happy being out here? You don't think we all don't want to go home?"

The argument didn't move Smith and when, as if he hadn't been listening, he said, "I'm still hungry," he found himself flat on his back with Kellyn standing over him. "That hurt," he moaned, rubbing his chest.

"So, what next?" asked Chandler.

"Don't you start too," said Kellyn and walked away to sit alone at the edge of the water where he ripped at the weeds. Ham was at hand and he asked him, "Did you bring your fishing line?" Ham shook his head. "Well, fuck off then!" Ham scampered away and found a place to sit with the rest of the group.

"Who was that back there, you think? Yesterday in the fog, I mean?" asked Chandler of no one in particular.

"Who or what more like," said Smith and Ham nodded, while Chandler waved off the comment.

"It was my father," said Ford. Everyone sat up and stared at him.

"You're sure?" asked Chandler.

"Pretty sure."

"How do you know?"

"Who else has reason to come for us? For me? He's after this." He held up the ax and frowned at it.

"Why didn't he come and get it then?"

"Because," jumped in Smith, who was still lying on his back staring up through the trees, "like as not it were a ghost, and not your da."

"I tell you, it was him!" snapped Ford. "I stole his ax and now he's come after me to get it back." Ford threw down the ax and dropped his head into his hands, resting his elbows on his knees. Smith had set him off and everyone knew it, even Smith. In these tense moments, some whimsical distortion of good intentions propelled the clownish young boy into foolish acts. So, no one but Ford was surprised when Smith crept up behind him, snagged the ax and danced amongst the boys, holding the ax head aloft and covering his lips with it as he sang out, "Ford, why did you do it? Why, Ford? Why did you steal my ax? Why?" Smith found it hysterical, some of the boys laughed too, so the song was repeated, then again twice more before

Ford grabbed back the ax on one of Smith's twirling passes.

"Hey," the boy protested, but Ford just pushed him aside, strode to the water's edge and hurled the ax overhead as far into the lake as he could.

"Leave him alone, let him be," Jakes implored all those curious to know what was eating Ford that he'd do such a thing. "Give him space. That's always best when you got worries loading you down." They watched Ford kneeling at the shore, not moving for the longest time and wondered when he might snap out of it. Eventually they lured him away from the water when an old man came in sight, poling a small, flat-bottomed boat the length of the lake and checking traps along the way.

"He's nearly blind. See?" said Chandler to the others in the bushes spying upon the fisherman, who hauled in a rotting trap and pressed his nose up to it to examine its contents.

"Better not chance it," said Kellyn and they withdrew into the forest, where they spent the time scavenging berries, the odd mushroom they were sure of, even roots and snails. Kellyn balanced a spikey horse-chestnut in his hand and considered throwing it at Ford, who was absentmindedly pulling up a tree root. "Put that down," he said tossing the chestnut into the bushes, "and listen up. It weren't your da back there following us." He held up a hand, forestalling Ford's angry reply. "I don't know what it was, maybe nothing, maybe something, but I do know what your real problem is. Guilt." He let the word hang in the air. Nearby Chandler nodded and Kellyn was glad, glad to have Ford listening and Chandler agreeing, for he'd learned from Jakes that followers keep a flock together. "You need to forget about that and look out for you. Take what's yours and forget everybody else. That's the way the world works. But right now what you got to do is, you got to stop making a big deal about it. Why? Because we got more important business. You was telling once about that place your folks is from."

"Barlow?"

"Nah, I mean that market town where your father's folks come from."

"Lewiston."

"Right. You remember how to get there?"

"From Barlow, sure. But it's a long ways south, even from Barlow."

"Perfect. Just what I'm looking for. I've got an idea. We take whatever they got up there," Kellyn said, tossing his head at the village on the other end of the lake, "goats, cows, chickens…fish maybe. Damn. I hope they ain't got nothing but fish. Any road, if they got animals, we got Jakes. He's good with an animal. Then we take them fast as lightning far out of here and sell them at market in this Lewis town where nobody's heard nothing about stock gone missing up this way."

Kellyn clapped his hands together and laid out his plan to the others, setting it and them into motion the instant he finished. Ford did not ready himself like the others, but went back to the lake and stared out over the water. The fisherman was gone.

"You should never have thrown it away," said Chandler joining him and gesturing towards the lake. "All you had to do was give the ax back and you wouldn't feel so bad about it anymore."

Ford looked from the water to Chandler and back to the water again, and then dove into the lake. The boys raced to the water's edge, some cheering Ford on, some imploring him to give it up as he splashed about and dove time and again in search of the ax.

"He's mad through and through," said Kellyn.

"Something awful's bound to drag him under," said Smith holding the side of his head in one hand and a handful of Chandler's shirt in the other as he stared unblinking out at Ford. "He's good as dead!"

"Get out of the water!" screamed Ham, his voice so shrill it made the others flinch. Ford broke the surface with a desperate gasp and floundered back on to the bank empty-handed.

"Give it up. It's lost," said Kellyn shaking him by his wet clothes. "Now come on, we got work to do. Everybody, let's go. Bring everything. Maybe we'll come back here and maybe we won't, so take everything."

"Jakes can't go. His foot," Chandler reminded him.

"Right, right. Jakes, you stay behind and keep a low and I mean low fire going. Nothing that can be seen across the lake and no smoke. Now listen, the rest of you, I don't have to tell you all how important this one is." He looked them over, one by one. "I can see you're hurting. We all are, so it's important we get this one right. No messing around. We got to get something out of this—" A weighty splash behind them cut Kellyn off and they turned to see Ford swimming out into the lake.

The sun went down and the shoreline morphed into an indistinct mass of trees and bush, and though he couldn't be sure if he was near the right spot anymore, Ford went on treading water, his lungs all but spent and his limbs tiring as he swept his legs and reached with his feet. Something clipped his heel and he swung his foot back to feel for it again. A burst of renewed strength surged through him and he stretched himself out, lifting his chin to keep his head clear as he reached down as far as he could. Around and around he swirled his leg until he felt it twining about something rope-like. He kicked and it coiled around his ankle. He tugged and it held fast. His arms frantically beat the surface and he panted fast as he struggled to keep his chin above water. He wanted to shout, but his breath came only spurts. Yanking and yanking, he went under and came up spluttering. Deep, wheezing breaths, thrashing, and then it was over. His leg pulled free.

"It's a weed, only a weed," he repeated, willing himself to believe it.

The night fell so black that when he broke the surface for the last time, only the dimmest orange glow deep between the trees guided him to shore. Exhausted and soaked, he flopped down beside Jakes, who was sitting alone and poking at a weak fire.

A lifeless sleep overtook Ford immediately. For how long he'd been sleeping he could not say when an agonized wailing forced him awake. Lifting one eyelid he beheld a ghostly pale Smith he hardly recognized, a black void appearing where the boy's lower jaw, neck and chest once were. Ford jumped and fell back.

"Quit your moaning," said Chandler emerging from the trees. Seeing the horrified faces of Ford and Jakes, he laughed. "Oh he's fine, though he did lose some teeth. Smile for them." Smith's eyes welled with tears and Chandler was the only one smiling. "Some of the bottom ones were kicked out by a mule that didn't want to leave home."

Ford stirred the fire and could see that by a shadow's trick, the blood that had flowed from Smith's mouth and down his chest had dried into a dark mass, creating the illusion of a void in the poor light.

"Why don't you go wash yourself?" said Jakes. Like one defeated, Smith drifted off towards the lake, shunning offers of help.

"Where's everybody else?" asked Ford.

"They should be coming."

"Did anybody get anything?"

"Doubt it. He woke up the whole village with his bellyaching, and we just took off in all directions and fast."

"Did they come after you? Should we be getting out of here?"

"If I was in charge, I'd say yes, sometime soon. But we're okay for a bit. Look at that, you found it!"

Ford patted the ax next to him with an irrepressible grin.

"That's just great. We got one problem solved," said Kellyn standing at the edge of the fire light, "but what do we do with this one?" He held by the neck a sullen, emaciated little creature quivering in filthy tatters. Ford leapt up.

"Runt!"

He took a step forward, ready to wrap Runt in a bear hug, but one look at Kellyn was enough to ward him off. One of his eyelids twitched and he fought to blink it away. His lips were pulled back from his gritting teeth, his hands shook and Runt winced under his tightening grip. Too much had gone wrong in too little a time and Kellyn's patience was at an end. In fact, Ford grew quite worried for Runt. Stepping back so as not to anger Kellyn, he found Ham at his elbow.

"You all right?"

"Yeah," replied the boy, neither taking their eyes from Kellyn and Runt.

A crashing through brush out in the forest had everyone drawing weapons and ducking for cover until Duff broke into the circle of light drenched in sweat. Cook followed soon after. Most of the boys stood on one side like an audience watching and waiting to see what might happen next. Kellyn's mouth worked in a grimace full of unspoken fury, and his reddening eyes swept over the boys. They waited, no one moving, no one speaking. Tears streamed down Runt's cheeks and he cried out. Reawakened to what was in his grasp, Kellyn redoubled his grip upon the boy and his knife. Ford lunged to grab Runt away, but Kellyn whipped up his knife.

"Don't try me!"

Ford backed off.

"Calm down," Jakes implored, trying to hoist himself up with the help of a stick.

"You're not thinking straight," said Chandler.

"You don't know what I'm thinking!" Kellyn said and spat at Chandler's feet. "No. And I'll tell you another thing you don't know. It was him," he shook Runt, "this little shit's been following us around this whole time. He was the one we saw out there in the fog. And him," he snarled, pointing his knife at a shame-faced Cook, "he's been feeding the son of a bitch this whole time. Anyone else want to tell me about how they been lying and going around behind my back? Anybody?" Most of them averted their eyes in some way, not out of guilt, but rather to avoid the vehemence staring back at them.

"I knew about it," Jakes admitted and all were stunned that the most open and honest among them had it in him to deceive. Kellyn's face contorted as he swallowed this new, bitter draft. He jerked Runt around to face Jakes.

"He," stated Kellyn and Runt's teeth rattled from being shaken by the neck, "is not part of this gang. But it looks damn near impossible to get rid of him." The little boy squirmed and Kellyn shook him harder. "So, what do we do with this worm?"

By now everyone knew well enough to keep their mouths shut. At least it seemed everyone knew well enough until Duff let loose a giddy chortle filled with sinister joy that finally ended with him saying the first two words he'd said all day.

"Fish food."

Chapter 11
The Tears of the Earth

Three bored riders swayed and rocked atop a loaded cart drawn by two equally bored horses. The more passive of the two horses was happy for the long-in-the-tooth mare to set the pace with plodding steps over the rutted road passing through an orchard disused and overgrown until quite recently. Dead and rotting apple trees cut and piled upon the newly scythed slopes to either side of the road were left to be cleared away as a part of Barwnig Blackoak's recent plans to reclaim this plot of land before the wilderness took it back entirely.

The riders had often made this long, dull trek. Just the week prior, they'd been to Melynbren on a special delivery for the wedding feast. So absolutely familiar were the horses with this stretch of road that the riders, including the driver, could sleep for long stretches. So, when the cart stopped for no apparent reason, each man was roused enough to look about for the cause. Their sleepy eyes found nothing ahead or among the heaps of stumps and branches to the sides. They even looked behind them and still found nothing.

"What's wrong, old Clopper, Dandy?" the driver asked and received muffled sniffles in reply. The man in the leather jerkin guarding the load from a reclining position at the back of the cart sat up and fumbled with his spear and the dagger at his side while he got to his knees.

"Can horses cry?" he asked, blinking at the backsides of both horses. Sitting beside the driver, a lazy-eyed merchant of modest means, cleaner under the fingernails and better dressed than his two companions, pushed back his floppy flat cap and leaned over for a look between the horses' legs.

"It's a boy," he said and the driver, an old man of spent body and brackish soul, gave him a queer look.

"And the other's a girl. Could've told you that without looking between they legs."

"No, down there. A boy in the road."

All three men leaned over to one side to have a look between the horses' legs. Indeed there was a boy, not more than two strides in front of the horses. Dandy sniffed with a tentative and twitchy nose, but Clopper had seen a great deal and wasn't spooked by a crying boy, even one sitting on the grass and weeds between the ruts in the middle of the road. Slump-shouldered and red-eyed, Runt peered up at the horses and the men leaning around them. When he spoke above a mumble his voice trembled, but he kept on repeating the same question.

"Can you help me find my mama and pa?" His lips shivered into a crooked smile, almost hopeful. His hailing hand pled for answering salvation. Dandy reared back.

"Stop that, boy!" hollered the driver. "You're frightening the poor beast!"

"Go on, young man, quit the road!" commanded the merchant.

"Who's that?" asked the guard, pointing his spear at a youthful, smiling man hobbling down the road towards them with the help of a stick. "Hey there, you! You this boy's kin?"

"Yes, sir, in a manner," replied Jakes.

"Come get him out of the road then."

"Hello there, hello," said Jakes, shuffling and limping along the road at a pace the men in the cart found infuriating. He faltered, went to one knee and, grabbing a handful of grass, offered it to the horses.

"Never mind that. Get the boy out of the way," said the merchant. The horses sniffed at the grass Jakes offered and took it from him by lip and tooth with gentle precision. The cart's guard had enough.

"Get off the road!" he shouted and jumped down to meet Jakes at the head of the horses. "You hear me?" A choked squeal from behind made him swivel back around. The Wayward Boys, masked and armed, held the men in the cart at knife-point. Smith hoisted the guard's spear above his head in triumph. The guard patted his empty scabbard.

"Looking for this?" Jakes asked with the dagger held up next to his impishly raised eyebrow. A flick of the wrist and the slender knife was sailing over the guard's grasping hands and over the cart, where it fell near Duff. When the guard ran around to retrieve it, there was Duff holding the dagger like an ax, two hands crammed upon the handle and poised over his shoulder for a downward chop. The guard backed down. All three of the men gave in and surrendered the cart to the boys, who began tearing through it to see what they'd won. All the while, Runt remained alone in the road as ignored as his own tears.

"Cheese," said Kellyn, hoisting aside some of the heavy wheels, "it's all cheese and nothing else."

"Cheese? Ugh, I hate cheese!" said Smith, though few understood the lisping coming from his blubbery lips.

"Cheese does not set well with me," said Chandler.

"More for me then," said Ford with a big smile that stretched out on either side of his hastily-made cloth mask.

The boys poked their knives through the dusty mold into a surprisingly orange cheese, solid and unveined.

"It's Wulfford Red," said Ford with his nose to the cut.

"How do you know?" asked Chandler.

"My rich cousins over Lewiston way would buy a wheel and give us a wedge now and again."

"Is this a joke?" said Kellyn palms up. "We can have a nice chat together about this after. Come on!" He kept pressing them on, warning that anyone could happen upon the road at any moment. They worked fast, but binding all three men to each other was tricky for a bunch of boys who'd never done it before. And since their own rope was in short supply, they had to use some which had been holding down the cheese at the back end of the cart. Then there were the horses. If ever the pair had any concept of time they obviously lost respect for it at some point. The boys coaxed the beasts up the slope at the kind of leisurely pace that sapped Kellyn's patience. With Jakes taking the lead and the rest pushing the cart from behind, they had nearly reached the cover of the trees when the horses stopped and refused to go on.

"It's too steep. They're finished," said Jakes patting the horses' dewy necks with tender strokes.

"Unhook them and we'll pull the cart the rest of the way," said Kellyn. "We just need to get it hidden."

"There's no way we can move it ourselves," said Chandler. Kellyn knew he was right, but for a moment it looked like he might punch the bearer of bad tidings between the eyes.

"Hurry up and unload some of the cheese then!"

Smith threw down the spear and leapt onto to the cart. Groaning under the weight, he managed to toss two wheels over the side. Cook grabbed one and made for the trees with it. The other eluded them by rolling on its side all the way down the hill and bounding in a great leap over the ducking heads of the men on the road.

"Wa-hey! So close!" exclaimed Smith and then rolled another off the cart aiming for the men. Everyone stopped to watch, but this wheel hit a tuft of grass and veered into a pile of wood.

"Game's over," said Kellyn, who had also been caught up in the fun, but now his fingers fussed with the buckles in a frustrated attempt to separate the horses from the cart that ended with him pulling out his knife and hacking at the straps and ropes until the beasts were free. All the strongest boys pulled as one, but the cart rocked forward only a foot and would have rolled backwards if not for the straining efforts of Ford and Duff to hold it in place. Sweat poured off them and the straps dug into their skin.

"Take off more weight," said Kellyn and Smith went back to dumping the cheese from the cart. Ham and Runt dodged the cumbersome wheels and stopped the ones they could from rolling away.

"Help!" The cry came from one of the three men tied together on the road.

"They're getting loose," said Chandler.

"Look!" Ford shouted. From where a thin curl of smoke could be seen above the low hill, a team of laborers with an ox pulling a long sledge were coming to take away some of the wood. Kellyn turned from them to the men on the road who were breaking free of their bonds and back again.

"We're finished if we don't do something," said Chandler pulling his new mask tighter over his face and backing away towards the forest.

"Grab all you can," Kellyn commanded, "and make for the trees!"

"Get away from my cheese!" hollered the merchant. "Thieves! Stop them!"

"Go! Go! Go!" shouted Kellyn. Smith chucked cheese wheels left and right. Jakes took a large wheel under one arm, grabbed up his stick and hobbled off for the trees with Chandler, Ham and Runt on his heels. Duff followed with a load twice the size of anyone else's. That left Ford the only one holding the cart back.

"Hey! Hey!" he called after Duff just as a cheese wheel knocked him down. He scurried to his knees and dove for the cart, but it rolled away and took off down the slope, rapidly gaining speed.

"Jump!" he and Kellyn shouted. Smith had a foot on one side, ready to leap, but a lurch threw him back. The cart picked up its pace and, while

Smith was regaining his feet, his mask blew off and revealed a ghastly yet irrepressible smile of fat purpled lips, darkened teeth and the gaps between. The tremendous speed thrilled him and when the cart clipped a pile of cut apple trees, sending shattered twigs and branches flying, he let out a wild, "Whoop!"

The laborers starting up the slope stopped to watch in amazement as the cart and cheering boy flew by them straight for the wide-eyed men in the road. They turned and ran after him. Ford picked himself off the ground and Kellyn dumped wheels of cheese into his arms.

"Let's go!" he shouted in Ford's ear, spinning him around and forcing him into the woods at the moment the cart vaulted over the road between the scattering men and sped straight for a pile of wood.

. . . .

"Stop that!" said Ham with his fishing pole in one hand while the other swatted the fetid air between him and Runt. For weeks it had been cheese for every meal. Cheese all day. Cheese every day. Some of the boys did not take well to this unvarying diet.

"That's awful," said Ford sitting nearby with his back to a tree, whittling away with more determination than skill the missing pieces to the game Smith had stolen and Ford had inherited. Smith's capture, or just as likely his death, whether a foolhardy accident or a brave act, had saved the boys. Either way, Ford resolved to make something of these pieces to honor that sacrifice.

"I can't help it," explained Runt. "Chandler says it's 'cause of the cheese."

"Well, stop eating it then."

"You can have this fish I caught," offered Ham. Runt scrunched up his nose at the trout that wasn't much longer than the length of Ham's outstretched hand.

"I'm not hungry," he said and walked off rubbing his stomach. "I don't feel good."

"There's plenty else, too," said Ford, scraping and turning then scraping some more a miniature ogre, not realizing the time elapsed. He looked up to find Runt gone and Ham staring at him.

"Plenty what?"

"Nothing. Never mind."

Uncomfortably bloated, but content because he was once again welcomed into the Wayward Boys for doing his part in what they had dubbed "the big cheese holdup," Runt leisurely made his way back home through the awakening Valley. Almost overnight the whole of the forest had turned into a veritable well-stocked pantry. The boys could reach out in any direction and pull back a handful of blueberries or the tart grapes no one but Duff could stomach, enduring them mostly so he could spit the seeds at the others. Mushrooms sprouted in every moist nook, leafy greens swirled in Cook's stews, and the churning waters of spring cleared, keeping Ham busy at his favorite fishing holes.

In these warmer days of plenty, the boys did as little as possible. They might spend all day wallowing by the stream or enjoying themselves in whatever way they wished, except for Ford. Upon their return to the Valley, he'd made it known he wanted to return to Barlow in order to bring back his father's ax, and Kellyn had concocted an unending list of chores designed to keep Ford in the Valley.

"It's like he doesn't want me to go." While venting, Ford kept his concentration on his carving. Ham never took his eyes from his bobber, the floating piece of wood attached to his fishing line that he hoped to see dunk under the water, but he didn't miss a single word of Ford's complaints. "It wouldn't take long. I could be there and back again in a day."

"Maybe he's afraid you won't come back." That was exactly what Kellyn feared; however, Ham feared it more. With so few friends, he didn't want to chance losing one, even going so far as to give Kellyn ideas that kept Ford busy and rooted to the Valley.

"Maybe he is," said Ford, considering the idea and taking a bite out of the fist-sized hunk of cheese he'd brought along. "But how come Jakes can go wherever he likes all the time and we can't? Or I can't, anyways."

"You can't what?" asked Chandler coming up from behind and surprising them both. "We can go," he said when Ford finished explaining, "all of us, wherever whenever we like. It's only Jakes that likes to go off and do whatever he does. You can go if you want. Hold on." He took a few steps away, passed gas behind a tree and returned. "Pardon me. I was sure I'd heard the end of that on the way over here."

"So I can go?"

"Yes, of course. Kellyn won't stop you. Probably. You see, the thing is, he just doesn't want you to leave for good."

"I'd come back."

"I'm sure you would, but Kellyn might not be so sure."

The light, almost apologetic tinkle of the stream through the rocks Ham had piled to create the pool he now fished grew into an obnoxious splashing as Duff shuffled into view, poking at the banks and overhanging bushes with a heavy-ended stick.

"You're scaring the fish," said Ham. Duff brought his stick down with a slap and spray.

"Cut it out," said Ford without taking his eyes off his whittling. Duff sneered and smacked the water again. Ford kept on carving. Duff frowned, looked around for frogs and then waded upstream to a still pool.

"Thanks," Ham said as he dipped his drowned worm back in the water. Ford shrugged. Duff flopped belly first after a frog and came up choking.

"Stupid as a stick, that one," murmured Chandler. Always flashy, whip-smart and happy to speak his mind, Chandler's confidence had risen even higher since thinking of the idea to use Runt as bait after Duff suggested turning the boy into "fish food." When Runt had distracted the cheese merchants enough for the other boys to take the cart by surprise, Chandler took great pride in knowing his plan had worked perfectly. His inflated ego pushed him to root around until he found part of a pine branch, which he aimed at Duff's back. His end-over-end toss fell short. Duff plucked the stick out of the water and whipped it back, catching Ham with a sharp crack on the shin. Ham leapt about, wincing, Duff bent over laughing, and only when he quit did he notice Ham sniffling. "Willow." He spat the insult, common where he grew up around the prevalent weeping willow, and went back to his frog hunting.

The bushes rustled and Kellyn emerged, pulling up his pants.

"Any left?" he called out to Duff, snapping off a branch and jumping into the stream with him. Ham yanked his line out of the water and threw himself with the pole on the ground, rubbing his shin and wiping his nose. After much clumsy flopping about on Duff's part, he and Kellyn managed to herd a few puny frogs back down the stream. Chandler took off his shoes, rolled up his pant legs and stepped into the water, scooping up one of the frogs in a single fluid swoop.

"Easy," he said holding it aloft for all to see. Duff's stick flew by Chandler's head.

"That un mine!" he hollered. At the sight of a cross Duff, charging and snorting like a taunted bull, Chandler dropped his frog and was about to flee when Duff was doused down one side, the side where Ham stood with an exultant smirk on his face.

"Ha, ha! He got you!" The words were barely out of Chandler's mouth when Duff picked Ham up by the neck, threw him down and pinned him half-submerged, thrashing and gurgling. Everyone was shouting. Ford pulled Duff off Ham, who emerged coughing and convulsing, his mouth working in a fight between fear and hatred as streaks of blood formed on a scrape over one cheek. Out of the fray, Ham had come up holding Duff's stick in one hand. He cocked it back to swing and when he didn't, Duff stuck out his chin and dared the much smaller boy to hit him. Ham hesitated.

"Go on, do it!" Chandler encouraged, but Ham felt every bit of the overwhelming, pent-up power in Duff waiting to be released by his feeble blow. Even his strongest, luckiest hit would do nothing but worsen the beating he'd receive. Ham's whole body began shaking. He turned ashamedly away and shuffled off. Before him a frog glided over the settling water to the edge, its two bubble eyes visible above the surface. Down went the stick and up came the frog, its white belly like an egg floating on the surface. Kellyn cheered and Duff laughed, but Ham wasn't finished. With awkward swings, he flailed at it again and again, each swing faster, sometimes hitting, sometimes missing. The mangled frog was pressed into the bank and Ham, emitting exasperated whimpers, beat it until it was no longer a frog, but a yellow, browning mess soon indistinguishable from the mud. Sucking up his runny nose, Ham dropped the stick and ran upstream with his head bowed.

The other boys didn't have much to say after that. Duff kept on looking for frogs, but the rest sat beside the stream and wrung out their clothes in the afternoon sun.

"One of us should go talk to him," said Ford, arriving at the notion because it was the sort of thing Leo used to do when Ford's world weighed heavily upon him. No one else could talk him out of a bad mood quite like his brother.

"Don't bother," said Kellyn "He's mad in the head."

"Maybe."

"Definitely."

"All the same," said Ford. He grabbed his knife and the little ogre, and finished off the last of his cheese as he headed upstream where he found Ham. The boy was crouched in a ball with his head resting upon his knees on a flat rock atop the step-like waterfall that marked what the boys considered to be the westernmost edge of their Valley. Warmth and light streamed through the leaves and twinkled off the bubbling water. In this cheerful spot, the miserable boy stood out like a dark cloud in an otherwise sunny sky.

Ham hadn't seen him yet and for an instant Ford considered walking back, because he could think of nothing to say and had no idea how to say it even if he did. This brand of kindness had been practiced more upon him than by him. Put to it, he recalled vague recollections of Leo's soothing words that had brought on a heart-lightening tingle throughout his body, but nothing of practical use.

"I hate them."

"What?" said Ford emerging from a trance, his eyes refocusing and falling on Ham. The boy had his head up, but faced away seeking the singer of the warbling song in the branches over the water.

"I don't like them."

"You don't like birds?" Ford studied the boy.

"No, them." Ham nodded downstream. His crisis was over, Ford realized, and so he took the liberty to sit next to him.

"They're a bunch of oafish louts."

"Sometimes."

"They are *all* the time to me." Ford couldn't disagree with that. Ham wasn't targeted and picked upon inordinately, but he did take more hurtful gibes than Ford. The problem was, he was no one's favorite. Nothing about him stood out. He wasn't the strongest, fastest, smartest or even the funniest. Ham was the sort who did his bit and got on, but he was too small to be seen as truly useful and too shy to make friends in this environment. His desire for friendship and affection came off as needy, and was his own problem as far as the rest of them were concerned. The honest truth was that Ham remained a Wayward Boy because he wasn't a nuisance.

Ford became aware of the lengthening silence between them, but struggled to come up with anything more to say; certainly nothing comforting came to mind. He sucked air through his teeth, picked at his fingernails and began wishing he hadn't come.

"Questions," he bellowed in a rush when the idea finally came to him.

"Awyr bless you," Ham said and Ford wondered why, but he didn't wonder for long. When juggling two thoughts at once, one or even both dropped from his memory like it'd never existed. The main point was questioning, a thing Leo often did, and in doing so, somehow answered Ford's problems. Never having tried it, he blurted out the first question he could think of.

"They're louts, huh?"

"Yeah."

"What, um, what's the, uh…" Ford trailed off in a slurred cluster of nonsensical words and phrases that, as luck would have it, Ham wasn't listening to.

"I don't want to be here anymore."

"No?"

"No."

"So," Ford said when more of the dreaded silence crept between them, "if you don't want to be here, where do you want to be?"

"I don't know."

"You don't know?" asked Ford and Ham only shook his head. "Oh. Well, then what?"

"What do you mean?"

"I don't know, I mean, I guess, what will you do?"

"I'm going to run away."

"But where? Where to?"

"I'll go with you," Ham said and sat up straight. His eyes glowed with a new optimism and searched Ford's bewildered face in expectation.

"Go with me? Go with me where?"

"You said you were going home, to your home. Barlow? Where you came from." The boy's excitement built word by word into a towering monument of hope that Ford feared to topple. "So, if it's all the same, I'll go with you!"

"Nobody's going nowhere," said Kellyn picking his way along the stream with Duff and Chandler trailing behind. He climbed the rocks and stood over Ford and Ham, glowering down and sizing them up. "I don't know all of what you two were talking about, but I can guess and I tell you to forget it. Put it out of your minds. You know why?" Ford expected the worst, but Kellyn surveyed all he saw before him and said, "Because there ain't nothing better than this life. You can work yourself into the grave and get nothing for it. Not even for kin. Better to be your own man, out here, free. Nah, you don't want to go nowhere." He leaned back to take in the sun, closed his eyes and let loose his ugly smile that had a way of looking cruel when he meant to be kind. "Now come on, we're going."

"Where we going?" asked Ford, jumping from the rock with Ham to follow Kellyn and the others upstream.

"To the Tears of the Earth," sang out Chandler with a flourish of the hand.

"What's that?"

The Tears of the Earth was the name the boys had given to what some of them thought was the source of their stream, an ice-cold spring that dribbled from a crack in a rock.

"Why we going there?"

"Because Duff said Ham was probably out here weeping big girl's tears," said Kellyn, which made Ford look to Ham and Ham look away, "and that made me think of it." Chandler shook his head and pointed to his own chest. "Besides, we figured it might help them that's sick."

Anticipating Ford's next question, Chandler said, "They think water from the source of the stream has healing powers, if you drink it."

"Does it work?"

"I don't think so, but it can't hurt."

"It works," said Kellyn over his shoulder, slowing to let Ford catch up, then grabbing his arm and falling into step with him. "I once heard tell of a woman, healthy as anything, she falls down dead in the middle of a field on the nicest summer day you could imagine for no reason at all. They bring her water—"

"Water from the Tears," asked Chandler.

"Course! Why you think I'm telling this story? Ignore him. So they bring her this water and what do think happened? She comes back to life. Jumps right up and starts hoeing the field again."

"Honest?" asked Ford.

"Search my soul, I tell you it's true."

Ford's world went still and blurry. If these waters could bring back the dead as Kellyn claimed, Ford asked himself, why not Gwen? "Milda, too, come to think of it."

"Who's Milda?" the other boys speculated as they watched Ford fly off into the woods. At the camp, he frantically filled his arms with extra waterskins.

"Why not put them in one of these bags?" Cook shouted at Ford's rapidly fleeing form. "Damn fool."

Ford heard nothing. His breathing came too fast and loud, his thoughts faster and louder still. All might be made well again. The past could be, if not erased, at least mended. Somewhere between the camp and the spot above the waterfall where he caught up with the boys, it occurred to him how long it had been since the passing of Gwen and Milda and his spirits dampened. Images of dead and rotting creatures he'd found in the forest came to mind. The skeletons littering the crypt in the woods could not be forgotten. Every step of the way his conviction shrank, but he held on to enough hope that when they passed a split in the stream and took the lesser of the two waterways, Ford was just as happy to overlook it as the rest of the boys.

The trip to the Tears wasn't long from the waterfall. They should have made it there and back again before dark, but because of Ford's delay and more petty fighting, they didn't reach the spring until sundown. Still, they were in time for Ford to see the domed portion of rock, gray and veined, protruding from the side of a hill like a scalped skull, its bare surface cleft at the center from which drooled out a clear and continuous stream of water.

"See, the ground is crying," Ham whispered to Ford, who thought it resembled a slobbering baby more than gushing tears. However, the boy had spoken in such a hushed, reverent tone that it humbled Ford, so when all the others fell to their knees at the base of the dribbling dome to say prayers and give thanks, he was on his knees next to them. Afterwards each climbed as high upon the rock as he could and drank a mouthful before respectfully moving aside for the next person. When the last of them had drunk from the Tears of the Earth they sat about the spring peacefully staring until Kellyn stirred.

"Fill up your skins and let's get back before it's dark."

By the time he was on the last of the waterskins, Ford had to rely on feel to make sure it was filling and then rush to catch the others, stumbling along the stream and sometimes into it. The boys swore their way home with every poke to the face by a branch or trip over a root.

"The wood's no place to be without a light after dark," said Ham holding his eyes open as wide as they'd go.

"Can't believe none of you thought to bring a lantern or nothing," said Kellyn releasing his shirt from a snag.

Ford stopped and ran a hand over his eyes, trying to rub away what he thought must be an illusion. Ahead the trees glowed as if the sun was rising in the middle of the forest.

"Fire!"

The shout came from the heart of the Valley, within their very camp, where a wall of flames waved and snapped in a wicked dance upon the palisade. A horror-stricken Jakes raced back and forth from the stream, throwing useless buckets of water on a fire that only grew stronger.

"Help!" he screamed repeatedly and when he saw them tearing through the trees towards him, he babbled a jumble of words, rapid and shaky. "It won't, I can't…help me!" The flames, starting at the cooking fire, were spreading around the wooden wall.

"Stop gawking! Do something!" shouted Kellyn. Ford dropped his waterskins and ran about trying to find anything to carry water in. Duff pulled the bucket out of Jakes' hand, but stumbled to the stream and came back much slower. Ham picked up the waterskins and flicked weak splashes at the fire; much of the water landed uselessly on the ground until he had emptied all the waterskins. Kellyn pulled at the posts as if he might rip them from the ground. Stumbling back from the heat, he pointed to the roof of the building, "It'll catch on fire!"

The palisade was a lost cause and there was no stopping the blaze upon it, which was drawing ever closer to the roof. Ford shot past Kellyn and drove his shoulder into the post closest to the house. It lurched and flames licked his back. Again he slammed into the palisade and the post clipped the corner of the roof, collapsing it with a crash. The scorched post was left tilted inward; fire ran up its length and threatened what was left of the roof.

"Pull it away! This way! Pull!" Kellyn shouted, jumping in beside Ford and hacking at the charred bindings. They pulled together until the post leaned outward, and with Duff's help, they dragged the posts closest to the house to the ground where new fires sprang up. Sparks snapped free of the timbers, setting leaves alight. All the boys ran about stamping the ground, putting out what they could and kicking away dry leaves and anything else combustible.

A gusty howl blew through the Valley and coalesced into a lilting whistle before diving deep to root itself in a subterranean groan that spoke with a tongue foreign to them all of doom and condemnation.

"What is it?" shrieked Ham. Chandler fell to his knees and grabbed his ears. His face closed in a tight grimace. The others stood dumbfounded and trapped in confusion. From what abyss this disembodied voice emanated was uncertain at first, but as it spoke they beheld within the Face an emerald illumination shining out of the mouth like the green glow of foxfire. None could speak. Some pointed. Ham fled to the edge of the firelight and wrapped himself around a tree. The voice growled one last time and died away in a trailing rumble, the green glow and the flames upon the palisade fading with it. Kellyn shuddered violently and grabbed his stomach as if he'd been stabbed.

"What is it? What's wrong?" asked Ford and followed his friend's shocked gaze through the posts left standing to where Cook lie sprawled on the ground, his gut ripped open, blood saturating the ground under his head, dripping from where his face had once been.

Chapter 12
Into the Wild

The boys spent the rest of the night awash in tears, on the verge of bolting at the next provocation, shaking beside a fire built out of sight from the ruins of their camp. Kellyn beat his fists and occasionally shouted or cast accusations about until he was hoarse. No one was exempt. Everyone was to blame. He even accused Jakes of murder, because he and Cook had been at odds recently. Jakes explained with red-tipped ears that his fight with Cook had only been about whether or not to admit that they'd been secretly feeding Runt after he'd been turned out of the group. The deception plainly stung Kellyn, but it did answer his doubts.

"I didn't really think you'd done nothing. Just forget about it." His readiness to relent and move on paralleled everyone's willingness to stick together. They were afraid and sought safety in numbers.

In the morning, the boys woke to find Kellyn gone and the smoldering palisade sending up a thick trail of smoke plainly visible above the trees. Barely had they begun arguing amongst themselves about what to do when Kellyn strode into view along the bank of the stream. He held a waterskin newly filled from the Tears of the Earth and stepped gingerly into the ruins of the palisade to kneel beside Cook's body. From the periphery, the boys watched in awe and a silent respect as he poured the water over the corpse. Then they waited. When nothing happened, Kellyn said a prayer. Still nothing.

"Pray, damn you!" Kellyn commanded and the boys followed along with him. When it was over some shut their eyes, others held their breath. Kellyn bowed his head and shielded his eyes. A few of his tears, true tears, fell upon the body. Eventually he got up, kicked over a charred post and threw down the waterskin as he walked up to the boys. "The longer we stay, the more likely we get caught."

The magic of the Tears had not worked and it didn't take much more convincing that the thick, rising smoke would give them away and that they'd soon be discovered by curious villagers. Not that any of the boys wanted to stay. In fact, none would go near the Face, nor did they wish to look upon the mutilated corpse of Cook, so their stores of cheese went untouched and many of their possessions they left for lost amongst the ashes of their home.

"Where are you going? Don't!" implored Ham soon after they had started off when Ford turned about and headed back.

"What's he think he's doing?" asked Chandler and received his answer a moment later when Ford returned pale and shaken, but with a measure of subdued triumph and the ax in hand. Ham, too, found his fishing gear where he'd left it upstream the day before and Kellyn went out to retrieve his traps.

"All busted to pieces," he said with a kick to the crushed remains of a wooden cage when Ford finally found him. "All of them, all smashed."

"Who did it, do you think?" Ford ventured to ask, trailing at a safe distance while Kellyn moved on to the next trap.

"I don't know who…or what it was," Kellyn finally said after blowing out long breaths and looking around the forest for answers. "Someone or something don't want us here, that's for damn sure or they wouldn't a done what they did. Cook, me and him been together a long time." He picked up a piece of a trap and threw it down in a clattering of broken wood. "God and demon, damn them! Why? Why'd they go and do something like that?" Ford realized he wasn't talking about the traps but rather Cook when Kellyn buried his face against a tree and let himself go.

Ford turned away and knelt by the broken pieces of the trap. He was trying to push two snapped ends of wood into one another when he caught sight of the other boys standing at a distance in an awkward jumble looking on with cautious and concerned curiosity. Even Runt was with them. Earlier, when everyone was readying to leave the Valley, Ham came back from the lookout tree and said Runt wouldn't come.

"He's too frightened to move, I think."

"I can't imagine what that poor boy saw," said Jakes with tears building in the corners of his eyes. "I wish I'd been there for him, but I was off on one of my walks when it happened," he explained. Ford didn't blame him, but he could have wished Jakes were more dependable.

"What do you mean *he won't come*?" Kellyn had bellowed and cursed on his way to drag Runt from the tree, if necessary, only to return soon after alone. "He won't come."

Ford and Jakes climbed the tree to the lookout and found him, as Ham and Kellyn claimed, lying on his side in a ball, shaking.

"What's wrong, Runt? What's troubling you?" they asked until they could see, truly see the vacant stare in his hollowed-eyes and their questions turned to, "What happened? What'd you see?" Those too went unanswered and all the compassion they could muster was in vain. The boy would not speak or even acknowledge them. Besides his involuntary convulsions, he wouldn't move either. It took Ford and Jakes to carry him out of the tree.

Now Runt clutched at Jakes' sleeve and watched with the rest of the boys as Kellyn broke down before them in a way they'd never seen. The clustered crowd of boys leaning silently out from behind a forked tree jumped when Duff blew the mucus in his nose in and out until it cleared. Kellyn heard too and wiped his face before joining them with a throat-clearing cough.

"We're off for the Lost City," he declared and no one objected.

Ruins of past civilizations were common enough, but Ford thought this Lost City sounded like a fantasy of the boys' making. None knew it firsthand. Jakes heard it described as "a beautiful place on a mountain that overlooks all the land around with lakes and water everywhere and safe grazing land that's always green all year round." Kellyn built the city up with castles, marble fountains, silver statues, golden temples, and the loot to be had. "They say it's packed to the gills with coin."

"I've never heard of it. Where is it?" Ford asked.

"Somewhere to the north," said Kellyn.

"Somewhere?"

"Calm yourself. We'll find it."

Having trodden much of this land in his lone wanderings, it made sense for Jakes to take the lead as pathfinder on the first day, but by the second day he faded into the pack and others offered random ideas of their own, often picking paths for the sake of ease.

"We're going this way! Got it?" Kellyn shouted with an unnecessary insistence to put an end to Chandler's persistent suggestions. The boys would've obeyed without the underlying threat. If anything, the threat tainted their trust in him, for they knew that when pressured Kellyn would make a choice, even a poor one, just to show he was still in charge. And yet, they followed him, a quiet file of boys delving deeper into the unknown wilderness upon narrow deer paths that led through lowland thickets over hills and back into marshy valleys. An unforeseen, impassable drop-off upon the summit of a sharp hill turned them eastward for nearly a mile and drove them, frustrated and exhausted, into a swamp made by a languorous river already dead this early in the year.

"Glowing!" said Chandler rising in elation. "Mushrooms!"

"What is he on about? Somebody hit him for me," said Kellyn from the far end of a downed cedar on which the boys were sitting during a long rest.

"Remember when we found those mushrooms that were glowing underneath?"

"Sure do," said Jakes. "I remember them lit up all blue and green like."

"I'll bet whoever did it must've used a bunch of those to make that weird glow we saw."

The boys hadn't talked much since leaving the Valley, but when they did it was usually to toss about guesses on what caused the tragedy. Blame for Cook's death was placed upon villagers, wolves or a bear, or Smith ratting them out to the law, but there had been no answers for what made the strange sounds and what caused the bright green glow. Kellyn latched on to the idea of wind for the sounds and now these mushrooms of Chandler's would do for the glow coming from the Face, both satisfying his need to provide non-threatening explanations for unknown terrors.

"If it's nothing, then why don't we go back?" asked Ford, not for the first time trying to change their course back to the Valley. It was not that he wanted to go back there, he merely wished to be closer to Barlow. "It might not be too late. We could find a mender, a true mender, one of them one's that heal with the hands of the gods. They could make Cook all right."

"Great idea. You know where we can get one?" Ford didn't know and Kellyn's rhetorical question reminded him that this wasn't even the first time he or one of the others suggested it. "Don't be sore. I ain't mad. It's a good thought, but even if we found one, you think they'd twiddle they fingers and put Cook's face back on? Forget all that. Besides, whoever done the deed, they know where the Valley is now and they just might come back any day. We can't be hanging around there. Maybe we'll go back some day, but not for a damn long while." And that was the last they spoke of that.

"Too many bones," Duff said gnawing on the remains of a fish.

"Mine's burned on the outside and raw inside," said Chandler.

"Burned part's the best part," said Ford, their newly dubbed cook. "It's got more flavor." He took a swig from Ham's waterskin to clear the taste and his parched throat. Complain or not, they all ate every last bit of the perch and pickerel Ham caught for them on slugs and grubs. He'd done well, even received a pat on the shoulder from Kellyn while has was pulling in the last of his catch, and now he sat alongside them watching the water and grinning, the first smile for any of them in days.

"It's slippery right there," said Chandler to Ford over his shoulder for the fifth time. "Take care or you'll drop that." They waded through waist-high water with the rest of the boys in a line that stretched across the swamp. No one liked the idea. They were still unnerved by the pickerel fins ripping through the inky-black surface like the mysterious serpents that sometimes haunted their dreams. The other concern was the torch Ford held aloft. Having forgotten their flints, they had no other way of starting a fire anew except by torchlight, so they kept one going at all times. Ford was chosen to carry the lit torch from one side of the swamp to the other and as Chandler predicted, his foot slipped and he floundered face first. He reemerged to the sounds of Kellyn swearing.

"Light another!" he shouted at Ham standing guard over the small fire pit they cooked the fish upon. Though it smoked feebly, some stirring and blowing brought the coals back to life enough to ignite another torch from the pile of simple branch and bark extras kept at the ready. This one Kellyn carried, making everyone else wait by the fire until he'd safely crossed the swamp. He entrusted Duff with the last spares and Duff held the bundle ludicrously high above his head as if walking tiptoe and reaching for the sky. However odd he may have looked, it proved effective. When he slipped and his head went under, the torches stayed dry.

The shallowest points in the crossing still came up to Runt's neck. Seeing only the little terror-stricken face bobbing and his quivering lips lifted just above the surface was too much for Ford. He hoisted the boy on to his back and carried him across. Whenever Ford faltered or when the swamp let forth a huge belch, Runt tensed up and whimpered in his ear. It reminded him of that morning when some of them were gathered around talking about how Runt had laid awake in an unresponsive, zombie-stare all night before finally falling asleep only when the sun rose. "He's afraid of everything," Jakes had said. To which Ford replied, "It's like he died when Cook died," and thought it as clever as something Chandler might say, if a little morbid. He hadn't meant to connect Runt to the mysterious circumstances of Cook's gruesome death, but that's exactly what the other boys did, and Ford had regretted making the comment ever since. From then on they wanted nothing to do with Runt. They stopped talking to him, stopped trying to feed him and some wouldn't so much as touch him. In essence, he became dead to them. Ford tried to make up for it by sticking with the boy and making sure he at least had water at hand and offered food when there was any. At night Runt continued to sleep curled up next to him and during the day Ford kept an eye on him.

That evening, while trying to dry out, Ford watched Runt over the fire and noticed that he wouldn't meet the eye of another even when spoken to. He stared into the distance as if seeing something others could not. Ford guessed Runt had seen Cook's killer, tried to imagine what visions of evil enslaved the boy, and knew he could not leave him. For however long it took Runt to return to the boy he'd once been, Ford felt honor-bound to play father to him.

That afternoon they climbed the tallest hill in a range crossing their northward route hoping for a clear view of the area, hoping they might see their Lost City. Where the top leveled off they found a sharp ravine cutting across the ridge with a gap small enough that a leap across might be possible, but a deadly drop to the unseen bottom was more probable.

"Smith'd give it a go if he was here," said Kellyn. The offhand comment tempted Ford to ask again the question that still nagged him, why hadn't they gone to see what became of Smith. Kellyn's response the first time had been that no good could come of it. "He's dead, one way or the other, he's dead now." Pointless as it may have been, Ford felt they should have done something.

"It splits the whole hill in half," said Chandler stepping to the very edge with the others for an angry look over the side. He threw up his hands in agitation. "That's unbelievable. Utterly ridiculous!"

"Is this as far as we can go?" Ford inquired after a while of following alongside the ravine. "Do we have to go back?"

"Nah, said Kellyn, "either it ends soon or we go and try the other end. Someone, Jakes, get up one of these trees and have a look around. See if you can't tell which end of this damn hole is closer."

While Jakes shimmied up a tree, the rest of them scavenged the few tart blueberries from the low bushes growing along the ravine's edge where the trees drew back to leave bare rock riddled with fissures and cracks covered here and there by leaves, twigs and scrub. Ford grimaced and grabbed his legs. He sat to stretch them and massage out the aches from all the walking followed by sudden bending and squatting to pick berries.

"What's a matter?" asked Ham gravitating towards Ford like he always did when his big friend showed any sign of weakness. This irritated Ford. He preferred being left alone with his pain and misery.

"I don't know, they just hurt. It's nothing. Don't worry about it," he said when Ham shuffled closer and reached towards Ford's leg with a moist hand. "Listen, I found these." Ford held out some dark berries. "I don't know if they're blueberries. Go ask Chandler for me."

"Looks like bilberries of a sort."

"Just ask." Ford didn't care about the berries, he wanted to avoid Ham's embarrassingly fawning pity. His legs felt better already and his attention turned to Runt, sitting by himself continually picking the berries, each one plucked with a precision too slow to be worth the effort.

"He said maybe, maybe not," said Ham coming right back with a hop over a crack in the rock, "he said it's probably a mountain bilberry, like I said."

Ford let out a defeated sigh and his head slumped forward. Other than being a clingy nuisance, nothing was inherently wrong with Ham, there was just no getting away from him these days. Only Ford keeping close to Runt kept Ham at bay. At one point, Ham tried to separate Ford from Runt by warning Ford away with claims the boy was cursed. Ford ignored him as he did now, taking a deep breath and walking off to where Jakes, having climbed a fair way, scanned the country all around them.

"Hard to tell, but I think I see…" Jakes shouted down, but what Jakes saw Ford never heard, because the ground fell out from under him. On his backside with arms and legs flailing about, he slid with an avalanche of dirt and leaves down through a fissure. His fingers clutched at the retreating earth. What didn't give way ripped at his clothes and skin. Roots whipped his face and he bounced off rock. Everything around him snapped and rumbled. The more he struggled, the faster he slipped into the ravine where the light piercing his clamped-shut eyelids grew faint. He slowed, his eyes popped open and he slammed on to one side, was flipped upside down and dropped into emptiness.

Ford awoke to the world once again with a garble of groans, a blurred view of his dim surroundings, and an incredibly distant voice repeating his name. Lying on his back, he cupped his throbbing elbow and winced when he flexed his leg. It seemed every part of his body ached in someway, so he stopped checking himself and ran his hands over the ground, brushing against the stones and crisp leaves that had fallen with him, and probing the damp and spongy ravine floor with his fingers. After adjusting to the low light, he could make out the ravine walls draped in vines and hanging tree moss. Where bare, the wet rock glistened. High overhead the sky was framed by the top of the ravine, open and jagged like a never-ending jack-o-lantern smile. Discreet warbling twittered about him, as if polite birds were having a private word by his ear.

He hoisted himself on to one elbow, nearly bumped his head and realized he was lying at the mouth of a low-ceilinged cave, no more than a cavity in the rock wall the size of an animal den. The warbling fluttered from some secret, dark corner. Ford blinked, squinted, saw nothing, and patted the ground for his ax. It wasn't there. A prickly heat irritated the back of his head. A sweep of the hand found nothing and vigorous scratching gave no relief. He twisted about for a look and a searing glare blinded him. He threw up his arms to protect his head and waited for an attack that never came. When his sight gradually returned, he peered from behind his shielding hand and found the glare came from the sun reflecting off of a polished bronze hand mirror lying on the ground. A mounting thrill momentarily dulled his aches and pains at the sight of a slender band of silver wound around its handle. To find something this valuable in the middle of nowhere was pure luck. The silver adornment looked to be an afterthought to improve upon an otherwise plain mirror and, being in good shape, Ford hoped it would fetch a decent price at market. He had a quick, unhappy look with it at the scrape marks on his bloodied and dirty face. He caught himself in the eyes with the glare again.

"Damn it."

After his vision cleared once more, he flashed the light around, turning it on the cave, which lit up in a dazzling shimmer of color and twinkling reflections. Silver necklaces tied to roots dangled in lines and inverted arches from the ceiling. Prisms flashed a rainbow of light off gemstones fitted into the cracks. The head of a farmer's two-pronged pitchfork buried in the ground held dozens of gold and copper rings upon each of its tines. This was more wealth than Ford had ever seen, enough to set his family up for life and many generations after. Using his elbows, he scooted a few inches farther into the cave to reach for a gem and his sleeve snagged a necklace. Many of them came with tiny hooks attached to both ends. He untangled it, pushed up his other sleeve, wrapped the necklace around his upper arm, pinched the hooks tight and covered it with his sleeve.

"Perfect!" he said flexing the arm and looking around the cave guessing at how much of it he could hoard away upon his body. Certainly not all. Even if he could, he wouldn't deprive the others of their share. "At least *a* share. No, there's plenty for all and then some," he said at the sight of coins overflowing an old boot leaning against a rock. From behind the rock a moon-faced and astonished creature stared back through almost entirely black eyes. They both let out a resounding yelp and the diminutive creature scurried from the rock to the back of the cave, revealing a pale and gangly body naked but for bracelets and chains about its neck. Ford toppled on to his back with his legs flying up and yelped again when he saw that another of the pale creatures had been trampled under one of his thighs. He held his legs up because he didn't want to crush it or touch it at all if he could help it. With a thrust, he rolled on to his knees and grabbed a rock. The creature lie sprawled face down. Ford watched and waited for it to move, this thing the size of a newborn baby, yet with arms, legs and body cut like a full-grown man's. Only its head was oversized like an infant's. Ford dropped the rock, found a stick and tapped the creature gently. He tried again and when he got no response, he flipped it over. Its eyelids were open and the large, round eyes themselves were light colored in the extreme compared to the other creature, looking like green grapes set into a white coconut. Even its stringy and coarse hair had a texture much like a coconut's husk. Its staring eyes disconcerted him and so he flipped the body face down again. The warbling Ford had heard before fluttered out from the cave in a chirping symphony. He turned the mirror reflection upon it and found a hole rounded out of a crack at the far back. From it shown pair after pair of bulbous eyes. Ford watched the eyes. The eyes watched Ford.

"Ford?" came an echo through the ravine.

"Hello!" he shouted up to the surface.

"Ford?" The shadow of a head appeared high above.

"I'm down here!"

"Ford! He's alive!"

"I guess so," said Ford to himself still wondering if it were true.

"We'll get you out!"

"Hurry up, there's something down here!" Ford glanced at the tiny body and all around him. "Maybe lots of somethings."

"Hold on!" The head disappeared.

"Don't have much choice, do I?" he said to himself, scanning what he could see of the ravine with its impossibly steep walls and the vines that gave way to the slightest tug. Since no one brought a rope, he worried he might be trapped forever.

The tiny creature laid out at the mouth of the cave hadn't moved. Ford ducked and directed light from the mirror into the darkness. There were no little eyes staring back at him this time. Afraid, he figured. Strangely though, even the hole in the wall at the back was missing. Where once was a void, now appeared solid rock. "What in the name? Where'd the hole go?" he said, shining the light around. "Weird." He glanced down at the unmoving body, trying to avoid looking at its naked rear. "You didn't do this. Did you?" More than anything he wanted to crawl inside and take some of the gems and jewelry, especially now that the boys were on their way, but it was such a tight squeeze and the thought of the naked little men running around in there worried him. He leaned farther in and flashed the light around the cave. "I better not be imagining all this."

Something peculiar struck him. When pointing the light directly at where he remembered the hole in the wall being, the rock turned somewhat transparent and the hole could be vaguely made out through the rock.

"It's magic!" he said in awe, then turned to the little naked body on the ground. "Is it? It's strange whatever it is." It took Ford some crouching, crawling and sliding to get his unwieldy body into the tight nook while staying out of the beam of light. Once in, he waved his hand in front of the hole. Nothing happened. He poked at it, not even coming close to touching the rock. "You little coward." He reached out with a grimace that anticipated the worst and pushed his hand right through the place where the rock should have been. His hand touched nothing and vanished. He yanked it back with a frightened start. When he saw his fingers wiggling about in the mirror's reflected light, all of them where they ought to be, his thumping heart slowed some. Everything seemed fine and he didn't feel any different. He gave a low whistle. "Well now, that right there is…I don't know, but boy, that sure is something."

Folks like Ford and his family didn't get the chance to see much magic, if ever. One of his cousins, a Goldsmith from his father's side of the family, had been sent to learn the craft in Port Morton. No one with the gift stayed in country villages. Now, here it was right in front of him, a bit of magic he could touch. He did so, darting his hand in and out, and waving it around.

"Aw, sick. What is this?" Drawing back his hand, he found it coated in a yellow-tinted slim. The nectar-like goop clung firmly to his skin and webbed his fingers. He wiped it on the boot filled with coins and it stuck. Lifting the boot, he whipped it about until eventually it came loose, long after most of the coins had flown jingling all around the cave.

Three, four, then five of the scrawny, moon-faced men dashed from the hole protectively wrapped in silk noil and without their jewelry. They darted at Ford, throwing puny handfuls of purple dust at him and scurrying away. The dust floated harmlessly to the ground. He sneezed and they jumped back. While Ford swatted away the lazy purple clouds the largest of them ran right up to him and hurled dust straight into Ford's face. The cloud enveloped him and when he rolled away to elude it, he flopped forehead-first on to the rock wall.

"Ford. Ford?" Could these sweet words be from his mother, Ford wondered. More lovely, ethereal sounds were never heard he decided in this, his most benevolent of moods. Not even a mammoth of the deep's monotonous slurp and snuffle could ruin his good humor. Airy compassion, generosity of heart, these worthy traits he would live by upon this cloud-cushioned bed floating over an affectionate world of hope and forgiveness.

"Is he snoring?"

"Wake up, stupid!"

Slaps to the cheek finally roused Ford to wet clothes and a painful body. Kellyn and Jakes stood over him where he'd been laid out on the damp ravine floor with lumpy rocks prodding his back.

"What is...who...I'm," he stuttered. Breathing in quick and sharp, he tried again with no more success and soon surrendered to his exhaustion of mind.

"Good time for a nap. Smart thinking," said Kellyn. "I mean, we're only trying to help you out this hole. But hey, you have yourself a nice little sleep."

"The little people," said Ford getting to his hands and knees and peeking into the cave, "where are they? There was one right here."

"The *what*?" asked Jakes. Not only were the scrawny men gone, including the naked one sprawled upon the ground, but all of the treasure was missing, too.

"Oh, no! No, no, no," Ford moaned as he searched the ground. "Even the mirror's gone. It was nothing but a dream, wasn't it?"

"You looking for this?" Kellyn moved aside to show a short stack of coins on top of a mossy rock. The pile contained only half of what the boot had held and there were no gems, no pieces of jewelry.

"There was more," said Ford, wanting to explain what had befallen him, but he pulled up quick and cut himself short at the sight of Kellyn, who he knew wouldn't want to hear about little magical men. Besides, any more details about silver necklaces and golden rings might end with him having to give up the one wrapped around his arm.

"You mean this?" asked Kellyn holding up by one end a spiraling necklace with a serpentine clasp. "Found it stuck to your arm." Ford groped his upper arm, feeling for his necklace. "No, the other arm, hanging off the back side, snagged on there just barely." Ford located the delicate chain under his sleeve and relaxed. "Yeah, don't worry. It's safe." Kellyn dropped his serpentine-clasped necklace into a pocket. "Looks like someone stored away their goods and forgot about them. Oh well, finders win the fortune!"

"What did you mean about the little people?" Jakes pressed while they wound their way through the tight crevices of the ravine to a crack in the rock wall with sturdy vines and footholds enough to climb back out. Ford frowned, shrugged.

"The kid smacked his head and was out of his senses," said Kellyn helping Ford with a leg up. "Leave him be."

"Just strange is all. I heard him say—"

"Enough talk. Let's get out of this place already!"

By the time they climbed out of the ravine and rejoined the others, the sticky substance on Ford's hand had collected a thick coat of dirt and debris. The boys dubbed it his "snotty hand."

"I found it for you," Ham said handing Ford the ax. The gesture meant more indebtedness to the one boy who tallied these things most closely, but when Ford's fingers slid over the wood and wrapped around the comfortable grips his father had worked into the handle, he was grateful to have the ax back in his hands.

"It's a good haul," said Kellyn over the shoulders of the others examining the newly found coins in a better light, "but we can't eat none of it and it won't keep us warm and dry. We keep moving while there's still sunlight left in the day."

Getting beyond the ravine meant a long detour that drove them into wetlands infested with mosquitos.

"Wonderful! Just wonderful!" said Chandler slapping at his exposed skin and waving over his head the torch he willingly offered to hold in hopes the smoke would drive away the buzzing pests. "There's no end of them! And now it's starting to rain. Really, really great!" Some of the boys rolled their eyes at each other. This included Ford, though he worried for Chandler, who was complaining more than usual these days and had all but lost his dramatic flair. He'd rather have Chandler's odd, sometimes vexing flourishes rather than this irritable monster he'd become.

"Try annoying them and see if they don't go away," said Kellyn. His jesting tone turned serious. "Whatever you do, just keep the torch dry."

"What do you think I'm doing?" After they entered the tangled bushes of the thick forest surrounding the boggy patch of land, Chandler didn't have to do much to keep the torch dry. The canvas-like cover of trees overhead did the work for him.

"It's very dark all of a sudden," said Ham to Ford.

"It's just the trees."

"It's getting late, too."

The day had grown old while Ford was trapped in the ravine. Plus, he'd been out cold twice and the lapse in time confused him. In his mind it should have been noon at the latest, but it was already early evening.

"When are we stopping?" barked Chandler, halting with a hand on one hip. Kellyn barked back and the two went at each other, tossing hurtful jabs, but saying nothing of importance.

"We'll camp soon as we put some distance between us and them swarms by the water," said Kellyn when he calmed down.

"They've followed us this far, I don't see why they won't follow us to the ends of the earth." Like the rest, Chandler was tiring and his rant trailed off to such a humble finish that Kellyn let the argument die.

Though still shaken by the mystifying and brutal death of Cook, Jakes was closer than any of them to being back to his old self, happy to be hiking about the countryside. His foot was much better and, like in the old days, he out-paced them all, occasionally scouting ahead out of sight, scampering up a tree or skipping to the top of a rise for a better look around, then sprinting back down to report what he'd seen. Long stretches would pass before he'd reappear, maybe not with his former carefree flippancy, but at least some optimistic word about what awaited the dreary column of sullen boys pressing on through an increasingly unforgiving wilderness. Late that day in a thickening forest he'd come crashing back through the bushes wearing his most irrepressible smile.

"We found it! The Lost City!"

What they found, after fighting through a wiry thicket into a natural and quite peaceful clearing, was a very small hut made from deadwood with living roots and vines crawling through out.

"That's not what I thought the Lost City would look like," said Ford.

"That's not it, you idiot. That's just an old pile of wood," said Kellyn turning on Jakes. "Why'd you think this was anything but an old pile of wood?"

"I didn't get a good look," said Jakes. "Just saw the roof and came back and told you guys." Though constructed like a man's hovel, the only part of the hut clearly manmade was the door, a fragile fence gate that hung loose and creaked when moved.

"What's it doing out here?" asked Ham, the last to poke his head into the hut and see the collection of bird feathers, piles of seeds, and dead rabbit peacefully laid to rest in wool.

"Maybe an old hermit lives or lived out here, that is, if we're getting close to Rock Harbor on the other side," said Chandler, speaking of a trade port far to the northeast.

"Could be," said Kellyn.

"We'll probably find this Lost City tomorrow," Ford said laying his hand on Jakes' shoulder.

The patter of rain upon the leaves overhead melded into a hiss while they used the stub of their torch to light a fire in the center of the clearing.

"This'll have to be camp for the night," said Kellyn as they sat about the fire facing the hut.

"We could stay dry in there," said Jakes.

"There'd barely be room for half of us."

"The smallest ones could fit all right."

"You want to sleep in there tonight?" Ford asked Runt. The little boy shook his head and wrapped his arms tighter around his knees. The almost ritualistic placement of items within the hut spooked all of the boys, so instead they stretched out upon on the ground as comfortably as they could and a few of them nodded off. Lacking dry wood, the occasional loud pop from the fire woke the light sleepers, which included most of them since the tragedy at the Valley. No one needed to be assigned to watch, because someone was always awake.

"The rain is slow—"

"Hush," said Chandler, cutting off Ham while cupping an ear and tilting his head towards the woods. He thought he heard footsteps in the trees crunching between the snapping of the fire and the dripping rain, but couldn't be sure. Runt sat up beside Ford's prone body. The sound became regular, too steady to be anything but footsteps. Chandler nudged Kellyn with his toe.

"I hear it," Kellyn muttered without stirring. Out of the dark came the crinkling of leaves and the snap of twigs in an arc around them. When the footsteps receded behind the hut, Kellyn crawled around shaking the sleepers, who awoke spouting incoherent babble or asking loudly what was wrong as they fumbled about in the dark. However, when Kellyn gave a tremulous order both urgent and desperate to "shut up and listen," they did. For the longest time there was nothing and Kellyn started to doubt what he'd heard enough to hope that indeed there was nothing actually out there, but he knew better. Lifting up a stick poking from the fire pit, he blew hard on the embers until they flickered into a wavering flame. He then stepped towards the encircling forest with his weak torch outstretched to cast whatever glimmer of light he could upon the darkness. From just beyond the clearing came a sniff, a snort and a growl so close it sent a petrifying shock of panic through the boys. The smell of urine tainted the air. Kellyn pressed half burnt branches into their hands and those who had knives drew them. Ford gripped tight his father's ax. Everyone pressed into a constricting circle with their backs to the fire pit.

"Hold them up," said Kellyn. "Wave them around. Don't let the flame go out."

A squeak escaped Ham and they saw that off to his side a husky mound of fur on all fours stalked the edge of the clearing. It kept up a deliberate, plodding gait circling around them.

"What is it?" cried Chandler.

"Go on! Get!" Kellyn shouted and flung his flaming stick at it. It dodged aside, its eyes flashing a brilliant yellow before it slipped from sight behind a cluster of trees. The boys crowded together. A wind kicked up the leaves. Treetops swayed and bushes shimmied. Their clothes flapped about and no one could see or hear the creature in the woods anymore. Overhead the clouds sailed by and the moonlight broke through casting a rich blue light upon the ground that mingled with the shadows in confusing patterns.

"Where is it? Where'd it go?" Kellyn hollered, trying to pick out their antagonist from the forest shroud. The wind carried leaves into the clearing where they danced around the boys. The swirling air quickened and flung raindrops like stinging darts. Around and around, faster and faster flew wind and water like a funnel squeezing in on the boys, knocking them about, sucking up the flames of their fire, and extinguishing light, sight and sound, all but the whipping of wind.

In a paroxysm of screams and terror they dropped their weapons and ran for the hut, shoving each other and packing themselves inside. No sooner did Ford slam the door than the strength of the wind ripped it open and dashed it so hard against the side of the hut that it shattered and blew away. The gusty howl soared into a deafening whistle of words spoke in a quiver teased too shrill to comprehend beyond a conveyed sense of the contempt and scorn it felt for the intruders of its sanctuary. Ford's ears throbbed, but it was an inner anguish that doubled him over and made him grasp his stomach.

"Where is it coming from?" cried Jakes with his hands over his ears.

"Someone's screeching in my head!" Chandler wailed just before falling to the ground where he thrashed about their feet and pulled at his hair. So crowded was it that all Kellyn and then Ford could do was kneel on Chandler to keep him from hurting himself or others. Pressed against a wall and sweating profusely, Ham threw up and fell in a limp mass upon Ford's back.

"Somebody's out there," muttered Duff as he braced himself in the doorway. No one heard him, but Ford had already made out through Duff's legs the outline of a bearded, willow of a robed man leaning upon a tree at the edge of the clearing with what looked like thorny horns upon his head. The man's arms sailed up, unfurling impossibly long fingers and his entire being burned an emerald splendor that clothed the clearing in a radiant spring of new-growth green. A heady warmth flushed the evening's chill and evaporated the rain into a steamy mist.

The shrieking whistle sailed with the raging whirlwind that coiled into a tight vortex and sprang like a cobra upon the hut. The boys covered their heads and crouched while wood tore away and whipped spinning into the air. Some screamed and shouted, some buried their faces in the ground. A snapped branch dug into Ford's back, another rapped him on the shin. So often was he hit that his anger soon surpassed his fear. The interwoven vines and roots released their hold upon the remaining deadwood and when there was almost nothing left of the hut, Ford was the first to bolt. He pushed Duff aside and ran into the clearing, grabbing up his father's ax and raising it high. He was going to bury it in the head of the old man, warlock, devil or whatever it might be, but he stopped and stood there dumbfounded as the other boys fled around him into the trees. The old man had vanished.

Ford chased after the boys. Their panicked flight through the forest was soon joined by a flanking, ever-looming, ever-changing green glow. The glow grew and at one moment the old man appeared to be floating beside them, then it changed into an enormous face with huge tree-ring eyes and vast oval mouth frozen into an indignant horror. Any notion Ford had of venting his anger upon it fled along with him as he ran and the otherworldly creature kept stride. It melted into a tree and came out the other side as a loping, leafy giant covered in malleable bark, stalking crab-wise upon roots showing beneath a blanketing moss beard. In one wooded hand it held a log like a club that it beat upon the ground, sending out reverberating shockwaves that drove ground-dwelling rodents from their holes to nip at the boys' feet as they hurried by. A snake slithered in front of Ham and the boy skipped over it, but fell in a somersault on to the ground. Sitting up, he saw what none of the others had yet seen, the four-legged and yellow-eyed beast chasing after them. He screamed and pointed. Ford lifted him to his feet and they took off once more.

The boys stumbled through the woods in a slow moving clump, huddling for safety, because they realized that no matter how far or fast they ran, they could not escape. The old man and the furry beast following behind could keep pace without effort, without tiring, while almost every one of the boys gasped for breath and clutched at their chests and the searing lungs within. None were aware of the subsiding wind and rain, or the moon breaking free of the clouds once more, lighting up the night steel blue.

"Stop! Stop!" shouted Kellyn after a while, holding up both hands. They turned and looked about.

"It's gone," Chandler said with some relief as he let go of his forehead and opened his clenched eyes.

"Everyone just calm yourselves," said Kellyn. Ford dropped to his knees. Duff collapsed on the ground. Jakes rejoined them through a thicket, leading Runt by the hand. Kellyn cautiously stepped back towards where they'd come from. He leaned forward with ear and eye to penetrate the night and make sure the distant snaps, clicks and cracks were nothing more than normal forest noises amplified by the dark. "It is. It's gone."

"But it could come back," said Chandler to no one in particular. "What if it comes back?" He looked to Kellyn, then the others from one to the next. "We should keep going. We have to get out of here."

"Calm down! I tell you it's gone," said Kellyn.

"Whatever that thing is, it'll come back. We'll all be killed!"

"Shut up!" hollered Kellyn grabbing hold of Chandler by the chest. Chandler wouldn't relent and Kellyn began shaking him, then shouting him down. Away in the woods, a howl like that of a wolf yet deeper and throatier silenced them and got everyone to their feet. Kellyn commanded them all, "Go. Now!"

The moon lit their ceaseless hike on through the night. Hours passed. Aching feet and exhaustion slowed them to a shuffle, and then Chandler stopped altogether, followed by Duff.

"Keep going, you slugs," said Kellyn through barely parted lips with his chin resting on his chest. When he saw Duff leaning against a tree, he shouted at him, but no matter what Kellyn said, Duff would not move.

"Don't piss him off," said Ford, coming up from behind and giving Duff a shove in the back. Like a falling tree, Duff crashed to the ground. He snorted and jerked about, his eyes popping open and blinking.

"He was sleeping on his feet," said Ford. A dry croak of mirth hiccupped out of him. This loosened them up somewhat. Even Kellyn smirked. Their situation was bleak and they needed release, even this minute amount. Lightening their load by losing and leaving behind most of their possessions might have been a saving grace, since they could go further for longer and escape the danger, but it was not by choice. They had almost nothing now, neither food, nor fire. Nearly all of their weapons were gone, as well as many of the coins they'd found in the ravine. They'd even lost their way.

Tripping down the backside of a small hill, the boys found a thick tree with muscular, tentacle-like roots clinging on to two boulders; the tree had grown up between them and was now slowly enveloping them, like an octopus gripping conch shells. The boys nestled in between the roots, the rounded curves of which seemed to hug them back.

Kellyn curled up by himself and knew sleep would not come easy, not with the weight of his own failures pressing upon him. A leader was supposed to point the way, yet he'd only managed to get them lost and sink them deeper into danger. If he could only explain away the bizarre night, but there was no denying what they'd all seen, no denying even his own fear. Answers were needed and he was out of them.

"Listen," he said, "I don't know what that was. And I don't know where we are. I don't even know where the Lost City is, or if it even exists. It don't even matter if we don't find it. All I know is, sooner or later we'll find a new place, new towns. Somewheres over these hills we'll find a new life."

No one replied, and Kellyn felt it wasn't enough, and yet it had been just enough. They'd gleaned the reassurance a bunch of exhausted boys needed to relax, close their eyes and sleep for a welcome few hours.

From the biggest to the smallest, they were tired to the bone, so when the sun rose and a peculiar kind of bird-song twittered about them, they slept on, quite dead to the world and the approaching footsteps. Ford grumbled at some unknown annoyance and threw one leg over a particularly rotund root. Repeated nudges woke him, but it was a hard kick to his heel that actually opened his eyes to the arrow pointed at his face, mere inches away.

Chapter 13
The Lost City

"What's this? What's your game?" The lisping, saliva-sucking demand hissed from a scarred-over upper lip that curled back to reveal a clutter of chipped, yellow teeth crowding one side of the mouth of a lean, thick-browed man flanked by two foul-eyed, grubby men.

"Why you out here?" asked the tallest, most cadaverous of them, swaying like a branch in the wind over Ham with a hungry leer as he poked the boy in the gut with a rusty knife tied to the end of a staff.

"You Mellek's men?" asked the one with the wounded lip. "Mellek send you out here after us?"

"We ain't anyone's men. We don't even know a Mellek," said Kellyn standing to confront them. They were full-grown men and armed, but the boys still had the numbers, and Kellyn was aware of Ford's firm grip upon his ax. "What's the deal? What's this all about? Point that somewheres else." Kellyn pushed away the makeshift spear. The third man, pinched-face and crouching badger-like, backed up and swept his bow with its drawn arrow left to right and back again, taking in all the boys with one lazy eye and one hawk-sharp.

"You, get over there," he grumbled in a voice divulging years of hard drinking, and Chandler did as he was told. Likewise, the others were shuffled together into a tight group. "I don't want none o' you sneaking up behind us." The three men completed a triangle, covering each of the boys with a weapon. There was no easy escape.

"We're not out to get you, if that's what you think," said Chandler holding up his empty hands.

"Yeah, we ain't with the law or nothing," said Kellyn. "Nobody tells us what to do." He released his balled fists and, making a shrewd guess, drew two fingers from one hand in a slow arc over his head. One might think nothing of it, that he was doing nothing more than smoothing back his hair, but the man with the wounded lip caught the signal and the two of them ran through an intricate series of precise hand gestures at the end of which the wounded lip stretched into a sneering smile.

"We're brothers then!" he bellowed while locking wrists with Kellyn. The men lowered their weapons and the boys relaxed at hearing words of friendship, even from an unpleasant voice. "Well, brothers it is. What do you call yourselves? What name do you go by?"

Kellyn introduced the boys and finished by saying, "We're called the Wayward Boys."

"Boys, indeed," said the tall, cadaverous one and an involuntarily, rippling quiver shook him from head to toe, which the boys couldn't help but notice, though it didn't faze the other two men in the least. "Not a girl among you," he said passing an intent gaze over the boys that landed on Runt, whose untended hair had grown quite long since last being cut. "Or what's this, a cute boy or an ugly girl?"

"Leave him be, Jorgi!" said the wounded lip man and added, "That's Jorgi. This here's Noll. Noll Cotter." The bowman grunted. "And I'm, well, you can call me Neb. Neb of, I suppose Towns, it is." Chandler snorted and covered it up with another longer one while blowing his dry nose into his sleeve. Nobody was named Neb and Towns was a surname the elusive adopted so they couldn't be pinned down. Neb ignored Chandler and went on, "We was called the Minurs." Minur came too close to sounding like manure for the boys to hold back from snickering, but this name neither Chandler nor Kellyn found funny. They knew its origin came from those craftsmen of antiquity who were not only skilled at sharpening blades, but also notoriously handy at using them. Perhaps these men weren't craftsmen, but a name like that left no doubt that they were cutthroats.

"You said you *were* known as the Minurs," said Chandler, "so you're not anymore?"

"That were our name when we made up twice this number," said Neb.

"There was seven," said Noll.

"Same thing. No difference at all. Point is, there once was more of us just but recent."

"What happened?" asked Kellyn. Neb thought about it before answering.

"Call it a difference of opinion or a misunderstanding that led to...I suppose, the end of a few friendships."

Neb wheedled out the boys' history and Kellyn's explanation for why they'd been driven from their normal territory. He then lifted their spirits with light banter riddled with subtle flattery that softened the last of the edge between them before ferreting out what they were doing in his territory.

"We're looking for the Lost City," said Kellyn and Neb raised a questioning eyebrow.

"Lost City? Never heard of no Lost City," he said, and rubbed his chin. "Or maybe you mean the ruins? You think they mean the ruins?" His two cohorts shrugged as if they didn't know or care. "Wait just...hold up." He stepped a few paces away with his hands on the shoulders of Noll and Jorgi. They turned away and shielded their mouths as they went back and forth, shaking their heads and then eventually nodding. "Here's the deal. We got a place, a sweet little spot not too far off."

"Sweet little spot," Ford overheard Noll say mockingly into the hood bunched around his neck.

"Maybe it's what you're looking for," Neb went on, "and maybe not. The thing is, it just happens we're putting together a new gang and we need more bodies. Maybe not this many," he said, looking down at the smaller boys, "so I make no promises. None. But come with us and we'll think on matters and see what can be done. Come on, this way. Follow me!"

"We'll feel it out," said Kellyn falling back for a private word with the boys, while Neb led and the other two Minurs took up the rear. "You know, see about these guys and what they're all about and if it's all right, we stay. If we don't like it, we go. Nobody's got a hold on us." Only Chandler voiced dissent. He was sick of the woods and he didn't like these men, but he fell into line like the rest.

"How'd you find us out here in the middle of nowhere?" Ford asked later after they leisurely hiked between thick-trunked, evenly spaced trees and passed into a wilder wood dotted with thickets and vines.

"Middle of nowhere," scoffed Jorgi. "You really got no clue where you are, do you?"

"We heard screaming," said Neb, "lots of screaming last night. So, when morning come, we come looking."

For the better part of a mile, the land dipped to the east at a gradual slant before it leveled out and the first signs of civilization came into view.

"Does this look like your Lost City?" asked Neb walking into a vast expanse of ruined foundations, knee-high walls, corners of houses and piles of stone that blotted the land as far as could be seen between the trees. The roofs of buildings still standing were caved in or completely missing. In some places all that remained was the outline of a foundation in the ground. If this was the Lost City they sought, it was a disappointment, and Kellyn couldn't keep the sour expression from his face.

"It's not quite a city," said Chandler.

"Ha! That's true, quite," said Neb. To have a look around, Jakes skipped up a stairway ending in rubble after the fourth step. At its base, Ham pressed his toe into a once mighty now sodden plank that lay rotting where it had fallen.

"What are these?" asked Ford, pointing to one of the long gullies crisscrossing the ruins.

"These here," said Neb, "they was canals. They was, but now…" He gestured at the mud and leaves filling them in. A portion of one canal was so full of debris it could be crossed with barely a noticeable step down. "This is home," he continued, pointing to one of the few remaining lodgings, "least it's what we call home for now. It is what it is." It was in fact the best house still standing and that wasn't saying much. Though as long as a barwnig's great hall, little remained of its past glory aside from a wide fireplace with decorative bricks in a bird's eye pattern. The decrepit walls appeared ready to topple at any moment and the roof was nothing more than cloth draped over branches, barely tied down securely enough to keep it from blowing away. Soiled clothes, half-buried blankets, broken tools, empty wineskins, smashed pottery and bottles littered the house inside and out. "That's the shithouse," said Neb pointing through a gap in the wall to a small, round building that had once been a dovecote, but from which a stench of urine and feces now assaulted them even from a dozen yards away. "You go in there. Only in there. If I hadn't set down that law these two'd be shitting wherever they pleased. Wherever, I tell you."

Neb abandoned the tour and flopped down on a log lying across two others to comprise a wobbly bench. "At night you want to use the shithouse even for a piss. Trust me. Especially at night. There's briars just over there," he pointed in the obvious direction one would head in order to relieve themselves, "and you don't want to get your wee pricks pricked, do you?" He laughed and laughed harder when he repeated it.

"Thanks," said Kellyn.

"Fire and food! Food and fire!" said Neb, wiping away spittle from his lip. "Be quick about it!" His two companions looked at him as if they'd been unjustly wounded.

"What about this lot?" asked Jorgi, "They just going to sit round and do nothing?"

"These are guests, you lout. Don't you know how to treat guests? On the other hand, I'm sure our new friends would want to lend a hand."

Kellyn sent the boys off to help. Ford volunteered for woodcutting and wished he'd picked trap duty, because Jakes more than any of them disliked handling mangled and dead animals.

"I'll do it," Ford offered. "I got experience with traps."

"Hear that, Noll?" said Jorgi on the hike into the woods to do their various duties. "Big boy thinks he can do both at the same time. I'd like to see that. Come on," he said to Jakes, "your daddy can't do everything for you."

"It ain't true," was the first thing Noll said to Ford when they were on their own, hacking away at a downed tree. Ford waited, but Noll only ripped away at small branches and rolled the log out of some bushes with his head down and his mouth shut.

"What's not true?"

"What he said," replied Noll jerking his thumb over his shoulder back towards the house. "He's a fucking liar, that Neb. I never shit everywhere wherever I pleased. Born liar. Neb's not even his real name." He grimaced as if swallowing something disagreeable and after that he spoke little. Having had his say, he seemed at peace and became a more pleasant person, perhaps not jovial, but at least bearable and a steady worker, who pulled his own weight. "You spread horse hair?" he inquired when Ford asked what he knew about the area, specially weird glowing things, strange voices on the wind and little magic men.

"Not regular like, but we use to, when we could get it."

"There's your problem. Got to keep up with it, got to keep them happy or there'll be trouble." Noll gave a serious wink and nod and went straight back to work without another word until they were done.

Some of the other boys walked back to the house with armloads of kindling alongside Ford and Noll, who each carried one end of the log and found Ham talking to Neb about the valuables they'd found in the ravine. Kellyn sat by quite annoyed.

"Coins, you say," said Neb, handing Ham another strip of seasoned beef from an opened parcel laid out on the ground beside him. Sacks full of dried meat, bread and grain lay near at hand. "That's a strange place to find coins. Ah, they return."

Ford dropped his log on the ground and straddled it for a seat. Neb pushed the parcel towards him and said, "Help yourselves. We don't have much, a little, not much, but what little we got is yours, brothers." Ford looked from the smiling Neb to the unhappy Kellyn and grabbed a fistful of meat, downing it in painful mouthfuls almost without chewing. It was salty and full of smoky flavor; he couldn't get enough to satiate his hunger and dug into the bag time and again, not noticing Jorgi coming back carrying a pair of squirrels with a downcast Jakes trailing behind.

"So, looks like we got a sheep fucker here," Jorgi said with a mischievous grin while nodding towards Jakes, whose demeanor completely deflated. "I don't hear him denying it. Come on, Sheepfucker, tell us that ain't what you did out there to them poor little lambs whilst no one was looking."

"I was a herder," said Jakes taking a seat with the other boys, "that's all."

"See?" said Jorgi, who'd been itching to hear some juicy tidbit that proved his theory. "What'd I tell you? And why else leave a cushy job like that if but he couldn't keep his wee willy to himself? Poor unfortunate beasts, you dirty little fucker." Jorgi convulsed with a dry, inward giggle more suited to a prepubescent girl than a grown man.

"Lay off him!" said Kellyn standing and facing off with Jorgi.

"It's all right. It's all right," said Neb slipping in between them. "No one blames him. It's the usual story and no one blames you, boy. Herders get lonely and seek comfort, but sooner or later they get caught, don't they? Get caught and course he loses his job, loses it, and the family don't want nothing to do with him. Family and friends all desert him, leave him on his own. Nobody, nothing, and all on his own."

That left the boys in a somewhat stunned, uncomfortable silence and it was fast becoming apparent to them that cruelty was a commodity these men traded well in.

"Does he," said Nebs pointing at Jakes, but speaking to Ham, "spend a lot of time on his own?"

"Yeah."

Kellyn's open palm swung around and connected with the back of Ham's head so fast no one realized what had happened until the boy cried out and rubbed the spot where he'd been smacked. The men fell about laughing and

Ham fought back tears.

"Don't get yours feathers ruffled," said Neb. "Have a bit of this." From a box in a shaded corner he drew forth a bottle half-filled with an amber liquid and passed it to Kellyn. Neb made sure Ham had a sip next, and then from there it went around. Jorgi took a long swig, finishing it off and tossing the bottle over the wall.

The drink may have smoothed over some hard feelings, but Kellyn remained irritated, Ham sulked, and Jakes kept to himself. With Runt still in his shell and Chandler not pleased with their new company, the evening would have been somber indeed if not for Ford and Duff happily conquering their hunger and enjoying another drink with the men. Once they'd had their fill, Neb cleared his throat.

"Now, it's only right," he said with upheld palms balancing invisible weights equally, "only fair since we shared what's ours, now you share yours. Share and share alike."

"What you getting at?" asked Kellyn and Neb's eyes narrowed at him.

"Even if the boy hadn't blabbed, I heard your pockets jingle. That sweet, sweet jingle. Hand it over." Kellyn sought a sign of jest in Neb, but met only a cold sobriety.

"Fuck off!" Every head turned toward Kellyn.

"What you say?" asked Neb.

"You heard me."

"I couldn't o' heard right."

"You say we're brothers and now you want us to pay, what, a tribute?"

"No, no, no," said Neb, trailing into a chuckle, "as brothers we share everything. Everything."

"We haven't even decided we're staying here with you people," said Chandler.

"I'm not so sure you all's invited," said Jorgi turning his sneer on Chandler.

"Don't let's spoil the mood," said Neb, standing and taking a clumsy step toward Kellyn with an outstretched hand. "We can talk about it later, settle up some other time."

Before the sun set fully, Ford went off to relieve himself. A nauseating sight and smell drove him away from the dovecote to a private spot at a distance. On his way back he found a comfortable crook in a tree and, instead of rejoining the rest, decided to linger, giving himself time away from the noise and tension. No sooner had his chin rested upon his chest than he felt the presence of company. His eyelids fluttered open and his head rocked back at the sight of Kellyn and Chandler in close conference over him.

"I don't like this," said Chandler. Kellyn gave a sharp nod. "I think we should get clear of them soon as we can."

"So do I. Tomorrow we'll clear out."

"What are you whispering about over there?" asked Neb wearing a poor imitation of a pleasant grin while he walked between the trees in an arc around them as if he were passing along elsewhere. "Whispering, whispering away."

"Us? We're just fighting over who gets the best bed tonight," said Chandler.

"Come back to the house," Neb hissed. "I've got a treat for you, a sort of surprise. Come on back to the house."

The surprise was a bottle filled with a liquid clear as water, an alcohol more potent and harsh than anything the boys had ever tasted. There was another surprise and one that Ford took to immediately. From a roll, Neb produced a sheet of parchment upon which he sprinkled dried, brown, crumbled leaf from a pouch. Rolling the parchment tight, moistening the end and sealing it, he then lit one end and sucked on the other, inhaling and exhaling the smoke as if he were savoring the most intoxicatingly delicious of flavors. He passed it around the circle after the bottle. It took some time, well after the moon rose along with an intense bonfire, but eventually most of the boys warmed to the new experiences.

"What's wrong with this one?" asked Neb of Runt, who was still mute and refusing to drink or smoke. "He don't speak? Something wrong with him?"

"He'll better drink with, with us," slurred Jorgi between nips from the bottle. He'd taken to spitting half his mouthfuls out in a dribbling spray over the fire until finally holding the lit end of a stick close to his lips and blowing out a long, bursting fireball for the spellbound boys who'd never seen it done before.

"Stop wasting it, you dog! You're spitting more than you're drinking." When the first bottle was finished and another appeared, more was splashed about the house, coating the rubbish strewn so liberally about. Jorgi wrapped his arm around Runt compelling him to go on and have a smoke, but the boy balked after the first inhaled breath. Staggering to a corner, he bent over coughing convulsively and dropped the smoking butt into the refuse which immediately caught fire. The drunken boys and men fell about one another trying to put it out, but Jorgi splashed it with the remainder of the bottle and the blaze flared up and spread to the flimsy cloth roof, incinerating it at an incredible speed.

They stood outside the house, sobering up quickly at the sight of it engulfed in flames. The boys felt terrible about what one of their number had done, but by morning they all felt much worse. Jakes just wanted to be left alone and it didn't seem Chandler would ever stop retching. Ford slept it off and Duff twirled a squirrel-laden stick over the smoldering embers of the house. Neb sat with his head in his hands, not pained so much from the drink as from the sight of his band's former home in smoke floating up through the trees. He tucked in his hands, hiding them close to his body while struggling to roll and light another of his dried-leaf creations with slightly shaking fingers. Soon after he began smoking his nerves calmed with each long, slow exhaled stream of smoke as if he were blowing away all of his cares.

"We ain't been here that long, ain't married to it. Anyway, it's time for a new place. It was getting filthy." He pondered for a moment before continuing. "Maybe it's time to go, I mean, really go. Getting a little hot around here, if you know what I mean? Time to find new territory. I don't know, maybe I'm just talking."

The calming affects smoking had on him continued in a most palpable way. Not only did his hand-tremors taper off, but his sneering grin came easily and he spoke casually about himself and his two comrades at length, freely explaining how some trouble they'd "gotten mixed up with in town" had brought them out here to the ruins.

In a brief moment when Jorgi and Noll were busy and Neb had his back turned, Chandler poked a discreet elbow into Kellyn's ribs.

"Watch it!"

"You said—"

"I know."

"Hush!" said Neb. His sudden insistence startled the boys into a silence that brought to their ears the voices of a whole village reaching out of the forest.

"Who is it?" asked Ham jumping to his feet and immediately sitting as an eerie sensation overcame him. After that, no one spoke. They just stared into the trees. Kellyn looked around for Neb, but he and the other men were nowhere to be seen. Through shoving and manic gestures, he commanded the boys to duck behind walls and trees. Seeing the last of them safely away, he leapt over a jumble of broken jugs and jars, half burying himself in the clutter piled in a ruined corner wall.

A sharp gasp and curse broke out from the briars on the parameter. Annoyed grumbles, thrashing brush and a graceless grunt preceded a scowling, bent-backed man in a farmer's smock blundering forth from the bushes. Driving his pitchfork into the ground, he dug a thorn out of his hand, poked a finger angrily through a new hole in his sleeve, and stole back his hat from the thieving briars.

"Death and demons, your mother's bloody…" his muttering trailed off and he fell back a step at his first sight of the ruins before him. Clutching the pitchfork tight to his chest, the man crept forward amongst the old buildings, taking care not to tread on the broken jugs and jars. A man half his weight could not have tiptoed more delicately than he did in his approach to the ruined corner wall. It took a great deal of courage and time before he peered over the top. A crunch of leaves at a distance sent him into a defensive crouch, where he waited trembling against the wall. Cowering so low, he did not see well off to one side the four horsemen appear through the trees and continue on their way at a steady pace. Other footsteps could be heard in the opposite direction. After what seemed an eternity to the boys hiding all around him, the man with the pitchfork craned his neck for a better look about.

"Keep your head, man," he said, stumbling to his feet and walking right into the burnt-out house. They could hear him sniff the air and prod with his pitchfork in the ashes. Smoke rose from charred wood and he gasped, jumped back and pivoted to the left and right with his weapon outstretched. Cupping a hand around his mouth, he took a deep breath, and then Jorgi had a hand over his mouth from behind and the point of a knife pressed to the side of this head.

"Say nothing!" Jorgi hissed in the man's ear as he dragged him behind a wall, "or this goes through your fucking skull." Neb and Noll pulled him down, secured his arms and the ruins went still once more. The boys peered around walls and peeked from behind trees watching and listening as men and women appeared on foot or riding, all armed and searching the ruins. They kicked over boxes, stabbed into piles of cloth and bushes, and came ever closer. One young, redheaded woman was picking through a coffer filled with wooden hairpins, combs with missing teeth and countless trinkets of little worth.

"These are my cousin Shiona's!" she exclaimed, holding up a pair of shears with initials engraved on one of the blades.

"Bah, most of it's broken junk," exclaimed her companion, tossing a piece of pottery over a partial wall and clipping Chandler's shoulder. "No use to no one no more. Not worth bothering with. I mean look at this place. The damn filthy pigs."

Soon a dozen searchers and then two dozen had gathered together in the vicinity of the smoldering house to pass on information and decide what to do. A farmer on a pony rode up on the side of the partial wall where Chandler crouched examining a shard of pottery with his back turned towards the rider.

"Find something interesting?" asked the farmer. Chandler stood and half turned toward the man.

"It's my cousin's shears," cried the young redhead. "Can you believe it?"

"You don't say," answered the farmer riding closer to her as Chandler faded deeper into the ruins and slipped away unnoticed.

With a plan in place, one half of the searchers rode off to the far end of the ruins while the other half returned the way they'd come. More than an hour passed, during which the boys remained hidden. Ford could hear Runt trying to hold his breath the entire time. When they did finally come out of hiding at Neb's signal, Jorgi and Noll were quick to bind the man they'd caught and all three prodded him with questions.

"Who you with? You with Mellek?" Neb demanded to know. The man searched his questioner's face before shaking his head and replying in the negative. Whether from fear, misunderstanding or simply a dry throat, his hesitation and mute answer irked Neb. It created an unknown and he was a man who freely conjured worst-case scenarios for the unknown.

"He's hiding something," Jorgi said with an accompanying leer and a snarl.

"You're hiding something," lisped out Neb, somewhere between a question and a statement. The man repeatedly claimed not to be, but he couldn't make eye-contact with them or stop squirming. "Then why you out here with them friends o' yours? Why?"

"We," the man coughed and forced out, "hunting."

"Hunting with a pitchfork? Hunting what, wild cows? Wild cows, is it?" Neb turned to the boys gathered around in a tight circle, "He's hunting wild cows!"

"Boar."

"Bull," Jorgi said and lifted up both of the man's hands behind his back level to his shoulders. He cried out and tore away from Jorgi's grip, collapsing in a heap on the ground. Jorgi cackled over him. "That's how you do ones that want to be funny," he explained to Ford and Duff, who stood near at hand, absorbing it all.

Neb walked around considering the matter, weaving this way and that as if moving with his thoughts. "Boar," he said finally, letting the word hang in a pregnant pause. "You sure you wasn't hunting us? Yeah, I think you was hunting us."

"Nay, I swear, we were after boar." The man cried out when a slap caught him by surprise. Neb yanked his hand back, wincing and shaking off the pain.

"String him up! String this bastard up high!" he shouted. Jorgi and Noll each took the man by an arm and dragged him off. "We'll show you we're not messing around."

Neb passed by Ford and gave him a sly wink. Ford felt so assured this was all an act that when the nervous man, whether hunter or seeker, dug his heels into the ground, continued to deny their accusations and refused to go where they were taking him, Ford pushed him in the back and shouted, "Go on!"

"That's right!" cried Neb in delight.

They took the man beyond the ruins to a secluded worshippers' grove, a ring of massive golden maples still growing strong after a thousand years. In their center stood a waist-high altar of rectangular stone blocks decorated with wavy lines and jumping fish, the signs and symbols of Afonyda, the benevolent goddess of rivers. They threw the man to his knees and he leaned his bowed head against the altar repeating his innocence as he waited out a quarter hour's search for a musty rope that was finally dug out from under a mound of mildewed sacking. With his arms folded, Kellyn stood by the other boys sitting outside of the holy ring, watching Ford and Duff help the men hang the rope from one of the lowest branches some thirty feet above the ground. Neb tied a noose and slipped it over the man's head.

"No, no, no! Please!" he begged when they lifted him onto the altar. His legs gave out and he fell to his knees.

"Stand up. Stand up!" Neb shouted at the man, who was clasping his hands in supplication and deaf from fear. Neb commanded the others to pull him up. Jorgi happily directed Ford and Duff on how hold and anchor the rope. It yanked at the man's head, tore at the skin around his neck and obliged him to stand. All slack was pulled out of the rope and the questioning began again. Neb paced before the altar jabbing his accusations at the bound and dangling man, whose unsatisfactory answers were curtailed by a lack of breath and an uncontrollable panic that had him dancing at the end of the rope on his toes. "Now you're making me mad, very mad." Neb spoke with an edge and Ford noticed his flexing fists. The boys looking on, Ford saw, were all downcast, even horrorstruck. What seemed a jolly entertainment to the likes of the giddy Jorgi, was revolting to Ford's friends. He let go of the rope, walked away from the altar and sat with the other boys. The hanging man dropped to his feet and sucked in a long, grateful breath.

"What you do that for? Where you going?" demanded Jorgi.

"Damn it," shouted Neb, "haul up that rope!" Jorgi and Duff strained against the weight. The man gasped, but his feet remained firmly upon the alter. "Weak as old ladies." Neb took Ford's vacated place and with a heave, the rope jerked the man's head up. Choking and sputtering with mucus running from his nose, he struggled to keep even a single toe on the altar.

Ford felt sure these must be his last breaths. Something twitched by his leg; it was Runt, shaking violently in Jakes' arms, shaking as he had done after Cook's death. This was too much. Fast and fluid, Ford ran and leapt onto the altar, wrapping his arms around the hanging man's legs, lifting him, easing the tension of the noose, and slipping as his momentum sent his foot off the edge of the stone. He would have fallen from the altar, but instinctively he gripped hard upon the man's legs and the rope went taut, tightening the noose into a death grip. Ford regained his balance and lifted the man, whose jerking turned to fluttering twitches. Ford wondered if any of the others would ever come to his aid and his legs began trembling under the strain. He looked up and saw that the man had gone purple in the face, and he realized he'd stopped moving. Neb and Jorgi shook their heads and laughed and Duff joined in.

"Oh my, did you see that?" Neb asked the boys while rubbing his belly. "Hard work and a job well done always gives me an appetite."

"This isn't right," said Jakes. He'd long since stopped watching. One of his hands absentmindedly stroked the top of Runt's head. Ford, having dropped to the ground by the altar, found Noll beside him.

"Some get what they get," Noll muttered, never taking his eyes from the hanged man above them, while pulling back the hood bunched around his neck to reveal a rope-burn scar from some years past. "And some get out of it."

"We ain't murderers!" Kellyn hollered, and all eyes fell upon on his every stride straight up to Neb. The two met chest to chest, eyes flaring, mouths blazing. A fight seemed inevitable, but Kellyn broke away before it erupted. "We don't want nothing to do with this! And we don't want nothing to do with you!" He walked off, leaving Neb with a twitching eyelid and a stymied animosity upon his lips.

Duff remained standing in front of the altar, following the slow swinging of the hanged man back and forth, but the other boys caught up with Kellyn on his determined march back into the ruins.

"We're leaving," he said. "We'll grab what we can and get."

The boys were more than ready to go. They didn't want to be with these men any longer than need be. Back at the burnt-out house, they sifted through the rubble and the poor stash of goods that hadn't been lost in the fire. Neb came running back into the ruins.

"Wait, wait!"

"We're leaving," said Kellyn.

"Fine. Fine," said Neb between breaths. "You speak for everyone? For all these boys?"

"They do what I say," said Kellyn. He expected Neb to be angry and try to stop them. At the very least he didn't think Neb would allow them to take from him the food and weapons they'd gathered together so far. However, like the sun breaking through clouds, Neb's entire being softened and he even smiled.

"Fine. Do what you got to do, whatever you think's best. Sign of a good leader, that is. A good leader." It was a strange transformation, an unnatural yet inviting charm. One could see the warmer side of the man, perhaps the reason Jorgi and Noll had taken to following him in the first place. "But wait. Rest a while. Cool down and give it some thought. Think on it." Kellyn had but one thought now.

"Can you spare us what we got here?"

"You're set on going then? Well then, let's see, it's all in such a mess now after what your boy did." Neb glanced over the items they'd scrounged. "Who's to say what's left. Listen, forget all that. The least we can do is give our brothers one last meal before you go. Will you allow us that much?"

Kellyn didn't want to, but had little choice but to agree. The boys needed whatever they could get out of these men before they trekked off into the unforgiving wilderness once more, and if placating this man got them what they needed, he'd play along for a little while longer.

"All right then."

"Fine. That's fine. My boys will take care of that," he said and called to Jorgi and Noll who'd just made it back from the hanging site. "Take these lads and dig up what you can for them. You," he said, turning back to Kellyn, "you come with me. You and I, we'll talk." Kellyn raised his hands to protest. "Please, before you go, give me one more chance. Come and listen." He took Kellyn by the elbow and led him off for a private word along the briars and into the trees beyond.

Jorgi and Noll were quite generous, giving freely whatever they had scavenged about the ruins, filling moldy sacks with waterskins, extra cloaks, a length of rope and various other items, some more useful than others.

"It's small," said Noll handing Ford a whetstone, "but maybe it'll work on your ax."

"Thanks. I'll give it a try."

Sweating and short of breath, Neb raced from the briars in a feverish agitation, a spray of fresh blood speckled one side of his torn shirt. "Hurry up, grab everything. We're getting out." He spoke quick, but his voice was steady, his resolve steadier.

"Why? What happened?" Ford shouted along with the rest of the boys.

"Them from town, they jumped us. I fought them off, but they'll be back. If I know Mellek's men, they'll be back."

Even more panic and questions flew about.

"What do we do?"

"We got to go."

"Where?"

"It don't matter! We got to go!"

"Where's Kellyn?" Chandler had been repeating the question louder and louder until he finally got an answer.

"They got him," Neb said.

"What do you mean?"

"He's dead. They killed him."

CHAPTER 14
FOREST TICKS TO SAND FLEAS

A bliss of green rivers and wild flowers, cool showers and a warm sun, bushy tails on the run and vibrant songs upon the wing accompanied the nine intruders infiltrating the outskirts of a land that didn't want them, a living wood thought to house a god or demon of the earth, a force of the unnatural they came to call the Glowing Devil of the Wood.

"We're going to this Valley of yours. No question," Neb announced when Jakes let it be known that they were traversing the frightening forest they'd been run out of by the supernatural spirit that no one wanted to encounter again. Neb was willing to risk it, but the boys able to rise above a despondent lethargy in the wake of Kellyn's passing balked at the idea. Runt shook his head and had to be carried for a time. At the other end of the spectrum, Ham brightened at the thought of returning to the place he loved, even though Cook's massacre was still fresh in all the boys' minds. Getting closer to Barlow revived Ford's once forlorn hopes of returning his father's ax.

Neb's knowledge of this area didn't extend very far, so he handed over the lead to Jakes. For his troubles, Jakes took the brunt of Neb's wrath hours later upon explaining how he'd led them on a different path than the way the boys had originally come, an arc miles wide around the Glowing Devil's forest.

"Don't be smart with me!" Neb shouted in his face. He turned to Ford, "Where's the damn hole you fell in? That's where I want to go. You tell me where it is now."

"Search me," said Ford truly perplexed by the sudden attack. "What you want to go there for?"

"Don't try that nonsense with me. You're too much the fool to play that kind of fool, boy. I know it's where you all hid your loot. Don't" —both of his hands shot up as if to dam Ford's mouth— "don't try denying it."

But deny it they did, all of the boys. As evidence, Ford even offered up the true story of finding the pale ones of the ravine. This made the other boys smirk. Neb clenched a fist, turned red and released all his tension in a burst of maniacal laughter.

"You got balls to bullshit me to my face like that. Straight face and all, like you believe your own bull. Fine. I'll find it." Neb took off over a hilly land of broken rock, leaving the rest to hurry after.

"Nobody'd stash loot out here for anybody to find!" Jorgi hollered at Neb's back, spreading his arms out to the desolate landscape around them.

"It was all lost," put in Chandler after hurrying to catch them. "I told you that. Even if we did stash it, we wouldn't walk away from it for good."

"Stands to reason," added Noll. They argued about it back and forth until it ended with Neb snapping off a branch, breaking it in half over his knee, hurling the pieces into the forest with a growl and telling Jakes to take the lead again.

"Good!" said Chandler "Get us out of here."

For his own reasons, Jakes wanted to placate Neb by finding the ravine. Being the only recognizable landmark around, it would have headed them in the right direction back to the Valley. Instead, he floundered forward into the unknown. At the edge of a rock ledge on the side of a hill, he stood upon a pile of stones placed there by some past visitor and strained his neck and eyes for a better view.

"I thought the ravine might've been here," he said squinting so hard it looked like a wince, "or over there, but—"

"Sheepfucker's gone and got us lost," Jorgi said for the third time that afternoon. The fleet-footed Jakes said nothing to that; he merely hung his head, leapt from the rock and disappeared below it just as the sun dipped over the horizon.

"Where's he gone off to?" asked Neb, dropping his sack of provisions into Duff's arms and striding ahead of everyone else.

"He does that," said Chandler. "He scouts ahead and then he comes back and tells us which is the best way."

"That's all I need to hear," said Jorgi from the ground, where he tore off his shoes and began rubbing his feet. "I'm staying right here until Sheepfucker gets back."

While they waited, Ford marveled at the casualness with which Chandler took the news of Kellyn's death. Everyone else still reeled from it to some degree, yet Chandler appeared unfazed. He perched alone upon a rock picking twigs and bits of leaves from his pants with an air of utter indifference. Back at the ruins, upon hearing Kellyn was dead, Ford and Duff had immediately made for where they'd last seen him walk off into the woods. Neb had chased them down, yanked Ford back around by the arm and told him, "Don't go that way, unless you want to die." Even now, with the shock of the news subsiding, Ford couldn't be sure if it was a warning or a threat.

They waited, and before they knew it, it was too late in the day to go any further. By morning, Jakes still hadn't returned.

"Fuck it!" said Neb stomping around the camp, knocking over whatever was in his path. "I knew that little shit wouldn't come back. Can't trust nobody. Nobody. Well that's fine. Don't need him. Don't need no one that'd take off and leave his brothers." Ford seriously doubted Neb was fine. His creasing lines of worry deepened when he discovered that none of the remaining boys had the slightest idea how to get to the Valley.

"What do we do?" asked Noll in a quiet voice with his head bowed.

"We keep going that way." Neb pointed his chin in a general, southerly direction.

"We can't leave without Jakes!" said Ford, his voice loud and his eyes locked on Neb's.

"We can and we will. He left you, didn't he? He left us all. You don't understand, boy. People like that, they don't mean shit. You got to learn to do for yourself and your brothers, always, 'cause no one'll do for you and yours. Now get ready. We're going soon as we're ready."

Ford sat back and crossed his arms while the others cleaned and packed.

"Come on," muttered Chandler behind him, "don't cause problems."

"We're not going anywhere," said Ford, "not until we find Jakes."

"He's never gone off all night. Face it, he's left us. You don't expect us to stay out here in the middle of nowhere forever waiting for someone that's not coming back, do you? I'm not, that's for certain. I wasn't made for this. I don't belong out here," Chandler said, with a dismissive flick of his hand at the trees. "I'm a townsman through and through. I never wanted to spend my whole life out in the damn trees with the bugs and the dirt."

"You liked the Valley though," put in Ham.

"That was different," Chandler explained. "We had comforts there. Here what do we have? We don't have anything. So, with or without Jakes, I'm going."

"Go then! I'm staying." Ford turned and spit at Chandler's foot.

"What was that for?"

"You don't care about nobody but yourself. First Cook, then Kellyn gets killed, now Jakes takes off, and you only think about yourself."

"That's not true!" said Chandler on his way around to kneel in front of Ford. "Look, Jakes isn't coming back, and the way they picked on him, do you blame him? I'm not surprised he left."

"Our friends leave or they die, and we keep on going like nothing happened."

"Because, that's how it's always been. People come and go. A little before you joined, this kid we called Wulf took off. He said"—and here Chandler adopted a twangy accent— "*I's off for Mortre Porth!* That's what he called Port Morton. He thought he could do better in the city, I suppose." Chandler went on a while longer, but Ford heard none of it. He was busy coming to terms with the fact that Port Morton might be the same city as Mortre Porth, that place from his father's story about the mysterious woman, the story he'd figured out was really about his mother.

"So Mortre Porth is the same as Port Morton?"

"Yes," said Chandler, a little perturbed by this sudden interruption. "I think it's the old way to say it. Why?" Again, Ford appeared lost in his own thoughts. "Look, if you're going to ignore me, I'll gladly return the favor."

"Why didn't he just say my mother went to Port Morton?"

"Arswyd the unholy terror, it's a mystery to me what you're even on about." Not hearing what he said, but catching the exasperation in Chandler's tone, Ford tried to appear more attentive. "Look now, Jakes was great. I'll miss him as much as anyone. I miss Cook and even Smith in a way. Kellyn," he added with a shrug, "I'm sorry what happened to him."

After that, they wandered at random with Neb guiding them and though he did not know the way, luck proved to be on his side when they encountered few of the rivers, swamps and rugged hills that had troubled the boys' northward passage. Instead, they blundered into outlying settlements, pockets of fringe civilization similar to Barlow in their insignificance, poor farmers scraping a living from the earth, risking their family's safety by taking up on the edge of the wilderness where the living was cheap but dangerous.

A lone Rover spotted them skirting a field from a half mile's distance and, upon seeing their number, veered away in the opposite direction as if he had meant all along to check on the broken wheel left to rot in the tall grass by a pond. Neb drove his band back into the woods and along a natural hedge sufficiently tall and thick enough to mask their movements. Beyond the Rover's range, they happened upon a crimson carpet of late strawberries that supplemented dried meat for their day's meal.

"Don't eat it all. It won't last forever," Neb said, ripping into a tough piece from a bag he held to his body. He'd spoken almost directly to the youngest and smallest, making Ham and Runt shy away and nibble mouse-like. Even the somewhat undersized Chandler felt uncomfortable. "Too many, too, too many of you. Maybe that sheep fucker was on to something. Maybe it's time to lighten the load."

Ford was happy to see Ham no longer shunning Runt, but Neb's hints and matter of fact weariness worried him. He worried, because he now understood that he didn't want to see his little family torn asunder. Each exit, Smith then Cook, Kellyn and finally Jakes, evoked the same kind of wrenching pain that had dug at his innards the day he discovered Gwen had died.

"We got useless weight here, too damn useless!" Neb went on, chewing his words with the same vigor as the stringy mass in his jowls.

The boys were the only family Ford had left and he was responsible for them. Tough as he was, Duff certainly couldn't be trusted to look after them. After Kellyn's death, Duff had stumbled after the group in a daze, lost without the welcome yoke that steered his life's direction. But when Neb jerked the proverbial reins, Duff came alive and followed this new master with a happy, quickening step. With Kellyn gone, Duff's shifting allegiance and the loss of Jakes, Neb had all the command he needed to jettison any one of them at will.

"Chandler's as smart as they come," Ford found himself saying in a sudden outburst that was a surprise to himself and a curiosity to everyone else. Chandler took a long, hard look at him, trying to figure out what he could be thinking now. "And Ham, he can fish a hole clean. Runt, he...he...." The youngest boys couldn't have been more grateful for Ford's loving praise until he floundered over Runt's accomplishments, trailed off and Jorgi's unnaturally boyish mocking giggle filled the air and dampened their hearts.

"What a sweetheart," began Neb, but Ford cut him off.

"Runt stopped a whole caravan on the road. Tricked them better than anybody could've. He's a sneaky one." Ford found little Runt's face fixed upon his with a sort of reverence. "And if you throw him out, I'm going too." The words were out of his mouth before he realized what they meant. If he was thrown out, he'd be separated from the very people he intended to keep together. The dark cast over Neb's features and the way he turned his back on them and walked away for a while had Ford so convinced he was about to be tossed out of the band that he began gathering his things to leave.

"That's right," said Neb, coming back, "get yourself ready. You're heading out. If you want to keep your happy little family together, you got work to do."

Ford was picking up the ax and throwing an old musty blanket containing his few possessions over one shoulder when what Neb said finally sank in.

"What do you mean?"

"You stock the larder and we'll keep the kids," Neb explained and later that night Ford found himself flat on his belly creeping from the edge of a field to a barn near the top of a sloped field. Though the house below was dark and no movement or sound came from within, he kept himself shielded by the barn until the moment he dashed through the door. Marble-white eyes rolled as the cows within huffed and struggled to get up. Ford slid a foot forward with his arms raised out to the dark. Something coiled hanging from the rafters brushed his head and he ducked. A rope, he realized. The cows pressed against the walls. He felt for them, passing his hand along the warm, heaving flank of one and seeing a flash of blinding light when another kicked him in the shin. The pain was enough to make him quit, but so much was hanging on his success that he rubbed at his shin and plunged in amongst the beasts again. His perseverance paid off when a calf, more daring than its elders, nuzzled his hand. With much fumbling about and arm waving, Ford found the hanging coil of rope, slipped a noose around the calf's neck and led it out just as if he'd done it a hundred times before. The smile creeping up his face vanished when the cows in the barn followed him out and trailed right behind him with snorting heads lowered. The temptation of a handful of grass led the calf only so far, and pulling on the rope dragged it further, but it had to be carried the final few feet with the cows' thumping hoofs and grunts at his back before Ford was able to heave the calf over a stone wall to the waiting arms of the others.

They led the calf deep into the woods, slit its throat and the next day roasted it in pieces over a fire. Much of the meat was still raw when they ate it, and little time was spent dallying afterwards, just enough for Neb to have a smoke. After returning from a stint on lookout duty, Ford stood before him, gnawing on scraps.

"I've done my part," he said between ravenous bites.

"Calm down. Calm yourself down. Have a smoke." A much more relaxed Neb let a long, satisfied sigh trail after the smoke drifting away from his lips. "I give no guarantees, but they're safe for now." He gave a small nod at the smallest boys. "They're yours now and after a time you'll mayhap find the burden too heavy, but it's your burden, all yours, my friend."

It was the best Ford could do for them. The boys could stay, but even so, Ham reverted to his quieter ways. Chandler remained aloof, as if none of this had anything to do with him. Runt obviously felt every bit of his tenuous situation, and without Jakes, he seemed particularly lost. Even on a warm night like the previous one, he shivered himself to sleep.

On the following day and the next, village after village fell into their way and nothing looked familiar to any of them.

"You recognize this place?" Neb would ask them each and every time. As if they could will the foreign land into an old friend, they would squint harder at a cluster of houses or along a stretch of field bisected by orderly stone walls. This was supposed to be the boys' territory, argued Neb, and they should know it by sight.

"None of you seen this before?" he asked of a random mill. "Not one of you?"

"It looks like a mill," Chandler said. None one else answered.

"Damn it and damn you, you worthless sons of bitches! Worthless whores' sons, every one of you!" His cursing streak continued with him down to the village beyond the mill and returned with him an hour later.

"What you find out?" asked Jorgi like an eager dog about to be fed.

"It's as miserable a place as all the rest. Not worth the wood it's made of." Neb took back his bag of personal possessions from Duff, not a single item within touched. "Every last one of them is poor as a pauper. But I got some value out o' the place."

"What you nab?" asked Jorgi.

"Didn't I just get done saying they got nothing? Shut up one time and let a man say what he's got to say. Listen now. Them bumpkins down there say a port town's not far south o' here. Big town. Lots o' trade."

"I knew I could smell salt," said Chandler cracking his biggest, truest smile since Ford could remember. "I'm going to eat a belly full of crab and then eat some more." His excitement infected the others, even the men.

"I bet they got some of that tasty hadas from over the water," said Neb, licking his lips at the thought of the astringent foreign wine.

"I bet they got some of them tasty clams down there, too. Dock girls is the best kind," said Jorgi with a lecherous smile that made his meaning clear enough even to the boys of pure mind.

Since Ford had never seen the sea before, his anticipation swelled when the forest dissolved into scrub and sandy ground. The boys quickened their pace along a pebbly path crowded with seaside bushes and raced up to the crest of a sand dune, where they stopped almost as one, shoulder to shoulder, panting and sweating under an unrelenting sun, none daring to move an inch closer to the undulating leviathan of water before them. None backed away either, such was the dazzling enthrallment of the twinkle of light playing upon its surface.

"It shines so bright!" said Ford with his mouth falling open. "It's like the ground is moving!"

"What's that white junk?" asked Duff.

"Waves," said Chandler. "They churn up the water like foam on a beer."

"Can you drink it?" Duff leaned forward with hope and desire.

"Sure can," Jorgi said laughing. Ford looked to Chandler and Chandler shook his head.

"It's too big to take all in," said Ford, shielding his eyes from the sun's glare.

"Is it going to fall?" asked Ham with frightened eyes glued to the blue-green mass below them, which oddly seemed to rise above them.

"Is it what?" asked Chandler.

"Fall. It looks like it's going to fall over."

"No. A little bit falls over on to the sand down there, but that's it."

Below them the land dropped steadily away. With nothing but water stretching off to the endless horizon, it gave the sensation of a world on tilt.

"I feel dizzy," said Ham and Chandler nodded.

"I guess it is like looking down from a tree and feeling like you're going to fall, but fall forever and ever."

Each flurry of steps and skips closer expanded the blue vista, until at last the land met the sea in a slurry of rocks, weed, churning mud and water. They flipped over the clumps of seaweed, collected shells, laughed when a tiny crab clamped onto Ford's finger and laughed all the harder when Duff tried drinking the salt water.

"Enough fooling around," said Neb, forcing their attention back to business, to the town of Dror Bae within sight two miles away along the coast. Between breaths on the hard climb back up the bluffs overlooking the sea, he said, "Let's have us a good long look and see what these fishermen have to offer."

The town coated the inner rim of the bay with houses built like rows of stacked boxes upon the hill down to the water and along a thin, curving peninsula. Weather-beaten shacks perching upon stilts or left to tumble into the sea dotted the shore. Narrow, single-plank docks reaching out like arthritic fingers rocked with the push and pull of the waves, yet the townsfolk traversed these rickety structures with sure-footed confidence.

The boys took careful steps over huge boulders, broken rock, and slippery stones covered in torn netting, frayed rope and battered wood fragments; a huge mass of wreckage decorated the shore with the grace of a seaman's hand. They picked their way back down to the water where boats that had seen better days covered the few available yards of pebbly beach. The rotting frame of a partially submerged, capsized vessel arced out of the shallows like the stripped ribs of a whale carcass. A man scraping the barnacles off the bottom of his boat with a monotonous back-and-forth grinding clapped a mistrusting eye upon them until they passed. Near to shore, fishermen cast weighted nets, while others in wide-brimmed hats mended theirs. Next to crouching figures with flashing knives, butterflied and filleted fish lay on rocks or spread out on sheets. More hung from lines tied post to post. Boys and girls toted poles strung with flatfish towards the town. Small, white fish filled baskets minded by children, whose curiosity for the strangers earned them loud reprimands across the beach from their parents until their tiny, brown hands resumed swishing away at the flies and encroaching birds.

Such a large group of idle boys and men stood out and drew looks from all. It had been simplicity itself to fool the farmers of the inland villages with lines like "We seek work in the fishing trade," and "Ship's crew heading for the coast," but now that they were among fishermen and the shipping trade, a new alibi was needed. So far, Neb had none.

"This place stinks," said Jorgi holding a hand over his nose.

"Those fucking birds!" Neb shouted at the circling gulls. "I can't hear myself think!"

Upon a massive ledge of rock at the foot of the town's sturdiest, longest dock stood a thirty-foot tower topped with a bell and brazier. It created a clear divide between where the fishermen's beach ended and the town began. Under the tower flowed a steady stream of men and women, many in tattered foreigners' clothes, hauling cargo from longboats working back and forth from a ship anchored out in the bay.

"We're getting the eye from the boss," Noll muttered and nodded to a paunchy man wearing a small fancy hat and a tightly buttoned-up coat, neither of which made him particularly comfortable under the sun. As foreman of the dock, he felt that upholding an appearance of dignity while pacing the planks was more important than comfort.

Neb signaled the boys to keep their heads down and move on.

"What are you all doing?" asked the foreman, pointing the end of a roll of papers at them.

"We've got trade," said Neb indicating the sack on his back and what the others carried. "We're off to market."

"All of ye?"

"Yeah, what of it?"

"I could use a couple two hands is all."

"Oh, that's fine then. Yes sir, I could spare as many of my boys as you need."

"Two'll do."

Neb happily dispatched Ford and Duff to the loading and unloading of barrels of whale oil and boxes that smelled of springtime and cut, dried grass if one put his nose to the cracks and breathed in deep, as Ford often did. For hours they trudged back and forth, while Runt sat out of the way on the dock between two barrels watching Ford until the work was finished. Once released and paid for their labor, the three boys entered the town in search of the others.

Most of Dror Bae's trade took place on one street running parallel to the shoreline. The less reputable taverns and the town's few brothels filled the side streets, above and behind tradesmen's shops or down the slick lanes to the water. The weathered buildings and faded hanging signs spoke falsely of the town's prosperity. The occasional new cloth awning and a steady flow of custom told a truer tale. Never a rich town, neither was Dror Bae infested with beggars, at least not above the norm for a town with so many craftsmen, merchants and shopkeepers.

Ford took a look inside The Cracked Scull and found sailors at leisure sitting elbow to elbow with town servants sneaking a quick one. It was in just such a place that he expected to find Neb and the others, and eventually they did find all but Noll at The Rusty Hoop, making mugs of weak ale last for the free bread brought out by the landlord now and then for paying drinkers. They shoved in together on the benches and reached for the bread, but Neb pulled it away.

"Hand it over first," he said and they laid their newly earned coins in his palm. Ford grumbled and took his time about it, but paid up. "What was that?"

"We get stuck doing all the hard work while you all have a good time."

"Watch it boy," said Jorgi. "Your lips flap too free."

"We've been working hard, maybe harder," said Neb laying a hand on Jorgi's shoulder.

"Looks like it," said Ford with a sniff and an eye on their mugs.

"You little shit!"

Neb pulled Jorgi back into his seat and lowered his voice, "We been working our eyes and ears, seeing what's on offer here."

The tavern grew fuller and noisier the more the day darkened. The scant news of the bay was passed about, tall tales were told of impossibly large fish caught and inevitably lost; at last someone even sang a song and others joined in.

"Neb's been showing us tricks," Ham told Ford when little could be heard above what the nearest neighbor said in one's ear. "That's how we paid for all this." He stuffed bread in his mouth and washed the dry stuff down. Neb sensed the nature of their conspiratorial conversation and slid along the bench toward them.

"Look, you done good work today," he said to Ford and nodded at Duff. "We needed a cover and you did what had to be done. To show my appreciation, I'll make it up to you, show you the ropes, as the sailors say." To Ford's surprise, right then and there he began by going over the basics of pickpocketing, some of which they'd already learned from Kellyn. "Oh, smart fellows, are you? Well then, you'll have heard of the press?" They hadn't, so he obliged them with a lesson and was getting into the finer points of lifting without detection when the door opened and in walked four men in leather jerkins branded with a barwnig's mark. Four mugs were conjured and placed in their hands as if the barman had expected them at that very moment. They looked around the room, disappointed at not seeing any empty seats.

"Ah fuck," said Jorgi with a few rapid taps on the table.

"I see, I see," said Neb. "Come on, let's go. This place just got too crowded, too crowded for us." And in a honeyed voice he added while passing the newcomers, "Sirs, my boys and I are leaving. Please." He waved the newcomers to the table they had just vacated.

During their walk up and down the length of Dror Bae in search of a spot to sleep that night, they saw that all the shops were closed or closing. Traveling as one, with Noll slipping into the group almost unnoticed, they might have drawn attention upon the emptying street if the townspeople hadn't already withdrawn into their homes. The lingering odors of home-cooked meals floated across their path and mingled with a misty fog until both were carried off upon a chilling wind blowing in from the sea. Only the waves and occasional laughter erupting from a tavern broke the relative quiet.

Halfway along the lane that traversed the length of the peninsula, they spotted a hooded figure wrapped in a cloak trying the door-handle of a shuttered shop. The door rattled but held, and the figure went on to the next door with a faint lantern dangling from one hand.

"Night watchman," remarked Neb when they'd passed beyond the lane and out of earshot. "That's good to know. Something to remember." He turned to the boys. "Know what you're up against before you try your luck."

Before the town completely dissolved into dilapidated fishermen's huts and a field of frayed tents housing whole families locked in their poverty, they came upon a house set amongst rocks like a nesting bird with too many eggs. The fading words "Pit Jist Spat" scrawled above the door wouldn't have meant anything to them if they could have seen them, but they understood well enough the jug hanging from the eaves. The inn's faded and cracked boards, its broken shutters, and the general disrepair of its exterior mirrored the squalor within. The narrow common room had a gaping hole in the roof and a sticky floor littered by toppled mugs and fragments of crockery swept under tables topped with a layer of grime.

In this damp room with mold in the dark corners, a ship's drunken crew hogged the space in front of the fire. Clustered in the far corner, a family of four threw timid glances from the sailors to the door when Neb and the others entered. They dressed in clothes lighter than the region's norm and their naturally dark-lidded eyes looked heavily made up. They were known as Amita, a southern people, the likes of which Ford had seen at Lewiston in the past and earlier that day upon the dock. The sailors grumbled when a wind blew through the open door and the family certainly weren't happy to see newcomers crowding into a room already cramped for space. Neb and his band noticed little of this, being absorbed in the peculiarity of the inn's odd tables and bench seating, all built low to the ground as if for children. Instead of a barrel, its diminutive cousin the firkin was tapped and placed upon a bar no more than a foot off the ground and made of a plank set upon two rocks. At the end of this bar perched a bald boy of indeterminate age swaying back and forth. When they entered the place, his swaying turned into a sharp rocking that grew quicker as more people packed in.

"Is there room?" Neb asked him and he smiled, his roaming eye rolling back to show the white, while his good eye shied away to a vacant corner. Laughter broke out at the sailors' table.

"You got anything to drink?" asked Jorgi. "Beer, anything?" The bald boy giggled, hid his face in one hand and rang a little bell at his side.

"Who runs this place?" asked Neb. "Where's the landlord?" He looked toward the family, but they faced inward to one another, presenting a defensive circle around their possessions.

"He's coming," said one of the sailors and they all fell to laughing once again.

"Something's real funny," said Noll as he, Neb, Jorgi and Duff crowded on to the only remaining bench. Ford breathed in and out a slow, calming sigh as the division within the group tested his patience.

"Prok? Prok?" came snippy from the same doorway through which spread scents of fish stew, setting off a groaning chorus from the boys' stomachs. From the doorway emerged, what Ford took to be half a man carrying a pot in his cloth-wrapped hands, struggling with its weight partly because it was full and partly because he held it away from the apron over his bright white clothes. His large head, round features, and expansive eyebrows should have adorned a man twice his size. He placed the pot on the bar and threw down the cloth, revealing fingers so stumpy that Ford wondered if they lacked knuckles.

"Is it a dwarf?" asked Ham in a whisper behind his hand.

"It's a nightmare is what it is, a Sever Man," said Jorgi, referring to the common nightmares brought on by those cautionary tales used by parents for generations across the land to get their troublesome children to behave. "Trouble me again and the Sever Man will come take you away tonight," Milda would threaten young Ford. In truth, it wasn't the Sever Man of the Severn people, but rather their cousin the Skala, raiders and slave traders of women and children. The Skala hadn't come raiding this far west in ages, but that didn't stop mothers and fathers from perpetuating the legend. It was too handy a tool to neglect. In any case, this short man before them was a Kamen and only loosely related to the nightmare.

"Vy? Vy for de bell?" he demanded of the bald boy, whose rapid nod targeted Neb. "I hear! I know dis. Get for eat." He jerked an elbow at the doorway. The bald boy hopped off the bar and ran into the back room, returning almost instantly with an armload of bowls that were grabbed up by the family and sailors converging upon the pot like pigs on a trough filled with slop. With the meal served out and everyone else attended, the short man turned back to Neb's band.

"Viktor is me. Velcome my inn!" said Viktor the innkeeper, smiling at them all and curling and uncurling his fingers in a sign of welcome commonly used in his homeland. "Vaht for you I do?"

"Some place to sleep and something to eat," said Neb. Viktor now looked them over more closely and was not pleased with their appearance.

"Vaht you do?" he asked.

"We're traveling tradesmen," said Neb pointing out the old dirty sacks with them.

"Vaht you heff? For sell, vaht?"

"Little of this, little of that." Neb was elusive, Viktor was persistent and Ford feared they would get no dinner as he watched the fish stew draining fast with every ladled bowl. "Weapons," said Neb, showing his knife. "We trade in weapons, among other things." Viktor, however, appeared unimpressed by the plain knife. "The rest of you, come on, let's have them." Noll and Jorgi placed their weapons upon the bench nearest them and the boys followed suit. Viktor looked them over, nodded and a deal was struck for accommodations and a meal. Whether or not they were weapons merchants didn't matter to the innkeeper. While not overly particular about whose money he took, Viktor did prefer his guests weaponless.

"I don't want to," said Ford gripping his ax tight.

"Fine!" said Neb. "Go hungry and sleep outside. Your choice. But everyone that wants to stay and eat has to pay up."

"We'll get them back," asked Ford, his powerful hunger ruling his will.

"Of course!" said Neb, and with that everyone was soon fed and content. Content that is, until the firkin ran dry and a brief fight broke out with the sailors, because Jorgi intentionally guzzled the last of the ale.

"Anudder tomorrow! Anudder vun tomorrow!" promised Viktor, and with the patrons once again calmed, the sailors claimed the benches by the fire, the family cowered in their corner and Neb's band made do with the remaining space. Aside from Runt tossing, turning and crying out from Glowing Devil nightmares, most of the others slept soundly. Ford was an exception. He lay awake pondering how he'd get the pawned ax back. Then thoughts of his own mother came unbidden as he watched the family barely illuminated by the flickering hearth fire; he contemplated the exhausted woman with her arms draped over her children even as she kept watch over a chest containing the family's worldly possessions without the protection of a lock.

In the morning the boys woke up itching. Red bite marks dotted their bodies.

"Marvelous," said Chandler. "Looks like we've exchanged ticks for sand fleas."

"You boys stop messing about and go out and do your thing, that thing you boys do," said Neb referring obliquely to Chandler's idea to play the street waif. Ford followed the smaller boys to the door. "Where you going?"

"With them," replied Ford.

"Look at yourself." Neb lowered his voice and checked to make sure the room was clear of the other patrons and the innkeeper. "You're too damn big for them games. No one'll believe you're a kid. Stick with me today and I'll show you a thing or two. I said I'd show you something."

Neb dove back into the topic of better pickpocketing methods for the benefit of Ford and Duff, this time with practice. Their attempts upon his own pockets proved so clumsy that he turned the focus to distractions. "You remember I told you about the press? Right well, a good bump, a good solid shake rattles them. They don't know what's up, and when you work with a buddy, it lets the other guy go to work. One bumps, the other grabs. You don't even need clever hands for that. Not very clever anyways."

As soon as Neb had finished, Ford rushed out the door and down the road back to the market. Seeing this newfound knowledge as the best and quickest way to buy back his ax, he sought the crowds and a likely target, but neither was to be found. The morning had moved on, and with it the people.

"Slow down!" said Neb coming up and putting an arm around Ford's shoulder. With Duff dallying behind, they strolled between a smithy and a shop that traded in spices.

"We're too late. Everyone's gone," said Ford, his last words punctuated by the tower bell tolling into the fog upon the bay.

"Don't worry, don't you worry. We'll find something. Something or other will…look at me." Ford saw Neb's eyes dart over the road to Noll and Jorgi as they stood close on either side of a young man in clothes plain, yet clean and new, examining the hanging fowl, leg of mutton and side of beef through a butcher's window. Ford took him for some nobleman's servant, probably the local barwnig's. Noll pressed in, spoke to the servant and blocked the view of Jorgi's hand reaching around from the other side to slip a pouch from the man's belt. A smiling fishmonger pulled his cart to rest behind the servant to entice him with his spread of the morning's catch. Louder than Ford had yet heard him, Noll said, "Ho, look at that!" as if surprised to see fish in a town like this. Jorgi was already gone by the time the servant leaned his nose out over the cart. Noll took off around the nearest corner.

"You see that? You got to learn to use your voice like that," said Neb pulling Ford into a lane and behind a tavern, where he caught Jorgi on his way in the back door. "Hand it over!"

"Fuck yourself!" Jorgi said and let slip a tiny yelp when Neb whipped his knife up to his chin. "Aw, have a heart, my old friend," he begged with a child's pout. Neb snatched away the pouch and stashed his knife.

"You'll get your share."

"Give us a little something now, to wet our whistle."

Neb dug out three of the smallest coins, repeated their number and value to himself and handed them over. Jorgi grabbed them and disappeared through the door.

"Not so much as a thanks," said Neb walking on, "and after all I do. No thanks."

"Your knife, how'd you get it back?" asked Ford. Duff stared up at the glaringly white sky until his eyes watered and was oblivious to what they were talking about.

"Oh that? Never really gave it to old Viktor. Nay, grabbed it back before he made off with our gear."

"He never noticed?"

"Suppose not. And neither did you. You got to be more, what's the word? More…you got to use your eyes better, is what. Now where were we? Voice. You got to use your voice. You got a plenty big one if you'd only use it, like how Noll did back there. A good, loud shout in the ear can work real good. Scares them but good. Scares the piss out of them," he laughed, "but the main thing is they can't hear nothing." Neb looked Ford up and down. "Speak up. You're too old and too big to be acting like a boy anymore. Now come on. We can't all three be hanging around here with this, waiting for the wrong people to come along." He tucked the pouch into his pants on their way back to the main road.

From ahead leapt the acrobatic notes of an energetic piper on the corner of the busiest intersection. A group gathered around him with a scrubbed clean Chandler amongst them, almost unrecognizable in a new, white tunic and spotless breeches. For all his zeal, the piper played a repetitious melody that threatened to drive away his audience if not for Chandler, who clapped along, creating a rhythm out of the pattern. His broad smile and enthusiasm encouraged the others to join in and soon he had all the young women reeling about in a frolicsome dance.

"What in all the world is your damned friend up to?" Neb demanded in dazed bemusement, but got no reply.

The music, the success of Noll and Jorgi and even Neb's backhanded encouragement all bolstered Ford's confidence and his eagerness was bubbling over at the sight of an old man leaning on a stick beside the bell tower. Ford guessed that the bulge in his pants, the result of a drooping stomach roped off mid-belly, must be from a purse filled with coins.

"Follow me," he said to Duff, and gave some brief instruction on the way to the tower. Before Neb could stop them, the boys were on either side of the old man. Ford bumped him into Duff, Duff bumped him back, and Ford bellowed in his ear, "Hello!" The old man tottered about holding one hand over his ear while beating Ford and Duff with his stick. Neither came away with anything but the beating.

"You're not very smart, are you?" said Neb down on the beach by the boats soon after. "That weren't no mark. You even know what's a mark?" Ford and Duff were too shocked and breathing too hard to reply. Neb wouldn't have waited for an answer anyhow. He dove into a tiresome explanation, which only confused Duff and bore Ford. "Oh, it's useless. Both of you are useless! Go see if you can get more work on the dock or take a leap off the end."

That night, Viktor's inn had a different crowd. Gone was the foreign family, and drunken sailors from another vessel took up residence by the fire. The bald boy perched upon the bench as before and the innkeeper sat in the common room talking to a friend, the piper they'd seen that morning. Neb's band kept their backs to the room and pretended to play chuck-a-coin, while turning out their pockets and discovering they'd made next to nothing beyond Noll and Jorgi's one success, most of which they had already drunk away.

"This town is dry," said Neb, rapping his knuckles too hard on the bench and shaking off the pain with a curse. Nothing pleased Neb that night and with nothing to smoke, he grew more irritable.

"Maybe," Noll said and thought a moment longer before moving in closer, "maybe that spice man's got something hidden away."

"Maybe? Maybe? Well maybe you should check instead of giving me nothing but your maybes," said Neb catching Noll with a spray of spittle. Ham, Runt and Ford stopped tossing their wooden coin at the wall and watched without appearing to watch. Noll got up and walked out.

"No women," said Jorgi, "and no drink." Viktor's supply had run out again. "What a rotten town this is."

"Tomorrow you all better do a lot better than this," said Neb, "or there'll be trouble. There'll be changes tomorrow if it don't look up."

Early the next morning, as Neb instructed, Ford waited by the dock, leaning against the bell tower with Duff and a few other of the town's poor looking for work. Carts of fish and shellfish went by, the menders bent over their nets, the foreman of the dock turned away scores of people because no ship had come in. The sun rose, the fog burned off and the heat drove Ford to ladle water from a barrel placed there for fishermen and dockworkers alike. Soon he had to relieve himself.

Hurrying back through the market, he turned on to a side road and, feeling the urge press in on him, slunk into a back lane and around the first building, a two-story house with a shop on the ground floor and living quarters above. It belonged to a weaver who made the heavy wool sweaters the fishermen wore out to sea. The weaver would likely be working, but the windows facing Ford were shuttered. So urgent was his need, Ford wouldn't have cared if the weaver was watching. He lowered his pants, shuffled closer to a tall bush growing from the base of the house and let loose a blissful release that not even a girlish giggle from the other side of the bush could stop.

"What are you doing?" hollered Chandler as he and an older girl he'd been dancing with the day before peered over the bush at him. She found the scene much more amusing than either of the boys and giggled again when Ford jerked away and sprayed the side of the building.

"I...," started Ford, but he really had nothing to say beyond the obvious.

"This is her parents' shop!" shouted Chandler. The girl took off around the far corner. He let out an exasperated gasp and chased after her. Ford thought he understood now why Chandler had come back to the inn so late the night before and why he had been in such a better mood than all the rest.

While Ford was tying up his pants, a quick-footed and wiry shellfish-monger's daughter, who'd been "almost eight" for months now, appeared a ways off along the back lane, stopping door to door to drop off pots and sacks of crabs at certain houses and shops along her usual route. "Pot here!" or "Crab!" would ring out shrilly, the door would open and the crab would disappear. Most were gone immediately and eventually all but one sack vanished within the long line of houses.

Ford followed behind the crabber's daughter, who sprinted ahead and doubled back at the end of the lane, knocking on the door with the remaining sack and calling out once more, before returning to her loose-wheeled barrow. Ford dragged his feet. His palms grew sweaty and his fingernails picked at one another without his noticing. He hovered by the door with the lone remaining sack. The girl scooped up more pots and sacks and was off in the opposite direction. More calling out, more doors opening and closing, and the breath whipped through Ford's nose, whistling so sharply that he clapped a hand over it. Back and forth his head turned, looking up and down the street. He couldn't be sure no one was looking when he reached out for the sack at his feet. A creak of words from behind the door remained a mystery to the monstrous and lopsided boy thumping away with the sack shoved under his shirt, wincing from the pricks the points on the crabs' hard shells inflicted.

Ford made straight for Viktor's, but the conspicuous lump under his clothes worried him and blending into the crowd was impossible with the street being nearly empty. So, he darted into a lane and out to the backlands, where blueberry-pickers bent over the low bushes in open fields. The harvest was being gathered by those poor from the tent village east of town. They viewed Ford with mild curiosity as he hustled along the footpaths, but asked him nothing and made no comment.

"Vunderfool!" Viktor exclaimed when Ford burst into the empty inn and showed the innkeeper the small green crabs. He rubbed his belly and hummed with pleasure. "I make stew. You eat good, tonight, very good."

"I want my ax back." If Viktor understood him, Ford couldn't tell. The man merely gaped at him. He did his best to make himself clear. When Viktor's reply came, it took a long while before Ford understood. "You mean you sold it?"

"Yes. To pay," Viktor waved around at the inn, showing the luxuries he'd provided them, "For you friends to sleep, to eat."

Oblivious to all else and with a manner the locals were becoming accustomed to, Ford marched straight to the shop of Gof, the blacksmith to whom Viktor had sold their weapons.

"You got my ax. I want it back."

The husky blacksmith and his somewhat starved assistant kept on working and left Ford standing there looking about the room, large and nearly empty, only containing what they needed to work and what they were working on. When Gof put down his hammer and finally acknowledged him, Ford explained that he was after what Viktor had traded in. The blacksmith went to a room behind a door at the back and emerged with the ax.

"This it?"

"Yes. He gave it away, but he shouldn't have," said Ford with outstretched hands.

The blacksmith appraised the ax and said, "It's twenty-five of the Harans' copper."

"I don't have that." The smith headed for the back door. "Wait. It's my father's. I have to get it back to him."

The blacksmith appraised Ford and said, "One solid silver and that's the least I can take."

"I don't have it."

"Then you have no business here."

The blacksmith returned the ax to the back room, locked the door and went back to work. Ford's body sagged with his whole spirit, but his heavy feet stayed glued to the floor. His gaze followed the smith's motions and fell upon the weighty chain being fashioned.

"Stop gawking and get on with you!" commanded the smith and Ford sprang to life, grasping about his body, feeling about his own arm, frantically seeking but finding nothing under his shirt. He fished up his sleeve until, frustrated, he tore the shirt off entirely and checked both of his arms. The necklace he'd found in the ravine and wrapped around his upper arm was no longer there. He searched the ground, he checked his shirt and was looking down his pants when the smith and his assistant bodily removed him from the shop and threw him into the road.

"Stay clear of my shop, you Odd Jonson!"

Ford left the smithy amid laughter and astonished faces, heading towards the fishermen's beach for no other reason than to get away. A team of workers stacking long wooden boxes at the head of the stairway down to the beach made him veer away along the dock, where he stopped midway upon catching sight of Ham and Runt climbing among the rocks far beyond the fishermen. A push from Duff followed by a hoot of laughter carried Ford off the dock and down on to the gravel-strewn beach some yards below. It wasn't a pleasant landing, but he'd felt worse and, lying there on his side thinking how this had not been his best day, he knew at the very least that nothing was broken.

"Are you alive?" came the voice of the foreman of the dock from above.

"I think so," Ford replied. "Do you have any work?"

"No."

The waves rolled in, soaking his legs, but he didn't care. He wondered where he'd lost the necklace, gave that up and pondered ways to get the ax back. All of this was Neb's fault. He should be the one to get it back, but Ford figured Neb's solution would be to make him work on the dock. He pulled himself up on to a rock and dried out in the sun.

Back upon the main road, he found the market quiet in the midday. Even the piper sat resting against a wall with his instrument upon his legs. A frail old woman selling unappetizing green apples napped on the back of her cart with her leathery, red-brown legs swinging in a breeze that occasionally blew her skirt up.

Ford leaned against the building behind the apple cart to get out of the sun and closed his eyes. For almost an hour, he rested, felt the rumbling in his stomach grow and watched the blacksmith work from a distance. His ax was in the room at the back of the shop and somehow he was going to get it.

The blacksmith's assistant pointed a finger at him and said something to get his boss's attention. Only then did Ford realize he'd been glaring at the men in the shop with a penetrating ferocity. He lowered his eyes, feigning interest in something on the ground. A man came to the old woman's cart to haggle for a basket of apples and thankfully stood directly between Ford and the blacksmith's.

"They're not even ripe."

"They are good! I sell only the best, juiciest, sweetest…"

The woman had many ways to describe the deliciousness of her apples, each one deepening Ford's craving. He realized the woman was completely distracted, so he palmed one of the smaller fruits and took off across the road, up the lane towards the backlands before turning the corner and ducking behind the blacksmith's building. A single window stood head-high. Mashing the apple in his mouth, he checked both ways to see that no one was around, and then he reached for the shutters. They were barred from the inside, but even if they had not been, it would have been too tight a squeeze for him. He bit into the apple again and sized up the window. Runt could fit through with no problem.

"Aha!" The piper stood at the corner of the building pointing at him. "Call the thief-taker!" Before he could explain himself, Ford was bustled out to the road, where the market flooded with people at the piper's call.

"I wasn't doing nothing!"

"I caught him at it!"

Hands clamped on to him, pulling and pushing him to a hitching post, where he was bound at the wrists.

"I knew he was trouble!" the blacksmith called out above the others, whose jeers ranged from "Run him out of town!" to "Sink him in the harbor!"

"You'll pay with a flogging. Yes sir, boy, that's what you'll get!" said a sailor, sneering in Ford's face and relishing it all.

"What about a fine?" asked someone from the back of the crowd.

"Fuck your fine!"

"You'll get nothing out of him if he's dead."

"He ought to pay the fine *and* get a flogging," the sailor all but demanded.

"What'd he do?"

"I caught him stealing apples," said the piper, standing tall among them.

"Apples?"

"An apple."

"An apple?" was repeated throughout the crowd, who had trouble coping with the fact that they'd been riled up over a single piece of fruit.

"It's only an apple," said Neb, holding up a coin for all to see and placing it in the apple seller's palm.

"A theft is a theft!" cried the piper.

"Oh, go blow your horn," said the sailor drifting off with the rest of the deflated crowd.

"That was an expensive apple," Neb said to Ford when they'd gotten away. "You owe me. You owe me big."

"I can make it up," said Ford.

"Yeah? How?"

"I know how to get our things back."

"What are you talking about?"

Ford explained how the innkeeper Viktor had sold their weapons to Gof and how the blacksmith was keeping them in a room in the shop. "He locks it, but there's a back window and I think Runt can fit through."

Strolling by the back of the smith's, Neb glanced at the window. "It's small, but maybe the little one can fit."

"That's what I thought. Only thing is, it's barred from the inside."

"That's nothing," Neb sniffed, "nothing at all. All right now, keep quiet and let me think on this."

Neb thought all the way back to the inn, where he complained loudly and got into an argument with the innkeeper about selling off their possessions. Ford tried in vain to pull him away, to get him to spend the time conceiving plans for getting back what had been theirs.

"I told you I saw him a heading this way," said Noll to Jorgi as they shoved through the door. Neb gave up the fight with Viktor and they all sat by the hearth, even though the fire had gone out.

"What's going on?" asked Jorgi.

"Go round up your boys," Neb said to Ford.

"What about—?"

"I said, go find them!"

Ford took the backland paths, not particularly wanting to see or be seen by the townspeople who had been so recently out for his blood. Along the way it occurred to him that Neb had called the boys "your boys," referring to them, not for the first time, as if they were his gang. It was something to think about later, but now he was concentrating only on getting the ax back.

Finding Ham and Runt was easy, and even Duff came along when told it was Neb's orders, but locating Chandler proved impossible. By the time they returned to the inn, the others had a plan well in hand.

"That's good and all," said Jorgi, "but we need coin to pull it off."

"Don't worry about that," said Neb, "don't you worry."

"Pull what off?" asked Ford.

"Come on," said Neb heading out the door. "I'll tell you on the way."

"So what is it?" asked Ford after trailing Neb into the center of town with Ham and Runt scampering after them like ducklings. Neb gave vague details of a diversion of some sort, leaving Ford without a notion of the overall plan and doubting just how well-thought-out this plan actually was.

"Why we stopping here?" asked Ford when Neb stepped up to the spice merchant's door.

"Because this place is the next best thing to a moneylender's in this stinking town."

Gershon, the spice merchant confirmed as much when he said, "There is no other place around to sell jewelry, precious stones and the like, unless one makes the trip all the way up to Lewiston." He tittered at such a preposterous distance, but when Neb didn't appear amused, Gershon grew concerned. Business was not what he wished. Losing a customer would be bad, especially one who looked as desperate as the shoddy character before him.

The boys invaded the shop in a way that displeased the spice merchant's elderly father, a man whose lined features had a built-in leer he would cast upon customers from his stool in a back corner, where he leaned against a table tapping his fingers in a monotonous rhythm. His tapping grew quicker and his vigil upon the boys sharper the deeper into the room they ventured, circling the tables, ogling the small wooden boxes stacked in open cupboards and breathing in the wide variety of aromas. On a table in the center of the room sat thick and fine-woven sacks opened and rolled back to reveal the spices within.

"It tickles," said Ham rubbing his nose after it had passed over mustard and pepper. Coming to the nutmeg, cloves and cinnamon he declared them all his favorites. Runt was getting a second whiff of ginger when Gershon's father leaned forward on to his creaking legs.

"Eadric," he rasped without removing his eyes from the boys, "get them away from the stock."

Eadric, hired to guard the shop, was a mobile mound of solid bone and abundant flesh over muscle, attired in ringed mail and leather with a sword buckled to his side. Regardless of his immense girth, he often went undetected by new customers entering the shop, because his employers hid him around a corner that led to the family's living quarters. Groaning seemed a necessary part of getting himself up from his stool set a few convenient feet away from Gershon's counting-table where transactions were conducted and upon which sat a strongbox full of coins.

"You boys wait outside," rumbled out of Eadric in a surprisingly quick, clipped manner of speaking Ford had never heard before. Ham and Runt fled the shop and Ford turned to go, but tripped over his own feet at the sight of Neb handing over to Gershon a spiraling necklace with a serpentine clasp, the very same necklace Kellyn had found in the ravine.

"Clumsy boy!" croaked Gershon's father when Ford slammed against the doorway. He could barely see or walk straight for the revelations flooding in on him. Out in the road the evidence threaded together into one inevitable and horrid conclusion.

"Isn't it?" Ham kept asking him. "Isn't it, Ford?"

"Isn't it what?"

"Lewiston, isn't that the town near the Valley some of your folks are from?"

"It's a long way from the Valley, but yeah, that's the place."

"But if we get there, we can lead them all back home now! Neb will be happy." Neb. The name stabbed at Ford's heart. He grabbed hold of Ham.

"Neb has Kellyn's necklace. He just sold it. You know what that means?"

"No," said Ham shying away from Ford's intensity.

"It means he killed Kellyn."

"What?"

"He must've killed Kellyn and swiped the necklace off him."

"Maybe he got it some other how." That was enough doubt to throw off Ford's conviction. He needed someone smarter to sort the whole thing out and give a final ruling.

"Where's Chandler?"

"I-I don't know, maybe with that woman."

"The weaver's daughter," said Ford, thumping Ham on the shoulder before running off.

Before he made any accusations, he wanted to be absolutely sure. If he was right, he wanted to know what to do about it. Chandler was the smartest of them. Ford hoped he had answers, but it was the kind of ambivalent hope that leaves one unsure of one's desire for the truth due to its consequences.

The sun crept towards the bay and touched the horizon when Ford reached the weaver's. He stalked about the building, sneaking a peek through the windows where he made out a man, a woman and at least one or two others working in the shop. Circling once more, he stopped at the back beside the large bush and hissed, "Chandler…Chandler!" The window above was open and a plank stood below it, propped against the wall. It was the sort of thing one might shimmy up to gain a hold upon the window, if that person was attempting to sneak in. Ford tested the plank. The wood was soft with age and damp. Someone half his size might climb it, but not he. He called Chandler's name again, a little louder this time. A cat brushed against his leg and tried the plank with one front paw, then the other, but seeing no benefit in a climb, prowled about the bush instead. When next Ford looked up, Chandler was staring down at him from the window. He appeared in good spirits, though slightly disheveled. His new tunic was pulled down over one shoulder.

"Come down," whispered Ford. "I need to tell you something."

The weaver's daughter appeared behind Chandler and didn't seem pleased to see Ford. Chandler smiled down at him, waved with a grand flourish and closed the window shutters.

"Chandler! Chandler!"

A neighbor's door cracked open and a head was thrust out. Ford held back from calling out again, pretended to examine the plank and walked away.

Beyond the dock he seated himself on the rocks and took his time considering the situation in the rapidly cooling air. Without Chandler's help, he felt truly on his own and at a loss for what to do. Whatever was going on and whatever was to be done about it, he'd have to figure it out for himself now. At first all he could think of was how happy he'd be to be anywhere else, to be doing anything else. Forcing out the idle wishes, he went over all he knew, gathering the facts he was certain of and any possibilities he could think of. Ham had a point; maybe Neb had gotten the necklace by some other means. No, he decided, there wasn't time, and Kellyn wouldn't have given it up. Maybe he'd been wrong and it wasn't the same necklace. "What are the chances?" he said into the crash of the waves. The design alone was unusual, but the snake-shaped hook clasp was nothing he'd ever seen before, not even on visits to his uncle's shop in Lewiston, where the family worked in jewelry. He hoped he was wrong, but he knew what he'd seen and there was little chance but that it had been Kellyn's necklace. "Then what now? Call the thief-taker on him?" If he were not so tense and agitated he might have chuckled at the thought. In the end, he decided to go along with Neb's plan for tonight, so he could get his ax back. After that he'd figure out what to do. Having the ax in hand would give him more options.

After a tumultuous anger and anxiety-filled stop at Viktor's inn that night, Ford found himself with Noll and Runt in a tavern within sight of the blacksmith's. He ran his fingers in circles around his temples, trying to rub away the throbbing caused by dehydration and a head full of confusion.

"What if it doesn't work?" he asked Noll.

"It'll work."

"What if somebody's left in there after? How do we know how many are in there?"

"What you think we done the last couple days?" Noll lowered his naturally discreet voice. "We know this town inside out and been planning for something like this." His lips lifted in a half smile. "We're going to bleed that fat sucker."

Across the smoke-filled room, a droopy-eyed woman in a coarse smock encrusted with fish scales down the front stretched out on a bench, leaned her back against the wall and let out a loud, contagious yawn that started a ripple effect throughout the few remaining patrons.

"Time for home," said a scarlet-cheeked fisherman, rocking himself to his feet and shuffling across the room to the door. He pulled it open, but instead of walking through, he swayed in the doorway and almost fell back into the room. "That doesn't look right." A ray of yellow light, like the rising of a brilliant dawn come too soon, streamed through the door and windows.

"Save us!" muttered the woman covered in fish scales, her eyes widening the closer she crept to a window. "What's happening? What is it?" The rest of the patrons swarmed around the door and windows, gawking and gasping at the bell tower, which was lit up like a torch and crowned by an engulfing flame. Ford ran to the window with them, then ran back and took a seat again.

"Cool down, boy!" Noll snarled out each word as he pulled Ford up, so that all three of them stood at the window by their table at the back.

"Sorry."

The fire spread along the tower's length to the ground, flickering in an arch around the door. People ran towards the inferno shouting, "Fire! Fire!" Clearer heads called for buckets and water. Noll counted on his fingers as the blacksmith and each of his household emerged with sloshing buckets. The fish-scale woman rallied the rest of the patrons and soon they had mugs filled from the tavern's water barrel. Buckets were brought out, and all stumbled through the door, splashing half of what they carried on their way to the blaze.

"Let's go," said Noll dragging Ford and pushing Runt through the tavern's back door. In the shadows of the lane, a raccoon scurried away with a crab carapace. They slipped across the road and pressed themselves against the back wall of the blacksmith's. Noll reached up to the window, slid a knife between the shutters, lifted the blade and gave it a flick. From the other side of the wall came a dull thud, barely audible for all the crazed shouting on the main road. The narrow window now open, Ford hoisted Runt up and shoved him through. The boy was dangling halfway in and would have landed head first on the floor inside, but Ford pulled him back out and flipped him about. Runt vigorously shook his head.

"What's the matter?" asked Ford.

"It's no good," said Noll standing on his toes and looking through the window. "It's not the store room. Damn."

"What do we do?"

"Come on." They stole up to the front of the shop and peered around the corner. Noll turned back and, seeing Ford crouched and pressed to the side of the building, smacked him on the arm. "Don't stand like that. Looks like you're up to no good."

The townspeople, still attempting to put together a bucket brigade, ran back and forth, some towards the fire and some away from it, few of them paying any mind to what the others were doing. A terrified howl, like a man under attack, rose shrieking above the general din. A woman's piercing screams followed. A figure sprinted from the dark lane behind Noll, Ford and Runt.

"Fire! There's a fire!" shouted a young, tremulous voice as the figure flew by.

"Oh," groaned Noll clutching his chest, "that about did me in!" He looked about one last time. "Let's go." The two boys followed him around the corner and right into the blacksmith's.

Partially lit by the fire and its own glowing forge, the shop where Gof did his work was always open since nothing of value was left in it, aside from permanent fixtures like his stone forge, a wide and deep quenching trough and a sturdy anvil that hadn't been moved in ages.

"This one," said Ford running up to one of two doors at the back, "but it'll be locked." He tried the knob and sure enough, the door wouldn't budge.

"Never been a lock I couldn't handle," said Noll.

A group of people ran by the shop and all three of them instinctively ducked behind the tall water trough. Ford eased around the edge for a look.

"See anyone?" asked Noll.

"No."

Noll got to his knees and into the shop rushed the blacksmith's wife with the smith's assistant, heading straight for the family's living quarters, barely missing Noll as he scampered back. A metal pan clanged, a pot shattered on the floor and the wife spat out her regret with a curse. There was some scraping before the assistant came back into the shop carrying a large washbasin and proceeded into the road with it.

"Wait!" shouted the smith's wife. "Fill it here. Here, give me that end!" Their shuffling feet neared and Ford tensed, ready to run or fight if necessary. With a thump and a splash, in went the basin into the trough, spilling water over the edge of the tub that soaked Ford, Noll and Runt on the other side.

"It's too heavy," said the straining assistant.

"Dump some!" said the wife and more water splashed about the trough. "Heave!" The shuffling passed from the shop to the road.

Noll's head was up with his flashing eyes assessing the danger, and in an instant he was working at the door-lock with a slim pick. He flinched at every shout from the people fighting the fire and shadows darting by the shop sent him diving for cover.

"Hurry!" Ford implored.

"I am!" hissed Noll digging and jabbing at the lock with an erratic urgency. "It's not easy. If those damn people…"

"Come on, they'll be back!"

"This fucking thing won't budge!" Huffing loudly, Noll stabbed viciously at the lock. "Shit!" He pulled out the pick, held it to the light and blinked at the broken stub.

"What do we do now? Wait!" Ford called after the silhouette of Noll flashing away through the shop and out to the fire-lit road. Ford turned back to the locked door. How could such a little thing stand in his way? So close. So close to the ax. So close to home. A light pressure upon his arm brought him back to the present. Runt was tugging at his sleeve. A mad desire to flee distorted the little boy's face. Only fear of abandonment held him back from leaving on his own. Ford let the boy draw him out into the road, but there he stopped and ran back into the shop, flinging himself with such force against the back door that the wood shattered. He kicked and knocked away the broken pieces until little else remained besides the lock and handle which still held tight.

The storeroom had no windows, but the light from the fire was enough to illuminate various racks of hammers and tongs in numerous shapes and sizes, an assortment of chisels and files, barrel hoops hanging over shelves and tables well organized with boxes, coffers, buckets of nails and a few tools for other professions. Gaffs and a variety of fishing hooks hung beside anchors. Even a few weapons and pieces of armor were collected in one corner. And there was his father's ax propped against a wall among spades and hoes. He grabbed it and made off with Runt close behind him, tripping out into the road where they found the townspeople. Most were slowed by exhaustion and quieter now that the hysteria had worn away. For a moment, the two boys stood together with them and watched the fire burning itself out. Halfway to Viktor's, Ford recalled Neb's plan and they hurried between the houses out into the fields behind the town, groping their way along a path in the dark.

With the interior of the bell-tower gutted and charred, leaving only its stone base and the thick framing beams, the nearly spent and distraught people of Dror Bae bemoaned the loss of their pride and joy, a symbol of the town's prosperity. All those years of labor were lost. The gold and silver sunk into its construction drifted away with the smoke. Not only that, but it would hurt trade, for ships relied upon the beacon at night and on its bell when fog blanketed the bay and the camouflaged coast deceived the pilot's eye.

"How did it happen?" became "Who did it?" when the unmistakable stench of whale oil was detected upon the smoke and it surfaced that a quantity of the stuff had gone missing that afternoon. Resentment burned hotter than the destructive flames themselves. Accusations flew. "Drunken sailors?" No. "Them filthy foreigners?" To what end? Rumors of the band of shady newcomers spread. With a voice soaring clear and high over the increasingly agitated crowd, the piper reminded everyone of Ford's apple theft. Gof the blacksmith's discovery of a break-in heightened suspicion. The newcomers were known to be staying at the ramshackle inn at the end of town, but when a mob burst into Viktor's, the stunted innkeeper explained that his patrons had suddenly left without warning. The mob broke into search parties that scoured the town. Word got around of a child who'd seen the newcomers fleeing. The child led the townspeople to the last of the fishing boats at the far end of the beach, where all that remained beyond were a few wrecked vessels upon tidal flats and the paths leading off to the country beyond.

"They're making for Lewiston," ventured Gershon the spice merchant, relaying the story of his transaction with the newcomers, which further solidified their guilt in the people's mind. They sought the help of the law. The barwnig promised to send out a party to bring the culprits to justice in the morning. That was not good enough. The people took it upon themselves to set out immediately with torches and on horseback or afoot, it didn't matter to them how or with what, as long as something was being done. The captain of the fastest trading vessel, a sloop that had plied the coast for years, prepared to sail for Lewiston and bring the criminals to justice.

Chapter 15
The Rat and the Killer

Footsteps squished through the mudflats. Riders trotted by upon the bluffs. Sleek boats slid out of the bay. Hours later the footsteps and riders returned and nothing more was heard but the surf amongst the wrecked vessels beyond the fishermen's beach until well past midnight, when seven figures threw off musty scraps of damp canvas, emerged from under the remains of rotting boats, and slipped away from Dror Bae.

"We got to go back for Chandler," Ford told Neb from behind a muffling hand.

"Go back and risk your own neck if you want," was all Neb would say, blocking out the insistent Ford and everything else while he guided his band with dogged persistence away from the coast and into the country, avoiding towns and villages whenever possible. They all breathed more easily once they found themselves among the trees, even though they still trod the fringes of civilization.

"Why don't we go deeper in where it's safer?" asked Noll.

"I'm looking for this Lewiston town," said Neb. "That backwater town back there was a waste of time. We're worse off for bothering with the damned place. But you did all right," he added, looking at Ford's ax. "Did just fine for yourself, didn't you?" The fact that Ford had grabbed only the ax and none of the others' weapons had been brought up more than once that morning, and it irritated Ford.

"What about you?" he complained. "All you all did was burn down that tower." To his surprise, the gibe did not have the intended effect. Neb and Jorgi were too distracted by their disappointment to pay any attention at all.

"We was all set to do that spice man," Jorgi said and spat on the ground.

"That's right," said Neb through pinched lips, "but that old fart and his muscle-bound bear never left the damn place the whole time."

"Woulda been a nice prize," said Noll.

"Don't worry, we'll get ours back in Lewiston." Disappointed though he was with Dror Bae, Neb felt the drive of confidence in his new scheme. Not all shared his enthusiasm, however.

"I've been there. People know my face there," said Ford.

"Shame. Guess you don't get to go into town then, do you?"

Keeping Neb's gang away from Lewiston for the sake of Ford's family on his father's side living in Lewiston was his true concern. As he trudged step after step through thin forests between back fields and overgrown glens, it littered his thoughts along with Chandler's disappearance and the reappearance of Kellyn's necklace, all of it mixing in a brew of anxiety and anger. He thought of Neb, of how he had most likely killed Kellyn, and he picked up his pace, passing Jorgi, Noll and Duff. The back of Neb's head made an inviting target. It would be just like the battle, he told himself, hefting the ax and balancing its weight, readying it for a vicious, downward stroke.

"Why are you running?" asked Ham racing up alongside him and placing a hand upon his rising forearm, staying the rising ax head. Shocked out of his single-minded ambition, Ford met the boy's eyes, remembering in Ham's face that single ounce of doubt about Kellyn's death and Neb's hand in it.

"Leave me be," he said and shook off Ham's hand. "I'm not running."

"Noll!" Neb called over his shoulder, then stopped upon catching sight of Ford and Ham at his heels. "What you two want?" Ham slipped back into the pack.

"Nothing," said Ford and he too fell behind with the others, his passion spent in frustrated confusion. Noll made his way to the front and Neb called a halt. While the two spoke, the others sat where they stopped. With his desire to know the truth still not sated, Ford spent the time debating whether he should come out and ask Neb if he had killed Kellyn. But, he wondered, what then? If it came to a fight, Ford had only Ham and Runt on his side and he didn't like those odds. No resolution came readily to him, so the problem continued to fester.

Neb smirked and then snickered. He was fitting Noll out in a disguise and had just wrapped a piece of torn cloth around his head, covering one eye. "Give me a smile. A smile. Wider. Perfect! You don't look anything like your ugly self. Do that when you're in town. Smile big and they'll love you like a brother or any road, no one'll recognize you," said Neb slapping Noll on the back and sending him off towards a village along a river that would have to be crossed soon.

Such an insignificant settlement as this, barely glimpsed at a distance through the trees by passing travelers, caught the attention of passersby only because of its laboring inhabitants' perpetual stamping and clubbing of woolen cloth by a broad framework of cloth-stretching tenters. Upon the banks upriver and only just within sight, carpenters rested in the shade by a fulling mill in the early stages of construction. Neb kept his band out of sight of both groups while they waited.

"Your Lewiston is five mile west," said Noll upon his return.

"There we go," said Neb with a pat on the back for his spy. "Hear that Jorgi? Good times are coming!"

"Better be worth the walk," said Jorgi.

"From what I understand, it's a good sized town. A good deal more to it than that last stinking hole."

"They got a bridge over yonder," said Noll nodding to the village, "Narrow, but we can cross without wetting our asses." Neb looked at him sideways.

"Great!" he said with exaggerated bravado and a puffed-out chest. "Let's all march merrily on into town, waving and smiling as we go and having a grand old time. 'Here come the villains of the Dror Bae fire,' they'll say. 'Let's give 'em beer and bread and send 'em on their merry way!' You idiot, think!"

Leaving them to follow in his wake, Neb led his band of boys and men northward up the river in search of a ford. The mere presence of the few villages all along the way repelled them back into the woods and further north. Repeatedly Neb edged them cautiously back to the river, but as it was such a hot day, the villagers were finding work under shade whenever possible and the band blundered upon almost the whole population of one settlement gathering withies from willows. They were mostly women, sturdy and unafraid, but wary and watchful.

"The whole countryside will know about us now," grumbled Noll when the women sent off a pair of fleet-footed youngsters. "The law'll be after us."

"You think I don't know? I know!" shouted Neb. Noll had gone sour since being called an idiot, but he had a point, so Neb changed course, heading eastward until they were well out of sight before turning back to the north. It was the last word any of them uttered for the long while it took them to find a fordable spot. Neb's choice of crossing, where the river narrowed and remained calm upon the surface, seemed ideal at first glance, but it was not as shallow as the shortest of them could wish. The high, rounded banks made crawling into and out of the river more treacherous.

"Don't see one, but must be a village or something like about. The bushes is all cut back," said Neb of the newly shorn greenery where Noll lowered himself into the water. If the current was any stronger, the water any deeper, Ford had a mind to push Neb in and hope it swept him under. If he bumped him in a way that it looked enough like an accident, he might even get away with it. But instead he dropped down next, splashing into the water and leaning back on to the bank so Runt could climb on to his shoulders. There was no question of the little boy being able to cross on his own. Two confident strides into the river and the water already surged well over Ford's waist. After that, the undercurrent dragged his legs downstream every time he lifted his feet.

"Watch the rocks! It's damn near impossible to keep your footing," Noll called back to the others, cutting himself short when he slipped and sank to his chin. Ford was finding the extra, unbalanced weight of a boy wobbling and swaying about his head unmanageable. More than halfway across the river he took Runt in his arms. "Grab for them roots. Ready?" And with that, he launched Runt towards the riverbank. The boy flopped, half in the water and half on land, catching hold of roots and grass and not letting go. Lightening the load helped considerably, and from then on Ford navigated the rocks to the other side without further incident.

"Bunch of foolish nonsense, I say," said Noll while they watched the others work their agonizingly slow way across. Something in Ford's grunt encouraged him to lean closer and speak lower. "We're good as dead if we go down to this Lewiston." If there was one thing Ford yearned for right now it was a strong ally, and what passed for open, frankness in Noll was all the incentive he needed to speak freely.

"I don't want to go neither. I got family there and they'd spot me."

"Family," said the man with a wistful air. "If I had a place to go, I'd quit all this."

"I want to, but they wouldn't take me in." After that Ford went mum, feeling he'd perhaps said too much. Anything he let slip now might be too much amongst this band of ruthless men he barely knew, so he held his tongue, wrung out his clothes and saw to it that Runt did the same.

"I oughtn't say," said Noll leaning closer and speaking almost too quietly to be heard, "but seems Neb's got plans for you."

What was meant by this and what those plans were was never said, because Ford leapt off the bank into the river. Ham's head, bobbing about and slipping downstream, had plunged underwater and not resurfaced. Someone cried out, but no one made a move to help the boy until Ford jumped in. He lurched about, lost his footing and tumbled along with the current. Ham's back broke the surface and his hands flapped upon the water until he flipped about and gasped for breath before sinking again. Ford made a useless dive for the boy, who was swept just out of reach. Ham's body rolled about, his feet kicked and his fingers reached hopelessly for the riverbank. Ford sloshed along a bend in knee-deep water until catching the boy and hauling him on to dry land where he lay on his back, coughing and spitting up water.

"Get enough to drink, did you?" Neb's jest was all the soaked and miserable band had to say afterwards of Ham's ordeal while they squeezed water out of their shirts and poured it from their shoes. Yet again Jorgi asked how much farther it was to Lewiston, as if they'd traveled countless miles instead of the fifty feet of fording they'd managed since last he asked the question. "Shut up about it. We'll get there when we get there."

"A man needs a bit of fun, and all we've had is shit and misery."

"You and your fun, you'll get us killed," said Noll sparking a walking argument about whether or not to go to Lewiston. Jorgi's almost mad desire for fun and Neb's lust for profit pressed them on closer and closer to the town regardless of everyone else's worry about getting caught by the barwnig of Dror Bae's men, who had had plenty of time by now to spread word about them over the countryside. However, thieves can be dissuaded from greater prizes by the ease of low hanging fruit, such as what dangled in front of them along a desolate road not far from the river.

"Must lead to town," Neb said, surveying the wheel-rutted track winding through the overhanging trees on a roughly parallel course to the river. He crossed his arms and tapped his elbow for a time in thought. This was not another of the many footpaths that checkered the land, but a road capable of supporting trade; a concealed road with plenty of cover nearby. His lips stretched in a greedy smile as he formed a robber's banquet of an idea. "Maybe we don't have to go all the way to town. Maybe we let the town come to us."

A twitter of birdsong from Noll sent the three men diving for cover.

Ford barely corralled the boys behind a bush before a troop of marchogs thundered into sight, pushing their horses south, where they would pass within feet of Duff standing dumbfounded in plain sight by the side of the road. Like all the others, Ford held his breath and feared the worst, but he also half hoped the hard-charging warriors would see Duff and stop. His visions of escaping with the boys, while Neb and his cronies were captured, beat in his heart to the pounding of the hooves drawing alongside Duff. The warriors' sheathed swords bounced at their sides, the horses frothed at the mouth, and the men's cloaks whipped out behind them on their flying passage southwards. Ford blinked uncomprehendingly as they passed out of sight. He couldn't believe they hadn't seen Duff.

"More than like they didn't much care," said Neb later when they all gathered together, spying upon the road from afar. "Them boys is looking for a whole bunch, a whole band of us, not just the one. I wager they never even suspected our old boy here," he said squeezing the back of Duff's neck and putting an arm around his shoulder. The creaking of wheels and axles drew their eyes to a point up the road where they could make out a caravan of six covered wagons sluggishly bumping and rocking into view, each with a man-at-arms and two more guards leading and following.

"A tasty apple," Neb mused when they'd passed out of sight. "Tasty indeed, but too big a bite for us."

Over the following few hours, all that passed them upon the road was a farmer driving a haywain and the occasional villager shuffling by bent-backed under shouldered faggot bundles, targets too poor to bother with. The boys' heads began to nod and Jorgi snorted himself out of a nap. Their eyes fluttered wide open at a tinkling through the trees. Up the road ambled a horse with a bell around its neck leading a train of a dozen more horses in single file, all with loose packs hanging at their sides. On one of the horses rode a man in well-dyed clothes, clean but for the ubiquitous muddy bottoms. Walking alongside were two stocky young men, one carrying a spear and the other holding a pitchfork and a whip; these were farmhands, so unaccustomed to riding that they preferred to make the journey on foot.

At Neb's command, his band descended upon the caravan, hurling rocks, sticks and whatever came to hand, frightening the horses and overwhelming the men by numbers. A brief struggle ended with the guards disarmed and some of the bandits taking superficial cuts and bruises. Duff suffered the worst, having received a lash across the face that drew blood about his eyes, tore away skin from the bridge of his nose and left a white line of missing hair along one side of his head.

"Where is it?" Neb asked the man in the clean clothes after pulling him from his horse. He was a barwnig's overseer in charge of transacting the chief's various contracted business. What that business was, he wouldn't say, but whatever it was, it had already been concluded, so Neb knew the man had coin he was withholding. "Where's your purse? Where is it?" The overseer's face went as innocent as a newborn babe's, while he raised his hands and shook his head.

"I have but little," he relented with a pitiful grimace under Neb's persistent pressure, and eventually handed over a light purse with a few copper coins, the sort of prize Ford and the boys had reaped from their attempts at waylaying merchants when Kellyn was in charge. "That is all. I have nothing more." Neb cracked the overseer on the chin.

"Keep it up and you'll get more and worse. Now where is it?" Holding a hand to his face, the overseer pointed to the road north where the tinkling bell of the lead horse had long since died away. "Bullshit! Boys, check the packs of every horse you can lay hands on and hurry. We got to get off this road." Ford grabbed the horse closest at hand. Pack after empty pack was searched, until a bulging purse was found wrapped in cloth and stowed in a secret flap in the pack of a horse so docile it had never moved a step during the attack. "Good, good. Now strip them!" They took weapons, clothes and even shoes, but the horses were driven off. They'd been marked and would be difficult to keep, trade or sell without raising suspicion.

"Pity," said Noll as they melted back into the forest. "We'd get a fair bit of silver for beauties like that."

"Pity it is, but we did good. You did real good," Neb said and a chuckle burbled out of him. "You all see how old Noll took down the big lad back there? Good work, cousin!" Noll beamed like an embarrassed but proud boy.

Cousin? This was the first Ford had heard that Neb and Noll were kin. It shed a whole new light on their bond, an uncomfortably bright light.

"Good enough so as we don't need that Lewiston?" asked Noll.

"Nay, we don't need that stinking place. It'd be nothing but trouble. On to this Valley of yours!" Neb said to the boys, with a snap of his fingers so merry it was as if the overseer and his two companions hadn't been bound, dragged into the woods and had their throats slit but moments before.

A few miles north they came upon a village in a clearing where they found a flimsy dogcart by the forest's edge. When they were sure no one was looking, they carried it off to a footpath and drove it north, where it was piled high with provisions bought at the next two villages. Wherever and whenever they could, Neb, Jorgi and Noll traded in their newly acquired weapons for sharpened knives. Duff pulled the cart with a will over grassy fields, muddy paths and even the road when Neb declared they were "safe as safe could be this far on." So weak and overloaded was the cart that it threatened to break apart or topple over at every bump, and often it sank stubbornly into ruts. Duff pushed and yanked at it until his face was awash in sweat and blood from wounds poorly tended to.

"This is madness!" yelled Neb propping a foot against the cart and finally bringing it and Duff to an exhausted halt. "Madness! Where's this Valley? You said it wasn't far north of Lewiston and it's already too far." Though the complaint was directed his way, Ford ignored him. Neb didn't care. He only wanted to vent his bad mood. "How'll we get this stupid cart through the woods? This thing ain't going through no woods. We ought to break up the useless thing for firewood." Neb shoved the cart with his heel and went on berating it, but few listened, least of all Ford, who was distracted by familiar sights.

Since the robbery, every village they passed had become more recognizable. The Barlow to Lewiston trip was not one Ford had made often, but now they were entering territory his father occasionally provided with timber. They were loads he had helped haul, and though one field or wooded path might look much like another, he knew this was Blackoak land and in the presence of his own people a deep shame came over him at the thought of being an outlaw. He would not meet the eye of the farmers or any local inhabitants they passed. When Rodulf of Leofford, one of his fellow warriors in the Battle by the Llyn, waved them closer to entice them with the head and haunch of a newly slaughtered sow, Ford held back, let his straggly hair mask his face, and feigned interest in a duck pond he had once splashed about in as a child.

The bright yellow timbers of a newly completed wall surrounding a village atop a gently sloping hill came into view as Neb led them from a forest path into a stretch of fields. Upon reaching the top where the path forked off to an easily missed footpath, Ford could resist the urge no longer and turned his gaze towards the tiny cluster of houses where he had grown up. Barlow sat below just over the stream, where Aedalin the old woodcutter's daughter-in-law knelt by the water doing the washing. She looked up at them and shielded her eyes for a better view. Ford faced away at first, but realizing she couldn't possibly recognize him from this distance, so he turned back to watch her until they passed from view.

A few of Oren's inhabitants cast quizzical looks their way, but Neb's band followed the path away from the village down through the spindly trees to the stream and made as if they planned to fill their waterskins and rest by the water. The ruse formed of its own accord, for here the path ended and the cart's wheels ground into the soft earth. Duff collapsed, regained his footing, threw his bulk against the cart and fell to his knees.

"Hold up, hold up!" said Neb after walking about the clearing where the people of Oren came to do their washing. "Your Valley is straight this way?"

"Right that way," said Ford with a nod north.

"Right then." Neb took a few spongy steps amongst the trees. "Wood's too thick, ground's too soft. Unload the cart and we'll go back and sell it. Sell it and see what we can't get for it."

"There's a marchog in that village," Ford warned.

"That's what I feared. Well that's the last of that," he said, and kicked one of the wheels. "We ought to be off soon as soon can be, so pack up all this mess and hurry up about it!" The boys and men unloaded and redistributed the goods as Neb saw fit. Ford bore the brunt, partly because he could and partly because he wasn't paying attention. While the others made sure to avoid the heaviest of the provisions, he stood at the edge of the clearing staring into the trees in the direction of Barlow, holding back a wry smile and trembling lips.

"What are you looking at?" asked Ham, squinting but seeing nothing of interest amongst the trees. "Are you sick?"

"No," said Ford wiping at his running nose and watering eyes. "Well, maybe."

"They're almost ready."

"Go on. I'm coming."

Ham drifted back to the others and Ford drew in great breaths, trying in vain to suppress the pain and any happy memories that came back to him, because even the happiness hurt. He blinked his eyes clear, and then blinked again. A tree some hundred and more feet away grew a limb, then sprouted a head and torso off one side. The shadows of the forest had a funny way of camouflaging the ordinary things of the forest and turning them extraordinary, but even so, he was sure he had made out an eye and would have guessed it to be a deer if not for the limb rising and taking hold of the tree. "A dryad," he said in a worried murmur, "or no, Father." He stepped back and bumped into Neb.

"What's that you say? Is that your folks' place back there, in one of them villages?" Neb waved at the trees in front of Ford.

"No."

"No? I figure that for a lie, elsewise how was you so certain about the marchog back there, eh?"

"I didn't come from there."

"Must've been that other rotten hole. Mind if I pay them a visit?" Neb mockingly took a jaunty step towards Barlow and Ford planted a hand upon his chest.

"That's not my home. But I know them people and they got nothing worth the trouble."

"That's all right. Only a joke," Neb said brushing off Ford's hand and gritting his teeth, "but don't you ever lay hands on me like that again." He looked Ford straight in the eye, dotted his chest with a pointed finger and returned to the others. "Let's go!" Ford scanned the forest, but whoever it had been behind the distant tree was no longer there.

The straps of saddlebags they'd lifted off the overseer's horses dug into Ford's shoulders, but with his head down and his mind elsewhere, he managed to stumble on along the side of the stream, slowing the line behind him. Mercifully, this leg of their journey proved to be short.

"This is where we first found you, wasn't it?" Ham said to Ford when they stopped at the bend in the stream with the high arching bank just north of Barlow. Ford couldn't have cared less, but he looked about him, remembered the spot and agreed. "So, was that your home back there?" Ford nodded. "Oh." The others dropped their packs, drank from the stream and dug out something to eat.

"I'm going back," said Ford patting the ax. "I'm bringing this back."

"Oh."

Ford stopped, made sure no one was listening and lowered his voice, "Don't tell no one." Ham nodded. Ford might not have been a part of his father's family any longer, but they were family nonetheless and he wasn't about to lead a band of outlaws into Barlow, not a second time.

"Let's have a drink. I'm dead thirsty," said Jorgi, pulling out the jug of ale they'd bought in Leofford when Neb had donned the overseer's clothes and posed as a merchant.

"Not the jug. Here," said Neb taking the jug and handing him a smaller bottle, "And don't get too comfortable. You can put your feet up and drink all you want when we get to this Valley." He turned to the boys. "So where is this Valley?"

"It's not far," Ham burst out in his uncontainable excitement.

"You said that before. How many miles?"

"I don't know."

"Five? Ten? Twenty?"

"I don't know."

"Well shit. Shit. Shit. Shit." Neb walked circles about the bend, kicking pebbles and thinking. "All right. We camp here tonight." He threw himself down by the water and pulled off the new shoes he'd recently acquired courtesy of the overseer. "Somebody, Noll, get up there!" he said, pointing to the top of the steep bank on the other side of the stream. "We're too close to people. We need a lookout."

Relief could not be found even under the trees that humid summer evening. While the men and Duff drank ale, the younger boys waded in the water. Ford did neither, preferring to sit, fully clothed and sweating profusely, away from everyone else.

"This goes to the winner," Jorgi declared with a lazy, thick tongue. He propped himself upon unsteady legs before the campfire and held a bottle over his head. "Whoever can get it, gets it." No one responded. "Come on. Come get it!"

"Everyone's tired and you're drunk," said Neb. He was trying to smoke, but getting frustrated by damp leaves. "Bah!"

Duff crawled to his feet and exhausted as he was, he knocked Jorgi down with ease, the two of them rolling about on the ground, emitting an odd mix of giggles, grunts and pained growls.

"I got to go," said Ford grabbing at his groin and getting up while the wrestling carried on. He turned away from the firelight and in the dark his fingers slipped around the handle of the ax leaning against the tree behind him. He pressed it against his leg and walked awkwardly away from the group towards the bushes. Behind him, Jorgi let out a giddy screech and lurched into the water with Duff. Ford looked back to see them both naked from the waist up and splashing water at Ham and Runt. He brought the ax around, held it in both hands in front of him and stood straight-backed and stiff, facing a shadowy clump of bushes with his back to the pealing maniacal laughter and splashing at the camp. *Now, go now!* he urged himself, but his nerves were so rattled that he actually needed to relieve himself. Fumbling with the ax, he pulled down his pants and let loose an urgent stream upon the dry leaves. A tremendous splash behind him preceded a string of Jorgi's foulest oaths. Ford yanked up his pants and was ready to bolt, but all the noise and commotion behind him vanished in an eerie silence that froze him in place. An eternity elapsed in his mind before he tried a step, but the leaves under foot crunched in an agonizingly loud chorus. Jorgi's quivering titter sprang up again and Ford sped away, running straight into the thorny brambles that walled off most of the bend in the stream.

Dragging himself out and picking the clinging thorns from his clothes and skin took time, too much time he feared. Indeed, footsteps approached. Immediately, he squatted behind a tree.

"I'm busy!"

The footsteps came on. He grunted and groaned, hoping to ward off whoever was coming. When he stopped, the footsteps were no more, so he got up and made for Barlow.

"Where you think you're going?" Neb demanded from just the other side of the tree.

"Nowhere. I was taking a shit."

"With your pants up and that ax in your hands? I don't smell shit neither, but I *do* smell bullshit. Come on, kid," he said, and waved for Ford to follow him back to camp. But Ford didn't move. "Look, you don't want to leave."

"Maybe I do."

"Nah! Listen, you're one of us. We're family. We got to stick together. Look out for each other. You know what I mean? You don't want to leave." Ford remained unmoved in body and spirit. Even with the darkness between masking the implacable features of Ford's long, drawn face, Neb was left in little doubt as to where Ford stood on the matter. If he didn't persuade him, he'd be stuck with the thick-headed one, whose worth was only slightly more than that of the two useless boys. "Fact is we need you and you need us. We're all the family you got. You can't trust nobody else. Nobody. They'll rob you, treat you like dirt. But us? You can trust us. There's nobody in this world you can trust but us."

"How do you know I was leaving? Maybe I wanted to be alone."

"I knew. I got a tip." Neb laughed as he drew Ford back to the campsite where Ford saw Noll upon the high bank overlooking the camp.

"Oh."

"Oh? Oh, Noll? No, Noll didn't rat you out. Noll's blood, but he don't rat nobody. It was your little friend, the piggy."

"Ham?" When Ford turned his malevolent gaze upon the boy, Ham stepped back, back from Ford, back from everyone else.

"I didn't want you to go," he said bowing his head and fidgeting with his fingers, "I was afraid you'd leave forever."

"Isn't that nice?" Neb hissed and his smile went absurdly wide. "He'd miss you. That's real nice. Like one happy family. See, you don't need nobody else. You got family aplenty right here," and he repeated his whole speech on family again.

That night while a snore flapped and fluttered out of Jorgi as he lay with his face in the leaves and everyone else found the best possible sleeping spots, Ham inched closer to Ford and remarked on the warm evening. Ford moved away, going to the stream to urinate and find a patch of ground to lie upon which wasn't too damp or littered with sacks, wasted food and bottles.

"Keep an eye on him," Neb told Noll and Duff, and Ford rolled over facing away from the group. A volatile temper, primed by exhaustion, pumped irritation through him and dampened any further plans for slipping out of camp, as well as souring his thoughts of what might come of him after delivering up the ax. Straining to bring it all to order only left him spent, and at last he dropped into a deep sleep that lasted until dawn.

"From what I hear," Neb started in again before the cobwebs were swept away from Ford's sluggish waking mind, "your folks don't even want you no more, not after what you done."

Again Ham had betrayed his confidence, thought Ford, staring into the back of the head of the boy leading them on the last leg of their hike to the Valley. He wished something with awful fangs would jump out from behind a tree and devour Ham. To make matters worse, he was angry at himself for sleeping through the night and annoyed at Neb, who wouldn't stop talking.

"Yup, the way I see it, if you leave us and they don't want you, that leaves you all alone. Alone, and where's that get you? Nowhere. Know what I mean? When you're by yourself people walk all over you. I'm telling you, that's what they do, I know. They treat you like dirt."

"Oh shut up!" said Jorgi, who carried next to nothing and used one of his free hands to hold his forehead while shuffling along behind everyone. Occasionally his moaning could be heard above the dragging of his feet. "How much longer?"

"Not much," Ham said with a joy slightly dulled only by the cold wedge that kept Ford from him all that morning. Ham's memory proved true and their arrival soon after brought them all relief, if not the kind of pleasure Ham himself was experiencing. By appearances he was the only one truly happy to see the Valley again and even his happiness died away at first sight of the state of the place. Many of the foundation stones had been knocked in upon the ashes of their home, which had been burnt beyond what the boys recalled. Not a scrap of the roof remained. Runt's watchtower in the tree had been pulled down and evidently burned as well. Neb kicked at what little was left of the foundation.

"Some place you got here."

"It wasn't like this," said Ford, but that was all the answer he cared to offer.

Murder, death, betrayal, theft and everything to do with this gypsy banditry was wearing on him, and now the summer poured on a humidity so muggy one had to strip down or sit about in sweat-soaked clothes. Ford found a boulder to sit on away from everyone else and started in on a skin of wine. He left the defense of the Valley to Ham. The only positive Ford could see in all this was what couldn't be seen. Cook's body was gone. Good, he thought, leaning back for another swig. No one needed a reminder of that horror, least of all Runt. The boy sat on the far side of the stream, refusing to come any closer.

"Don't mind if I do," said Jorgi taking the wineskin and downing half of it. "Why's he doing that?" He slapped at a mosquito and waved the skin in Runt's direction, then slouched against the nearest tree, shielding his eyes from the little light slanting down through the leaves.

"He seen some things here that frightened him."

"Still, it ain't natural." Jorgi winced. "Fuck the gods, my head! This is the only cure right here," he said holding up the wine. "You should get you some. There's plenty more. I made sure of that." His words were growing unsteady again, like his step as he tramped off, watching the ground in the way one would keep an eye on a shifty trickster.

Sliding to the ground with his back against the boulder, Ford closed his eyes to enjoy what peace could be had. To him it seemed half a heartbeat's time before he jerked awake at the shattering of glass. The whole scene in the Valley had changed drastically. Noll and Duff swayed and rocked by the ash pile while Jorgi danced around them like a three-legged colt. Each hoisted his own bottle or jug, swung it about and sang his own song in the discordant harmony of the drunk. Ham waded in a pool downstream with his pants rolled up over his knees. Runt still sat alone on the opposite bank, but now he had stripped to the waist and was dangling his feet in the water.

"Damn fool." Ford whipped his head around and there was Neb sitting next to him casting a scowl of annoyance back at Jorgi. "Idiot'll have the lot drunk up by morning." In glancing at Neb, Ford noted the bladder of wine resting against his far leg, but afterwards would not look his way and even scooted off. After exhaustedly complaining about Jorgi's unrelenting antics, Neb moved on to his main complaint. "This place is too far from anything. We'll have to go back and forth again and again every damn day just to keep from starving."

"Cook kept us fed."

"Cook?"

"He died. Right there." Ford pointed to the ashes. Neb followed his finger, contemplated the pile of rock and ash, and sighed.

"We got some meal to boil down, but no pot. Even if we did, it won't last long."

Kellyn may not have been perfect, but he was a better all-around leader than Neb, in Ford's opinion. How these men had kept themselves alive all this time begged some speculation.

"I can catch fish," Ham slipped into the pause from just behind Neb, making him flinch.

"Go on, get, you sneaky little bastard!" Neb's anger vanished along with Ham. "Might make a thief out of him yet." Neb pondered the notion a while longer. "The big boy's not useless either," he added, nodding at Duff. "That one though." Ford didn't have to look to know he was talking about Runt. He stopped listening altogether when Neb went back to complaining about the Valley's remoteness. "Back and forth, back and forth. We'll be needing new shoes. On top of that I got to find an honest tradesman who won't cheat a man." Neb threw down the parcel of leaves he'd purchased the day before. "What I'd do for a good smoke right now." Ford hadn't thought about it for days, but now that he did, there was nothing else he wanted more.

"Hey! Hey! Drink!" shouted Jorgi at Ford and Neb. The drunken revelers shambled in their direction. A bobble-headed Duff dropped in next to Ford, smiled and rammed him shoulder to shoulder. Ford caught himself from falling over and then slid away to put some space between him and Duff.

"All right, all right!" Neb muttered, drinking from the bottle being shoved at his mouth and handing it back. "Show me the Face," he said to Ford when the revelers commenced their flopping, oafish dance around him.

"It's right there. Go yourself."

"Ah, don't be like that."

All it took was another aggressively playful shot to the shoulder from Duff to get Ford on his feet and over the stream, leaving behind the annoying Jorgi who was imploring them to drink with him and "my friends, the best friends in all the land!"

"I don't see no monster," said Neb grinning at the entryway of the Face, that massive carved rock glowering down upon the Valley from its hill. "The pig told me all about it, what happened and all. Sounds like a bunch of hogwash." He dropped one foot across the doorway while Ford held back. "But by the looks of you, you believe it, don't you? It's the sort of thing Noll'd believe. Bah, mists and imagination is all it was." He laughed off such nonsense and the laugh gave him the confidence to go in alone.

If Ford had been in the mood to talk, he would have said he was not afraid. Certainly he was apprehensive to be revisiting the site of the tragedy, but whatever it was that had killed Cook and caused the bizarre lights and sounds that frightened the boys away, Ford had seen it vanish with his own eyes. It was gone, and maybe that wasn't courage, but it was common sense, plain and simple.

No, what really was bothering Ford at the moment was the idea of spending any more time around these men. He most definitely did not what to jam himself into a tight spot like the inside of the Face with the man who had most likely killed his friend. He sneered down at the drunken men cavorting about and wished they'd drink themselves to sleep. There was hope in that. Noll slunk off to be sick. Duff danced a few more waddling steps, fell over, tried to get up, fell again and stayed there. Jorgi, however, seemed inexhaustible. With his pants pulled down to his thighs, he stumbled backwards using his hands to manipulate his cheeks while performing a sort of bawdy puppet show.

"Beware the one-eyed warrior! He's a fighter and a fucker!" he shouted repeatedly, but no one was paying much attention or enjoying it, aside from a guffawing Duff and Runt. The little boy's giggle tinkled so pleasantly in Ford's ears that it had tears brimming in his eyes.

"Aha!" echoed Neb's triumph from within, spreading throughout the Valley and frightening Runt into silence until Jorgi distracted him again. "That flat stone out there, I knew there'd be a good flat spot for rolling somewheres. There's something like it back at our place. Oh yeah, you remember that, where we strung up that liar."

"You think that's pretty funny," Jorgi slurred to Runt. "Well why don't you come and play? Come and play, boy. Have a drink and dance with us." He offered a wooden jug. "Come boy, don't make me beg. Just one little drink and one little dance. Here!" He threw the jug over the stream. Runt watched its high arcing flight, cringed when it landed with a thud beside him and was not ready for the oncoming Jorgi splashing through the stream. The gangly drunk man lost his footing and fell on to the far bank scrabbling for Runt's ankles. "Got you, you slippery fish." He let loose an ear-piercing squeal and pulled Runt into the stream. The twisting boy slipped away and Jorgi leapt on to him, pinning him under the shallow water.

"Let him up!" Ford shouted.

"What damn nonsense are they up to now?" asked Neb from within the Face. "You know, this here'd be a good cold place for storing, oh, this and that."

Jorgi wobbled on to one knee, avoiding Runt's thrashing arms and legs. He wiped the splashing water from his eyes and Runt wriggled out from under him. As Runt was crawling on to the bank, Jorgi jumped on him, but their wet half-naked bodies slid away from one another. Runt got to his feet, but Jorgi had him by the ankle again and this time he dragged the boy toward the camp.

"No, no!" begged Runt as he slid over leaves, clutching at loose earth and saplings that slipped through his small fingers. An unbridled terror enveloped him the closer he was pulled to the ashes and stone. Letting loose a shocking screech, he flailed free and ran floundering into the stream. Jorgi tottered after him like a marionette with tangled strings, diving into the water and catching the boy by the back of the pants. With repeated yanks exposing the glaring white skin of his pale backside, Jorgi dragged the boy screaming and crying back to the camp, his lunatic laughter madder than ever. He threw Runt down and sat on him, trying to catch his breath and suppress the squirming beneath him. His balance was off and he fell over backwards, but before Runt could escape, Jorgi rolled over on top of him. Excitedly panting, he pounced again and again, making a cat-and-mouse game of it, letting the boy scratch away a few inches before jumping on his nearly naked body, wheezing gleefully and sucking back oozing saliva. Almost exhausted, Runt tried to buck him off, but Jorgi held on, riding him as if breaking a horse, spanking the boy's bare buttocks.

Through his tears Runt saw nothing but the burnt ruins and Cook's blood still clinging to the leaves and pine needles under him as he struggled to get away on his elbows and knees, his mouth opened wide in a breathless scream of anguished horror so unnatural in a child and starkly contrasted by his tormentor's joyous face, absolutely ecstasy-filled before it smashed into the ground. A deep red fountain sprayed many feet in the air before subsiding into a turbulent bubble and finally a calm trickle from the back of Jorgi's head.

Runt pulled himself out from under the dead weight and ran into the forest without looking back. Ford bent over Jorgi's body with the ax in hand, the deathblow sapping his contempt and anger almost immediately. The ax was wrenched away. The world around him flew forward while he wallowed in the moment of the murder. The changing scene and players in it whirled about him, and then all that was chaos snapped into a sobering realignment of order restored by Neb.

"What have you done? What have you done?" Questions and threats flew about the camp. Neb wits and rage fought a tug-of-war battle for supremacy, while Noll bound Ford with Jorgi's torn shirt and volunteered to be lookout, leaving Duff to watch their prisoner. Ham was all but chained to fire duty, collecting wood and building a pit with loose stones. Runt was still nowhere to be seen, but Jorgi's body remained, dragged a few yards from the camp.

By early evening a fire was lit, the lookout and watch switched, and Neb and Noll continued arguing about what to do with Ford. Whispered and contentious, it went on and on without decision. Ford caught a word here, a phrase there, occasionally more.

"Slit his throat and be done with it."

"No, for this he deserves something special. Give me time and I'll think up some real good."

Did they plan to torture him? Perhaps he misheard the word *sacrifice*.

One thing was certain, it wouldn't be a hanging. Their lone length of rope was only long enough to secure him to a thin tree, not nearly long or strong enough to break his neck or let him swing for the time it would take to suffocate to death. He quit listening and worked at freeing his wrists from the cloth wound tightly around them.

In obedience to Neb's orders, Ham piled on the fuel on a night when they would have been sweating without a fire. What was left of Neb's band bedded down for the night and it was clear that whatever end they planned for Ford would wait for the morning. To Neb's thinking, the wait was part of the punishment.

Not everyone slept, nor would they. The bonfire obscured Ford's sight, but he thought Neb and Noll lay by the edge of the light in close counsel. Ham diligently kept his promise to Neb to keep the fire stoked, stirring the coals, throwing another stick on from time to time and stealing glances at Ford when he didn't think he was looking. It occurred to Ford then that Ham was on watch. It was his former friend's duty to keep an eye on him. Knowing that stung him, and it would have angered him even more if he were not already frustrated by the knotting of the tie binding his wrists. Each twist and pull only made it tighter, and even if his hands were free he couldn't imagine a way of extricating himself from the rope holding him fast to the tree.

Sleep hardly entered his thoughts that night. Though he didn't feel in the least bit drowsy, a strange calm did come over him as time wore on. Knowing you're as good as dead will do that, he supposed when he'd abandoned the idea of getting free and spent the time reflecting on how he had ended up in this situation, what he'd become, what he was before and what he might have been. He felt no love for this life. More might have been made of it, but it seemed beyond his power, even before this day. The accident with Milda had seen to that. He regretted that day now. Yes, he'd loved his dog and that was hard to take, but her death need not have happened. *No*, he thought, *I could've walked away, just like today. Just like today.* The fire burned down and gave off a smoke that floated low across the ground, drying his eyes and forcing them shut.

"What I'd give to walk away now," he murmured to himself. Between the crackling of the fire, his heart started at the sound of footsteps behind him.

"Shhh!" hissed in his ear. The rope about him tightened, then loosened and fell free. Fingers fought with the knot at his wrist. Thunder thudded upon the ground. A monstrous growl erupted behind him and two bodies vaulted into the center of the camp, summersaulting right through the fire. The others arose, startled and confused at the sight of a hulking creature rolling over and over, kicking and punching someone slender, a young man. A half-charred log kicked into the coals stirred the fire into a blaze, and revealed Duff pinning down Ford's brother Leo.

Chapter 16
Severing Ties

"He's a spy!"

"He meant to cut our throats in our sleep!"

"Kill him!"

Knives flashed and bodies descended upon Leo, ripping at his clothes and limbs, and stretching out his neck for an eager blade.

"He's my brother!" Ford's shout, so desperate and determined, drew a metallic hint of blood to his mouth. The Valley froze in time. All hung in a cloud of indecision. The knife over Leo's throat waited for Neb, who bared his clenched teeth to speak before turning his back on them.

"Hold," he said bowing his head as he took a few steps away. With a nod to himself, he came back and said, "Tie him with the other. Back to back."

The scant rope was wound around Ford and Leo's necks with the slender tree between them. Strips of Jorgi's shirt were tied about their wrists.

"What are you doing here? How'd you find us?" Ford asked and gasped as the rope was pulled tighter. Neb struck him hard across the jaw and commanded Duff to do the same should Ford speak again. The hideous visage of Duff hovered over him, almost begging in its plain eagerness for Ford to say something. Ford slowly worked his painful jaw and ran his tongue over his teeth, sure he would find cracks and new jagged fragments. Leo straining for air could plainly be heard on the other side of the tree.

"He can't breathe," said Ford and Duff hit him exactly as Neb had done. Neb and Noll hardly noticed though, so deep were they in discussion on what to do next. Ford remembered Noll saying Neb had plans for him. Just what those plans might be now, he feared to guess. Neb kept his head bowed in thought, while Noll fed him with hushed suggestions. Occasionally Neb swatted Noll away and paced about, and then the two would speak again, repeating the cycle for the better part of an hour during which Ford and Leo found themselves drenched in nervous sweat.

"Not much. Not much," Neb muttered, looking around at what was left of his dwindling band of outlaws. A sullen and sly comrade from the old days and a strong, loyal but dull-witted boy, the only two he could still rely on, didn't add up to much. Maybe one day the little pig boy would be good for something, but now Neb viewed him as useless, perhaps even part of the problem. When Ham had ratted out Ford it had made Ford want to leave all the more and Neb didn't want to lose the fast-growing young man, who was already larger and probably stronger than them all. The wood-cracking chop of Ford's ax in the hands of Ham cut the air as it split another spindly tree limb. He was busy making stick and bark torches as commanded. The boy carried the wood back to the fire, trimmed away the twigs and split the ends of branches.

Neb's gaze fell upon the back of the head of Ford's admittedly brave brother. Yes, very brave and crafty of him to sneak into their camp and nearly free his brother. Neb hummed a tune of his own making, one that he felt sang of possibility.

"I wonder." Perhaps mischievous Gwency, the cagey goddess of cunning and luck, had dropped fortune into his lap. He bounced up and strode to the Barlow brothers. "After what you done," he said, motioning to Jorgi's body, "we ought to cut your hearts out." Duff grunted encouragement. "The least you deserve is to have your throats slit. If we had the rope, I'd o' hang you both already. But we don't. And maybe that's for the best, because I got a better idea." He stalked around Ford and squatted in front of Leo. "Calm down, kid, I won't bite. Listen. We could use a good, sneaky kid like you. Good and sneaky, you are. You snuck right up and just about stole away with our dear old Ford here." He slapped Ford's shoulder. "We can't let you do that. We love our old buddy Ford. He's important to our little band of brothers here, too important for us to just let him sneak off with you. Oh no, can't let that happen. So listen. I'm going to make you a deal and it's a fair deal," he said, weighing his words, "a damn fair deal for someone in your position. I feel like I'm owed something for what your brother did to my man over there, something in return, a fair trade. And you, you can help your brother out of a bad situation. Wouldn't you like to help your brother out?" Leo nodded cautiously. "Good, good. I knew you would. I just knew by the look o' you that you was a smart fella, a real smart fella." He pulled the rope tighter around Ford's neck so that it loosened around Leo's. "Here's the deal.

It's simple. Join us. Simple as that. You join us and we'll forget the whole…" Leo shook his head violently.

"You stole from my family. You took my brother away. I'll never have anything to do with you people!"

Neb recoiled like a man stung by wrongful accusation, and then frowned at Leo's vehement and absolute refusal. Ford sighed. If only he'd been able to speak with his brother he would have told him to agree. Agree now and they could flee together some other day. But Leo was so averse to the very idea of becoming an outlaw that he couldn't think beyond his basic instinct. *No doubt our father would be proud of him,* thought Ford with a resigned admiration.

"My family and no one in it would have anything to do with outlaws," went on Leo. Had Leo forgotten that his brother had done just that very thing, Ford wondered, or was he no longer considered part of the family?

"Shut this one up!" Neb commanded and Duff gladly drove a knee into the side of Leo's head, knocking him unconscious. "I gave him a chance," Neb said with a shrug to Ford as he returned to the fire, where he picked out the biggest of Ham's torches and lit it. "I just decided how to finish you, you and him at the same time." The torch flame licked the air as if tasting for something to devour. Neb walked up to Ford, crouched beside him and looked into his eyes almost tenderly. "Such a waste." Ford jerked away when the flame touched his leg. Even with Duff sitting on his ankles and Neb applying the torch directly to Ford's pants, all that came of it was a tortured yelp and a great deal of smoke. The pants were too soaked with sweat. Neb gave up and walked around to Leo to try his luck there. Ford writhed about, wanting to massage his searingly hot leg and at the same time trying to keep the scorched skin from touching anything. He opened his tearing eyes and saw Neb about to apply the torch to his brother.

"Wait! Don't!"

"What?" asked Neb, staying the fist of the eager Duff. "What do you want?"

"I want…" and the words caught in Ford's throat. "I want to live."

"We all want to live, boy."

"I want to stay here. I won't leave."

Neb pulled back the torch and stood by Ford again.

"Why should I trust you? You'll leave first chance you get."

"I won't."

"Liar." Neb stepped over to Leo again.

"Wait! I'll prove it. I'll prove I'm loyal."

"How?"

"I'll…" Ford trailed off. At first he wasn't sure what he was going to do, but amongst the myriad of thoughts racing through his head, an idea was forming that he wasn't sure he could execute. He'd have to try, since he could think of nothing else.

"Bah, he's stalling," said Neb, turning his back on him. "I want a pile of the driest wood around right here." Neb pointed at the base of the tree where Ford and Leo sat.

"Wait!" Ford cried out.

"I'm done waiting."

"I'll do it."

"Eh? What?"

"I'll do it."

"You'll do what?"

"I'll kill him."

A short, disbelieving chortle burst from Neb.

"You're going to kill your own brother?"

"Yes."

Neb's long, harsh laugh filled with the utter delight of one who'd received a surprise gift was not the reaction Ford would have expected, but then again, Neb had done quite a few unexpected things since they'd met.

"Well, that is coldhearted. You surprise me, boy. I didn't take you for a survivor. Not at this cost. Well, well. Should I let him?" he asked the even more surprised Noll, who had no idea what to do and only threw up his hands. "Why not? It'll be some fun, something to remember!" Ford was freed. "Mind you, no messing about or one of these two," —Neb indicated Duff and Noll who were gathered close— "will put an end to you, to him, to the whole fucking show!"

Ford got to his feet, rubbed his leg and gritted his teeth against the returning circulation enflaming the throbbing skin on his thigh. Neb held out the torch, but Ford refused it.

"Fine, that wasn't working anyway. Get his knife," said Neb to Noll, flicking a finger at Jorgi's body, while keeping his eyes on Ford.

"He don't have one."

"What do you mean?"

"He sold it for a skin of wine."

"Fine then, give him yours."

"But—"

"Give it to him!"

Noll handed over his butcher's blade.

"Now, cut out his heart."

"No," said Ford a little too firmly.

"You cut out his heart or I'll cut out yours!" Neb pointed his knife at Ford's chest.

"In the old way. I'll do it the old way."

"What's he on about?" asked Noll.

"He means to take his head off, is what he means," said Neb spreading an appreciative smile. "Well, well! More surprises! We got ourselves a warrior here, a real warrior. I'm really starting to enjoy this! All right then, do it your way."

While Duff hauled Leo's limp body closer to the fire, Ford flipped the blade over, checking out its sharpened side and feeling the grip of its handle. He wasn't particularly handy with a knife and he hoped he could manage this. His breath came faster and harder than he could control. He tried to block out where he was, spoke a quick prayer, and hoped the gods were on his side. Duff dropped Leo at his feet and he lurched to catch him before he hit the ground.

"Get on with it!" said Neb.

Leo flopped about like a newly-slain corpse in Ford's arms, but otherwise he found him surprisingly easy to lift, much easier than it had been when they'd wrestled in years past. A corpse in his arms. That idea sank in and Ford imagined what it would feel like to hold his dead brother in his arms and what it would mean to him. It would be worse than any death he'd ever endured before.

"Go on, do it!" shouted Neb, stepping forward. "What you waiting for?"

In one fluid motion, Ford wrapped his free arm under Leo's chin and around his neck, lifted his head and slid the blade over his throat. Those around the fire watched him in a subdued hush. Ham stopped passing out torches and stood with two of them lit in each hand while staring aghast at Ford.

"Cut off his fucking head!" Neb demanded. Ford grimaced and let out a howl like a wounded wolf baying at the moon as he jerked back the blade, cutting just the way the mender had shown him after the Battle by the Llyn. Blood ran freely down Leo's neck into his shirt.

"Shit!" said Noll, absentmindedly dropping his torch and picking it back up. "He did it." Duff looked from Leo to Ford and an admiring awe shone in his scarred features. Ham shuddered and dryheaved.

"You two," Neb said to Noll and Duff, take the body and pile it next to the other."

"Keep your hands off him!" Ford growled and stepped back from them all. "He's my brother, I'll do it myself."

"His head's not off," said Duff, and just then Leo's eyes flickered open.

"He's come back to life!" screeched Noll falling over backwards and scrambling away. Ham ran for the nearest tree, but Duff looked on, immensely confused. Leo slurred something and tried to stand, but his legs wobbled under him and Ford had to hold him from falling.

"It ain't no ghost or nothing like that at all," said Neb pulling out his knife. "The boy ain't dead and never was. It's a trick." He lunged at Ford.

"Get back!" Ford shouted and swiped the air before him with the knife. Holding Neb at bay, he beckoned to Ham. "Get that!" He pointed at the ax and Ham picked it up, but merely stood with it at a distance. "Come here!" Ham inched closer and closer until he was close enough that Ford was able to snatch away the ax and knock him on his back with a kick to the chest. Forcing the knife into Leo's hands, Ford left him to stand on his own. Leo swayed about and looked dazed, but kept his feet.

"See," said Neb pointing his knife at the gash along Ford's arm, "it's his own blood and nothing but a trick, like I said."

Ford picked up a torch and pressed it into Leo's hand. Neb and Duff edged closer and Ford swung the ax in a broad arc. "Take another step and I'll gut you!"

Tree limbs scratched their faces and ripped at their arms and legs in their reckless retreat through the forest. Leo loped along behind, holding the torch lazily at his side and crashing into bushes.

"Hold that up higher!" Ford pleaded, picking himself off the ground a second time. Shouts from behind reached them from unexpected angles in the dark. "They're coming. Let's go!"

"Ford, they found us." Leo had his knife aimed at a figure in the dark. Ford readied his ax and stepped wide to give himself room to swing. Leo lifted the torch and its light shone upon the wraith-like face of a half-naked boy.

"It's Runt," Ford exclaimed. "He's a friend!"

"Here!" shouted someone behind them. "They're over here!"

"Come with us!" said Ford pushing Leo ahead and grabbing Runt's arm. The three of them stumbled down one hill and up another. Ford looked back and saw two, then three torches appear atop the hill behind them.

"There!" called out a voice. Ford urged them along the crest of the hill, through a thick wall of laurel and then down the back slope.

"They see the light. Get rid of it!" he said and Leo blinked at the torch as if seeing it for the first time before hurling it away into the woods. Its circle of light diminished as they ran in the opposite direction, guided only by moonlight.

"There they go!"

"Over there!"

The cluster of following torches veered away for the discarded torch, but soon afterward someone yelled, "They ain't here!" and Ford heard Neb call, "Quiet!" The forest behind them went silent. Neither Ford, nor Leo, nor Runt spoke, but their labored breathing, the ax handle knocking against a trunk, and involuntary grunts and muffled cries caused by the lashing of tree limbs gave them away and put the hunters back on their trail.

Sweat poured down their backs as they shimmied along the edge of a hollow, tore through bushes and splashed into a morass of muddy water and sodden leaves. Ford's feet squished and sucked through the mire until he looked back and saw Leo helping Runt.

"He's stuck!" Leo tugged and one of Runt's legs came free. The rim of the hill above the hollow glowed an intensifying orange.

"Get down," Ford whispered and plunged into the watery layers of musty, decaying leaves. A deafening thunder of water sloshed into his ears just before the otherworldly deadening of earthly sound. Only his nose, mouth and eyes remained above the surface. All he could hear was Leo and Runt splashing and his own rapid, straining breath just above the screaming prayer he repeated to himself that they might not be caught. In the cool water, the searing burn on his thigh eased immeasurably, but he would have endured twice the agony if only they might not be spotted. If they were, it was the end. They couldn't hope to crawl out of this muddy pool and escape.

Torchlights hung high like floating fireballs in the sky. Ford wished them away back over the far side of the hill, but they bobbed down into the hollow and hovered by the water's edge flickering and waving upon the muddy pool. A gush and a sizzle, and one of the fireballs died.

"You idiot!"

"I lost a shoe."

"Fuck your shoe! Come on!"

Footsteps tramped away and the light receded. Time dragged slowly by before Ford exhaled in relief and began to rise, but Leo's gasp stopped him with his head half out of the water. A peculiar orb of light drifted towards them amongst the spindly trees and bushes. All three boys imaginations flooded with fears of the will o' the wisp, those seekers of souls lost in deep, murky forests and lonely places such as this. Ford's fingers curled tight about the ax handle and mushed the leaves beneath him to pulp. All three boys remained perfectly still. Water rolled down the back of Ford's head and dripped into the pool. To him, it sounded like a torrential rain. A shiver shot through him and the lurch sloshed water across the pool. The orb ceased swaying, whipped about and erupted into flame. The boys clamped their eyes shut, but Ford couldn't resist. He cracked one eye open just as the flame faded to nothing, leaving the glowing orb and a pair of lips that blew on the ember at the end of a stick. It flared up and died again.

"Damn," grumbled the lips and then both they and the ember flittered off like a skipping deer through the woods. When peace resumed, the peepers around the pool relaxed and recommenced their high-pitched croaking for only a moment before the boys climbed from the pool. Ford took a few steps, bent and shook the muddy water from his ears. Standing erect, a silvery haze cast over all before him and he pitched forward into the ground. When he came to, Leo was at his side tearing a strip of cloth from his own wet shirt.

"Are you all right?" Leo whispered.

"Yeah."

"Are you sure?"

"Sure, just…lightheaded."

"Well it's no wonder, you have a nasty cut here on your arm." Leo held Ford's arm in the scant moonlight. "Did you know that? You probably lost too much blood." He wrapped the cloth tight around the wound. "That's no good. We got to wash it out and get out of here." Gripping a tree and adopting a wide stance, he helped Ford to his feet, only for both of them to fall back down immediately.

"My legs," said Ford, dismayed by his quivering limbs. "I'll be fine. Just let me get my legs."

"Be quick as you can. We've got to get you home."

On their way out of the hollow over and down a rock ledge, a weariness overcame Ford in which he keenly felt the drag of his soaked clothes. He tugged at his brother's arm, motioning him to stop just as the faint veil of a cloud passing over the moon drew away and exposed them in a crisp light that penetrated the few trees growing upon the granite outcrop. A shout in the distance and a returning call much closer to the brothers drove them and Runt down into troughs and valleys until there was nothing but flat land and a wildly meandering, soundless stream. Ford dropped to his belly and drank. Leo unwrapped the wound, washed it and hurriedly wrapped it again.

"I don't like the look of this place," he whispered as he hunched over Ford, twisting about to see in all directions and shivering in his wet clothes despite the warm night. "There's no place to hide. We should keep going."

"Yeah," was all Ford said between gulps of water, giving no sign of moving on. Leo was right, he knew, but that didn't help Ford's wobbly legs and flagging energy any. Runt knelt beside him, sipping from his cupped hands and it reminded Ford that he wasn't alone, that someone depended upon him. He splashed handfuls of refreshing water over his face, heaved himself up with the help of the ax handle and nodded for his brother to take the lead.

Runt stayed by Ford, while Leo raced ahead, stopping quite often to listen; he let them catch up or halted in fear when Ford's heavy heel snapped a twig under the fir tree canopy. Leo would stumble to an abrupt stop pressed against a tree trunk or lean against his brother, scanning the darkness for their pursuers. At one point he wouldn't go on even after the other two had caught up. He was lost. His wide, searching eyes and worried glances all about him said it plainly enough.

"If we keep heading south," Ford guessed, "we'll be all right."

"Which way is south?"

That was a good question, but one to which Ford had no answer. The land was familiar enough. He and the Wayward Boys had passed over it months ago, but with only trees and more trees for landmarks, he had no idea what direction he was facing. Feeling about the base of trunks for moss showed him only that moss grew everywhere in this damp part of the country. The lethargic, seemingly unmoving stream was no help either.

Determining its downstream flow would lead them out of the forest and to a village, but it dove underground much of the time, appearing only in sporadic still pools. The clear, repetitious whistle of a titmouse sang above Ford as he sprawled out beside a plate-sized puddle watching a leaf drift one way, turn around and drift back. How long the bird had been singing was anyone's guess until a second titmouse chimed in, waking Ford to the beautiful and horrible harbinger.

"Morning's coming," he said with the regret of one with too many unfulfilled dreams and a life fast expiring. The morning would bring light, and in the light they could see and be seen. All three boys looked up and made out individual branches and leaves against a sky turned a shade grayer than pure black. As if suddenly ungagged, a chorus of birdsong twittered throughout the forest.

Fleeing between the trees in a crouching gait in order to make themselves as inconspicuous as possible, the boys fumbled forward in a reckless dash for Barlow. Dawn birthed shadows and strange apparitions more terrifying than the mysterious black of night. More than once all three boys gasped and felt their chests seize up at the sight of some specter or phantom looming before them, only to discover it to be a fallen tree, malformed bush or rotting stump. In their minds, the flutter of a bird's wings, the crack of a stick snapped, or thump of a heavy footfall took on exaggerated significance and heralded the coming of a demon or their pursuers. When the land rose gradually into hillier terrain once again, Leo slowed and stopped.

"What's wrong?" asked Ford coming up and huddling together with the other two.

"I don't know," Leo said with a quiver of hesitation and indecision. "This might be the way or well, I don't know, we might be heading back the way we came."

"How'd you even find us if you don't even know which way is which?" Ford immediately regretted wounding his brother so, knowing that it was nothing more than the frustration and fear overtaking him, as it did all three boys.

"I followed all the noise and mess you people made." Leo laid emphasis on "you people" and Ford took the fair retaliation without complaint, and moved on.

"We can't stop here," he said taking in the lightening forest all around them. "It's one way or the other." They would either press on into Blackoak territory or retrace their steps towards the Valley. Leo had no answer and seemed rooted to the ground. "This way," Ford said, taking the lead and scrambling up a low, slowly rising hill that would have winded him hours ago, but now he guided the little group at a steady pace. These visions in the shadows, these terrors of the night were nothing to what he'd witnessed over the past year. Pushing on was the only answer. Leaves and drying mud flaked off his damp clothes and dropped upon the layer of pine needles coating the ground passing beneath him. His focus remained glued to the natural carpet whether they turned left or right, or kept straight on until he was compelled to lift his head by a sense of something unusual lying ahead.

Above him towered an enormous oak with its crown aglow in the tender, pale light of dawn. Beyond it the sky opened clear and bright, and just visible over the hill could be seen a wooden palisade with the peaks of houses poking above. Fields stretched down the slope to where the boys crept slowly to the edge of the forest. Leo shot up.

"Oren!" he cried out. "We're as good as home!" From the top of the hill ahead they would be able to see Barlow. Leo strode on, taking in the familiar village and letting all the tension within flow out of him. Behind him, Ford dropped to the ground. Leo and Runt rushed to kneel at his side. "Are you all right?"

"I feel..." Ford steadied himself to rise, but fell on to his side and propped himself up on one arm.

"We're almost there." With help maddeningly in sight, Leo all but willed Ford to his feet. Clearly his brother was hurting and so he stopped. "Rest a bit and then we'll go. But let's not dally." They sat back and Leo tried to master his returning nerves. Somewhere deeper in the woods, a strange bird called out. Another answered. The calls repeated, but closer. Ford caught his brother's concerned, questioning eye.

"I'm all right."

"Are you sure?" Leo laid a hand on Ford's forehead. "You're heating up and you look miles away."

"I'll be all right," Ford insisted, but Leo had hit the mark. In his mind at least, Ford was miles away. Miles away and yet his thoughts rested on that tiny village just over the hill, that home which was not home and might never be home to him again.

Leo fidgeted, but tried to calm himself by concentrating on Ford, looking his brother over, really seeing him for the first time in the long months since Ford had run away.

"I don't understand why you took up with them, those outlaws," he said, breaking in on Ford's distant, depressing musings.

"I didn't choose to, I just kind of fell in with them."

"But they're horrible!"

"It weren't so bad, not at first."

Leo didn't think much of that, but kept his opinion to himself and asked the question he'd pondered since the day Ford left. "Why did you even go in the first place?"

"Why?" Ford couldn't believe the question and blurted out, "Because I killed your mother."

A stab of the old wound struck Leo's core and flashed in a grimace. He'd spent months getting over it, hating Ford for what he'd done. A part of him still did. However, time had calloused over this wound. With time, reflection and forgiveness it had nearly healed.

"It was an accident," murmured Leo by rote, repeating the line he'd drilled into his subconscious mind for months. "So why did you run off?"

Accident. It was a relief to hear his brother say that. Ford gave a small shuddering sigh and bowed his head. Although he appeared to be contemplating the question, it was the struggle of his elation pitted against his guilt that gripped him. He'd killed Leo's mother. The shame came back to him as if that horrible day had been only yesterday.

"I don't know," he eventually said. "Figured I'd get blamed for it, I guess." The words, tainted by exhaustion, came out flat and sounded cowardly to his ears, but Leo couldn't argue. Some did blame Ford and would never forgive him.

"You could have come back," was Leo's muttered, halting reply. Ford read the unsteadiness in the statement and doubted the truth of it. Could he go back home? Would he be welcome? "It'll be just like it was before." Ford fought to suppress a bitter laugh, for he was absolutely sure it would never be the same. And even if life could go back to the way it was before the accident, the thought of how things had once been hardly felt more inviting.

"They'll be happy you're back. Trust me." Ford studied his brother's smile and doubted if anything could suppress Leo's upbeat outlook on life. As he looked at him, really looked at him, he was struck with a full appreciation of the risks Leo had taken for his sole benefit. He leaned forward and threw his arms around his brother's neck.

"It's good to see you again, brother."

"It's good to see you, even though you look like a ghost," Leo said, pulling away and grabbing hold of Ford's arm to examine the blood-soaked wrapping. "It's hard to tell if the bleeding's stopped. Can you walk?"

"Not yet."

"Maybe I should go get help?"

"That sounds like a real good idea."

"I'll get Father and you stay right here. You'll be all right?" Ford waved him on. "I'll be back fast as a fox!"

Runt scooted closer to Ford and the two watched Leo hurry up the hill, his pace slowing near the top, where he was greeted by the squawks of geese and a pony's whinny. Runt poked Ford's leg and handed him three light pink raspberries, then shuffled back to the bush to pluck more. Ford savored the tart berries as Leo's head bobbed over the hill and was gone.

"I feel a lot better," he said with a smile as proof and thanks to Runt. "I'm ready to move on. You?" The little boy's face lit up some and he jumped to his feet. Ford handed him the ax. "Take this for me and I'll catch up." Runt was confused and didn't move. Ford nudged the boy in the direction Leo had gone. "Hurry! You can still catch him. And when you're with him, stick with him. He's,"—Ford sought the best possible way to describe his brother— "good." Runt's uneasy eyes searched Ford's. When it was obvious he wouldn't budge, Ford locked his gaze on the boy with a reptilian coldness and all it took was another soft, persuasive shove to send Runt skittering away up the hill to chase after Leo.

The strange, ever-nearing birdcalls crept closer tree by tree while Ford said a silent prayer that faded into a plea that his family might take the boy in. If there was anything else, absolutely anything more he could do for him, he was at a loss. As for his own future, Ford figured the best he could hope for was the life of an outlaw. Still, he took a cue from his brother and hoped for more.

The still-forbidding shadowy depths of the forest at his back weighed upon him. Runt scampered up the hill and passed over the top out of sight. Ford closed his eyes, took a deep breath and staggered to his feet. His cramped, stiff legs steadied as he hobbled along the edge of the forest, keeping hidden within the trees. The birdcalls ceased and from behind came his name, hollered from some distance at first and later repeated in a sing-song fashion. For a mile more this went on before the calls faded away. Only then did he step from the forest on to the road to Port Morton and walk away from Barlow.

View other Black Rose Writing titles at www.blackrosewriting.com/books and
use promo code **PRINT** to receive a **20% discount** when purchasing.

BLACK ROSE writing™